Vicki's Work of Heart

Born in Derby, Rosie Dean has been writing stories since she was a little girl. She studied ceramic design – gaining a 'degree in crockery' as the man-in-her-life likes to call it – which she put to good use as an Art & Pottery teacher.

After moving into the world of corporate communication, to write training courses and marketing copy, she finally gave it all up to write fiction, full-time.

Rosie is lucky enough to live partly in the UK and partly in southern Spain.

Also by Rosie Dean

Novels

Millie's Game Plan

Chloe's Rescue Mission

Gigi's Island Dream

Toni's Blind Date

Short Stories within

the following Anthologies

Truly, Madly, Deeply
publisher: Harper Collins
e-book

Roses are Red
publisher: Flint Productions

Let's Hear it for the Boys
publisher: ThornBerry Publishing

Vicki's Work of Heart

Rosie Dean

ISBN-13: 978-1495403620

ISBN-10: 1495403629

Copyright © Rosie Dean 2014

Rosie Dean has asserted her right under the Copyright, Designs and Patents Act 1988 to be identified as the author of this work.

The story contained within this book is a work of fiction. Names and characters are the product of the author's imagination and any resemblance to actual persons, living or dead, is entirely coincidental.

All rights reserved. No part of this book may be reproduced, stored in a retrieval system, or transmitted in any form or by any means, electronic, electrostatic, magnetic tape, mechanical, photocopying, recording or otherwise, without the prior written permission of the author: Rosie Dean, Rosiedean.author@gmail.com

For Emily

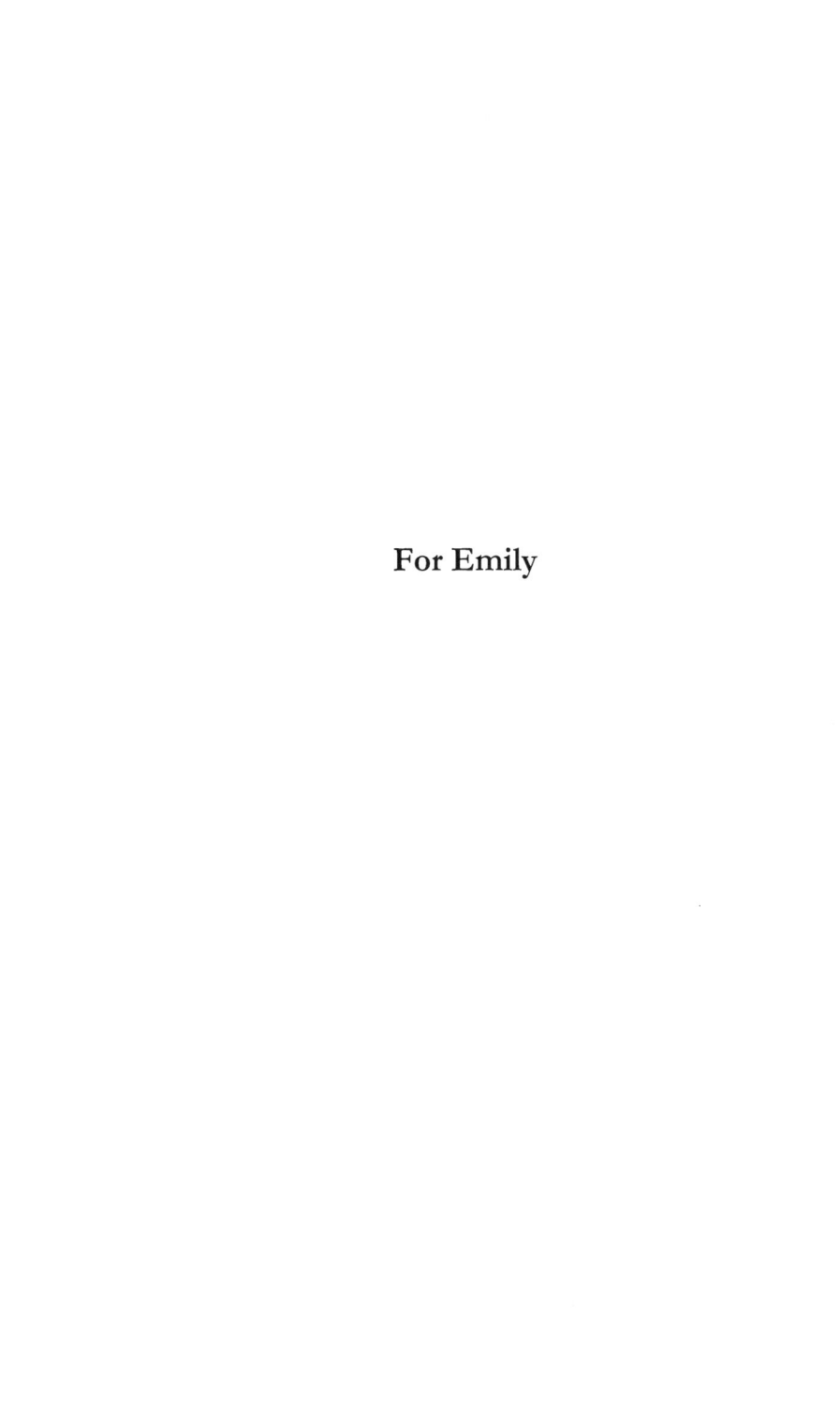

Chapter 1

There can't be many weddings involving eight sixth-formers dressed in black, carrying massive paintbrushes for the guard of honour; two red setters in cream ribbon and an organist bashing out I Will Survive.

To be truthful, the organist's performance was at the direct bidding of me, Victoria Emily Marchant, spinster – still – of a parish somewhere south of Bristol. After striding with whisky-fuelled confidence down to the altar rail, I turned, smiled to the assembled throng and announced, 'It may not have escaped your notice, but this is one wedding short of a bridegroom. The adorable, enigmatic and perpetually irresponsible Marc Morrison has got cold feet. So cold, in fact, he's fucked off to Barbados. Without me.' I couldn't be sure whether the gasps were for his solo exodus or my profanity in a holy place. 'However, as my parents and I have spent an absolute freaking fortune on smoked salmon, champagne and Trinidad Tyler's Steel Band, I would be even more devastated if you didn't stay and enjoy it with us. Whatever else has happened, this is still the first day of the rest of our lives. I'm young,' I threw an arm in the air; 'free,' the other arm; 'and still single. So let's shake it on down!' I believe I may have performed a neat shimmy of the hips.

There were shuffles and murmurings amongst the

congregation. Faces I knew smiled sympathetically when I caught their eye; faces I didn't know gawped in fascination.

Father Patrick, purveyor of whisky to the recently jilted, was approaching at a polite but urgent pace, followed closely by my mother, father and a pair of red setters – their tails wafting proudly, like plumes on circus ponies.

I continued. 'I'm serious. What do I always tell you guys?' I asked, appealing to the eight members of my A-level Art group, who were now sitting along the fourth pew. They glanced at each other. 'Come on, what do I say? "Always…"' there was a slight mumble. I beamed at them. 'You know what I'm talking about.' As Father Patrick and Co. reached the chancel steps, I held up my hand to halt their progress.

The youngest boy, Clark, spoke hesitantly. 'Always rinse your brushes thoroughly and don't leave…'

'Noooo!' Not wishing to humiliate him further, I added, 'Although you're right in one context. Now, Briony, help me out here. What did I tell you when you couldn't go on holiday because of that thingy in your ear?'

Briony blushed. 'Always make the most of the here and now?'

'Exactly. Work with the hand you've been dealt. Well, my lovely friends, Granny, Auntie Grace, Mum, Dad, this is my hand. The joker in the pack has fled and, I don't know about you, but I was really looking forward to a party; I absolutely love dancing to a steel band; and I have some wonderful friends here, who've travelled miles – continents even – to see me get hitched. Can't do much about the hitching, guys, but let's do the decent thing, get over to that marquee and make the most of what's left. Am I right?'

Nothing.

I noticed Father Patrick, his hands plaited in prayer position, turning to his public. I cut in before he could start an oration. 'Come on guys, help me out, here. Do you honestly want us to dump the food, the floral displays, the booze? Just look at me, all dressed up and nowhere to go.' I gave my veil a flick. The tiara glittered with paste jewels in blue, red and pearl – a nod to the day when I'd met Marc. It had been a Red, White & Blue party on Trafalgar Day. Back then, I'd worn a dress I'd made from the Union Flag, he'd worn a knotted American flag like a toga. I'd thought it was fate. Today, my dress was ivory coloured, halter-neck style and, because Marc hated long dresses and loved my legs, I'd opted for a knee-length one and cripplingly high, crimson stilettos. 'Let's make this a night to remember for something other than Marc Morrison's cowardly departure.' I glanced at the scattering of his family and friends to my left. 'No offence.'

My best friend, Isabelle, who had flown in from Paris, stepped out from the front pew, 'I think it is a wonderful idea.' She joined me on the steps and slid an arm around my waist. 'She deserves our support in any way she chooses. Don't you agree?'

I could practically see half the men soften and swell at the sound of Isabelle's French accent. She embodied Parisian chic with a dash of urban shock – dressed as she was in a figure-hugging navy dress, navy shoes, metallic handbag and a fascinator with fine metallic springs that seemed to vibrate on her head.

Mum and Dad looked at each other and closed in for a consultation. Finally, my dad faced the throng. 'It would seem a dreadful shame for you to have come all this way and for the caterers to dump all the food. If it's what Vicki wants, Betsy and I are happy to go along with it.'

As I marched down the aisle, with Isabelle at my side and a smile flickering on my face, I heard Father Patrick say, 'I'm thinking, maybe the whisky was a mistake.'

I woke up in the bridal suite, the following morning, with Isabelle by my side. I let out a long, low groan. 'It really happened, didn't it? I'm not married.'

Isabelle's head lolled over to look at me. '*Oui*. You're still single, *chérie*.'

I contemplated my status for a moment. 'Not a word. Not a hint. I never saw it coming.'

'*Non?*'

My eyes opened a fraction wider. 'Huh?'

Isabelle turned onto her side and put a hand on my shoulder. 'He had no job, Vicki. He just wasn't the settling down type.'

'You say that, now. Hindsight in twenty-twenty.'

'No. I told you, when you came to Paris. I asked you about his work and you told me about his little business venture.'

'And?'

'Didn't we discuss how weak it was? No investors. All those get-rich-quick schemes he used to come up with at college. None of those succeeded.'

'He's an entrepreneur.'

'He's a dreamer, Vicki. Charming, yes. He could

draw you in with his charisma but he is not a business man.'

'And apparently not a marrying man.'

We lay quietly for a moment. Finally, Isabelle spoke. 'I think he would make a great gigolo, you know.'

'He wouldn't. His legs are too bandy.'

For the first time since Marc's best man had delivered the bad news, I took a moment to reflect on what I'd lost. Isabelle was right – at least about the charm and charisma. But he had wanted to settle down. He'd said so. Many times. He'd loved my vision for a family home with a big garden for the kids to mess around in. We'd talked about the tree house we'd build; the vegetable garden; the playroom with a wall left bare for the children to draw and paint on. He'd even downloaded plans for the tree house and gift-wrapped them for me last Christmas. The memory of the light in his eyes as I'd opened it and giggled with joy, now closed my throat with sadness. And as we'd made love, later that day, he'd whispered, 'Imagine we're doing it in the tree house, and one of our nosy, sexy neighbours is watching.' I groaned again and rolled over, burying my face in the pillow.

I felt Isabelle's hand move in a circular motion over my back.

This was so wrong. Marc should have been here, and we should have been having slow, delicious, married sex. Me and Marc, that is, alone. Although, I could just imagine how thrilled he would be at the prospect of sex with the pair of us. My head bucked off the pillow.

'Did he ever make a pass at you?' The hand stilled, momentarily. 'He did, didn't he?'

Isabelle took a breath. 'It was ages ago, at your graduation party.'

Pre-engagement, I thought to myself. All the same... 'What happened?'

'He said some very flattering things and tried to kiss me. So I told him he was pissed and to leave me alone.'

'That's it?'

'That's it.'

I digested the information. We were fresh out of college, back then. If I thought really hard, I might be able to dredge up some inappropriate behaviour of my own. 'Sorry, Iz.'

'Don't be. I should have told you. Then, maybe this wouldn't have come as such a shock.'

'What? You think he made a habit of it?'

Isabelle shrugged. 'I don't know. Really, I don't.'

I felt a twist in my stomach. There had also been the time I'd seen him duelling tongues with another girl on our course – Maxine Dewar – but he'd confessed that was purely down to curiosity over the two piercings she had in her tongue; well, curiosity and a very potent spliff they'd been sharing.

'Oh, Izzy, how did I get it so wrong?' I looked down at the jagged mascara tracks my tears had left on the pillow and dropped my face back into it.

An hour later, as we shared stone-cold toast from the honeymoon breakfast and stared out over the river Avon, Isabelle said, 'You know, you could use this as an opportunity to change your future for something you really want.'

I managed a slow nod. It's hard to think of a new future when the one you were on the brink of has gone missing.

'Travel, write a book, take up sculpture, work towards that painting exhibition you've always dreamed about.'

My head moved from a nod into a slow shake. One had to be inspired to paint. An exhibition of blank canvases might not quite do it for the critics.

They say, as one door closes, another one whips your tits off, and so it transpired when I investigated the Internet History on the computer I'd shared with Marc: Vegas-Casino, Winner-Takes-All, BetsOn, Chase-the-Ace – you name it, Marc had tried it. That would account for the non-existent Malaysian honeymoon I'd tried to cancel. My money – that's my hard-earned loot from daily facing the delinquents at Darwin High School, and money which I'd signed over to Marc to make the booking – was gone. It was a 'man thing', he'd said. He'd wanted to choose the location and pick the hotel, so that at least some of it would be a surprise for me. Well, what a chuffing surprise. His activity would also account for a sudden and shocking avalanche of mail from debt collectors, and six thousand pounds sterling of that, in my name.

How had I been so stupid? Where had my mind been? Apparently in our fantasy future and not in our tawdry reality.

In the ensuing months, I kept myself together; working, staying positive, waiting for a call.

Nobody saw me lying on the sofa, i-Pod plugged into my ears to drown out my own sobbing. Nobody came to drag me out of bed at a weekend, as I pulled the duvet back over my head and waited for Monday. Nobody saw the catering packs of chocolate-chip cookies I consumed.

Offers from my parents to move back in with them were waved aside. 'I'm absolutely fine, Mum. Honestly. I'll get through this. Don't worry.'

I discovered Marc's mobile number now connected me to a Bill Millfield in Streatham – that's actually, Biw Miwfield – who'd 'never-eard-o Marc Morrison'.

Each time I rang his mother, the woman went to pieces. She pleaded poverty and threatened all manner of torture to her son, should he ever step over her threshold. All of which I knew was bollocks, since Marc had always been incapable of doing any wrong in his mother's eyes. A fact the woman had alluded to on our wedding day, when she'd held my hand, tilted her head in sympathy and intoned, 'Some men just need a little more understanding than others.'

His best man, Jamie, swore on his life he hadn't been in touch, which I was inclined to believe, since I'd always wondered at Marc's selection of Jamie as his best man; Jamie being the most abstemious of all Marc's friends but possibly the wealthiest. He too was in credit to my errant fiancé, to the tune of nine hundred quid.

No amount of petitions to the police or the debt collection agencies lowered my financial obligations, which meant I was expected to cough up every last penny.

I sold my car. I lived on BOGOFs. I turned the heating off and watched TV wrapped in a blanket with sleeves. My hair roots grew progressively darker, until a friend took pity on me and brought round a do-it-yourself highlighting kit, which not only bleached my hair the shade of straw, but rendered it so brittle I had a head like a dried thistle. At the end of the summer term, I signed the last cheque and faced my future.

It was a deep and depressing void.

No marriage to savour, no children to raise, no tree house to build.

Equally, no husband to support, no ego to stroke, no nebulous business venture to bankroll.

I picked up the phone and dialled.

'Izzy. I want to spend a year in France. I want to paint.'

Chapter 2

Christophe Dubois made his way through the chattering soirée, and leaned against the balcony balustrade to gaze out at the sun setting behind the Eiffel Tower, blissfully unaware of the future Isabelle was planning for him. She was the sister of his best friend, Xavier, and he had to admit, had blossomed into quite the stunner. She was curvaceous without being heavy and she knew how to dress to greatest effect. Tonight she wore a silver, beaded dress, which showed enough cleavage to tempt without being brazen, and her cropped, Audrey Hepburn hairstyle trod an interesting line between gamine and savvy – which she certainly was. He had, however, known her too long and too well to entertain any thoughts of pursuing her for his own pleasure. She was smart, she was funny but far too analytical. Many, long nights they'd spent in their youth, deep in meaningful and mind-bending discussions over life and its pitfalls; the writing of Stephen King; the varied works of Jean Cocteau and whether the human race was destined to fail, because frequent and repeated rebirths had not resulted in the soul progressing to a civilised level. Her belief in reincarnation alone was enough to put him off. There was also something disturbingly autocratic about the way she approached life.

'Christophe, here is your champagne,' she began. 'Wonderful sunset, isn't it?'

He smiled. 'Indeed. But you didn't set up this little chat to discuss the view, did you?'

'True. I have a favour to ask.'

'Go on.'

'Do you remember my English friend, Vicki?'

'Vaguely. Was she the one who threw up over Xavier at Euro Disney?'

Isabelle's expression froze, momentarily. 'Ah, yes. Who could forget?'

'What about her?'

She smiled and rested a hand on his arm. 'I'd like you to give her a room in your house, and in exchange she will cook for you.'

'What?'

'Can you cook?'

'I get by. It's quite easy to eat out, you know.'

'I know it's a lot to ask, but it would be so wonderful if you could help out.'

'Why should I? Can't she stay with you or Xavier, or even your parents?'

'Christophe, I live in a one-bedroom apartment in the centre of Paris; Xavier is a nightmare to live with – I wouldn't wish him on my enemy never mind my friend; as for my parents. Not for a whole year. It wouldn't be kind.'

'To them or her?'

'To her.'

His eyes narrowed. 'Why me?'

Isabelle rolled her eyes. 'To be honest, I'm desperate. I had a friend in Normandy lined up, but she lost her job and is having to downsize. Then I tried my cousin in le Puy but the house is being refurbished from top to bottom. And nobody on the company network showed any interest. You're my last hope.' Her hand on his arm was surprisingly tense.

'So, what's she running away from?'

'Huh?'

'The police must be on her tail for you to be so keen to sort this out. She's not in trouble is she?'

'Don't be silly. I don't have friends like that. She's an artist – a brilliant artist. She's given up her job to take a sabbatical and paint. She feels it's her last chance to succeed at something she dearly wants to do. I told her I could find her somewhere, easily. Unfortunately, she's out of work and soon she'll be homeless. If I don't sort something out, and fast, I will have blown her dream right out of the water.' Isabelle was giving him her most beseeching expression.

'So, it's you I'm getting out of a fix as much as your friend.'

'God, yes. I practically talked her into it. If I fail her now I'll feel guilty for ever.'

Christophe knew when he was being played. 'I doubt it,' he smiled. 'But I daresay you'll make me feel guilty for ever, if I refuse.'

Isabelle moved closer. 'You're a philanthropic man, Christophe. I'm just asking you to be charitable to another human being, instead of all those horses you lavish your funds and attention on.'

'Hmmm... What if she's a pain in the neck?'

'Vicki? Never. She's bright and funny and a very good cook. I know you have plenty of room in your house, you need hardly see her, except at meal times. Please say, yes.'

Christophe could see some small advantage in the arrangement. 'Is she pretty?'

Isabelle's eyebrows twitched. 'Very. But don't you

mess with her, Christophe, or I'll come down and chew your balls off.'

He laughed. That was exactly the reaction he'd expected.

'So, what do you say?'

'I'll only mess with her if she wants to be messed with, how's that?'

Isabelle's mouth knotted into a pout. 'Don't mess with her. This is my dearest friend, we're talking about. And one day, she will be godmother to my children. I don't want to choose who I can invite to their christening, just because you behaved with ungentlemanly conduct.'

Christophe grinned. 'Isabelle, I'm always a gentleman.'

'Just say, yes. Please. You're my last hope.'

Chapter 3

I checked my watch against the impressive clock tower of Limoges station. Quarter past five. No sign of Christophe Dubois. Brilliant. I could do Waiting For Men. I'd had practice.

Heaving a large bag onto my shoulder, and grabbing the suitcase trolley handle, I wandered back inside the station, where I began scanning every male face for evidence he might be looking for me – trying desperately not to appear as if I were up for trade. Not a single soul was holding a sign for Vicki Marchant. I took out my phone and re-read the email. It was there in black and white. He would pick me up outside the Bénédictins railway station at five o'clock. I turned, swapped my bag from one shoulder to the other and dragged the suitcase back outside.

Despite being September, it was so humid my tee-shirt was clinging intimately to my nothing-to-brag-about curves. I shrugged off my jacket, draped it over the suitcase, and began wafting air inside my shirt. Across from the station, I could see a beautiful garden with a cool, shimmering fountain – so inviting – and it certainly beat the aspect facing tourists on arrival at Bristol Templemeads.

I counted cars, I checked my watch, I chewed my lip.

Ten minutes later, as rain began to fall, I leaned against one of the huge, stone pillars and pulled out my phone, again. I rang his home number. After two rings, the answer-phone cut in. He had the kind of mellow, French accent that could bring a coach-load of diehard, female celibates to their hairy knees and convert them in a heartbeat. Apparently I'd met him, once, when I was thirteen. I had a hazy recollection of a generic French school boy in a parade of new people I'd met on my first visit to France.

As I peered out at the passing traffic, rain bounced off the ground, forcing me to retreat into the shelter of the entrance. Minutes ticked by. It was horribly familiar. Especially that sinking feeling, creeping through my stomach as I recalled the last time I'd sheltered from the rain, and waited. Where was Father Patrick now, with his bottle of Jameson's?

Of course, I had to examine the possibility I'd rushed into this and as I did so, all my gung-ho enthusiasm was evaporating faster than white spirit on a sunny day. A weedy art graduate, who wore an Oxfam Shop tweed suit, now sat in my art room at Darwin High. Plus, I'd let my flat to a lovely young couple with earnest faces, who were planning their own wedding.

My darling Isabelle had, after several false starts, found me a part-time job with accommodation... but only at the eleventh hour. I knew my friend's methods. Working at the sharp end of PR had given her the persuasive leanings of Torquemada. I suspected Christophe had been browbeaten into submission, and now had cold feet.

I tried the second phone number – his mobile. There was a barrage of rapid-fire, indecipherable French, which I assumed told me his phone was out of range, and left me mouthing like a guppy. It was becoming apparent my seven years of school French hadn't exactly set me up for life across the Channel. Luckily for me, Izzy had spent a gap year living with my family and working in Bristol, before going to Uni, so her English was almost faultless. I, on the other hand, had only made three exchange trips to stay with her family, and the occasional long weekend in Paris. Not surprisingly, we always spoke in English.

At quarter to six, I rang Isabelle. 'I've been waiting for Christophe to pick me up for nearly an hour. Do you know if he's changed his mind?'

'No. Why would he? I've told him about your excellent cooking skills.' Like I said – she's in PR. 'He's really looking forward to you staying with him. Have you called him?'

'Yes – just messages. Are you absolutely sure he was keen to do this? People say some rash things when they're at a party, especially if you had his arm twisted behind his back and your knee in his groin.'

'Don't be silly. I was on a mission to find you somewhere to stay, and he volunteered. Truly.'

'My cooking isn't excellent, Izzy. Not by French standards.'

'Bah! Christophe is no cook.'

'You said he lives alone, right?'

'Yes. But his veterinary surgery is next door, so there are other people about.'

Just then, my phone beeped.

'Isabelle, I have another call, hang on.'

I fumbled with my phone and lost both.

'Shit!' I glared at the little screen and waited a moment before checking my messages.

'Vicki, this is Christophe Dubois.' Like I got messages from French men all the time. 'I apologise for not meeting you. I have had an emergency. I suggest you take a taxi and I will be back later. You will…' The message cut out. Relief flooded through me. I grabbed my bags and headed for the taxi rank.

As I settled into the back of a cab, the rain came down like metal rods, beating off the roads and hammering on the car roof. The sky flashed intermittently before great, rolling belts of thunder shuddered around us. I had to keep wiping condensation away from the window to see out. Soon, we were leaving the bright lights of Limoges. Architecture spanning thousands of years gave way to rolling green countryside and grey stone cottages. They all merged and blurred beyond the rivulets of rain, like a painting by Monet in his final years.

My eyes dropped out of focus as I allowed myself to wonder about what I might achieve in the coming year. Never since I was at college had I had the opportunity to be creative without heavy responsibilities crowding in. I was giving myself a treat – the treat of a lifetime, really. And I knew, with absolute certainty, the year would fly by. In twelve months I'd be making this journey in the other direction. Only then would I know whether I'd mined the most out of this year. I allowed myself a quick peek into the future – a stack of completed canvases; an exhibition in Bristol… why limit myself to Bristol? How about London? Paris? Who knew how popular my work might become? Then, like the memory of a sensational dream dissolves on waking, the vision faded. Who said my work would be popular at all? What conceit.

I shifted in my damp coat. There was a lot of ground, not to mention canvas, to cover before anyone could even hope to judge my work. I wasn't certain it mattered whether it was good or not. No. I was here for me. This would be my phoenix year – time to rediscover the essential Vicki.

I would also be cooking every day for my landlord.

What did I know about Christophe? Isabelle described him as, 'Tall with dark hair. Not my type,' which was encouraging, since Isabelle always went for moody, academic types who sat brooding over books – even in company. Maybe he was an absolute dish and his looks had bypassed Isabelle. She'd called him a confirmed bachelor – with just one little blip last year when, to everyone's surprise, he'd moved a girlfriend in, but that was over.

And your point is? I asked myself. You haven't come to France to meet some dishy *homme*.

No. This was my time.

I reminded myself that Marc's departure had happened for a reason. I had to believe that, otherwise all his misdemeanours would be too painful to bear. No, his leaving had freed me up to pursue the life I was meant to follow. Until now, I had shelved my own artistic ambitions for the security of a teaching job, and saving for our future. Isabelle had known that too.

I was jostled from my thoughts as the taxi pulled to a halt outside a large, stone, detached house set back from the road. The uncommunicative driver lifted my bags from the boot and placed them on the pavement. He grunted the cost of the fare. I peered at him, '*Repetez, s'il vous plait*,' I said, so he had to repeat it. I still didn't get it. He said it louder and held up his fingers to indicate thirty-seven euros. I gave him forty and he grunted again before climbing back into his car and driving off.

The rain was lighter now – if you compare standing under a watering can with a power-shower. There were huge puddles in the road and a small lake on the driveway. I slung one bag over my arm and dragged the case towards the house. A deep bark, followed immediately by a higher yapping, answered my knock at the door. I waited and listened as the barking came closer and was interrupted now and again by exaggerated snuffling noises along the bottom of the door. Through the frosted glass at the top I could make out the shaggy head of some kind of hound. So I jabbered doggie-chat through the wooden panels until I reached their boredom threshold and they quietened down.

Still I waited. No point in knocking again – who needed a doorbell with security like that?

I looked for signs of human life. The brass plate by the door declared Christophe Dubois' credentials. Below it, was an arrow directing clients round to the side of the house. I followed it to the surgery door, which was locked and the interior in darkness. Extending from the house was a stone wall with a gate, also locked. Rain clouds were still dumping their contents on me and I had nowhere to shelter.

'*Merci*, Christophe,' I grumbled. '*Merci* chuffing *beaucoup*.'

Returning to the front of the house, I sat on my suitcase and looked up and down the road for any signs of life. If this were England, there would at least be a pub or a corner shop where I could seek refuge. Here, all I could see was a small bakery and an antique shop. Neither was open. I looked up at the darkening sky and waited for a flash of lightning to strike.

Should I call him again? Would that make me sound like an old nag? On the other hand, what kind of person agreed to collect someone from the station then left them to wait in a strange place, in the pouring rain? I pressed myself against the wall to avoid the full pelt of water from above. My hair was dripping, and droplets trickled down the side of my nose. Every joint in my body was stiffening with cold.

This was beyond miserable. A familiar ache clutched at the back of my throat as my ten-denier bravado began to ladder. I swallowed. Best not to think about that now. I was a big girl – well – a grown-up. It could be worse. I could be here all night.

Shit! I could be here all night.

I called him again and groaned at the beep of his messaging service. I spoke very slowly, in my best French and with a forced smile. 'Hello, Christophe. I have arrived at your house. I am waiting outside. It is raining. Please will you call and let me know when you will be arriving? Thank you.' I returned to staring broodily at the buildings across the street, where little shutters hung at odd angles.

A pair of headlights came into view. I watched as they drew closer and pulled onto the drive. The man at the wheel, who I assumed to be Christophe, was holding a mobile phone to his ear. He looked about as grumpy as I felt, which was a good start. As he pushed open the door, I noticed he was also just as soggy. His trousers were tucked into muddy boots and his damp hair had been pushed back off his face. Admittedly, quite a handsome face; good jaw-line, dark hair, dark eyes and a five o'clock shadow, which all made him look vaguely sinister. He nodded. 'You didn't find the key, then?' His voice was as deep as I remembered – though perhaps a little less silky.

'No. Why would I?'

He walked over to a plant pot by the front door. Stooping down, he moved it to reveal a key safe, punched in four numbers and retrieved the key. How was I supposed to know there was a key there? I wasn't a mind-reader. Then I remembered. His phone message had been cut short. I looked up at him – quite a long way up actually, he was easily a foot taller than me, I could feel vertigo taking a grip. 'I got your message but not all of it. I think the signal must have been weak.'

He nodded. 'I just listened to yours. You are not very happy, huh?' He looked down, his dark eyes fixing on mine. Boy! He didn't flinch from staring, did he? My pulse wobbled unnervingly. He spoke again. 'I see you are as wet as I am, non?'

'I'm not sure I've ever been wetter – fully clothed, that is.' As he cast his eyes down the length of my sodden figure, I could feel my mouth curl in embarrassment at such a stupid comment. Behind the door, the dogs had redoubled their barking. As he leaned over to unlock it, I smelt a faint hint of some cologne beyond the damp fabric of his clothes, which was battling with the undeniable pong of horse manure. Nice. He called something to his dogs, before he swung the door open. A large, sandy coloured wolfhound and a smaller dog of unclassified pedigree, rushed out. They were torn between greeting him and investigating me. Christophe introduced them, as he ruffled the large sandy head, 'This is Hercules, and the little guy is Boz.'

I stooped to scratch the smaller dog's ears. 'Hello,

Boz. You're a cutie.'

Christophe lifted my bags into the large hallway and placed them by the stairs while I paid attention to the dogs. When he clicked his tongue, they bounced back to him, circling expectantly. He crouched down and scratched their ears lovingly. I might have appreciated this touching little tableau, if I hadn't been wringing wet and sinking fast into pneumonia.

I cleared my throat and said quietly, 'Sorry to be such a nuisance, but I'm dripping on your floor.'

He looked at me for longer than I thought necessary, and something in his face suggested I might not be quite as welcome as I'd hoped. 'Of course.' Standing up, he commanded '*Allez*!' at which, the two pets skulked into a large basket, their paws hanging over the edge, alert for the next opportunity for attention.

'I see you are not a woman to be kept waiting.'

The cheek of him. 'Sorry. I just want to get out of these wet clothes. Don't you?'

I saw an eyebrow lift and the corners of his mouth twitch. I silently congratulated myself on plunging into a double-entendre with a wet Frenchman. Avoiding eye contact, I reached for one of my bags at exactly the same time as he did so our heads met like balls on a snooker table but without the satisfying 'click'. I recoiled.

He peered at me in concern, his hand touching my arm, 'I'm sorry, are you okay?'

'Yes. Thank you.'

His mouth lifted in a half smile and I saw the beginnings of fine lines radiating from his eyes. Nice eyes. 'Good,' he said, before lifting my bags and heading up the stairs. I followed him up and across the landing to a large room at the back of the house which was kitted out with heavy wooden furniture. He placed my bags on the floor and walked over to a door in the far corner. 'Your bathroom.'

I nodded. Despite having doubled my body weight with rainwater, I still couldn't wait to marinate in a hot bath.

'I hope you will be comfortable. If you need anything, just ask.'

The curtains and matching bedspread, in apple blossom print, reminded me of an old B&B I'd stayed in with Marc, at Ilfracombe, during a rare hot week when we were on a tight budget and fancied some sand, sea and sex. 'Thank you. It's lovely.'

'Now, you need to get out of those wet clothes and dry off so I will leave you.' He moved over to the door. 'Unfortunately, I have an evening appointment, so you will have to settle in on your own.'

'Oh.'

He ran a hand through his damp hair, forcing a stray lock back from his forehead. 'I had hoped to spend a little time with you, but one of my horses had an accident.'

'Oh.' I said again. This time, a breeze of guilt drifting across my heart. 'Is it going to be okay?'

'Yes. Unfortunately, he won't race again but I can still breed from him.' He glanced at his watch. 'Now, I'm afraid I really have to get ready.' He held out his hand. 'I'm pleased to meet you, Vicki *Marchant*.' He pronounced my surname with a soft 'ch' like the French word for walking.

I smiled and shook his hand, which was so much warmer than mine. 'Pleased to meet you, too. Thank you for letting me stay.'

He nodded and made a sweeping gesture with his hand. 'Please, find your way around the house. There is a room upstairs that I think you might like to use for your studio. I hope you will be comfortable here and, of course, productive.'

'Me too. I mean, I'm sure I will be. Comfortable. And productive. Thank you.'

There was that half smile again. Not quite the full blown Vicki-you're-very-welcome-here kind of smile, more an it-would-be-rude-of-me-not-to smile, before he walked out.

I wandered over to the window to peer out into the darkness and saw... well... darkness. I could explore the neighbourhood tomorrow. Right now, I desperately needed a hot bath.

In the bathroom, I was met by my reflection in the mirror. 'Aaargh!' The sight was as ghastly as Munch's Scream. My hair had been plastered to my head by the rain; splatters of mascara streaked my cheeks and my skin was as pale as cream. I checked my teeth. Thank God; no green debris. I swung away from my reflection, turned on the bath taps and watched the water gush out. I leaned over and inserted the plug and dispensed shower gel from an industrial-sized bottle into the flowing water. I stripped off and hung my wet clothes over the shower rail.

My first moment of bliss, in a very long time, came as I lowered my chilled backside into the spicily hot water, letting out a series of 'Ooh-ahs' as I did so. I lay back and closed my eyes and mentally flagged this moment as a key memory in the start of my new life.

Downstairs, I could hear Hercules and Boz fussing round Christophe. I heard the low rumble of his voice. Then, there was the sound of him mounting the stairs, two at a time, and the slam of a door, followed shortly by the hum of his shower. I slunk lower in the water and wondered what his evening appointment might entail. My best guess was a woman; he'd hardly be sprucing up for a night in the cow-shed.

When my body started to poach and beads of perspiration trickled over my temples, I sat up and washed my hair, rinsing through with cooler water from the shower attachment. On the back of the door I found a heavy bath-robe, which I wrapped around me. It was at least two sizes too big but deliciously snug. I towelled my hair and shook it loose.

There was more than enough room in the wardrobe for the limited selection of clothes I'd brought. I'd also had to carry paints, brushes and my old, telescopic easel.

There was a knock at my door. I tightened the sash of my robe and raked a hand through my hair. '*Entrez.*'

As he stepped into the room, I have a sneaking suspicion I may have gasped in surprise. He had transformed himself from soggy vet into Hollywood idol. He wore a white tuxedo, wing collar shirt, black trousers and bow tie – complete with satin cummerbund. His dark, wavy hair – slightly damp – now flicked over his collar and a stray curl flopped over his forehead. He looked even broader and taller than before. I diverted my attention to the wardrobe door, pushed it closed, locked it, unlocked it and pushed it again as it fell open. Was Izzy completely blind?

'I'm sorry. I forgot to offer you a drink. Very rude of me. Would you like a glass of wine, or maybe a cup of English tea? I bought some especially.'

'I'd love a glass of wine, thank you,' I croaked, that way you do when unexpected lust thickens your throat. That or lack of wine.

He nodded and headed off downstairs.

I turned to my reflection in the mirror, a gape of amazement on my face. I gave my cheeks a Scarlet O'Hara pinch, and ruffled my damp hair. 'Of course, I'm not interested in him,' I whispered to myself, 'but any self-respecting woman wants to look at least presentable.'

Moments later, he reappeared in the doorway, holding a large glass of white wine towards me. As I took it, I noticed the eau-de-manure had been replaced by shampoo and spicy cologne. 'Thank you,' I smiled and saw a tiny crop of stubble in the dimple of his chin, which in his haste to shave had been missed.

'Welcome to my home. Please, treat it as your own. There's a little food in the kitchen. And I promise, tomorrow, we will have time to talk.'

'Looks like you're going somewhere special.'

He shrugged. 'It's a horse racing dinner. Now, I'm afraid, I must go.'

As he turned away, I said, 'I hope you have a lovely evening.'

He looked back then and smiled, finally at full wattage, and another dimple appeared in his right cheek. 'I'm afraid I'm now keeping another woman waiting. Goodnight, Vicki, and sleep well.'

I watched him as he ran down the stairs, grabbed his car keys from the hallstand and disappeared from view. I stood, sipping my wine as I listened to the revving of his car and the crunch of tyres on gravel. I heard the drop of engine tone as he changed gear before roaring off into the night. And then it became very quiet – just the ticking of the hall clock and the occasional snuffle from one of the dogs. I shook my head and sighed. 'Just my luck. I've sworn off men for a year and he's drop dead gorgeous.'

I began my tour of the house, taking my bag of art materials up to the top floor. There were three rooms: a bathroom, a small room cluttered with boxes and old chairs, and the last was a large room with dormer windows on either side. It smelled like a dusty old attic but it was clean and tidy. There was a table, a huge and ancient mirror on the end wall, an old dining chair and an empty chest of drawers. Placing my bag on the table I looked around, nodding my head in appreciation. I tested out a little shimmy of the hips. 'This is my studio.' I announced to the four walls. 'Oh, lovely garret. Thou shalt be the platform for my talent to take wing!' I threw my arms out evangelically and pumped my hips. 'Vicki's back.'

Later, as I wandered from room to room, Hercules and Boz fussed around me – Hercules ramming his snout into my hand and Boz scuttling behind. I couldn't work out why a house with such old family charm could be so sparsely decorated, unless Christophe's former lover had legged it with half the contents. I should introduce her to Marc, it might be a match made in heaven. In the corner of the sitting room stood a piano, on which there was a group of framed photographs. All but one showed Christophe in the winner's circle, receiving trophies with different horses. Izzy had told me his family had bred race horses for years. Christophe specialised in equine vet work. Another photo was altogether more interesting;

it showed him holding a red-haired woman in his arms who he'd evidently just swept off her feet. She was clutching a huge Ascot-style hat on her head and kicking a very shapely leg in the air. After close scrutiny, I put the picture down and headed off to the kitchen – the room where I would earn my keep.

Old cupboards had been painted in duck-egg blue; a large American style fridge-freezer stood in the corner and a stainless-steel, five-burner hob was better than I'd hoped for. Despite these impressive facilities, I stuck a potato in the microwave and chopped some tomato and onion. I was too tired for anything fancy and I had nobody to impress tonight.

After supper I went back upstairs, where I couldn't resist taking a sneaky peek into Christophe's bedroom. It was decorated in blues and greens. A large dresser stood between two windows. On it were a couple of bottles of cologne, some loose change and a small, bronze sculpture of a horse. The doors of a large wooden wardrobe hung open, exposing a neat selection of clothes; sweaters in shades of bottle green, blue and deep pink hung beside an orderly row of trousers. European men were so much braver in their choice of colour. I wondered if their Mediterranean colouring helped. I thought about Marc's haphazard wardrobe, dull with khaki and navy, most of which would be spilling from the shelves like there'd been an earthquake.

On the bedside table was a biography of Jules Verne.

The light was still on in the en-suite and, as I approached it, I picked up the subtle, amber fragrance of his cologne. Guiltily, I turned away and my eyes drifted back over to the wide bed with its heavy blue bedspread.

Oh boy, I could just imagine the fun that might be had on there with Christophe. Maybe I'd tug his bow-tie loose with my teeth. Then again, maybe he'd do it himself – though not with his teeth, of course – in that confident way a true Hollywood idol would. Followed by the snapping open of tiny white buttons…

'Don't even think about it!' I screeched, and headed out of the room, clicking off the light and closing the door. 'Focus, Vicki! Focus!'

Chapter 4

The following morning, I woke with an ache across my shoulders. I sat on the side of the bed and wind-milled my arms to loosen the muscles. It was only six-thirty but I'd always been an early riser. Well… always since the first week of my first teaching term. I'd quickly learnt it didn't pay to face marauding year nines with the hang-over from Hades and a seat-of-the-pants lesson plan. They were experts at spotting weakness. It was a kind of jungle cunning. They might not all be destined to make eye-watering GCSE grades, but they were onto a fledgling teacher faster than a mean cat on a sickly sparrow. By getting an hour's head start, fuelled by a pint of coffee, I could just about keep on top of the little blighters.

Yawning, I wandered over to the window, lifted the curtain and looked out at the hazy morning light playing on the courtyard. There were buildings either side, which I assumed to be part of the veterinary practice. Beyond this, fields stretched into shallow hills dotted with trees. 'Heaven,' I said, thankful not to be looking out over a collage of rooftops, washing lines and satellite dishes.

Okay, this was it. I was embarking on an exciting journey into the unknown – my future. All I had to worry about was preparing regular, edible meals and unleashing my creative energy. With a rush of enthusiasm, I pulled on a pair of old jeans, a blue sweatshirt and a pair of sandals. I twisted my hair into a knot on the back of my head and fixed it with a clip. At least I had more colour in my cheeks this morning. I rubbed in some moisturiser. No reason for any make-up.

Okay. Maybe just a slick of lip-gloss.

As I descended the stairs, Hercules and Boz stepped from their beds, stretching and wagging their tails. I crouched down to give them some attention, before heading to the kitchen. The sun shone through the old windows, casting shafts of light onto the pale blue cupboards. I had no idea what Christophe would eat but thought a pot of coffee would be a good start. I also decided to make fruit salad and later, when I'd had time to go shopping, I would mix some home-made muesli.

By the time the fruit salad was in the fridge, and the coffee brewed, I heard the dogs on the move – a hint that Christophe was heading our way. I'm good, I thought. Sorted. The central, wooden table was set for breakfast, the fruit salad was colourful and nutritious, the smell of coffee was inviting…

Dear Doris! What was I turning into? Just pass me the twin-set and frilly apron!

Rebelliously, I slopped coffee into a mug and leaned against the work surface, just as Christophe sauntered in. He was wearing battered jeans and a loose-fitting, dark blue shirt. Yowser! He was still hot. Suddenly, I remembered how Marc could make an entrance – one flash of his boyish good looks, lit up by a dazzling smile and female heads would turn, knees weaken and pudenda would…

Oh no. I'm sooo not going there, I thought, gritting my teeth.

'Good morning, Vicki. Did you sleep well?' His brown eyes were almost black surrounded, as they were, by lashes the colour of tar.

'Like a baby,' I smiled. 'A good baby. Not a colicky one. I mean, it's so quiet here. Very peaceful. I had a long day yesterday. Long and tiring.' Oh crap. I was rambling, so I slurped some too-hot coffee and scalded my tongue.

'And getting soaked to the skin on my doorstep didn't help, huh?' Something about the way he said 'huh' at the end of his sentences was so very French.

He leaned against the worktop, hung his head over the coffee pot and sniffed. 'Mmm. Smells good.' He looked down at me. 'What a treat to come down to hot coffee. *C'est merveillieux.*'

The heat of his body was coming off him in wafts of shower gel and amber cologne. I lifted the coffee pot and carried it to the table. Realising his mug was still on the worktop, I carried it back and poured it out.

'How was your racing dinner?'

'Very good. But also tiring.'

'Was it a nice meal?'

'It was delicious – and should have been, the tickets were expensive.'

'Talking of food, what do you like to eat and where do you suggest I do the shopping?'

He shrugged. 'I eat most things. I will be happy with anything you make. We have some shops here, and you can borrow the car to go into Limoges. I will take you, some time, and show you round.'

'And... um... shall I buy the food and let you know what your share is?' He looked puzzled. 'I assume we're splitting the food bill fifty-fifty.'

'I know what you are saying. But, you do the cooking, I do the paying.'

He was a caveman. 'But I'm cooking in return for staying here. You can't pay for my food as well.'

'Vicki, I am perfectly happy to pay for the food.'

I shook my head. I had always paid my own way – not to mention Marc's. I appreciated his hospitality but this was taking it too far. 'That's very kind of you, but I really must pay for mine. I may not be working at the moment, but I do have money.' Not much, admittedly but there was a little spare each month from the rent on my flat.

He held out his hands in disbelief. 'But you don't have to. You are in my house and Isabelle tells me you are a very good cook. I shall eat well, non?'

'I hope so.' That really wasn't the point. 'But it still doesn't mean you can pay for my food. You won't even let me pay for my accommodation; I have to make some contribution.' There was something about being in debt, to anybody, which caused a clenching in the core of my being. I'd finally paid my dues for Marc's decadence, I wasn't about to put myself in a position where I was beholden to somebody else. I'd work for my rooms but I'd pay for my food.

For an absolute age he stared at me before saying, 'I'll tell you what: I'll give you some money each week and if it runs out, you can add to it. There, decision made.' He bent to sip his coffee.

I stared at the top of his head, where the dark hair swirled in textured waves. 'While we're on the subject, what do you usually have for breakfast?' I asked.

He held up his mug. 'Just this. I don't usually have time for breakfast.'

'Breakfast is the most important meal of the day. Let me guess, you take care of all those animals but don't look after yourself, am I right?'

He shrugged 'I have survived to thirty-four quite well, I think. Don't you?'

Oh. My. God. One of Marc's favourite phrases sprang to mind, You gotta love me, you know you do. My eyes dropped from his face to his tanned chest above the open neck of his shirt. I shrugged, 'You look okay, but I still say, breakfast is crucial and, if I prepare it, all you'll have to do is eat it. Now then,' I said, picking up a spoon and pointing to the bowl of fruit salad. 'Do you like fruit?'

He looked at it and up at me. I noticed a smile playing at the corners of his eyes as he asked, 'Do I have a choice?'

'Of course you have a choice. It'll keep in the fridge for days and I'll eat it myself.'

He held my gaze for a long moment before nodding at the bowl. 'Thank you. It looks delicious,' he said and watched while I attempted to serve the fruit graciously but my co-ordination was a little out of whack.

Unsettled by the silence as we sat eating, I said, 'Izzy told me you went to school in England, why was that?'

'My maternal grandmother was English. I was sent to school in Surrey for four years.'

'How old were you?'

'Seven.'

I coughed on a piece of banana that nearly choked me. 'You were sent away at seven? To a different country?'

He shrugged. 'It wasn't so bad. I had good times

and some nice teachers.' He grinned. 'You remind me of one of them.'

'I do?'

'Mrs Stafford. She was always making me eat things that were good for me.'

'Oh. Well, I'm sure she did it with the best of intentions. Children can be very picky.'

'This is true. And remember, I was used to French cuisine – steak and kidney pie with cabbage was a whole different thing for me. I'm afraid I still don't like cabbage.'

'If it's school cabbage, I don't blame you. There are much better ways of preparing it.'

'Then perhaps you will convert me.' He smiled that half smile again, the one that promises the full beam. 'So, Vicki, how is it you became such a competent cook, huh?'

'My nan taught me. She had a little restaurant in Clevedon – it's a holiday resort – I used to work there in the school holidays.'

He nodded but didn't say anything, he just appeared to be analysing my response. Then he looked at his watch. 'Excuse me. I have to walk the dogs before work. Thank you for breakfast.'

Standing up, he whistled. Immediately the dogs leapt to his side. As he stood in the doorway, he turned to me. 'I will leave you keys and some money. *Abientôt.*' he said; see you later.

'Christophe...' My shoulder flexed in surprise – it was the first time I'd called him by his name. 'Do I need to feed the dogs?'

He looked down at them and grinned. 'They will tell you "yes – all the time" but they only have one meal a day, at six o'clock. When I am not here, Louise comes in from the surgery to feed them. They will tell you when it's time. They are very good clock watchers.'

'Do you have surgery today?'

'Non. Today, I have three farm visits. But please, feel free to go in and say hello to Louise. She is a lovely girl. You will like her.'

I hoped so. I could do with a friend nearby. Isabelle was in Paris, 250 miles away. There would be no dropping in on her to share experiences and a bottle of wine. I'd called her last night, once I'd settled in.

'I told you Christophe would arrive,' she'd said. 'What do you think?'

'Great. It's a lovely old house and my studio is fabulous. I'd have been happy in an old shed.'

'And Christophe?'

The vision of him in his tuxedo had flashed before me. 'He seems nice. But we haven't really had time to talk and now he's gone out for the evening.'

'I hate to say it, *chérie*, I don't have time to talk either. Jean-Claude is here, we're watching 2001 A Space Odyssey, have you seen it?'

'Yes, I fell asleep after ten minutes and woke up when all the alarm clocks went off.'

'Oh Vicki, you're so funny. You must watch it some time, it's fascinating.'

'No, honestly. I'd rather watch paint dry.' And often did.

'Bye, honey. Love you.'

Just occasionally, I wondered how on earth Isabelle and I had become so close. Sixteen years ago, our friendship had an unusual beginning. Bristol had been twinned with Bordeaux for years, and my dad used to be very active in the city's twinning association. So, despite my hesitation to venture into another country alone – especially since I'd just had dental braces fitted – I'd been set up for an exchange. I'd arrived at Bordeaux airport, the youngest of fifteen Bristolian students, trembling in my short, lavender tartan kilt, lavender sweater, black tights and chunky black shoes – the height of fashion in the late nineties or so I thought – and waited with anxiety churning in my stomach. When the group leader began calling out names to partner us up, out of the crowd stepped a tall girl with short dark hair. She was wearing a bottle-green sweater over jeans and trainers but looked unutterably chic to my young eye. Isabelle Masson grinned in my direction and I was overjoyed to see her teeth were adorned with a comprehensive set of dental braces identical to mine. I hadn't smiled properly since I'd had the horrible things fitted but I beamed back at her with relief.

She'd made me a card, showing a hand-drawn, vaguely recognisable image of Bristol Suspension Bridge with the letters – V I C K I – hanging beneath. Inside the card was another bridge, that I later learned was Pont Pierre in Bordeaux, with the letters – I S A B E L L E – hanging beneath.

'We are the same,' she said in her best English.

'Yes,' I replied, delighted to think this girl would align herself with me. '*Oui.*'

Our friendship confirmed, she hugged me and took hold of my hand before leading me to her parents. As I'd never had a brother or sister – and coming from an English society where hugging was reserved for close family – the intimacy of this made me feel weirdly alien and yet totally accepted.

As if in anticipation of her future career, Isabelle already showed a knack for getting alongside others and gaining their confidence.

She was confident too, for a teenager. She had three brothers and read everything she could lay her hands on. I, on the other hand, was still finding my social feet, was an only child and read magazines – occasionally. While she would astonish me with her burgeoning philosophies of life, I would impress her with my drawing ability and early skills in the kitchen. My Somerset Apple Cake still remains a favourite with her family.

So, despite the miles which separated our homes, we became 'Sisters Under the Sun' and continued to enjoy a special bond in adulthood.

* * *

As Christophe walked up the hill with his dogs, he used the time to think about the newcomer in their household. 'What do you think, boys?' he asked them. 'Did I do the right thing, huh? Do you like having company around the house?' Hercules looked back at him, tongue flopping out of his mouth in a lazy, doggy smile. 'I did it for you, you know.' Although, he could see there were some benefits for him too.

He thought how vehemently Vicki had argued with him over the purchase of food. The girl certainly had spirit. Perhaps it was her artistic temperament coming out. The truth was, she probably didn't eat more than a mouse. She was tiny – that sweatshirt swamped her. Beautiful eyes though – were they blue or violet?

As the sun broke through a gap in the trees and warmed his face, he smiled.

Chapter 5

It didn't take long to unpack all my art materials and set up the studio. My greatest indecision was over where to place the easel in a room which lacked the preferred north light of a true artist's studio. All the same, I wasn't going to complain. I finally settled on the centre of the room, so I had light from either side, and it also gave me the ability to look out of all the windows.

Next to one of them, I hung a small, double-sided frame; on one side was a picture of my parents and, when I turned it over, there was a list of affirmations I'd written, which had been my mantras for the last few weeks. I stood with my arms stretched out and recited them:

'I am an artist.

'I am painting because I want to – I am a contented artist.

'I am painting for a living – I am a successful artist.

'I am painting for an exhibition.

'There is an audience for my work and the Universe is bringing us together.

'I am an artist.'

I bowed reverentially to the affirmations. 'And screw anybody who gets in my way.'

Yes. This was my time.

Throughout my college career, I'd imagined I would, some day, have an exhibition. Not, you understand, because I was a flashy cow (although some friends may beg to differ) but because I liked to capture the mood of a time, a place and the people within it – just as Impressionists like Lautrec, Manet and Renoir had done. I realise a camera does exactly that, but something about the colours and energy in their work added a mood – a feeling to the image. When I see something which seizes my heart and imagination, I want to capture everything about it; not just the scenery but how I feel about it at the time. So, I guess, I just wanted to share that excitement with everyone else.

I'd already googled art shops in Limoges but I had hoped there might be a small art supplier more locally. I'd only been able to carry sketch-pads so I decided to head out on a reccy of the town. But not before dropping into the surgery to invite The Lovely Louise over for her lunch break. And she was lovely; barely into her twenties, fresh-faced and with a smile for everyone. She had brown hair tied back in a pony-tail, barely-there make-up with a nude tone lip-gloss and she wore a non-too-flattering beige and cream nurse's overall. She was like a sepia toned Anne of Green Gables.

She welcomed me like she'd been looking forward to this day all her life. I doubted this could be due to Izzy's PR so I could only suppose it was Louise's default setting. She accepted my invitation like a shot and I trotted off cheerfully to discover the delights of the little town.

The morning sun was hitting the pavement at an angle, casting oblique shadows across the road. '*Quelle beau jour*,' I said out loud as the sun warmed my back. What a beautiful day. The smell of fresh bread floated out from the *boulangerie*, hooked me by the nostrils and drew me in to buy a baguette, still warm from the oven. Shops were dotted around the town, interspersed with quiet little houses, their window boxes still showing summer colour from red and pink geraniums. How did the French achieve it? I wondered. Wherever you went in France, there were geraniums spilling out of window boxes and traffic roundabouts ablaze with colour. Pride, God love 'em, they had pride.

After covering every square inch of the town, my hunch proved right – no shop selling art materials. The locals were cheerful enough, nodding in friendly greeting as I passed.

I picked up some fresh fish from the *poisonnier* – fishmonger to you and me – and stocked up on fruit and vegetables before heading back.

Today was like a rebirth. I'd promised myself a year in France, which meant another three hundred and sixty-four days to go.

I went back into the house with a broad grin on my face, and set about preparing a lunch of prawn salad. As I cut the bread, there was a tap at the kitchen door and I looked up to see Louise peering through the window. I beckoned her in.

To say conversation was stilted would be like saying the Matterhorn is big. Not surprising when you she wore consider my rusty French and Louise's near lack of English. Mind you, once I got into my stride, the muscles in my brain seemed to loosen up and work harder for me so I found myself firing off question after question. Looking back, I'm amazed she didn't run up a white flag and sprint out of the door. Instead she bore it all with remarkable good grace, a lot of smiles and the occasional frown. I did, however, learn Christophe only spent part of his time at the surgery, since he did the bulk of the equine and large animal work, while his partner, Philippe, kept to the domestic animal work.

'Did you go to the racing dinner, last night?' I asked.

'No, that is very much Christophe's thing. He loves horses.' There was so much emphasis in this statement, I couldn't work out whether she was a bit pissed off with his obsession or merely stressing the point. As I nodded she continued, 'I don't know why he doesn't just make a bed in the stables.' Then she giggled, 'Maybe he already has!'

She was even more pretty when she giggled. I wondered if Christophe's admiration for her went beyond the professional.

'Perhaps that's why he isn't married,' I suggested, boldly yet cunningly manoeuvring the conversation towards his love-life which, I realised, put me at risk of forming an unhealthy preoccupation.

At this, Louise's lovely smile slipped – just momentarily but enough for the finely tuned eye of a high school teacher to spot. She threw up her hands. 'Oh, that's men, isn't it?' she said, beaming again.

Hmmm. Had I plucked a tender nerve? I gave her my you-can-say-that-again look accompanied by a pair of hand flaps. I believe it is universally acknowledged that in a conversation between two strangers, a pair of men will gravitate to football and cars, while women enjoy a minute or two on the failings of men. So, in this moment of mutual disclosure, I said, 'Don't talk to me about men! I'm fed up with men. Right now, I prefer to stay single.'

'Why?'

If I'd had a better grasp of the French language, I could have done justice to the phrase 'right-royally shafted'. Instead I just shrugged. 'I was going to get married but it didn't happen.'

This drew a look of concern from Louise. 'So sad. But I'm sure it was for the best.'

'Yes. The end of a relationship is very painful but really proves just how wrong it was,' I said, sounding wiser than I felt. Louise nodded. 'Do you have a boyfriend?' I asked her, still hell-bent on satisfying my fascination with Christophe's status.

She smiled shyly and shrugged. 'Maybe.'

'My friend, Isabelle, who arranged for me to stay here, tells me that Christophe nearly got married last year.'

Louise frowned and shook her head. 'I don't know if he intended to get married.'

'What happened?' See how bold I was feeling?

Louise fidgeted with her coffee mug and shrugged. 'It's complicated. You should probably ask Christophe. I don't like to say.'

All credit to her, she wasn't indiscreet – more's the pity. 'Oh, it's not important,' I said, waving my hand dismissively. 'Just curious. It seemed like a coincidence, that's all. Two of us broken-hearted and moving on.'

'It's not that simple for him, she's still around.' With that, she pulled one of those flat smiles of defeat you see on the faces of a losing team and I was convinced, right there and then, that she had the hots for him. Before I could ask, she stood up and said, 'Thank you for the lunch, it was lovely. See you again.'

I waved her off at the door – watching her cross the ten metres or so back to the surgery. So the 'ex' was still around, eh? Was I perhaps about to witness a classic love triangle? I'm talking Louise, Christophe and the ex, of course, not *moi*. I felt a lofty sensation of maturity. I was so glad I'd stepped out of the mating game – at least for now. I drummed my fingers on the table as I considered it, before slamming them down firmly and making the dogs jump. 'What's it to me?' I stood up. 'In any case, I'm sure all will be revealed in due course.'

I cleared the lunch away and spoke to the dogs. 'How do you two fancy a breath of fresh air?' Hercules tilted his head to one side and I rubbed his ears. 'I'll get my camera and then we can go walkies.' The dogs might not have understood English but they definitely recognized my intention. They were milling around the hall until I came down and attached their leads, when their tails beat furiously with excitement.

The dogs knew the route, turning outside the kitchen door and heading off through the courtyard to a gate. I took in a deep lungful of fresh French air, smiled to myself and headed on up through the field. Ahead of me were rolling hills. To the far left was a densely wooded area. To the right was the town. I walked slowly, picking up stray pheasant feathers as I went. The dogs were far better trained than my mother's delinquent Red Setters. We stopped at a wooden stile where I sat on the wooden step and looked back at the little town. Gentle autumn sunlight was giving a warm glow to the red and grey rooftops. I lifted up my camera to capture it.

Gazing down at Christophe's house below but

particularly at the window of my studio, I smiled. I couldn't remember the last time I'd felt quite so content. 'Victoria Emily Marchant,' I said out loud. 'Down there, is your future.' Boz sat up and looked at me, his right ear cocked. 'Boz. I'm going to be an artist.' Boz stood up. 'Correction. I am an artist. I'm going to paint some fabulous pictures and you are going to be so proud of me.'

I'd be pretty proud of myself, too. But right now, I had a meal to prepare so I stood up and headed back down the hill.

I was standing in the kitchen, channelling Delia, and sucking cream from my fingers, when Christophe came home. I wiped my hand on my jeans and reached for the grater and lemon, ready to scatter zest over the mousse I'd created.

I heard him muttering to the dogs in his soft, baritone voice. I stepped back to peer out into the hall. Hercules and Boz were squirming round him as he crouched between them, all heads nuzzling and tails swishing – well, maybe just the two tails. He looked up at me. '*Bon soir*, Vicki,' he said with a smile for me too. 'Good evening. How was your day?'

'Great, thank you.'

'Have you begun your masterpiece?' he asked, standing up.

'Not yet. Just getting into the zone,' I said, indicating my zeal with a flick of the cheese-grater.

'Wonderful.' He came into the kitchen and glanced over at the lemon and passion fruit mousse. He raised his eyebrows in what I took to be appreciation. 'You look as if you have been busy here, too. Do I have time to go into the surgery to see Philippe?' he asked.

'Absolutely. You can have dinner whenever you like.'

'Thank you. I will be about fifteen minutes.' He smiled again and headed out into the courtyard.

'Cool,' I said, raising the cheese-grater in acknowledgement before setting to with the lemon.

I stopped grating for a moment. Should I set the table in the dining room or here in the kitchen? Maybe, on the nights he smelled of manure, we would take the rustic option. I sniffed the air. Cologne – so it was the dining room, then, which was a lovely room. It had a beautiful, old, circular table and heavy drapes at the window, which looked out towards the woodland. There was a large painting of a château on one wall and, on another, pencil drawings of two young boys. I looked around the room. Another dilemma – how many places should I set? Was it right to assume he would want me to eat with him? I was, after all, the cook and not a guest. Erring on the side of caution, I set only one place, directly opposite the window so he could enjoy the view in peace.

Back in the kitchen, as I readjusted the little plates of ingredients lined up by the hob, he came in, talking very quickly into his phone. I could only catch the odd word, which didn't add up to much of a story but, judging by the look on his face and his gruff tone, someone or something was seriously pissing him off. He glanced at the empty kitchen table, so I gestured to the dining room. He nodded and crossed the hall, sighing heavily into the phone.

I thought it best to wait until his conversation was over before taking him his bowl of soup. I listened till it all went quiet. I counted to ten, lifted the bowl and walked through to the dining room. He was standing by the window, scowling at the view. His conversation wasn't over; he was listening intently to the caller. I placed the soup carefully on the table and left him to it, closing the door quietly behind me.

Moments later, as I sat at the kitchen table with my own soup and a copy of French *Cosmopolitan*, the door opened and Christophe swept in. He stopped at the table and looked down at me, shaking his head. He picked up my bowl and held out his hand. 'Please. Give me your spoon.' I stared up at him. He flexed his hand again for the spoon. 'You think we are going to eat alone, huh? Like master and servant? Didn't you hear, the Revolution put an end to all that?' I felt my cheeks flush, and then he added, 'Unless, of course, you would prefer to eat alone?'

'No. I just didn't like to impose.'

'Not at all. Come, I want to hear what you have done today.' He pulled a quick but weary smile.

I'd lay bets it was possibly one of the last things he wanted to hear, but I moved anyway. He held my bowl and stood back to let me pass, so we did this silly 'you-go, no-you-go' routine because I felt awkward that somehow the roles had reversed. He won and I went ahead. He placed my bowl on the table beside his. 'So,' he began. 'What have you been doing?'

I filled him in on my walk around the town and the apparent lack of an art supplier.

'You need to go into Limoges. My good friend, François, is an artist. He will be able to help you.'

'Yay! Another artist? What does he paint?'

'Mostly horses. His wife, Marie, is an interior designer. I will call them after dinner.'

'Great. Thank you.'

I glanced, then, at his untouched soup willing him to taste it.

'And this is?' he asked.

'Melon and mint.'

His eyebrows twitched. He dipped the spoon in. I held my breath. He appeared to savour it for a moment and nodded. 'Very good.' He looked up and I breathed again. 'Unusual but delicious.'

Phew! One course down, two to go. After a polite silence, I told him about my lunch with Louise. 'You're right, she's lovely.'

'I'm glad you like her. It will be good for you to make some friends here. I assume you don't intend to spend all your time painting while you're in France, do you?'

'Well… it's my main focus but you're right, everyone needs a friend or two.'

'Good. Perhaps she will take you out with her. You can get to know her friends.'

I could feel my eyebrows lift. 'She's quite young though,' I said. Thinking she was closer in age to my sixth-formers – bursting with optimism and low on life's experiences.

'I think it's good to hang out with young people, non? They lift your spirits; remind you that life can be fun sometimes, huh?'

His smile was wickedly twinkling, now – and just a little intoxicating. Maybe he was remembering some fun he might have had, himself. Maybe he was imagining the kind of fun this sad, old, jilted art teacher might be crying out for. At this image, my cheeks roared up to maximum temperature and guess what; his smile registered the affect. Suddenly, I was catapulted back in time to the moment I'd come fact to face with my first big crush, Lawrence Harvey, outside the chip shop in Clifton. I'd run straight into his elbow and sent his chips flying. Then I'd performed a Tom & Jerry style juggling act to catch them before they hit the pavement, meeting a brutally vinegary chip full in the eye. As I'd squinted through the tears to clutch the greasy parcel to my duffel-coated chest, he'd said, 'Kids!' He was all of fifteen and I was eleven. On handing most of the chips back to him, he'd shrugged, looked me in the eye and grinned. 'Good catch, though,' he'd said and, for the first time in my young life, my heart boarded a roller coaster. My addiction to charmers had been launched.

Right now, as then, I could feel my equilibrium being seriously challenged. The difference being that on Whiteladies Road, I'd shoved the chips back into Lawrence's hands and legged it; now, under Christophe's scrutiny, I nudged a fraction closer, probably lowered my eyelids à la Miss Piggy and said, sotto voce, 'Do you think I might have forgotten how to have fun?' Our eyes locked. My focus did a slow pan from one of his eyes to the other. They were as dark as printer's ink.

'I think, the older we get, we can all be guilty of that, non?' he said. 'Tell me, what's the most fun you've had in the last week?' Week? We were talking seven days? I scanned my memory bank, tearing off imaginary calendar pages, one after the other. He must have spotted the rapid blinking of my eyes; I guess I looked like Richard Gere doing his I'm-in-a-tricky-spot-and-thinking-very-hard act, because Christophe added, 'Not much, I think.'

'Well, coming here has been a highlight. Last week

I was busy getting ready to leave.'

'Okay. Before that. What was the last fun thing you did?'

I'd got absolutely trashed at my leaving party in July. The theme was cartoon heroes. I'd gone as Madame Whiplash. Not because I had designs on subjugating any men, but because a certain level of bitterness had taken root. I think I was secretly hoping to keep them at arm's length by cracking my 120 centimetres of coiled leather if they got too close. In retrospect, I should have gone as Mrs Doubtfire. With term over, and several pints under their belts, some male members of staff were salivating at my apparently blatant come-on. In their eyes, I was back on the market. Three mojitos under my belt, and I'd become a proficient circus act; three more and all hostility towards the male species had been swilled away. I'm a happy drunk; everybody is my friend and I love them for it, which is probably not the most appropriate status when strutting around in cheap black latex and stockings.

'Well?' Christophe prompted.

Gah! 'We had a party at the end of term. That was fun.'

He nodded slowly but didn't seem too impressed. 'Did you dance?'

'Oh boy, yes. We also had a horse race – of sorts.'

'You did?' he looked puzzled.

'How do I explain? The men were the horses, the women were the riders. We raced through the car-park – piggy-back style.'

I omitted to say there was a grainy video of me on YouTube, frantically caning one of the PE teachers with my whip handle as we crashed across the finishing line. I'm not absolutely sure it didn't unearth some deep-seated masochistic tendency in my mount, since I swear his eyes shone quite brilliantly as he thanked me for the best ride of his life. You can hear him say so on YouTube; anonymously, of course. We're all responsible teachers who would never be caught doing anything unseemly after dark.

'So, the end of term was when – July?'

I knew what he was getting at. It was months ago. 'That was the most fun I've had recently. I've been busy preparing to come here. Although, I did treat myself to a weekend watching the entire boxed set of *Sex and the City* and eating my way through a large tub of Chunky Monkey ice cream. How about you?' I asked before he had chance to comment.

He smiled. 'Fun? Do you know what? I've probably not had that much fun myself, lately.'

'Think.'

He sat back in his chair. 'That would probably be when I kayaked down the river Tarn. Four of us went on a weekend away. I think you English would call it a stag weekend.' He nodded and smiled at the memory.

'When was that?'

He grinned. 'June.'

'You're right, Christophe, we need to get out more.' I stood up and reached for his empty dish. 'I'll go and fix the main course.'

From the kitchen, I could just make out him talking on the phone again. I figured he was calling his artist friend, until a loud and explosive stream of invective made Boz whimper with concern. By the time the main course was ready, all was quiet again. I entered the dining room cautiously but he was sitting with his elbows on the table, resting his chin on his fists and staring out of the window. I hovered. 'Are you ready for your main course? It's pork in apricot sauce with sage and onion rice.'

He sat back, and I could see from the set of his jaw that all sense of fun was forgotten. 'Absolutely. Thank you.'

He ate quickly, deep in thought while I wondered what was happening in his world to wind him up so. Should I distract him with conversation or leave him alone? It was hard to judge. You could practically twang the tension with a fingernail. Finally he spoke.

'You have no meat.'

I took my focus from the vegetable risotto on my plate and looked up at him. 'No. I'm a vegetarian.'

'Why is that?'

'Well… I think I was always a vegetarian at heart. I knew I could never actually take another creature's life just to satisfy my hunger; especially when there are so many other options. But I once heard someone explain he was a vegetarian because "animals are your friends, and you don't eat your friends".' I shrugged. 'Made sense to me.'

Christophe stared at me like he was assessing my sanity.

I continued, 'Well, I was stroking one of our dogs at the time, and I thought – he's right. So I haven't eaten meat since.'

Christophe repeated the phrase: 'You don't eat your friends.' And then he laughed. 'I would love to hear what Monsieur Bonnet would say about that – or Monsieur Laurent.'

'Let me guess – farmers?'

He nodded slowly. 'So, do you offer fish the same

respect?'

I wrinkled my nose. 'Not exactly.'

'You do not consider them your friends, then?'

'I know it is a tiny bit hypocritical, but I'm not sure there's much history of mankind bonding with fish. I'm not saying they don't have feelings or emotions – it's just not very easy to spot them.'

He smiled and studied me for a moment. It was that staring thing again. 'Vicki. Do you know what this meal is missing?'

I looked at his plate, confused both by his query but more by the intensity of his look. I shook my head. 'Salad?'

'Wine.'

Idiot. How could I have forgotten – in France of all places? I blushed, jumping up immediately. He closed his hand gently around my wrist. An electric surge shot up my arm. Yikes! This man could be dangerous.

'Vicki. please, sit down. Leave it to me.'

When he left I rubbed my wrist and shook it. I slid my plate a little further away from his and shuffled my chair into a new position. He returned with two large glasses and a bottle of Pinot Noir.

'I'm so sorry. I don't know why I forgot,' I said as he poured the wine.

'No matter. You have been busy.' He passed me a glass. '*A votre santé*. Good health.'

I took the glass from him, holding it by the stem to avoid his fingers, and sipped it immediately. The wine was smooth, buttery and just the right temperature. I could feel a warm glow spreading through my insides. Wine could do that to you, I reasoned, taking another swallow.

Outside the sun was setting behind the trees, forming a deep orange halo. I thought how lucky I was to be there, gazing out at such a lovely view. After a while, I asked, 'Who are the children in the pictures?'

'My father and his brother, Alain.'

'They're charming sketches.'

He nodded.

'And the château?'

'That was painted by a local artist.'

'It's beautiful. Is it near here? I'd like to go and see it for myself – or one like it.'

Christophe nodded. 'I can take you. It looks particularly beautiful in the autumn.'

'I don't want to put you to any trouble.'

'It's no trouble.' He smiled, the dimple in his cheek reappearing. 'It will be my pleasure.'

Pleasure. I suspected he was well able to find and give pleasure at the drop of a chapeau, which launched another rush of heat through my veins. 'Thank you,' I gushed. 'I'll take my camera. The more images I can gather, the more stimulation I'll have for my work.'

He raised an eyebrow as he lifted the bottle to refill our glasses. 'So, you have swapped teaching to make a living as a painter?'

'I hope so.' I remembered my affirmations. 'No. Yes. I am a painter. This year I plan on building a portfolio of paintings. I'm working towards an exhibition.'

He nodded. 'So, why the change and why now?'

Isabelle couldn't have told him the full story, then. Thumbs up to Izzy. I twiddled the stem of my wine glass as I considered my answer. 'Teaching art can be very satisfying but also frustrating. You come up with lots of ideas for the children to develop, and all the time you wish you could be working on them, too.'

'Really? Couldn't you paint while they were painting?'

'Not easily.' I thought of the pandemonium that had ensued the day I'd attempted to work on my own piece while the year nines were working on theirs. It had taken six hours and a large can of emulsion paint to cover up the graffiti. The standard of Banksy it wasn't. Nobs, balls and boobs proliferated, dappled with arcs of multicoloured spots and several blobs of chewing gum. No. Kids at Darwin High School had demanded my full and undivided attention. 'This way, I can really concentrate on my painting; no lesson plans, no reports, no detentions. I'll be free to enjoy the tactile pleasure of moving paint around the canvas. Sometimes, there's this glorious, serendipitous discovery, when you butt one colour up against another and it changes the whole mood of the image. It's amazing how just a line here or a highlight there can alter the picture. It's like a journey into the unknown.'

He smiled. 'Did you know, your eyes sparkle when you talk about your painting? You really lift the mood.'

'I do?'

'I think you could succeed at pretty much anything you chose to do.'

My inner thermostat went haywire as a rush of heat flared through me. 'Maybe. No, you're right. I want to prove something to myself.'

'So, Vicki, tell me, what do you do for pleasure?' He leaned back as he waited for me to reply. I looked down and could feel him watching me as I pushed rice around my plate.

'Well, painting, of course.'

He was still watching me as I lifted the fork to my mouth. 'But if painting becomes your work, you must do something else to unwind – what would that be?'

I rolled my eyes before reaching for my wine glass and took a gulp. After a moment I said, 'I love walking in the countryside and, of course, I like cooking.'

'And you cook very well. Everything has been delicious, and I'm looking forward to that lemon dessert you were making.' He smiled so charmingly I was reminded, again, of Marc.

I coughed to dislodge the rice sticking in my throat. 'How about you? Is it all horses and work?'

He nodded slowly and smiled. 'I have a lot of pleasure riding my horses.'

'Lovely. I can only imagine how wonderful it must be to gallop across the open countryside. I've never been on a horse in my life,' and there was a very good reason for that – horses terrified me.

'Really? Then you must learn while you're here.'

Not bloody likely. 'To be honest, I don't think I'd be very good at it. But thanks for the offer.' I chased the last of my risotto around the plate. 'What else do you do?'

'I go to watch my horses race. Now, that is a fantastic thrill and also a little tense. Have you ever been to the races?' I shook my head. He adjusted his position to face me fully as he began to describe the scene. 'But you can imagine the build up before the race, non? Everyone is excited and expectant; the traps go up and the adrenalin is pumping while you watch your horse charging round the course – ahead a little, then back, then ahead again. It's very intense and it's exhilarating. Then, when it finally crosses the finishing line – its head just in front of the rest – ah, it's like…' He leaned forward and his eyes narrowed as he looked for the words. I waited. '…it is the second best thing to making love.'

I just knew he was going to say that. I was toying with the idea of coming back at him with, 'You've clearly never skied down a red run, at dawn, stark naked,' but his phone rang again. He let out a groan and dragged his eyes away from mine but not quickly enough, I suspect, to miss the tell-tale heat scorching my flesh. 'Excuse me,' he smiled, before flicking open his phone.

I sipped at my wine as he sat back in the chair to take the call, saying very little, other than the odd 'oui' or 'non'. I could hear the caller's voice. It was a woman and, by the sound of it, an emotional one. I risked a glance in his direction but the strain on his face was so intense, I looked away quickly and gathered the plates together.

He snapped his phone shut. 'My apologies, Vicki. I must go,' he said, stood up and headed to the door, stopping briefly to say, 'Thank you for dinner.'

I sat for a moment and pondered. Could that have been the woman he used to live with? Was she still on the scene and raising the roof over my arrival? What news could affect him so strongly he had to rush off without trying my fabulous lemon mousse?

I let out a huge sigh and ran a cooling hand round the back of my neck.

Chapter 6

My host didn't come home that night or the following morning. I finally cleared the breakfast away at ten, tossing Hercules and Boz a small chunk of bread each. I took a mug of coffee out into the courtyard and sat on a wooden bench in the sunshine. I'd spent the morning reviewing my photographs and sketching ideas for my first canvas. The chances of Christophe having called his artist friend were pretty remote so I chewed over the idea of getting a taxi into Limoges. It would be pretty costly, though. I'd already shelled out on a taxi from the station.

Through one of the surgery windows, I could see Christophe's partner, Philippe, talking to Louise. Philippe was heavy-set, with a face like a young Gerard Depardieu, but without the 1970's hairstyle. Perhaps they knew where Christophe was. Not that it was important. He wasn't obliged to be around to eat every meal with me. But it would be nice to know if he was planning on coming home for dinner. I sipped at my coffee, mulling over my morning's work. There was no denying it – my sketches were stilted and dull. That's what comes of spending three years teaching the effect of viewpoint on elipses, or shading technique and how to show reflected light; I'd completely lost spontaneity in my own work.

I leaned back against the wall and closed my eyes. Thoughts of Marc and what he might be doing snuck into my brain. I'd heard he'd moved on from Barbados to Miami. And guess who lived there – Maxine Dewar – she of the double tongue piercing. That really niggled me. No wonder he hadn't wanted to invite her to the wedding. He'd said she wasn't 'into weddings' so why bother? She definitely wasn't into my wedding, any more than he was. Maxine did sculpture. She'd always been the wild one in our group. By the time she completed her degree, she'd had twenty-two piercings. I supposed they might come in handy for hanging her tools on.

I still didn't know whether Marc had made his decision to leave at the last minute, or planned it months ahead. Word had filtered through he'd felt pressured into the wedding; he would have been happy staying as we were. Oh, really? I thought. If that were true, where was he now? He could have talked it over with me and not taken the coward's way out. But that was Marc – never one to confront anything. He'd duck around a problem, sweep it under the carpet, never see anything to a conclusion. Where as I... I what?

It's not like I'd spotted his reluctance. I sure as hell hadn't been looking for it. We were a team, I'd thought, with me calling the shots, rallying the troops and saving the cash.

Yes. I was the kind of girl who saw things through to the bitter end. I was not a quitter.

I sighed. After everything Marc had done, I was surprised I couldn't hate him – not after spending so long in love with him. He'd always had this irresistible charm – even when he was totally in the wrong, he could make me laugh so I'd forgive him. I smiled a watery smile and groaned. 'May the universe deliver me from charming men.'

As I walked back across the courtyard, I could hear the unmistakable sound of a girl crying. It was coming from the surgery. A client grieving over the demise of a much-loved pet, perhaps? I paused. No, that was definitely Louise's voice I could hear between the sobs. Curious. Had it been her voice I'd overheard on the phone, last night? But why would she be crying on the phone to Christophe? No, surely it had been the ex calling? This idea nudged another thought into my mind – was Christophe the kind of guy who might use my stay to manipulate the women in his life?

I nodded to myself. Sure, he could be.

That pulled me up short. If my suspicions were right, it did put my sabbatical on a rather shaky footing.

I made myself a sandwich of goat's cheese and tomato, and tramped slowly back up to my studio, where I stared disconsolately at my sketches. So much for my new life. And it was hard to imagine a ticker-tape welcome on my return to Bristol, as I sloped down Victoria Street, shoulders drooping and an empty portfolio at my side.

I stared at the wall for ages, fighting my doubts with positive affirmations – with that tell-tale prickle in the back of my nose threatening tears. Had I kidded myself into thinking I could get over the storm of Marc's departure so easily?

Downstairs, the dogs began barking.

'*Allo!*' a man's voice called.

I wiped my face with my hands and sniffed, before running down the first flight of stairs. 'Hello!' I called back, sniffing again.

At the bottom of the second flight, I saw a large, sandy-haired man with a thick moustache looking up at me. 'Ahh!' he exclaimed. 'Vicki?'

'Oui.' I descended the stairs.

'I'm François,' he said, holding out his hand to me. 'Christophe tells me you want canvases.'

I opened my mouth in surprise. 'Yes. I do. Pleased to meet you.' I shook his hand.

He beamed at me. I could see he was a good deal older than Christophe, probably in his early fifties. His eyes were quite sexy in a dissipated way; creased as they were from laughter, and bloodshot, I suspected, from booze but his handshake was warm and strong. I felt like I was in the presence of a true lover of life – I could practically feel his energy recharging mine. 'I think you have been crying, Vicki.' he declared, in English; his frankness shocking yet welcome.

I brushed a strand of hair from my face. 'Just feeling a bit homesick, I suppose. Silly isn't it?'

'Nonsense. We are nothing without emotion. Come.' he embraced me firmly, kissing me on both cheeks, the tang of Gauloises cigarettes invading my nostrils. 'I have brought a canvas for you but it may not be the right size. If you like, I can take you to my supplier and you can choose exactly what you want.'

And we're off, I thought. I will get over Marc's departure. 'Absolutely. If you're happy to take me to your supplier, that would be great. Thank you.'

François, God love him, encouraged me to speak French during our journey. His enthusiasm for my efforts – not to mention his patience – had to be applauded. I watched him as he squinted through the smoke from his cigarette, while he concentrated on what I was trying to say. Whenever I grasped blindly for a missing word, he'd plug the gap.

The art shop was like an Aladdin's cave. It took all of my self control not to buy yet more paints and brushes – gleaming new brushes were always so tempting and utterly sensuous, especially when I stroked those silky, sable strands across my cheek.

As François closed the van doors on my materials, he said, 'Why don't we take all this back to my studio and stretch those canvases for you?'

'That would be fantastic. Christophe tells me you paint horses. I'd really love to see your work.'

'Well, I hope you like them. Not everybody does.'

As we set off, I asked, 'Have you painted Christophe's horses?'

'Many times. His father gave me my first commission. I was straight out of art school and full of enthusiasm – and angst. Hah! I like to think I've improved a little since then.'

'So you've known Christophe a long time?' I asked, masterminding a conversational path that led directly to the source of the recent drama.

'Since he was a baby. Always bright. Always thoughtful. And I think, often lonely.'

My head snapped up. 'Really?'

François nodded, tossing his cigarette filter out of the window. 'His parents were busy with their own lives. His father was a fine man – quiet but strong. Sadly, I don't think he was very affectionate. And yet his mother, ah...' he paused. 'What a beautiful woman.' A smile settled on his face and I could tell there was something going on behind his eyes, which I could only guess at.

And?

After a moment, I asked, 'So, they sent their only child away to school?'

François shrugged. 'His mother likes to travel. Having a baby doesn't automatically make you a good parent, you know.'

I leaned my head back on the seat and pictured a little seven year-old boy, packed off to a school in another country because his parents had better things to do than look after him. I would never do that to a child of mine. An image drifted across my inner vision of a beautiful boy, with dark eyes and a heartbreaking smile. Drawing a deep breath, I found it hard to imagine Christophe being lonely these days.

François steered his van through an avenue of poplar trees to a house and outbuildings that scrambled up the gentle gradient of a hill. 'A drink before we work,' he announced.

We sat on the terrace overlooking a lake, to enjoy a glass of Pouilly Fumé and munch olives. François rattled off stories of his time at art school and disasters he'd had with a foray into sculpture, 'Metal is not my friend,' he said. 'It's not forgiving like paint.'

The lake shimmered as the late afternoon sun played on a surface rippled by the breeze. I had just the one small glass of wine, while François downed two large glasses and filled himself a third before guiding me to his studio. I wondered if he'd be able to see straight enough to stretch the canvases and, more importantly, to drive me home.

His paintings, however, were superb. I stood back and marvelled at the huge images. They were vivid and full of his energy. Their vibrancy reminded me of the work of Gauguin, although François had a style of his own. In one, I could sense the horses straining to be off; in another I could almost feel the heat, and touch the sweat dripping off their flanks. If my paintings could have half of this power, I'd be deliriously happy.

In his vast barn of a studio we worked together, one holding the canvas while the other stapled it to the stretcher bars and finally, we were applying gesso with big, fat brushes. As we finished the last canvas, my phone rang. It was Christophe.

'*Salut.*' I chimed. 'How are you?'

'*Bien, merci.*' He sounded like he was in the car. 'Did François come to see you?'

'Yes, I'm with him now. We've just been preparing my canvases.'

'Where are you?'

'In his studio. His paintings are absolutely brilliant.'

'You like them, huh?' He continued. 'I will come and meet you. I expect François has had a couple of bottles of wine by now.'

'Nearly.' I smiled with relief. 'Thanks.'

'I will see you shortly.'

Twenty minutes later, Christophe was sauntering into the studio. He was tall, lean, undoubtedly sober and an Adonis alongside the haggard François. They greeted each other with hearty embraces and continental man-kisses. After a brief exchange of words, Christophe turned to me. 'François says you have had a good day together.'

'Yes, he's been really helpful and quite an inspiration.'

François offered Christophe a glass of wine.

He shook his head. 'Thanks but I've had a long day, we should be going.'

Not to mention – long night – I thought. Judging by the dark crescents under his eyes, he probably hadn't slept at all.

François continued, 'Vicki can speak French very well. We had quite a conversation, didn't we?'

I responded in slow but determined French, only getting one word wrong. Christophe corrected me so gently, I felt as if my attempts at French were perfectly okay. He smiled. 'Soon, you will be speaking like a native.'

'Well that, at least, would be one of my ambitions achieved.'

'And how many more are there?'

I scratched my head. Well, there was holding an art exhibition, somewhat difficult to declare in front of a talent like François; and then there was not allowing myself to be jilted again, which I certainly wouldn't own up to; and I supposed there was still the vague hope that, one day, I might meet a man – the right man – who wouldn't leave me at the altar. And there was no way I was making that confession, either. 'Certainly more than one.' Was all I would say.

Christophe raised an eyebrow and nodded. 'Do you want to put your canvases in the car?'

'I can't. They're still wet.'

François volunteered to deliver them the following day. 'It will be a pleasure and in time, I look forward to seeing your work.'

'Well don't expect too much. It's been ages since I put paint to canvas. But I've really found your work inspiring. It's wonderful.'

François took my hand, bowed and kissed it. 'Vicki, it has been an honour.'

We drove home in silence, me contemplating the

roller-coaster of moods I had experienced in the last forty-eight hours and Christophe, no doubt, reflecting on his torrid night at the hands (or possibly feet) of some hysterical woman. As we drew up alongside the house, without looking at me, he said very softly, 'Thank you.'

'Sorry?'

'Thank you for your quiet. I appreciate it.'

'Oh,' I responded, feeling like I'd just received an unexpected award. 'You're welcome.'

'I am dealing with a difficult situation at the moment.' He shrugged. 'No matter.' He turned and opened his car door.

I watched him head to the house. 'Well,' I murmured to myself, 'What's all that about?'

As we stood in the hallway being greeted by a frenzy of delight from Hercules and Boz, I asked, 'Are you hungry? I was going to make lasagne but I could do something quicker, if you prefer? A frittata, perhaps?'

He stood up, still caressing the larger dog's head and barely smiled. 'A frittata will be fine. Thank you.'

'Okay. I'll just pop up and get changed.' I guessed I was looking pretty shabby after stretching all those canvases. I stopped on the stairs. 'Could you feed the dogs?'

'But of course.'

The bathroom mirror revealed a couple of dirty smears on my face and strands of hair had escaped from various parts of my clasp. I washed quickly and changed into a long, cotton skirt and a scoop-necked tee-shirt in raspberry pink. The sun had drawn every last freckle out on my face and the tip of my nose matched my tee-shirt. I'd always been a great believer in coordinated accessories.

So, frittata on the menu tonight. Nice and simple. Simplicity was good. From what Christophe had said, I was guessing simplicity was something he was hoping for just now, too. But what, I wondered, was the difficult situation he was dealing with?

Chapter 7

Christophe felt the wine easing into his system and releasing the tension as he sat on the kitchen table, resting his feet on the seat of a chair. He would take time to savour the second glass. The last twenty-four hours had been quite an ordeal. Why did life have to be so complicated – especially where women were concerned? Oh for the simplicity of a few casual affairs. It had been so easy when he was younger; lots of pretty girls and so much fun with no strings attached. Last year, he had changed the pattern and what a mistake that had been. Now he was dealing with the fallout.

He heard Vicki running down the stairs and looked up as she came into the kitchen. At least she brightened his day a little. She smiled at him. He poured another glass of wine and offered it to her. As she clinked her glass against his, she said, 'So, what would you like in your frittata? Onions, mushrooms, tomato, peppers?'

'Anything. I'm sure it will be delicious.'

'Okay.' She sipped her wine. 'Hmm, that's lovely.' She raised her glass to him and placed it down on the counter.

Beside him on the table was a small vase containing a bunch of twigs and feathers which Vicki had arranged. He took another slug of his wine and pulled one of the feathers out, turning it between his fingers as he watched Vicki move about the kitchen.

Cute.

He clenched his teeth, reminding himself not to complicate things. Their set-up was nice and simple. She had come here to paint. The last thing he needed was another emotional complication.

* * *

I don't usually mind people watching while I'm preparing food, it was no different from teaching, really, but right then, I was acutely aware of everything I did. Not because I thought Christophe was judging me but because I wondered if he might be – and that was unnerving.

I glanced round and saw him sitting on the table, looking broodily into his glass and twirling one of the feathers from the vase. Heathcliffe in Armani.

I threw chopped onions into the frying pan and stepped back as they sizzled. Suddenly, I became aware of a change in temperature – not in front of me but behind. Christophe spoke so close to my ear, I swear I must have flinched.

'Perhaps I should watch you and learn to cook, myself, huh?'

I pulled a smile. 'Happy to teach you, if you want to learn.'

'Do you know what?' he said, smoothly. 'Standing this close…'

I held my breath.

'…I close my eyes and I think François is here.'

I turned and looked at up him. 'What?'

'It is the Gauloises. Yesterday you smelled of lemon and mint.' He moved round and leaned against the counter next to me. 'François smokes more than he breathes. He is not a healthy man but he is an interesting one. My father was very fond of him – even though he had an affair with my mother.'

My mind buzzed. First I was insulted by his practically saying I smelled like an old ashtray, then the lemon and mint comment and now, now he was telling me personal details about his mother's infidelities. How disturbing was this man? He was so close it was verging on intimate. He must be getting quite a lungful of my smoky hair, which was now absorbing tincture of allium as I stirred the onions unnecessarily. 'That was very magnanimous of your father. He must have loved her very much.'

'You think? Or perhaps he just wanted a quiet life. He was very preoccupied with his horses and racing. In many other ways she was an excellent wife. She was a superb hostess and brought many good contacts to him. You see, my father was a quiet man, he needed her social skills to further his business.'

'That's awful. You make it sound like a corporate merger.'

'This is often the case in marriage.'

'It won't be for me.' I said defiantly, then coloured at the irony of what I was saying. My own choice of husband had been seriously flawed and yet there I was, passing judgement on his parents' marriage.

'So, Vicki, you believe in love and marriage?'

I added garlic and peppers to the pan. 'Well…' What did I believe? He was looking at me expectantly. '…Marriage works for some people.'

Just not me, I thought.

'And it worked for my parents,' he said.

'Okay, point taken.'

'But?'

I shrugged. 'Marriage should be about two people really wanting to share their life. About commitment to a joint future. It's about teamwork.'

'So, if you're not a team player, you shouldn't get married, huh?'

'Exactly.'

'And are you a team player, Vicki?'

'Yes. But right now, I prefer a singles game.'

'You are impatient to paint, huh? What age are you, twenty-six?'

'Twenty-eight.'

'Interesting. Most women your age are starting to look around – they're like Meerkats.'

I shrugged. 'Then I guess I'm not like most women.' I jiggled the spatula vigorously through the onions and peppers.

'I guess not.' He heaved himself up to sit on the work surface next to the chopping board. I lifted the board, moved it to the opposite side of the hob, and set about quartering mushrooms. He sat, sipping his wine and watching me. I threw the mushrooms into the pan. As sizzling vegetables filled the weighty silence, I took a long, cool hit of white wine, he said, 'Some people rush into marriage, don't you think?'

'Possibly.' What was his obsession with marriage? Was he talking about mine? I was bloody sure Isabelle hadn't said anything, but maybe Louise had. 'Look, do you mind if we change the subject?'

He shrugged. 'Okay.'

Good.

I went over to the fridge for the eggs.

'It smells delicious,' he said quietly as I came back to the hob.

Now he's being nice, I thought with a pang of

guilt. I lowered the heat. 'It's not much, really,' I said, before looking up to meet the deep brown, unblinking gaze of his eyes.

'Since you're keen on a singles game, it's quite a compromise to worry about cooking for me, non?'

'No. I'm happy cooking.'

'But maybe that's why this subject bothers you – I'm thinking you'd rather not have to…'

'No. Not at all,' I said turning the heat down and stepping back. Before I knew it, some latent, Catholic desire for confession pulled an invisible chord in my back so I was spewing my story in bite-sized phrases, like a walky-talky doll. 'Izzy hasn't told you, has she? About my wedding day. Or rather, non-wedding day. My fiancé stood me up. He made off with my life's savings. He gambled money he didn't have. He used money I didn't have. There. Now you know why I'm here. It's a fresh start. Something for me. Nothing and nobody is going to screw it up. Not this time.' I drew a deep breath. 'That's it.' I took a gulp of wine, picked up the spatula and batted mushrooms from one side of the pan to the other.

'I'm very sorry to hear that. It must have been difficult.' His voice had dropped to a cosy, comforting level. I'd heard him muttering words of affection to his dogs in the same tone.

There was a tingle in the back of my nose. I lined up the bowl and whisk, ready for the eggs.

'Good for you, Vicki. You're making a change, you're moving forward.'

I walked across the kitchen to find something, anything, so I could blink the tears away before he saw them. I opened the napkin drawer. 'Well, I don't much fancy the alternatives. He's done me a favour, really.'

'I guess it didn't feel like that at the time.'

'No. And I could have done without the debts he left behind, too.' I slapped the napkins down on the table. By the time I'd put the cutlery out, I was back under control.

'Did he actually leave you waiting at the church?' he asked.

I looked across and was consoled to see his eyebrows dipped in a frown of concern rather than in that arched, are-you-shitting-me? way that so many others had adopted.

'Yes. Dad and I were shivering under a brolly in a horse and trap outside. His best man came up to us with this terrified look on his face, poor guy, and I knew.'

He shook his head. 'The man's a coward, huh?'

'Yes.' I had formed quite a list of other adjectives but coward was definitely on it.

'So, I'm guessing you don't trust men now. All of them are bastards, non?'

There was a twinkle in his eye so I guessed he was trying to lift the mood rather than flirt with me. 'After my recent and, it has to be said, most disastrous attempt at choosing a partner, I'll take my time and wait until I can identify someone with all the right qualities.'

'So you wouldn't have him back?'

'Marc?' I thought for a moment. Marc's mercurial character had fascinated me. No run-of-the-mill dependability there. Oh no. How had I described him? Enigmatic. Yes, well, it was a quality that didn't pay the bills and didn't turn up at church. But he'd probably love it here in France, with the new me. I wondered just how boring I had become; always banging on about school, or trawling through solid wood flooring brochures – not to mention adjusting seating plans for the wedding a hundred times. Maybe I'd moved so far from the girl he'd fallen in love with, he couldn't face the thought of spending the rest of his life with who I'd become. 'No. I don't want him back.' I cracked the eggs into the bowl with one hand and stirred vegetables with the other.

'So, you have come here to paint and to cook for me.'

'Yes.'

'And after that, how are you going to set about finding your perfect man?'

'I have no idea. I'm off men. For now,' I added out of self-respect. No woman wanted to be thought of as perpetually frigid.

'When was this wedding?'

'Last year. August.'

'Really? How long a break are you going to take?'

I stopped multi-tasking and stepped back to look at him. 'I don't feel the need to set a schedule.'

'No, but you seem like a woman who wouldn't wait around for too long.'

'Do I?' I asked, putting my hand out to adjust the heat, without taking my eyes from his.

'Well, you got impatient when I was delayed picking you up.'

'I was soaking wet.'

'You're eager to see me eating a healthy diet.'

'I know – Mrs Stafford.'

'You put your heartbreak behind you and travel to another country to pursue your ambitions; you get to work straight away on your paintings.'

He had a point. I picked up the whisk and began beating the eggs furiously.

He continued, 'I don't believe a woman with such passion can be fulfilled by work alone.'

I took a deep breath and slowed down on the egg-beating front. I turned and looked him in the eye. 'Is that so?' I poured the eggs into the pan so they filled the gaps between the vegetables. 'Well, I am also a very determined woman.'

He looked back at me, a smile lifting the corners of his mouth. Then he leaned forward, gently stroked the feather down my cheek and whispered, 'I believe you,' before slipping off the work surface to go and pour himself more wine.

I stirred mechanically, as my insides liquefied and my head span. The guy's charm was lethal. And I was pretty sure he knew it. Well, he might find that kind of trick worked in his bachelor world – and good luck to him – but I didn't have to fall for it.

Christophe headed out of the kitchen to put some music on, and I completed the frittata without further discussion. We sat at the kitchen table and, in my determination to act naturally, I brightly rattled on about how beautiful the countryside was in the Limousin region, 'It's so rural, it reminds me of England.'

'Then you should feel at home.' He refilled my glass. 'Tell me, how many paintings do you think you'll paint this year?'

'I don't know.'

'You have no target?'

'It's not that simple. It depends whether I'm swept away on a wave of inspiration… or not.' I lifted my glass and gestured to him. 'But what about your ambitions, Christophe? Is there a cup you haven't won or an operation you haven't performed?'

'Oh, many.'

'What are you goals?'

'Hah! There's always something more to be achieved. It's what keeps mankind going, don't you think?'

'Yes, probably, although that's very non-specific. Are you avoiding the question?'

'What do you want to know?'

Who is the woman in your life – or are there many? Why is your house so sparsely furnished and am I imagining it, or are you flirting with me? And, if I succumbed, do you think we could just be physical without getting involved?

I cleared my throat. 'You're how old, thirty-four?'

He nodded.

'You live here, all alone with your two dogs…'

'And you.'

'Okay, and me, at present. What does the next five years hold for you?'

'What you really want to know is, do I want to get married, non?'

'No.' I ran a hand over my hair. 'Although, it's a perfectly reasonable question – but I wasn't exactly asking that.'

'True, you were being non-specific.'

'And the answer is?'

He smiled. 'I guess I've decided I like things the way they are.'

There was a groan from the corner as Boz stretched his legs in sleep.

I'd had enough of this subject. 'Would you like some lemon mousse?'

'Pudding as well?'

'I made it last night, but you had to rush off.'

'Ah, yes.' A frown creased his brow. 'Lemon mousse sounds delightful. And then, I think I will take the dogs for a walk. I missed it this morning and it's such a beautiful evening.'

'Yes, it is,' I said, rather more wistfully than intended.

'Then you should come, too.'

Should I? I shrugged. 'Okay.'

We headed off towards the town and turned up a narrow lane, past a shabby house where an old sheep dog staggered from its kennel to greet us. We waited as all three dogs pushed their snouts up against the fence. '*Bonsoir, Emil*,' he said to the ragged old collie. 'Poor thing, he's very old and stiff, but he has a strong heart.'

'That's more than can be said for me,' I said, staring down at them. 'Look how matted and dusty he is. I bet he's never curled up on a sofa having his tummy rubbed or waited eagerly for an empty crisp packet to lick out.'

'I should hope not. Crisps packets are not for dogs.'

'Oh, well our Connie has a knack for turning them inside out. It's her party trick.'

Christophe moved on and whistled to his own dogs.

I threw my arm in the air. 'Look how brilliant the moon is tonight. See how it throws the trees into stark relief – can you see? It really brings out their texture in a completely different way from daylight.'

He looked up.

'And look at the grass, you'd never know it was green, would you? It's in such a cool light.'

'It's remarkable. All I can remember of art lessons is drawing buildings in perspective and making some very bad pots. Perhaps, if my teacher had had your enthusiasm, I might have enjoyed it more.'

I grinned. 'Maybe if I'd had the brain of a scientist, I might have understood physics.'

Back at the house, I thanked him for the guided tour.

'And thank you for a fascinating insight into the vision of an artist.'

'You're welcome. I just hope I didn't bore you – I can be a bit evangelical about these things.'

'Not at all. You were charming.'

Charming? I turned away and began unbuttoning my jacket. I was charming. That sounded nice. He moved to help me off with my jacket, and I noticed the soft, amber fragrance of his cologne and felt the warmth of his hands as they lightly touched my shoulders.

A shrill, repetitive note split the air. He stepped back, pulled a phone from his pocket and sighed. 'Bonsoir, Sylvie,' he said and walked towards his study, with a nod of dismissal to me.

I watched the door close and took off my own jacket.

Coffee. I needed coffee and an early night.

As I scooped up the coffee grounds, my chief thought was, 'Who is Sylvie?'

Chapter 8

François delivered my canvases late the following morning but didn't stop to chat. If I'd had a tail to wag it would've been going like a metronome. I hoisted a canvas onto the easel. Next, I squeezed large blobs of acrylic paint onto the palette. On the distant horizon was a line of trees crowning the hill. I would attempt to paint this. As a first work, the only objective was to flex those muscles I hadn't flexed for some time – both creative and physical. I'd studied my photographs and absorbed the mood of the season. Now, I just wanted to let loose and release my creative energy.

'You rock,' I crooned, sweeping blues and ochres across the canvas to obliterate its inhibiting purity. 'Go sister!' I mixed the paints, sweeping and daubing it in arcs and dashes. 'Feeling the mood, loving the vibe.' I knew my first effort would be weak. Hell, maybe even disastrous but, like an athlete, I just needed to limber up. I pushed and dragged the paint, imagining how Marc would have loved to watch me and revel in my liberation. Too late.

'Oh, bollocks to him!' I stabbed at the canvas. I didn't have to beat myself up over the failure of our relationship. 'I had to pay for our bloody lifestyle. I took responsibility. I'm not a loser,' I announced.

I painted. I wept. I laughed. Sometimes the brush strokes were thick and dynamic, other times fine and feathery. But through every one of them, I felt I was tuning in to the essential Vicki. It was like coming back into focus.

Only when the light began to fade and the dogs began to bleat for their meal did it dawn on me to stop. Six-thirty. Late dinner, then.

My mind was buzzing as I moved about the kitchen. There was no deadline for my artwork. No exam board to please – just freedom to explore. Could life get any better?

When Christophe came home, I very nearly leapt on him like his dogs did.

'*Bien*. You look like you had a good day,' he smiled at me as I paced about the kitchen.

'Fantastic. I spent the whole day painting.'

'Well, I'm glad you've been productive. It would have been a terrible waste for you to travel all this way only to feed me.'

He could say that again. I was no chef. 'Aha, well, after a few weeks of my cooking, you might think it was a waste me coming at all.'

'I doubt that but, tomorrow, you will be free to paint through the night, if you wish. I must leave early in the morning to go to the veterinary school in Toulouse. I go most weeks. I will not be back until Friday.'

'Really?' I maybe sounded a bit too thrilled at the prospect. 'Then, I shall definitely get stuck in.'

He moved over and took a chunk of carrot from the chopping board. 'And I will look forward to seeing the results.'

'Don't expect too much. I'm a bit rusty.'

'If you paint as well as you cook, I'm sure I will be impressed.'

I had much higher hopes for my painting.

He crunched on the carrot, all the time studying what I was doing. Just as I was mentally trawling through a range of topics to discuss, he glanced at his watch and excused himself. 'I'll be in my study,' he said, in what I can only describe as a very weary tone.

By the time I came down to breakfast, Christophe had already left. Two whole days of freedom to paint stretched ahead of me. In the morning sunshine, yesterday's canvas looked an absolute fright. There were haphazard attacks of colour, spiky strokes and areas of imbalance and yet... there was something I wanted to develop. I toiled over it, worrying small areas with new colour, until my jaw ached from being clenched in concentration. So I escaped into the fields with the dogs for a welcome breath of fresh air. I sat on the stile to watch the sun set behind the trees; Boz and Hercules sitting alert at my feet. The mobile in my pocket began to ring. I flipped it open and saw Christophe's number.

'*Salut*.' I chimed, feeling very French.

'Salut,' he returned, sounding preoccupied. 'We have an invitation to a private viewing of paintings by an artist called Florin. It is on Friday evening. Would you be interested in going?'

'Absolutely.'

'Good. Can you be ready for seven o'clock?'

'Yes.'

'Very good. I will arrange it. *Au revoir*.'

I closed the phone. 'Having a lovely time, thank you. Painting's coming along nicely. The dogs are fine.' Boz was watching me, his head tilting from side to side. I scratched behind his ear. 'Old Christophe's a bit of a mystery, isn't he?' I cast my mind back to a couple of nights ago – what was that face-stroking-with-the-feather all about? Nice boys didn't do that kind of thing to girls they hardly knew unless they were after something. I closed my eyes for a moment and allowed myself to relive the shocking, dizzying sensation. Well, even elective celibates could fantasize, couldn't they? But for now, I supposed I was in limbo but it was a good place to be. Limboland. Nice. Lacking in responsibility and furnished with hope.

I shook my head and stood up.

'Come on, boys. Let's go home.'

On Friday evening, I bathed early and took great care over my appearance. I'd just about managed to get the paint from around my nails, and covered up some of the staining with a blackberry coloured nail varnish. Not sure of the dress code for a private exhibition, I selected, navy trousers and a sky blue top I'd bought from a new designers' show in London. It was about six years old but I loved it.

By seven-thirty, there was no sign of Christophe so I called him, only to hear the messaging service. I hung up. He must know he was late. I was just stomping over to the bookshelf to find something to read, when the dogs began to bark. At last!

However, a knock at the door signalled it was not Christophe. As I opened the door, I swear to God, predatory music rippled through the house and thunder rattled the windows. The woman standing outside was tall and gaunt with short, spiky black hair and scarlet lipstick; her eyebrows dipped in the middle, suggesting a permanent state of irritation, and she made no attempt at a smile. Finally, she introduced herself as Jeanne. Since her canine teeth looked normal and there were no tell-tale scars on her neck, I invited her in.

'No need,' she said, chomping briefly on a piece of chewing gum, which seemed a little incongruous for someone wearing a sharp, black, business suit. 'Christophe asked me to pick you up and take you to the exhibition. He's running late.'

No surprises there, I thought.

'Thank you very much.' I grabbed my coat and bag.

The first thing I noticed when I sat in the car was a catering pack of nicotine gum in the central console. On the car radio, a current affairs programme was playing. Jeanne reached out a pewter-coloured, acrylic fingernail and pressed the off button. She then proceeded to quiz me about my home, my family and my view of life in France. Finally, and with some effort, I found an opportunity to fire off a couple of questions in return, and discovered she was a sporting journalist. Not surprising then, that I hadn't detected much genuine interest in her interrogation of me – it was probably habitual. Apparently, she knew Christophe well, from reporting on his horse-racing achievements. 'We've spent a lot of time celebrating his successes,' she crowed. 'Did he tell you about the Plat d'Or dinner?'

Ah. The tuxedo night. 'No. Was it good?'

'Well, we had a good time.' Which suggested she knew him very well. 'So, Christophe says you are an artist. What do you paint?'

They'd discussed me then? Better to be talked about than not, I supposed. 'I think my heart really lies in studies of people.'

'Portraiture. Have you done anybody famous?'

'No. But I don't do portraits, as such. I'm more interested showing something about people's lives. Showing them at work or relaxing.'

'I see.' And that was the last Jeanne uttered until we reached the gallery, when she snatched up two glasses of champagne, handed one to me and steered me towards the exhibits. 'Excuse me,' she said, 'there's someone I need to speak to,' before abandoning me in favour of a smart looking chap on the other side of the room.

The paintings were abstract in mixed media. Large strips of textured paper, woven back into itself and coloured in shades of dirt with jagged fragments of rusted metal nailed to them. Florin, the artist, was tall, skeletal and spent most of the evening out on the street, smoking. I was just trying to decide if I found his work entirely depressing or merely grim, when Jeanne reappeared.

'Vicki, this is Daniel Keane. He's an art critic from England.'

We shook hands and he studied my face briefly before saying, 'I hear you're also an artist. Might I have seen your work, somewhere?' His eyes were a cool, piercing blue, which echoed the blue of the Oxford shirt he was wearing beneath a sludge green tweed jacket. I decided he had to be ex public school; they had such a knack for lousy colour combinations and clashing patterns. I put it down to their being jettisoned from home at an early age and left to make their own choices from a bewildering wardrobe of clothes, added to which, poor laundry habits invariably left them wearing whatever had the fewest creases.

'No. Nowhere. I mean – I'm an artist but not a practising one.' That made me sound like a lapsed Catholic, which I was. 'I studied art, but took up teaching. Now, I'm just about to embark on a series of paintings.' Didn't that sound impressive?

He nodded and studied my face, which I found a bit disconcerting. 'So you're starting out on a voyage of creative discovery. Does it excite or daunt?'

'Both.'

'Well said!' He smiled, then, surprising me with this flash of normalness. It was good to be with a fellow Brit. 'So what part of England are you from and how did you end up in Limoges?'

I gave him the abridged version, before asking, 'Who do you write for?'

'I have a column in Modern Cultural Review and I produce the odd item for The Arts Programme.'

'On TV?' I asked. 'Sorry, obviously on TV. I always watch it, or I did when I was in the UK.'

He looked around the gallery. I did the same and noticed Jeanne had disappeared. 'So, Vicki, what do you make of Florin's work?'

I thought for a moment. 'Honestly?'

'Of course.'

I scanned the canvases again. Just because he was a serious art critic didn't mean I had to censor my opinions. All the same, I spoke very quietly. 'I think they're exceedingly gloomy, mind-numbingly dull and I can't believe he spent years painting them without topping himself.' I ended with a challenging smile.

He smiled back at me. He should smile more, it suited him. In repose, he looked severe, with his pale blue eyes and thin lips. But the smile... the smile softened his eyes and displayed two front teeth that were slightly crooked. I'd always found imperfect smiles rather appealing.

'You're assuming he finds them depressing, too. Perhaps he's exorcised the demons through this work and freed himself up for a whole new series of more stimulating pieces.'

I shrugged and looked outside, where Florin was drawing deeply on another cigarette, his sucked in cheeks appearing even more gaunt under the street light. 'He certainly looks refreshed, doesn't he?' We both laughed.

He held his hand out for my glass. 'Let me get you a top-up.'

Nice guy, I thought. Nowhere near as up himself as I would have expected an art critic to be; which just proved how judgemental I'd become. And that reminded me, where was my landlord?

When Daniel returned with my champagne, I asked, 'Are you in France for this exhibition?'

'No. I'm writing a book on private art collections. It's a labour of love, really, since nobody's paying me to do it. All being well, it'll get taken up by one of the publishing houses.'

'So you're living here?'

'Staying with an old school friend, Connor Kennedy. He's a bit of a reprobate but refuses to charge me rent. I just have to keep him supplied with good whisky and the fridge topped up with grub.'

'Sounds like my set-up; Christophe refuses rent in return for my culinary services. He's even funny about me contributing to the food bill.'

One eyebrow twitched, before Daniel said, 'I trust his intentions are honourable?'

'I hope so, too. I'm not sure I'd put him in the reprobate category but the jury's out on his honourability,' I said, just as Christophe materialised at my side. 'Hi,' I breezed, ramming a broad smile onto my face, feeling the guilt quivering through it.

'Salut,' he said, nodding at me before eyeing up Daniel as he introduced himself.

'Have we met before?' Christophe asked, through narrowed eyes.

'Not sure that we have,' Daniel replied. 'But then, I'm lousy at remembering faces. Listen, I'm going to see if I can grab an interview with Florin. You never know, I might get an article out of it for The Review.' He reached into his pocket and pulled out his phone. 'Vicki, would you like to give me your number, and we'll catch up again, next week?'

'Great. Love to.' I pulled out my phone. 'Call me, now, and then your number will be on mine, too.' As I recited my number and he tapped it into the phone, I was conscious of Christophe looking on in silence.

'Cheers.' Daniel said as my phone rang. 'I'll be in touch.'

'He won't,' Christophe breathed, as Daniel headed off in search of Florin.

'What? Why?'

Christophe shrugged. 'A hunch. Now, where's Jeanne?'

'I've no idea. She introduced me to Daniel and I haven't seen her since.' More importantly, I asked, 'Why won't he get in touch?'

Christophe waved his hand dismissively. 'Oh, maybe he will, but he looks to me like the kind of guy who collects women's numbers for fun.'

'Really? I've never met anyone who did that. Have

you?'

'One or two.' Christophe smiled then, and I detected a weariness in his face as he touched my arm. 'Ignore me, I'm probably wrong. Now…' he looked about him, his focus appearing to bounce from canvas to canvas, '…what do you think? Should I invest in a Florin?'

'If I said, 'yes', would you?'

He studied the closest piece. 'Non.'

'Art's not really your thing is it, Christophe?'

'No, although I can appreciate a good picture when I see one.'

'Is that why you asked Jeanne to bring me?'

'Not exactly. She rang to say she had invitations and would we like to come. I thought you would enjoy it. But maybe you didn't?'

'I don't like the results, but that doesn't stop me from appreciating the work that's gone into them. And of course, art can exist to stimulate and test the psyche.' Christophe nodded but I could tell he really wanted to be somewhere else, so I put a bright smile on my face and added, 'Plus, I met Daniel. He could be a useful contact, if I ever have an exhibition.'

'Excellent. So, does that mean you're ready to leave?'

I nodded. My feet ached and all I'd eaten since lunch was an apple and a couple of canapés. 'Don't you want to find Jeanne?'

'If I know Jeanne, she's already left. Art's not her thing, either.'

In the car, I kicked off my shoes and closed my eyes. So, poor old Jeanne had invited Christophe to the exhibition only to end up baby-sitting his lodger. No wonder she'd been so bloody cheerless and legged it at the earliest opportunity. Still, fair dos, by bouncing me off onto Daniel Keane, she'd done me a huge favour.

Christophe was wrong. Daniel, did call me, and he took me to see Limoges Museum's porcelain collection. 'I'm not a great connoisseur of ceramics,' he said. 'But the town's history is full of it, so I feel it would be rude not to go.'

'Absolutely,' I agreed. Anything for some creative stimulation and human company.

I couldn't quite work out whether Christophe had been avoiding me or perpetually busy. He'd invited his partner, Philippe, round for dinner on Sunday evening. 'His wife's away, do you mind?' he'd asked. Although I'd looked forward to the evening, it had been like watching a foreign movie without subtitles. I'd gone to bed exhausted from trying to follow the conversation. And in the morning, Christophe had gone back to the veterinary school in Toulouse.

Limoges museum didn't stimulate me half as much as Daniel's conversation did. The exhibits were fine – ornamental plates, urns and vases that wouldn't look out of place in a gypsy caravan – but Daniel, well! He was so connected. He had a sister at the BBC, an aunt at the Royal Academy, friends in two leading newspapers and a cousin on the Arts Council. Which sounded like he was name-dropping, which he sort of was but only because I was quizzing him on how he found subjects to write about. 'Word gets around in the art world, Vicki. Produce something fresh, interesting or just plain good, and people in the know get to hear about it.' He smiled. Was he hinting that if I could only produce something good?

Still, it couldn't hurt to know people in the know. 'I feel even more self-conscious about my paintings, now, than I did before,' I grinned.

'Don't be.' He touched me gently on the arm. 'There's such a lot of crap talked about art. I've done it myself often enough. Please don't try to produce something extraordinary. It'll only look self-conscious. Paint from the heart. That way, you'll paint what you enjoy, you'll produce more and by doing that, you'll develop a style all of your own. The best you should hope for, is to touch people.'

I felt my throat tighten at his sincerity but swallowed the lump down and beamed back at him and blinked a bit. 'Thanks. I'll try.'

'Excellent.' He squeezed my arm gently before moving his hand away and running it through his hair. 'Now, let's see if we can grab a coffee, somewhere.'

* * *

Later that evening, Daniel reflected on how Vicki had clearly been touched by his words of encouragement. It never ceased to amaze him how one person could so easily affect another. In the wrong hands, influential personalities could and did manipulate weaker ones. That was how teachers could inspire pupils; a few verbal strokes here and a pat on the back there. Equally, a barb or a sneer could squash any burgeoning talent. Maybe, in another life, he might have considered a career in teaching. He shook himself. Unlikely. He wouldn't have the patience. No. Teaching was for altruistic people, like Vicki. He smiled to himself. Beneath that bright, jokey exterior she was, genuinely, a sweetheart.

Jeanne had not done the English girl justice. Far

from being small and insipid, he found her bright and sparky. There was a mischief behind the eyes and a little awkwardness. His smile broadened when he remembered the flash of concern he'd detected when she'd realised she didn't recognise him or his name. But Jeanne had been right about one thing, as an aspiring artist, she was ideal. Yes, Vicki was a good find.

Chapter 9

On Thursday evening, to my surprise, Christophe was in a refreshingly chirpy mood. He asked about my trip to the museum. 'It's good that you have an acquaintance in the art world, non?'

'Very good. It's nice to talk to someone who understands what I do.'

'Not like me, huh?' he smiled.

'Ah, no, don't say that. It's just different. With Daniel I can talk about art and artists and all those things art snobs talk about. Not that I'm one of those. God forbid.'

'Don't worry. I can't imagine discussing Exertional Rhabdomyolysis with you, either.'

'Granted.' I thought for a moment. 'And that is?'

'Muscle disintegration. It can happen in horses that are exercised too much, too quickly.' We exchanged a smile and began clearing the plates away.

When the coffee was made and we took it through to the salon, I said, 'Do you play the piano or is it there for decoration?'

He cocked an eyebrow. 'It's a little too big for an ornament, don't you think?'

'So you do play.'

'Occasionally but like you and your painting, I'm a little rusty.'

'Could you play something now?'

He looked a little taken aback but placed his coffee

down and went over and drew back the piano stool. 'Don't expect too much.'

Like a joke pianist, he flexed his fingers, interlaced them and cracked his knuckles, which made me wince. Then he smiled, placed his fingers on the keyboard and faultlessly rippled through a classical piece I totally recognised but couldn't name.

'Wow! That was amazing. What was it?'

'Mozart. Rondo alla Turca.'

'You should practise more – you could give up your day job and tour the world.' As he made to get up, I said, 'Don't stop now. You're coffee's still hot. Play something else.'

He looked amused by this but settled down again, anyway. 'I think you'll know this one,' he said, and began to play the Harry Potter theme tune. Part-way through, he vamped it up into a honky-tonk style and ended, on his feet, hammering the keys with his fingers like a true pro.

'Bravo!' I exclaimed, clapping my hands. He looked over at me, a huge grin on his face. It was the first time I'd seen him truly cheerful since my arrival. The man was human, after all.

He closed the lid on the piano. Maybe he didn't believe in giving a girl too much of a good thing. Just considering how much of a good thing he could give me, made my pulse kick. 'You're so talented,' I said, to deflect my thoughts from where they were heading. 'You must have been playing for years.'

He stood over the table and picked up his coffee mug. 'Yes. It pleased my parents to hear me play. So I practised – very hard.' That was so sweet; to think of him as a little boy, eager to please his preoccupied parents by devoting himself to his music. 'My mother still has the grand piano I was taught on. It's a beautiful instrument but too big for this house.'

'Well, I think you should play every day – if you have time. I can't believe you play so well and yet I've been here two weeks and that's the first time I've heard you.'

'It's the first time I've played all year. I'm surprised the piano hasn't gone out of tune.'

I gaped up at him. Marc was forever tinkering with his guitar – and he was crap by comparison. Actually, on second thoughts, crap was too flattering. 'Then I shall insist you play more frequently.'

'Yes… Miss,' he nodded, a rather fascinating twinkle in his eye.

'Sorry.' I rolled my eyes and took a glug of coffee. I had hoped to leave my schoolteacher status behind me but maybe it was still my default setting.

'Would you like to visit the château on Saturday?' he asked.

'Would I?' I answered, registering how surprised I sounded. 'Yes please.'

'Good. Now, I must do some paperwork.' He moved off towards his study, coffee still in his hand. He turned in the doorway. 'I forgot to mention, Marie has invited us for dinner tomorrow night. Would you like to go?'

Marie? I thought. Marie?

'François and Marie.'

'Oh yes, of course. Love to. Thanks.'

'Good. I shall meet you there. Jeanne will come by and pick you up.'

There it was again, the Jeanne connection. The girl was clearly very much in Christophe's picture.

On Friday night, I pulled out the only smart dress I'd brought with me – the halter-neck wedding dress, now dyed a more appropriate shade of charcoal. As I zipped it up, I vowed the result of tonight's outing would be more positive. The cripplingly high, crimson stilettos were to have their second excursion, too. Although foxed slightly by the damp grass on my non-wedding day, I'd buffed them up with polish so you'd never notice from a distance. My hair had dried in random blonde waves around my face so I left it loose.

Jeanne displayed, I noted, monumental relief at having set me up with Daniel and was coming very close to being friendly. She was wearing a teal coloured trouser-suit, with a deep v-necked, cream vest beneath. Her long, gold stranded earrings, which draped over her collar bones, seemed surprisingly frivolous for her. The perfume she wore was pungent, a sort of musk verging on mothball. I suspected it was all for Christophe's benefit.

When I met Marie, I was surprised to see how tailored and trim she was in comparison with François. She was tall and elegant, her silver hair cut into a classic bob. Everything about her was slim, even her hands and feet. She wore a straight, magenta-coloured skirt and lilac blouse, which might have looked a tad secretarial on someone less graceful. She greeted me with a classic French double-kiss before introducing me to the other guests. There were to be twelve for dinner. 'I have seated you at the head of the table,' she confided in English. 'That way, you will be able to see everybody. If you're anything like François, you will love studying people. Am I right?'

'Yes. I'm a great people-watcher.' Although sitting at the head of the table sounded more conspicuous than I'd like for my first French dinner party. 'Thank you for inviting me, I just hope I can cope with the language.'

'Oh, we have quite a cosmopolitan crowd. Would you prefer to speak English, this evening?'

'No. I'll give French my best shot.'

Marie nodded and switched immediately to French. Thank heavens, she spoke slowly.

François, dressed in a bottle-green shirt with beige trousers and a scarlet cravat, pressed a tall flute of Kir Royale into my hand. He chinked glasses with me and took a large slug from his own. 'And how is your work progressing, Vicki?'

'Great, thank you. Nothing really outstanding yet but I'm enjoying exploring colour and movement again.'

'Wonderful,' He peered intently into my eyes. 'Never lose that joy for the medium. Now,' he placed a hand at my elbow, 'let me introduce you to our neighbours, Henri and Helene.'

Within seconds, the conversation shot up to warp speed and I struggled to comprehend but I nodded and smiled, all the time keeping a subtle eye out for Christophe's arrival. François left us for a moment then reappeared to top up our glasses. I was clinging to mine like a life preserver.

I'd just been introduced to a doctor and a TV executive, when Marie announced dinner and led us through to a long, blood-red dining room. It was like something out of *Vogue Living*. The table had been beautifully dressed and was lit by candles on tall candelabra. Four glass doors overlooked the terrace where I had shared lunch with François. It was too chilly to sit outside but we could all enjoy the magnificent view across the valley, where moonlight was glistening on the lake's surface.

Marie guided me to the head of the table. A vivid salad of lettuce, shredded peppers and tomato was already set at each place – along with a serving of prawns. Ah, so Christophe must have told Marie I was vegetarian – what a relief. She indicated that the seat to my left was for Christophe. I sincerely hoped he would turn up.

Around the table, conversation was animated. I tried tuning in to what was being said, but with so much noise, it was difficult. I tasted the white wine. It was delicious – light, crisp and very cool. The neighbours, Henri and Helene, were sat to my right. They were in their mid-forties; he a teacher and she a housewife. Suddenly, he was eager to try out his English and discuss various trips he had made to Britain. After a while, I could tell by Helene's travelling eyes, she'd lost interest so I endeavoured to draw her back into the conversation, asking if she too had enjoyed the same excursions.

'Helene speaks very little English,' Henri confided, before pressing on to relate a school trip he had recently organised to Edinburgh. 'Very interesting – but so cold,' he exclaimed.

'My mother is Scottish,' I announced.

'Really?' Henri raised his glass. 'A very friendly nation, I think.'

I raised my eyebrows. Good job he hadn't gone to Glasgow.

He continued to ignore his wife and struck up conversation with Jeanne, who was seated across from him and next to Christophe's empty chair. They spoke rapidly and, sometimes across each other's sentences, making it impossible for me to pick up. I sat with my elbows on the table, clutching my white wine and straining to grasp threads of their conversation. All I could hear was a barrage of chatter – occasional phrases made sense and then I would lose it again. It was like listening to a badly tuned radio – there one minute and gone the next.

Where was Christophe? Waylaid, en route, by one of his lady-friends? Maybe his mystery caller – Sylvie or possibly Louise? Perhaps they were having a highly-charged moment of passion, now that the English school-mistress was safely out of the way. I emptied my wine glass. It really was the most glorious wine.

Marie moved around the table gathering up the dishes, followed by François with another bottle of white wine. He sat briefly on Christophe's chair.

'My dear Vicki. Are you enjoying yourself?'

'Yes, thank you. That wine was delightful. What was it?' He held the bottle label towards me. 'Sancerre? I've had that at home but it never tasted as good as this.'

'This is an excellent vintage.' He refilled my glass. 'I hope Christophe will be here soon. It's a pity to see his lovely escort alone.' Jeanne glanced across and pulled a taut smile before returning to her conversation with Henri.

As François stood up to continue his round of the table, I felt a pang of isolation. Marie was right. People-watching was an entertaining pastime. I tried to remember all their names. Was the doctor called Raphael – or was that the financial director for the

French television company?

Jeanne was toying with her wine-glass, her pewter nails dancing round the rim. Was she flirting with Henri? I glanced at him. He was mildly good looking. My ears pricked up when I heard two names mentioned – Christophe et Sylvie. Who was this Sylvie and what did *croceuse dedi amant* mean? I knew *amant* had something to do with loving. I made a mental note to google it later.

Further along the table, a heavy-set woman with a cleavage a man could lose an arm in, rocked with an earthy laugh. Damn! Now I'd completely lost the thread of Jeanne and Henri's conversation.

Just beyond Jeanne was a tall, fair-haired Dutch man. Was he called Kurt or Karl? He had something to do with shipping – although why he was doing it in the middle of France, I couldn't imagine. I wondered if he had been invited to make up the numbers with Jeanne – who didn't seem remotely interested in him.

Marie reappeared pushing a trolley laden with plates. As my plate was put in front of me, I looked down in disbelief and horror. Seated in the middle of a circle of shallots and tiny potatoes, was the whole body (minus head and feet) of a small chicken – *poussin* – a French favourite. My heart began to hammer. Christophe had clearly said nothing to Marie. How was I going to deal with this? Perhaps I could shriek 'Fire!' then slip it into my handbag during the ensuing pandemonium. A small steak would have nestled neatly between the make-up bag and mobile phone but it would take a magician of David Copperfield's proficiency to disappear this little beauty. Where were Hercules and Boz when I needed them? Perhaps I could dissect it slowly and mash the meat into a small steak. I took another slug of wine and wondered if, with a little Dutch courage, I could actually eat it.

'Aha! *Mon ami. Bienvenue*!' François boomed, as the familiar and very welcome figure of Christophe walked in from the terrace.

He was wearing an open-neck, navy shirt, cream linen jacket and navy trousers. He glanced around the table, smiled and apologised for his lateness. François hugged him heartily and began introducing the guests. Clearly, the only person Christophe didn't know was Karl or Kurt from Holland. He made his way around the table, shaking hands with the men and kissing the women on both cheeks – including mine. His face was warm and I realised I was becoming familiar with his fragrance. I found I rather liked it tonight. When he kissed Jeanne, I noticed with a pang of acid resentment, the way her steel-tipped fingers caressed his neck as she accepted his kiss. I gulped more wine. No wonder poor Kurl (or was it Kart?) didn't get a look in – Jeanne had been honing her skills on the pathetic Henri in preparation for the main event. As Christophe sat down, Jeanne smiled triumphantly at me.

Well bully for her.

I drained my glass. Christophe turned and leaned forward to apologise. 'Vicki, I'm so sorry. It was unavoidable. I hope you have been okay?'

'Totally. Yes. Thank you. No worries. Famulous.' There was a kind of numbness to the letter 'B' in the word 'Fabulous' which was my first hint at inebriation. I'd have to pace myself. Leaning forward, I whispered. 'There is just one, small promlem.' There it was again; a bee that didn't buzz. I giggled.

'What?'

I looked down at my plate and back up.

His intense, brown eyes did the same, coming back to rest on mine – small creases just forming at their corners. 'This is one of your friends, huh?'

I pulled an apologetic face. 'Please, I don't want to make a fuss. Just help me smuggle it out.'

He smiled and my heart revved. Why did he have to do that?

'I think we can do something about this,' he murmured. 'I suggest you eat everything else. Just cut the meat off and move it around your plate for a while.'

I raised my eyebrows in question, which he answered with a nod of his head and the ghost of a smile.

François revisited his guests with rosé wine and new glasses. I tucked into the vegetables and made a wonderful job of carving my poussin. Suddenly when everyone was engaged in conversation, Christophe whipped my plate from under my nose and replaced it with his own – now only holding a stripped carcass.

'Nice work, monsieur,' I muttered.

'Lucky for you, I missed lunch.'

Unlucky for me, I was missing dinner. My stomach rumbled. Perhaps pudding would be something substantial – like rhubarb tart and custard or a big stack of Crêpes Suzette. The cheese course arrived. And since it was most unlikely that Marie had purchased special vegetarian cheese, I was stumped on this course too. '*Quel fromage*,' I muttered.

Out came another wine; this time, a Bordeaux. I hung my nose over the glass, inhaling its ferny vapour. I decided I'd better dig into the French bread to soak up the wine.

Speaking of digging in – Jeanne had her talons well and truly stuck into Christophe. She was talking animatedly on a quite fascinating subject, I was sure. For a few moments, I watched her flashing her eyes at him, stopping occasionally to listen, enthralled by his response.

Hmph! Wasn't it time they had some cheese? Go on, Jeanne, tuck into a wedge of Roquefort and breathe on him.

I corrected myself. Why on earth was I bothered? Christophe was nothing more than my landlord. I had absolutely no claim over him, whatsoever. He could talk to anybody. Have any woman he liked, and quite possibly did. Good for him.

So my feeling of triumph was totally unjustified when he excused himself from Jeanne's conversation and switched his attention to me.

'Hello, Christophe. D'you know, I'm really, really struggling,' I confessed. 'Everyone might as well be talking Greek.' I raised my glass. 'Fortunately, the wine is jolly good'

'And perhaps a little strong, on an empty stomach?'

'Does it show? Are my eyes all bloodshot and my nose red?' I went cross-eyed just to check.

He chuckled and shook his head. 'I think you will feel better in the morning if you stopped drinking wine and tried a little water.'

I nodded and placed my glass carefully on the table, giving him my very best, twinkly smile.

'Christophe!' François called from the other end of the table. 'Do you have any tips for the coming racing season?'

Everyone turned towards Christophe and I worked very hard to understand his take on horses and races. Every so often, he would turn and translate certain words, especially for me, so I wouldn't feel left out. Always thoughtful, I sighed to myself, *toujours attentif*.

Jeanne, however, was attentive only to Christophe. Like the world-class footballers about whom she probably wrote many column inches, she had spotted a new opportunity to seize the conversational ball, and now doggedly manoeuvred around him, fighting to retain his interest at all costs.

As if sensing I was being neglected, Marie beckoned to me to change places with François, so we could have a little chat. Grateful for her concern but reluctant to leave Christophe to Jeanne d'Arc there, I moved up to the far end of the table with some reluctance. I wondered if, like her namesake, Jeanne was on a secret mission to drive the English – *moi* – out of France.

Marie immediately engaged me in conversation, showing genuine interest in what I had to say and, at last, I felt comfortable. So comfortable, I ventured to bring up a subject that had been pressing on my brain for days. 'Louise, at the surgery, she seems very nice.'

'Louise? Yes a lovely girl. Nothing like her brother, Gerard.'

'Oh?'

Marie raised her hands. 'I should not say. It is not my business. All I will say is, Louise has all the character that Gerard lacks.'

I was confused. 'Does Gerard work at the vets, too? I haven't met him.'

'No. I'm sure you will meet him, he is Christophe's

cousin.'

So that made Louise his cousin too.

Ah. Aha. Ahahaha!

I nodded and toasted the discovery with some of the Bordeaux.

The pudding course, when it finally arrived was, to my dismay, a fruit plate. Delicate slices of melon, mango, pear and strawberries were arranged beautifully beneath a drizzling of fruit syrup, accompanied by another new glass – this time of dessert wine. Wow! These French certainly knew how to marry their dishes with their wines. Having sunk the Bordeaux, I sampled the Sauternes. It was delightful. I could get used to this.

Finally, sometime after midnight, Christophe rose from his chair and made his way around the table. In my peripheral vision, I tracked his progress – willing him to come to me. It worked. He came to a halt behind me. With a hand on each of our chairs, he turned to Marie. 'That was a beautiful meal, Marie. I must apologise, again, for being late.'

'Not at all, Christophe. I know you would have a very good reason.'

'Now, I'm afraid, I really must take Vicki away from you.'

Even though it made him sound like my carer, I felt a guilty ripple of satisfaction that he would be leaving with me and not Jeanne.

Christophe continued. 'I've had a very long week and tomorrow, I'm taking Vicki to see the château.'

'Ooh... that's right.' I beamed up at him.

Marie smiled at us both. 'I understand the weather tomorrow will be perfect. Vicki, you will love the château.'

'I'm really looking forward to it. And thank you so much for a lovely evening.'

'You're welcome. I hope we will see a lot more of you.'

Christophe moved to hold my chair as I stood up. I teetered on my stilettos, and he instantly caught my hand and rested his other on the small of my back.

'Ooops! I'm a bit out of practice with the heels, sorry,' I said, squeezing his hand to steady myself, although I hoped I passed it off as a gesture of gratitude.

I scanned the table and wished them all a very good night. François was now seated in my old chair at the end of the table with his head back and snoring softly.

Marie escorted us into the hallway and found my coat. She took my hands in hers. 'Vicki, it has been a pleasure to meet you. I think you are quite delightful, and I hope you find what you are looking for.'

'So do I, Marie, so do I.' I leaned forward and kissed her on both cheeks.

Once out in the cool night air, I held my face up and breathed in the musty, autumn scents of fading leaves and damp earth. Moonlight was picking out silhouettes of trees on the far hillside.

'Look!' I said, sweeping my arm out. 'Just look!'

* * *

Christophe was looking. At her. In the moonlight, her hair seemed more silver than gold. He cast his eyes down to her slender ankles, above the elegant crimson shoes which made her taller than he'd seen her before – although Vicki still only came up to his chin. There was so much energy in this English woman. He glanced back at her face as she turned towards him. Before tonight, he had thought she needed taking in hand by a stylist but her dress, with its halter neckline, displayed the fine edge of her collarbone and suited her frame so well. Her hair, usually scraped up and fastened in a clip, now fell in a soft cloud around her face and neck. The natural beauty of her eyes was accentuated by a lavender shadow.

'You're not looking at the view,' she chided him.

He gave her a long, lazy smile, blinked and turned to study the view. 'I've looked at it many times but perhaps not concentrated on it as you would.'

'You should start. It will enrich your life.'

He nodded slowly, before looking back at her. 'Maybe I should. Maybe I will.'

'No time like the present. Go on. What do you see?'

He scanned the view. 'I see trees against a moonlit sky.'

'Excellent. Very good.' She swayed in front of him. 'I think you can do better.'

'Maybe another time, huh? I'm tired and I want to make an early start tomorrow.'

She pulled her coat tight and headed off in the direction of his car. Although she appeared to be staring at the destination, her body kept veering off the edge of the path. He caught her with an arm around her waist and steered her back on track.

'Oops. Sorry. Not enough solids in my diet,' she said, leaning against him.

'It was my fault. I should have remembered to tell Marie. But you know, you could have told her tonight, I'm sure she would have been able to fix you something.'

'Nooo. I didn't want to make a fuss.' He felt her nestle into his body, her own arm sneaking round to hold onto his back. Suddenly, she stopped and threw her free arm forward. 'See those bushes? See how the moonlight makes them look like they're made of steel?'

'Steel? Non. Steel is too hard, too industrial.'

'Okay then. What would you say it looks like?' She gazed up at him.

'I'd say it looks like a plant that has been dipped in melted silver.'

'Molten.'

He looked down at her. 'Molten?'

'You could say molten rather than melted.' He could feel her heart was pounding beneath her ribs. 'A bit like your eyes being like molten chocolate,' she added.

He turned his body towards her, one hand still resting on her waist. 'You think my eyes are like molten chocolate?'

* * *

I gulped. 'Did I say that?'

'I think you must have. I'm not a mind-reader.'

As he smiled down at me, his eyes were creased wickedly at the corners. God, he was cool. I'd never been with a man who was so cool – as in sexy cool – before. My eyes dropped with embarrassment and now took in the breadth of his chest and the way the top of his shirt opened to expose fine, dark hairs beneath. There was a heat coming off him, bringing with it that delicious, spicy scent. I swallowed. He wasn't backing away, so either he liked being where he was or he thought I needed holding up. Judging by the jelly in my knees, he was right. What was my favourite saying? Always make the most of the here and now. My hand moved up to rest on the front of his shirt. Under the smooth fabric I could feel the heat and strength of his muscles. His breathing seemed to increase. I didn't dare look up in case I broke the spell. But he wasn't backing away. I moved my other hand so it skimmed across his abdomen till it came to rest on his hip. My thumb slipped naturally into the dip of his pelvis.

I felt a shudder run through him which meant there was only one way to go. I lifted my head up and felt his fingers lace into my hair, drawing me towards him. He was warm and firm and strong. Jeez! it had been a long time. He looked into my face. It was like he was debating whether to kiss me or not. Or maybe he just wanted to relish that delicious anticipation leading up to the first kiss. He circled my nose with his before gently brushing his lips over mine. I inhaled his breath. When my lips touched his, and I felt the moist tip of his tongue coaxing me to get closer, that was it.

His arms tightened around my waist. His mouth moved over mine with a heat and intensity I couldn't ever remember feeling before. I picked up the pace – tasting, sucking and nipping at his mouth. Sweet heaven. It was magnificent – far exceeding anything I'd ever felt with Marc.

Thank you, Marc, for leaving me so that I could find this.

Hang on a minute.
What?
This is NOT what you came to France for.

Oh, but it's so delicious.

Stop it! You might be attracted to him, but you can't have a fling with Christophe.

Why not?

You came here to paint. Remember?

I came here to paint. I did. And I still will.

You've got to live in the same house with him. Before you know it…

I pictured his wide bed with the heavy blue bedspread, and let out a little moan and dragged myself back from Chrisophe's oh-so-addictive kisses and took a deep breath. I held up both my hands as if to say, Enough! I glanced at him quickly but looked away again – his eyes were even darker now and the stray lock of hair that fell over his forehead looked more unruly than usual. My head was spinning but that could just as easily have been the wine. I blew the breath out of my lungs slowly. 'I… er… that was lovely and I'm not sorry it happened… but I…' Why was I making a speech? 'Sorry, I've drunk too much. I probably shouldn't have done that. Sorry.' I rammed my hands into my coat pockets.

'Don't apologise.' Christophe stroked the back of his fingers down my cheek.

My stomach flipped at his touch but I wouldn't be going back for more. 'You're tired and I'm drunk, so we really should be going.' I stepped away from him and stood by the car.

After a moment, I heard him let out a sigh as he walked round to the driver's side and got in. He leaned over and opened my door. I sat down without looking at him and fastened my safety belt. He started the car and reversed in a huge, sweeping arc, before accelerating down the drive – the tyres spitting stones in all directions. I dropped my head back and closed my eyes. Big mistake. I opened them again to suppress a rising wave of nausea, and fixed my eyes on the road ahead. It was a great relief when, moments later, Christophe turned on the CD player and made no demands on me for conversation.

Chapter 10

I peeled my eyes open and closed them again. Sunlight was streaming through a gap in the curtains. I rolled over to look at my bedside clock, and felt my brain follow a split-second later. Quarter past ten.

Quarter past ten.

I pushed myself up on one elbow. Eugh. My stomach was on slow spin and my skull had shrunk. Looking down, I discovered I had gone to bed in my underwear. I scanned the room. On the chair opposite was my handbag but where was my dress? I leaned over the side of the bed, catching hold of my head as I did so. No dress, just a bucket. Thankfully, it was an empty bucket. I sat up and dragged myself over to the wardrobe. My dress and coat were both hanging neatly on the rail. There was a jug of water next to my alarm clock too, which hadn't been there yesterday. I sat on the bed and poured myself a tumbler-full, which I glugged back.

Gradually, as the fog in my brain started to lift, little scenes from last night began to emerge. And the scene that absorbed me most, showed me making a pass at Christophe. I let out a heavy groan and lay back on the bed. What was that – remorse or excitement? I gulped. It was both. And added to the mix was the apprehension of dealing with him today and tomorrow and…

I pulled the pillow over my face and moaned.

There was a tap at the door. 'Vicki, how are you feeling?'

I snatched the pillow down to check he wasn't in the room. 'Okay. I think. Sorry, I overslept,' I croaked.

'Would you like some coffee?'

'Yes please.'

To my horror, the door opened and he entered, carrying a cafetière and a large mug. I stared at him wide-eyed, swiftly manoeuvring the pillow to cover my body.

His hair was still damp from the shower, and he wore a pair of jeans with a blue and white rugby shirt. 'It's always worse, first thing.' He moved the jug of water to the floor to make room for the coffee. I watched in fascination, unable to think of anything to say that might not expose me more than I already felt. Slowly, he depressed the plunger on the cafetière and decanted the steaming black coffee into the mug. I studied his capable hands as they worked, noticing the large silver and black watch on his wrist. He offered me the mug. 'Here, I think you need to flush the alcohol out of your system.'

I tried to sit up but it wasn't easy. I felt wobbly and was anxious not to flaunt my barely clothed body. Christophe seemed unperturbed and reached out a hand to pull me up. I flicked a brief smile at him and took the mug. Eager to get him out of the room, I said, 'Thank you. I'll have a shower. That should do the trick.'

He hesitated before asking, 'Do you still want to see the château?'

I held my mug with both hands, just another small barrier between my vulnerable self and him. Did I want to? If I said no, then it meant I'd kept him waiting when he probably had far more important things to do. And if I said yes, I'd have to haul this mother of a hangover with me. But, on reflection, it seemed better to be out in the fresh air and seeing the château than festering here all day. I glanced up, and those warm brown eyes were looking back at me. 'Do you still want to go?' I said.

He shrugged. 'Of course. I have to go anyway.'

Oh. Not quite the special excursion I'd imagined, then.

He continued. 'I see you have not been sick.'

I tossed him a sheepish look. 'No. Not that I remember.'

'Good. I put the bucket there as a precaution.'

My mouth and eyes popped open in unison. 'You put the bucket there?'

'I did.'

I gulped at the realisation of what must have happened last night. No wonder my room was so tidy. Usually, after a few glasses of wine, I abandoned my clothes in a heap on the floor. Last night, I'd lost count of the number of glasses. Christophe had clearly been the one who had put me to bed. Thank goodness I was wearing my matching, honeymoon underwear.

'Did I pass out?'

'Eventually. Before that, you were quite amusing.'

Dear Doris. What did that mean? 'In what way was I quite amusing?'

He smiled. 'You were singing a little song. It was about eating worms.'

Memories of Girl Guide camp came clanging into my brain. 'Ah. Yes. That is a funny little song.'

'I thought so – for a vegetarian.' Christophe stopped by the door. 'I'll be ready when you are.'

* * *

Christophe thought Vicki still looked remarkably good for someone with a hangover – maybe a little pale. Last night, despite her state of inebriation, she had insisted on removing her make-up. But then, she had sat back on the bed, handed him the cotton wool, closed her eyes and drifted into oblivion. It had been a strange experience for him, as he stroked the cleanser over her face. Her skin was smooth and delicate – with a scattering of freckles from the autumn sunshine. He had watched her sleep for a moment, resisting the temptation to steal another kiss. Then he'd faced a dilemma – should he leave her as she was or did her eagerness to remove her make-up indicate a girl who would never ruin her clothes by sleeping in them? Finally, the physician in him had taken over and he elected to remove her dress and place her in the recovery position. And, as an extra precaution, he had left both their doors ajar so he would hear if she was ill.

Even though he had been through a tiring week, somehow sleep had eluded him until it was nearly light. Unless he was mistaken, last night, Vicki had definitely taken the lead – even if it had been fuelled by the wine. Yet, it revealed another facet of her personality. He found he liked her spirit and passion, which had certainly come through in the heat of her kisses and, although he was reluctant to admit it, he wanted more. But that would be a really foolish direction to take.

Jeanne was already on his case, goading him with

comments like, 'Vicki is very attractive, aren't you tempted? After all, you are a free agent, now.'

However, Vicki was living in his house and, short of chucking her out, would be for the next twelve months. Involvement with a live-in artist was not on his agenda. And he knew it wasn't on hers. He threw the kitchen door open and walked into the courtyard for some fresh air.

* * *

I took a fast shower. Standing under the heavy jets of water increased my queasiness. I stepped out and wrapped the towelling robe around me and padded into the bedroom. I pulled one of the curtains back and swung a window open. A cool breeze found the exposed, damp parts of my body. Outside, Christophe was leaning against the wall of the surgery, his hands thrust deep into his pockets as he stared at the stone courtyard. At the sound of my opening window, he looked up. I jumped in surprise, clutching the robe tighter across my chest. Which seemed overly coy, bearing in mind only hours ago, he'd seen me in cream and red satin underwear. I watched as he pulled away from the wall and sauntered back towards the house, his focus not moving from me until he was out of sight.

I continued to clutch the robe, my heart hammering in my chest. There was something in that look which suggested there was more to come. A thrill ran up my spine and I swallowed hard as it reached the top. I listened, barely breathing, for the creak of the stairs. What would I do if he bounded back in and claimed me, Tarzan style, over the crumpled, rose-bud bedspread? Could I resist? I ruffled my hair and tried not to pant like an excited spaniel. I kicked the bucket – literally – under the bed. I scanned the room and fastened the wardrobe door. My reflection showed red, wine spiked eyes and an unhealthy mottle of pink on my cheeks. Ugh. It was probably too early in the day for me, anyway. I waited.

However, the stairs didn't creak and the door didn't burst open. After a few moments, as realisation dawned that my body was not in imminent danger of a good ravishing, I leaned against the wardrobe. My breath calmed and I muttered to myself, 'Christophe Dubois, you've got it in spades – but so help me, I am NOT going to succumb.' I caught my guilty look in the mirror. 'Again.'

Thank heavens, the château was only a few minutes' drive away so I wasn't obliged to make lengthy conversation with Christophe. Instead, I taunted myself with flashbacks to the night before – specifically one moment. This booted my hormones and a ton of guilt into circulation, which in turn triggered me to spit out phrases you'd only use if you were trapped on a bus with a complete stranger: 'What lovely scenery; We're so lucky with the weather today; Oh, what a pretty house; I do love autumn, it's my favourite season.'

As the acid in my stomach churned over, I gulped some water down and decided to keep the bottle close to my lips to prevent any more inane comments from spewing out.

The approach to the château was glorious. Red and copper beech trees illuminated the road on either side. As the car slowed to turn between two huge, stone pillars, Christophe reached into his pocket and took out a small plastic device and pressed a button. The impressive iron gates juddered apart to allow us through.

I looked at him. 'How come you have a clicker for the gates?'

'Why not? It's my home.'

I almost dislocated my neck in surprise. 'Your home?'

'I grew up here. Didn't Isabelle tell you?'

'No. I'd have remembered something like that.' I surveyed the wonderful biscuit coloured château, with its slate grey roof and circular towers. 'Wow! Does this make you a French aristocrat?'

He laughed. 'Non. My father and his brother bought it when it was in a very poor state. Both our families live here.'

We drove around the side of the château through a small parade of trees, to park in a large, gravelled area. To one side I could see stables and a paddock, to the other was a hedged path leading to the château. In the back of the car, Hercules and Boz had become restless. Christophe stepped out and opened the tailgate of the car to release them.

Throughout the short journey, my water bottle had never been far from my lips. Now, I drained the last remaining drops before stepping out into the sunshine. I shielded my eyes from the low-slanting glare as I surveyed my surroundings. It was so beautiful. I imagined setting up my easel in the shade of one of the old trees and painting here all day. I scanned the stable buildings, where two nodding horses peered inquisitively out of open doors. I looked beyond them to the paddock, and turned slowly to take in 360° of gorgeous French scenery – and, yes, that probably did include Christophe, who was watching me across the roof of the car. I smiled at him, my mouth still open in astonishment. 'This is amazing. I thought you were taking me to a château full of tourists.'

He smiled and nodded in the direction of the stables. 'Come. I will introduce you to the horses.'

I followed slowly, several steps behind, passing through a wooden gate towards the first horse. I'd not actually confessed to my fear of horses. I didn't mind them at a distance, behind a sturdy fence or shackled to a horse and cart but loose, that was another story. As we approached the first stable, a dark head bobbed in what I hoped was friendly greeting, whilst the lighter coloured horse in the neighbouring stable whinnied. Christophe held out his hand, '*Voici, le Magicien.*' The horse's head jerked unpredictably as Christophe patted its neck and cheek.

'He's a handsome boy,' I acknowledged, still standing a good three metres away.

Christophe stroked Magicien's nose. 'He is probably my best horse,' he said, looking up at me as I folded my arms and crossed my legs. 'Are you afraid of horses?'

'Kind of. I think they're really beautiful but I do get a bit nervous, close up.'

Magicien leaned in towards him in a remarkably intimate way – for a horse – and Christophe mumbled something into the horse's neck, before flashing me a wicked smile. 'Come closer. He'd like to get to know you better.'

I let out a half-hearted chuckle. 'Tell him I'm not that easy,' which in the light of last night's activity, was a pretty dumb statement to make – and not lost on Christophe, who raised an eyebrow. I swept an arm in the direction of the stables to distract him and asked, 'So, how many horses do you have?'

'Just ten.' He moved along to introduce some more of his four-legged friends. 'This is *le Léopard des Neiges* – or Snow Leopard in English; here is *le Roi de la Montagne* – King of the Mountain, and finally…' he held his hand out to a smaller, chestnut coloured horse. 'Here is the gentlest mare in my stable. Vicki, you need not be afraid of this one. This is *la Belle Amitié* or *Belle*.'

'Beautiful Friendship. That's a lovely name. How do you decide what to call them?'

'Sometimes we use an association to the sire and dam, sometimes it's just a personal association.' I watched as he stroked the filly's cheek with great tenderness.

'Why are there some horses in the paddock and some still in the stable?'

He left Belle and came over to join me. 'Just because they're all horses doesn't mean they get along. So we exercise them, groom them and rest them in different groups. There are four in the field now and there are two more out riding.'

'Do you race them all?'

'No. *Le Magicien*, *le Roi de Montagne* and *Crepuscule du Soir* – he is the black horse over in the paddock – are my top horses, the others are either too young or too old.'

'And which ones do you ride?'

'I don't often have the time, but Léopard. He may be too old to race but he still has a lot of power and he just loves to run.' He stared out across the paddock for a moment. 'I ride him when I want to exorcise the demons.'

I felt a little shiver. There were two faint grooves between his brows as he turned back to look at me. Just what exactly did he mean by demons?

His brows lifted and the lines evened out. 'But if I just want to relax, I take Belle.'

We heard the gate open behind us. An older man was approaching, clearly well known by the dogs. Christophe introduced him as his uncle, Alain. There was a strong family resemblance in their build; Alain was tall, like Christophe, but had grey hair and the weathered face of a man who spent his time in the open air. For an older guy, he was still quite handsome. I could picture Christophe in another thirty years.

Alain greeted us cordially enough but I detected a glacial breeze pass between them. 'Colette saw you arrive. I believe she is making preparations to receive you.'

'Then we'd better not keep her waiting.' They nodded briefly at each other and we left the two dogs with Alain.

I fell into step beside Christophe. 'Colette is your aunt?'

'Non. Colette is my mother.'

Aha. The great beauty who'd had the affair with François. This would be interesting. I imagined a tall, elegant brunette with beautiful eyes like her son – a French Catherine Zeta Jones. I considered my own appearance – best jeans, thin navy sweater and toffee-coloured, woollen jacket – more tourist class than supermodel. Add to that my large canvas camera bag, and one might be forgiven for thinking I was carrying a flask and sandwiches. Oh well. I lifted my chin and straightened my back as Christophe led me through a side door, down a stone floored corridor and through a heavy wooden door into a grand hallway. The walls were adorned with paintings, old and new; heavy drapes hung beside tall windows and somebody, somewhere, was playing the Bee Gees – loudly.

'Please excuse the interior styling. My mother is a woman of impulse. If she likes something, she buys it, never mind if it does not suit the rest.'

'Interesting though.'

He headed off up the wide staircase. The carpet, which was a deep pink, had seen better days. We were heading in the direction of the music. He stopped by a white panelled door, on which the detail had been picked out in gold. He tapped before pushing it open.

Shock horror! If I had expected a sophisticated brunette, I couldn't have been more surprised. Shimmying round the large room, in a knee-length, rust-coloured dress, tailored to an impressive hourglass figure, was a ravishing redhead. We stood in the doorway, waiting until she noticed us, when she paused, flashed us a traffic-stopping smile and gestured for us to join her. Then, she side-stepped to the CD player and turned the volume down. 'Christophe, *chéri*,' she crooned in a voice like *crème de marron*. She held out one hand to her son and another to me, before switching to flawless English. She spoke slowly, her voice caressing the words with just the hint of a French accent, which I imagined would set any red-blooded man's pulse racing. 'You must be our new English artist, Vicki. Welcome. It's a pleasure to meet you.' She air-kissed me, and then her son. 'Sorry, you caught me doing my exercises. Far better to dance in the comfort of one's own salon than put on hideous clothes and go to the gym, don't you think?'

'Absolutely.' I beamed back at her, recognising her as the woman I'd seen in Christophe's arms, in the photograph on his piano. 'And I'm sure this is a much better view, as well. Who wants to look at rows of sweaty bodies and pink faces?'

Colette took hold of my other hand and looked at her son. 'What did I tell you, Chéri? Only a woman could understand.' She turned her attention to me. 'In any case, carpet is much kinder to the knees and ankles, wouldn't you agree?'

Christophe's eyes creased softly at the corners. '*Maman*, I need to talk to Alain. I think Vicki might like a coffee and then, perhaps, you can show her round.'

'I would love to show you around the château, Vicki. Tell me, is that short for Victoria?'

'Yes.'

'Ah. Victoria is such a beautiful name. But your Queen Victoria was so plain and yet, I read somewhere, she was sex mad, non?'

Christophe rolled his eyes, placed a hand on his mother's shoulder and said, 'I will leave you to your conversation.'

'Apparently, I am an embarrassing mother.'

Christophe gave her a peck on the cheek. 'Not at all.' He turned and gave me an apologetic nod before leaving.

Colette picked up a telephone, pressed a button, and ordered coffee – like she was at The Ritz. I observed her – taking in the thick auburn hair, skilfully layered so it had height and movement. She wore several gold bracelets that slid up and down her wrist as she moved, and a necklace of amber, jade and gold. For a woman who was probably in her late fifties, she looked a good ten years younger. She gestured for me to join her on one of the sofas; old sofas, in a heavy chintz design of pink and cream roses on a saffron yellow background, were positioned opposite each other at right-angles to the window. A low, carved coffee table stood between them. She crossed her long legs, one foot still tapping to the music, and smiled encouragingly. 'It's so lovely to have female company. I always seem to be surrounded by men.' She gave a little chuckle. 'Not that I'm complaining but a woman needs the society of other women, don't you think?'

'Definitely. Girlfriends offer something a man never could.'

'This is so true. I do, of course have the company of Sylvie here, but I find her very much more like a man in her attitudes – very cool. She's away at the moment and I find I really don't miss her at all. You've heard of Sylvie, of course.'

My brain was pedalling fast to come up to speed on this one. Sylvie – the phone call to Christophe and the person I'd heard Jeanne mention, several times last night in the same breath as Christophe. 'Sylvie? No, I don't think so.'

'My son's ex-lover. She used to live with him. So surprising. He had always remained resolutely single.' She tutted. 'But it didn't work out.'

So that's what Louise had meant when she said his ex was still around. Dear old Christophe – what a guy. He even kept his ex-girlfriends simmering in the family château. I wondered if he had the name

Lothario tattooed across his chest. I summoned up the vision, just for the hell of it.

'Christophe thought it was time to settle down but personally, I always thought he'd picked the wrong girl. A mother can tell, you know.'

I nodded, taking it all in and rapidly assessing the situation. Christophe had wanted to settle down, then. So he must have felt a lot for Sylvie. Possibly still did. Louise had said things were complicated.

Colette ran both hands through her thick hair, bracelets jingling as she did so. 'Of course, it was devastating for him when she was discovered with Gerard.'

'Gerard? Isn't that his cousin?'

'Oui.'

I swallowed as I digested this revelation. First, we had Colette's affair with François and now Christophe's girlfriend had been cheating on him with his cousin. I wondered if he had been as magnanimous and forgiving of her infidelity as his father had of Colette's.

She shrugged. 'Oh well. Now Sylvie is married to Gerard, I will have to spend more time with her, I expect.'

What?! 'So, Christophe's girlfriend married his cousin, Gerard?'

'It's far more exciting than that, my dear. They eloped! Who would expect it these days? Unfortunately, Alain was very much against the marriage. It only happened a few days ago and threw everyone into turmoil.' She glanced across as an elderly woman appeared in the doorway. 'Ah, coffee.'

That must have accounted for why Louise had been crying, and for the tense phone calls Christophe had been having. Not only had his relationship failed but now his ex had married his own cousin, and was living under the same roof as his mother. But what, I wondered, had Sylvie been doing phoning Christophe only two nights ago?

Still, it certainly threw my own position into more favourable perspective. At least Marc had had the decency to move continents.

I was itching to know more, but waited until the coffee had been served before I asked, 'Why was Alain so against the marriage?'

Colette was perched on the edge of the sofa, holding her coffee cup and saucer. 'Gerard is a very passive man. Sylvie is a strong and determined woman. We all feel that, perhaps... well, no.' She turned the cup on her saucer. 'It's not fair to judge, is it? Alain believes that the marriage will fail. We will leave it at that.'

I stirred my coffee, even though I didn't take sugar.

Colette changed the subject. 'So, how did you come to be in France – and painting? Christophe tells me you gave up your job – that's a brave thing to do.'

'Not really. It was more an act of survival.' I wasn't exaggerating; a few more years at the mercy of Darwin High pupils and who knew what state I'd be in?

'And would I be correct in assuming you have no man in your life, at present?'

'There was one but we had a parting of the ways. He went to Barbados, I came to France.'

'Barbados... I once had a marvellous trip to Antigua, so beautiful – the colours. Why didn't you go with him? It is an artist's paradise.'

I pulled a face. 'I wasn't invited.'

Colette gasped. 'Non! He just went? You didn't know?'

And so, I spilled the whole story.

Colette was enthralled. 'And you still went ahead with the wedding reception – good for you.'

'Obviously, they thought I was mad but I'm a great believer in making the most of a situation.'

'Wasn't it awkward?'

'God, yes. Although in a funny way, everyone covered it up. There was a kind of hysteria took over. Most of it mine, probably. Lots of alcohol consumption. Also mine, I expect, and wall-to-wall jocularity.'

'What about his family – weren't they ashamed?'

'Well, his father had disappeared when Marc was a baby.'

Colette leaned across and touched my arm. 'Like father, like son, you see. You had a lucky escape. And his mother?'

'Embarrassed, naturally. Although I got the impression she was more miffed that he hadn't told her first, and saved her the humiliation of turning up at the church. She stayed long enough to be polite.' About twenty minutes as I recalled.

'But you're here now. And it's wonderful.'

'Thank you. I'm very happy to be here.'

Colette leaned forward and took my hand as she said, sotto voce, 'And what do you think of my son?'

'Erm…' I fought down the memory of his arms around me, and the sensation of his kisses.

Colette winked. 'He's adorable, non?'

I was trying to catch a rational thought. Finally, sounding as breezy as a holiday rep in the first week of the season, I said, 'Well, he's been very kind to give me a room in his house. I'm really grateful, and my studio is perfect.'

'Of course, as his mother, I adore him – but I think I should warn you, he has littered half of Limousin with broken hearts.'

No surprises there, then. 'Don't worry. I have absolutely no intention of losing my heart to anyone. I'm here to paint. I'm taking a sabbatical from men, too.'

Colette squeezed my hand. 'But chérie, make room for a little fun.'

I smiled back at her. 'I'm already having fun. I haven't felt this positive for ages. It's like I've been handed a second chance and the world is my oyster.'

'*Bien*. I feel I know you so much better, Vicki. I really look forward to spending more time with you. Now, you want to see the château. Let's go.'

Generations of French families had knocked the château about a bit, and now it was divided into five apartments; one for Colette, another for Alain and his wife, two for the cousins, Gerard and Louise and the other was Christophe's. It was the French equivalent of Southfork Ranch and almost as riddled with scandal. Colette had no access to Gerard's apartment but Alain's wife, Anne, showed us theirs. She was the polar opposite of Colette – very quiet and with seriously conservative taste, reflected in her furnishings of beige, sage and cream. Colette, on the other hand, worked with a more opulent palette. Paintings and sketches hung in every room alongside an eclectic mix of ceramics and sculptures. I was certain I saw two sketches by Picasso.

Louise's apartment was more of a bed-sit. Being

the youngest, I guess she drew the short straw. Mind you, at her age, I'd have been pretty glad to have a huge room with en-suite and kitchenette to take my friends to.

Christophe's apartment was a big surprise. In contrast to the homely, somewhat sparsely furnished house by the surgery, there was a glorious, modern spaciousness to the place. Sand-coloured carpet had been laid throughout. In the sitting room, huge squashy sofas in dark brown sat at right-angles, facing the floor-to-ceiling windows. There were big cushions in the same teal and brown fabric as the curtains and in the centre of the ceiling hung a massive multiple light in stainless steel. It was a very manly room – but comfortable. The bathroom was, possibly, the most luxurious I'd ever seen; with his-and-hers basins and the biggest bath you might find outside of a rugby changing room. The master bedroom had modern, dark brown and steel furnishings, cream and rust coloured fabrics and a bed wide enough to host half of said rugby team.

I was itching to have a good nosey around but Colette swept me out and back to her own salon, which pulsed to the beat of Jive Talkin'. 'This is one of my favourites,' I confessed.

Colette gasped with delight. 'Me too. But you're so young to like the Bee Gees.'

'My mother's a huge fan.'

'How marvellous.' She turned up the volume again. 'Come!' she clasped my hand and began dancing me around the room.

Within seconds, we were like a couple of seventies' schoolgirls – only without the flares. When I noticed Christophe standing in the doorway, I pulled a broad grin of embarrassment and stopped abruptly. Colette, on the other hand, swayed across, reached out and encouraged him to join us. Cool as you please, he cooperated in a few bars of perfect jive dancing with his mother, before the song ended.

Wow! He was good. Most guys I knew danced like lunatics. I applauded and Christophe nodded his head in acknowledgement. After reducing the volume he commented, 'I think you are feeling better, huh?'

'I'm feeling much better, thanks.'

'Chéri, Vicki is a fan of the Bee Gees. I think we must be due for a party, soon. Don't you?'

By the drop of his face and the slump of his shoulders, I guessed he didn't agree. Maybe it had something to do with the Sylvie situation. He shrugged and turned to me. 'Vicki, would you like to come for a walk outside; perhaps you could take some photographs?'

'Great!' I said and picked up my camera case.

Colette shook her magnificent auburn mane. 'I think the weather is good enough to have lunch on the terrace today. You are staying to lunch, chéri?'

Christophe glanced at me. I was more than happy to stay so I nodded. 'Oui,' he said, with a sigh. Rude bugger.

'That would be lovely,' I said. 'Thank you.'

Christophe nodded. '*Bien sur. Viens!*' He gestured for me to follow him. At the door he turned back to his mother. 'Vicki is a vegetarian – no meat, only fish.'

'*Vraiment?*' Colette drawled. 'That must be why you're so lovely and slim.' She studied herself in the large gilt mirror over the fireplace. 'I wonder if that would work for me?'

Chapter 11

I watched Christophe bounding down the staircase like he had the cavalry after him. I scuttled behind until we were outside, when he finally came to rest by the balustraded wall separating the terrace from the lawns. Aside from picking up on his strange mood, I couldn't help noticing how well the lichen-covered wall blended into its surroundings.

Christophe had his arms open wide, hands pressing on the stone slabs as he gazed over the grass. He'd hitched up the sleeves of his rugby shirt, displaying a fine pair of forearms, flecked with dark hairs. He turned and pulled a polite but incomplete smile. 'Feel free to take all the pictures you want.'

Like a Formula One racing driver, I gave him the thumbs up, 'Roger that,' I said before scrabbling about in my camera case.

After a few minutes, I'd walked the length of the terrace, looking for the best shots. From the far side I peered through my camera, training it on Christophe. Quickly, I swapped to telephoto lens and refocused, zooming in on his face. The lids of his eyes were half closed as he stared into the distance. I liked how the sunlight picked out the texture of his hair and the angular planes of his face. Click. He looked down. Click. And then, as if sensing my attention, he turned to look at me. Click. I lowered the camera and picked up my case, blushing like a Peeping Tom caught in the act.

'I thought you were interested in the château,' he said, as he walked towards me.

'I like human studies too. A telephoto lens is very good for that – it usually means the subject is unaware of the camera, so it makes for a more natural result.'

'Yes, I have personal experience of that.' His tone was deadly flat.

'Oh?'

'Journalists. It was a long time ago, but it was humiliating for my family. So forgive me if I don't get excited at the prospect.'

'Sorry.' I unscrewed the lens and placed it back in the case. Trust me to piss him off when he was already in such a sour mood.

He walked down the central steps that led onto the upper lawn so I caught up. He tucked his hands into the tops of his pockets and looked at me. 'I apologise. I'm a little distracted at the moment.'

'Can I ask why?'

We continued walking. 'It's just a family affair.'

Appropriate choice of phrase, I thought and shrugged, 'Okay,' and stopped halfway down the lawn and turned back to look at the château.

I got the message: it was nothing I needed to know about.

* * *

Christophe watched Vicki as she worked, changing her position; sometimes crouching down, sometimes swapping lenses but absorbed in her task. He liked the way her hair was loose again, and the colour was back in her cheeks.

As they walked to the end of the lower lawn, he led her to a seat under a rose arbour, now devoid of flowers. She placed her camera case down and leaned back with a satisfied sigh. 'This is such a lovely place. Do you know how lucky you are?'

Lucky? He could understand why she would think that, with her English love of history and her artistic imagination. He sat down beside her, forward on the seat with his arms resting on his knees, one hand inside the other. He was looking back at the château, his eyes narrowing against the sunlight. Was he lucky?

She filled the silence. 'I really like your mother. She's wonderfully eccentric.'

He nodded.

'What was your father like?'

Christophe's fist twisted back and forth in his palm. 'Much more serious. I used to think they were nothing like each other, but in a way, they were. They were both single-minded. He was passionate about horses…'

'And she's just passionate.' Vicki cut in, making light of the situation.

Finally, he smiled and sat up, stretching his arms to rest on the back of the bench. 'Yes. That certainly describes my mother.'

'She's very different from mine.'

He looked at her. 'What is she like?'

'Quieter. She's a lab technician at the hospital. Very organised, you know, writes lists and lists of lists.'

He nodded and smiled to himself. 'Like your little food inventory?' He saw her jaw drop. 'I've seen it on your notebook in the kitchen.' He wrote in the air, 'Dairy, Fruit, Vegetables. Very organised, I was impressed.'

'Oh, no. I'm turning into my mother.' She rolled her eyes. 'Moving on, did your father always breed horses?'

'Yes, and his father before him. The Dubois family were farmers. Grandpère Dubois acquired his first race-horse in a game of cards. It was very successful so he bred from it, and so he became more wealthy. And, of course, my father's marriage to my mother helped.'

'Your mother, the social butterfly.'

'Yes. My maternal grandmother was from a wealthy English family – a socialite who came over to France after the Second World War. She met Grandpère de Chatillon, fell in love with him and stayed here.'

'What did Grandpère de Chatillon do?'

'He had a pharmaceutical business.'

'So, did your grandmother go back to England when he died?'

'Non. Grandpère de Chatillon had, what you would call, a roving eye, which she ignored for many years, until… bah!' He ran a hand through his hair. 'You remember I told you about my concern over journalists? It was twenty-five years ago. There was a dispute between my grandpère's pharmaceutical company and a smaller one. Unfortunately, grandpère underestimated the determination of his opponent, who hired a journalist to grind the very dust out of the story. He discovered my grandpère with a fifteen-year old chambermaid in Milan. He caught some very explicit photographs with his telephoto lens.' He raised his hands in exclamation. 'There was an exposé and the name of Antoine de Chatillon, which was already known and respected throughout Europe, became known for a very different reason. Of course, it was a set-up. The girl in question was paid off by his adversary and disappeared into obscurity. But the whole story was too great a humiliation for my grandmère. She walked out on him, returned to England and never set foot in France again.'

'How awful for her.'

He turned back to focus again on the château. 'And not just for her. The family and the business suffered.'

'I can only imagine how that must have been.'

'I was just a young boy. I'd never seen an adult cry until I saw my grandmother, weeping with shame. She was a wonderful woman, she did good things for people. I loved her more than anybody. It was… bah! That's all.' He shrugged. Why was he telling her this? It was history, now. They had all moved on.

***

I would never have anticipated Christophe Dubois would bare his soul to me. The hunch of his shoulders and the drop of his head brought a shocking and unexpected lump to my throat. I sat forward, closing the gap between us. I could feel the muscles of my arm twitch as I resisted touching him but, after last night, I didn't trust myself, nor him for that matter. At such times of tension, I want to say something smart and profound, but all that came out was, 'You never know what's round the corner, do you?'

After a moment, he turned his head and looked at me. The gloom appeared to have lifted and as his gaze connected with mine, he said. 'You certainly don't.'

That glimmer in his eye could only be alluding to last night.

I swear I could feel the heat off him scorching my face, and I'm not absolutely sure I didn't flinch as his thigh moved against my knee. I swallowed and dragged my eyes away from his, clasping my now sweating hands securely together. His family history was littered with infidelities. As far as I knew, my own family had been steadfast to the point of calcification. I changed the subject. 'So, is Colette like your grandmother?'

He nodded slowly. 'In small ways. But she's more like my grandfather.'

'You mean, she has a roving eye, too?' He inclined his head and frowned as he looked across at me. Damn. Me and my big mouth. 'Sorry, it's just… the François thing…' My heart was starting to pound.

He studied me in an unnerving way. 'I imagine you're building up quite a picture of us all, huh? The Dubois and the de Chatillons – all loose morals and disloyalty.'

'No. Not at all.' I said, although he'd pretty much hit the nail on the head.

He continued staring at my face, his Bourneville-brown eyes judging me and drawing me in at the same time. I had the wild notion he was deciding whether or not to prove just how loose his morals could be, by ravaging me on the arbour seat in full view of the château. And I'm not sure I would have resisted. I could sense my body drifting towards him in slow motion.

'Is that what you were hoping for last night?' he murmured. 'Is that the kind of man you're looking for – a man with no strings to suit your new life?'

I lurched away and looked back at him. 'Hang on a minute. What happened last night was entirely a result of too much alcohol on an empty stomach. And you know it.'

'So you would have done the same thing if it had been François who walked you to the car, huh? Or Henri?'

I stared back at him. He had a point. There was no way I would have snogged Henri or François without a hefty financial reward to my favourite charity, which meant...

Without a response from me, he continued quietly. 'So does that make your morals any superior to Colette's or my grandfather's?'

I stood up clutching the camera case and drew in a deep breath. 'I think we're both adult enough to know that... that last night was a blip. You were my ally, my friend. I was seriously under the influence of François' entire wine cellar and yes, congratulations. From the selection of men on offer last night, you were the pick of the bunch.'

'And I'm delighted you picked me. It's always a pleasure when a beautiful woman takes the lead.'

Yes, oh Heartbreaker of Limousin. 'So I've heard.'

He raised an eyebrow. 'What have you heard?'

'That you have a reputation where women are concerned.'

He looked bewildered.

What on earth was I doing getting into this discussion? 'Never mind. Forget it.'

I spun round and stomped off – more annoyed with myself than anyone else. As I rapidly approached the paddock, I attracted the attention of the horses grazing there. Suddenly, the black one turned, raised his head and hit the gas, accelerating towards the fence, his mane dancing and mad eyes glaring as he approached. I stopped. Horses could jump fences. Wasn't that what the Grand National was all about? I watched in mounting horror as the enormous beast headed straight at me. I dropped to the ground and scrunched myself into a knot, waiting for the inevitable. I wasn't sure which was louder – the pounding in my ears or the hooves on the turf.

I waited.

Nothing.

I looked up. He was standing behind the fence, his head lurching and a snort billowing through his nostrils. I let out a whimper of relief, followed swiftly by a groan of humiliation. Finally, I sat back on my haunches and watched it from the safe distance of twenty metres. And the horse watched me. Before the moment was lost, I took out my camera.

Christophe appeared at my side. 'Did you think he was going to leap over the fence and eat you?' I ignored him and started taking photos. 'Equinophobia. We could help you get over that, you know.'

'Hmmm.'

'I could teach you to ride. I like a challenge.'

I stood up, and looked him in the eye. 'Yes. I have a fear of horses. You can blame a donkey at Weston-super-Mare.'

'What did it do?'

I hesitated. Could a donkey savage a three year old? I coughed. 'He dribbled on me.'

After a second's disbelief crossed his face, Christophe chuckled.

'He was big and I was very small. It was like a

monster. It gave me nightmares.'

Christophe studied me some more so I busied myself tidying away the camera. Eventually, he said, 'Are you okay?'

'I'm fine.'

'Good. Because I see the table is being prepared for lunch.'

'Lovely.'

'Should I tell my mother you'll only be drinking water?'

I zipped the bag up. 'Yes. Thank you.'

'Good. Then I won't have to worry about you getting so drunk that I have to fight you off.'

'Oh, per-lease!'

'Well, you appear to think I have no shame where women are concerned so if you were to make another pass at me, your honour would be seriously at risk. Although why you would make such a judgement about me, I cannot understand. Unless Isabelle has been very creative, and I know she can be.'

'Isabelle is a good friend of mine.'

'Well, she must have said something.'

'You don't have to look that far away from home. Your mother seems to think you've broken every heart in Limousin.'

He threw back his head and laughed. 'Now you're talking about someone even more creative than Isabelle.'

His smile was killing me. That's how men like him worked – one minute pissing you off, the next launching a massive charm offensive. How many times had Marc sweet-talked me round when I was fuming at his selfishness? 'Look, I'm sorry if I've offended you but you really do give off that whole 'love-em-and-leave-em' kind of vibe. And I'm even more sorry I was so stupid last night. It was purely biological. I'm a woman in my prime – what can I say?' I headed off towards the château, gesturing with my free arm. 'I have no intention of doing it again. I promise.'

Alain and Anne joined us for a lunch of salade Niçoise and tarte aux pommes. Despite Colette's relentless cheerfulness, and Louise's delight at seeing me again, the air between Alain and Christophe was so glacial you could have seen your breath in it. Neither met the other's eye and both said very little when spoken to. Anne was as quiet as a Carmelite nun, so the onus was on me, Louise and Colette to maintain the conversation. I plugged away with my interest in the château and its history. Colette seized on this by suggesting I spend a few days with her. 'There is a beautiful room overlooking the garden – well, you've seen it – I would love to have you here with me.'

'So would I,' added Louise.

Her offer was mighty tempting, in light of last night's little soap opera.

She continued. 'We could fly down to Nice for a few days – what do you think? I have some very good friends there.'

'Maman!' Christophe interrupted. 'Vicki is here to concentrate on her painting. She doesn't need you distracting her with shopping trips and soirées with your friends in Nice.'

I was surprised at the edge in his voice; surprised and somewhat miffed that he should be speaking for me. What was he – my manager? On the other hand, we did have a deal of sorts, and it would seem impolite and ungrateful if I cleared off to live it up with Colette – particularly when he'd gone to the trouble of setting up my studio.

Colette also raised her eyebrows at his reaction and looked over at me before saying, 'Everyone needs a little recreation, chéri.'

I imagined Colette could be wonderful and diverting company but Christophe was right – even if I did resent him speaking for me. I would tell him so later but, for now, I was possessed by pure devilment. 'Actually,' I said, looking from Colette to Christophe – who appeared to be fascinated by his empty plate – 'I'd really like to take you up on the offer…' I heard his deep intake of breath and saw the smile twinkle in his mother's eyes. 'It's so lovely here, with lots of stimulating scenery – and Nice. Wow! I'm very tempted but could we leave it for a few weeks? Only I do need to get my head down and work. I'm sure there'll come a point where I'll be desperate for a diversion and when I do, I'll be over like a shot.'

Colette raised her glass. 'Good. I shall look forward to it.'

I stole another glance at Christophe, who had sunk back in his chair. As he looked up at me, I raised my eyebrows over a benign smile. He merely narrowed his eyes and returned to studying his plate.

During the journey home, I said, 'I'm curious, Christophe, since when did you take responsibility for my painting?'

He looked across at me. 'I don't.'

'You told your mother I needed to concentrate on my painting – what are you, my agent?'

He briefly raised both hands off the wheel in exasperation. 'No. But you do want to concentrate on your painting, don't you? I thought I was helping. My mother can be quite formidable when she sets her mind on something. I didn't want to see you pushed into a corner by her.'

'I can speak up for myself – and have been doing for some time.'

'Yes, I can see that.'

I had the advantage of watching him while he concentrated on the road. He ran a hand through his hair in a futile attempt to keep the weight of it off his brow. Why did I have the distinct impression he didn't want me to stay at the château? Maybe he didn't like his mother cutting in on his territory – after all, he had quite a nice little arrangement with me being his resident cook. And then, of course, there would be Sylvie. If I went to stay at the château, I would get to know Sylvie and he probably didn't feel too good about that either.

In fairness, I did rather like staying at his house. Last week, when he was away, I'd been left to my own devices. If things continued in the same vein, I could be bashing out paintings at an impressive rate. A memory of last night shivered through my body. Or was it the chance of more shared intimacy that I didn't want to give up, and was he feeling the same? I swallowed and opened my window for air.

Christophe spoke. 'I apologise.'

'Oh.'

He continued. 'You're right. It was not my place to interfere. Perhaps you would do better at the château. You will have more stimulation there, more space, more inspiration. And you will have more company than you will at the surgery. The room at the top of my house is probably not suitable for a studio, anyway.'

'I like the studio at the top of your house.'

'You do?' he looked over at me.

'The wheels of my ambition started rolling in that room, I feel quite attached to it now. And as for company – you're absolutely right; I don't need any distractions if I'm going to paint.' I hoped he took the hint vis-à-vis last night's little aberration, too. 'So I'll stay put, if that's okay with you?'

He nodded in acceptance. 'Good.' Gradually, his frown lifted – as did the atmosphere in the car.

I shifted in my seat until I was almost facing him. 'So, did your mother teach you to dance?'

He glanced at me. 'Of course. It's one of the things she does best, that and spending money on travelling and parties.'

'She taught you well. You're quite a groovy little mover.'

Now he laughed. 'A groovy mover. I like that. And you – do you dance?'

'I love dancing but I've never learned to jive. I wish I could.'

'It's easy. Maybe I can teach you, sometime.'

I could let him teach me to dance. That would be fun. Just dancing. 'Maybe.'

'Of course, you would have to let me take the lead, which might be a problem for you.'

I gaped at him.

He laughed. 'I'm teasing. It would be a pleasure to teach you to jive.'

'Thank you.'

Around the next corner, there were half a dozen cyclists taking a break in a lay-by. They looked seriously fit, all lean and sculpted in their skin-tight vests and leggings. I let out a low whistle of appreciation as we passed – a shameful throw-back to my adolescence. A couple of guys looked up and waved.

'You like, huh?' Christophe asked.

'What's not to like?' I said, shrugging and settling back into my seat.

Christophe slowed the car, stopped and, to my horror, began a slow reverse back up the road.

'What?' I shrieked. 'What are you doing?'

He looked at me, all wide-eyed and innocent. 'Well, you seemed pretty keen to show your appreciation. Maybe you'd like an introduction, huh?'

'Noo! Stop it! Drive on!'

'What? You don't want another look? Maybe take a photo for your archive?'

'Christophe!'

He grinned at me. Stopped reversing, put the car into forward gear and set off again, chuckling at my mortification.

Just as we pulled into our little town, my mobile trilled into life. 'Excuse me,' I said to Christophe before answering it. 'Good afternoon, Daniel, how are you?'

'Pretty good, thanks,' he replied in his easy way. 'What are you up to?'

'I've just been out taking some photographs.'

'What of?'

'A château.'

'Where did you go, Lubersac?'

'No.' I didn't like to say more. I didn't want Christophe thinking I was a blabber-mouth as well as a loose woman. 'So, Daniel, why are you calling?'

'Are you busy, this evening?'

I looked at Christophe whose eyes were fixed on the road. 'What did you have in mind?'

'My friend, Connor, has a preview copy of the latest Jim Carrey movie so he can write a review. Wondered if you fancied joining us to watch it?'

'I do. I love Jim Carrey.' But I still had to cook dinner. 'What time?'

'It's flexible.'

'Could you pick me up at eight-thirty?'

'Of course,' he said and we ended the conversation.

After a few minutes silence, I said to Christophe, 'I'd quite like to get dinner finished by eight-fifteen. Is that okay?'

'Sure. If you love Jim Carrey.'

Chapter 12

Daniel looked better tonight. He was wearing navy jeans and an amethyst coloured sweater. He gave me a rueful look just before we entered his friend's house. 'I apologise, in advance, for the state of the place. Con considers himself too cerebral to tackle housework.'

Connor reminded me of a typical student, which would have been less disturbing if we'd all been eighteen. Instead, Connor – or Con – was nearer to forty. Born in Dublin, he'd arrived in France via Repton and Cambridge. They lived in an old farmhouse, once lovingly modernised but now a bit of a tip. An army of cleaners could probably get it up to habitable standard by Christmas.

A bottle of port had been opened and was sitting on the coffee table with some glasses. It was forming a new, glistening ring on the wooden surface, amongst dozens of similar, wine bottle rings. Con hauled his eighteen stone frame from his armchair as we entered. He smiled, a broad, welcoming smile and shook my hand before leaning forward to kiss my cheeks.

'Welcome to a Limousin Arts and Reprobates Social Event,' he said. 'Or L'ARSE as we like to call it. We're thinking of giving it official status and filing for government funding, what do you reckon?'

'Is that to buy the port,' I asked.

'Smart girl. Would you like one?'

'Don't suppose I could have coffee, could I?'

'Coffee? Good idea. You and Dan can stay sober and tell me what the film's all about.'

Daniel raised an eyebrow. 'Here, sit down,' he said, plumping a cushion on the sofa. 'How do you take your coffee?'

'Just black, please.'

'Settling in alright?' Con asked, thudding back into his armchair.

I perched on the vacant sofa. 'Yes, thanks.'

'Always good to meet a kindred spirit in this place – and a Brit. It's full of agricultural Frogs, of course.' He picked up the remote control for the TV and brought the set to life. 'I've cued up the DVD. Do you want to watch the trailer; get an idea of what we're watching?'

'Okay.'

'Always best, I think. Then if I nod off, at least I'll have the gist of it,' he laughed.

'Don't you enjoy reviewing films? I'd have thought it was a great job.'

'You get to see an awful lot of dross. That's why I like to share the load. I used to fly solo but, Christ, it was intense.'

Daniel came back with two mugs of coffee and sat next to me. 'So, this château you visited – I assume it's the one belonging to the Dubois family – what was it like?'

'Fabulous. Big rooms, tall windows. A bit crumbly round the edges, though. It could do with some money spending on it.'

'That's the home of the Dubois stables, isn't it?' Con asked. I nodded. 'Bloody loaded, so I've heard.

See the stables?'

'Yes, briefly but I'm not a horsey person, so please don't ask me about them. I don't know a fetlock from a nosebag.'

'Colette Dubois has quite a reputation, too. Don't suppose you met her, did you?' he asked.

I wondered if all journalists were chronically nosy. 'Yes. She was lovely. I liked her.'

'Bit of a man trap, I've heard,' he said, leaning forward to refill his glass. 'And an art collector, isn't she?'

'Come on, Con,' Daniel interjected, 'give the girl a break.'

'Just curious. Thought you might engineer yourself an invite, Dan. Check out her collection.'

Dan looked at me over his coffee, a smile playing round the corners of his eyes. 'Can I apologise for all Con's failings, here and now? Save repeating myself for the rest of the evening?'

I smiled back. 'Colette might enjoy showing you round. She's certainly not the shy, retiring kind.'

'Don't worry about it. I've plenty to keep me occupied.'

'He's playing it cool, Vicki. The man's personal obsession is private collections, isn't it, Dan?' Connor knocked back a hefty slug of port.

Daniel rolled his eyes and shook his head. If there were an Olympic sport for stirring up trouble, I reckon Connor would go for gold.

'I will try. If you'd like me to,' I said, smiling at Daniel.

'It's not important.' He turned to Connor. 'Come on, let's see this film before you nod off.'

I settled back onto the sofa next to Daniel, and

found I quite liked the companionable warmth of it. He didn't exude a dangerous heat like Christophe did. Around Daniel, I didn't feel that vertiginous threat – no desire to throw myself at him. So later, when he drove me home and suggested we might meet for lunch, the following week, I had no hesitation in accepting.

'There's a very pretty river valley near here. While the weather's still good, it's worth a visit. You never know, it might inspire you.'

'Daniel, you realise you could turn into my ancillary muse?'

'Ha! That'd be a first.' When he pulled up outside the house, he smiled across at me. 'Tell me, do you have a series of paintings in mind – a theme?'

'Absolutely... not.' I winced. 'Daniel, I haven't a clue where I'm going. I'm rusty, I'm... I'm shit-scared, to be honest. I've given myself this year but what if I waste it trying to find my creative mojo? What if I'm no better than a high-school art teacher? You know what they say, those who can, do, those who can't...'

He nudged my arm. 'Vicki, this is the year to find out. Give it a go. If it's not your destiny, you can go back to being a great art teacher and inspire the next generation.'

He made it sound simple, like it didn't matter whether I succeeded or not. Hell, I wished I could be so easy on myself. 'Right,' I said. 'I'll mull that over.'

'I'll pick you up on Tuesday, around twelve.'

As Daniel had promised, the river valley was gorgeous. At first sight I thought, if this doesn't spark something in me, I should jack it in and go home. I'm an artist, I told myself, wake up!

Either side of the valley, a blend of evergreen and deciduous trees made a haphazard patchwork of texture and colour, all reflected in the slow-moving surface of the water. 'Good shout, Daniel,' I said, reaching round for my camera bag. 'This place is beautiful.'

As we turned along a curve in the path, I stopped abruptly, and Daniel bumped into me. About a hundred metres away, a man and a young boy were fishing from the bank. 'Shh,' I put my finger to my lips and whispered, 'That is a picture.' I switched to telephoto lens and began to shoot.

When we finally reached the couple, I asked the father if he minded me taking a picture of the boy with his fish. Without hesitation, the youngster handed his rod to his father and lifted his booty into the air, his cheeky grin exposing a large gap between his front teeth. I took a couple of pictures and agreed to send them copies via email – jotting their address in my notepad.

Walking on, Daniel offered to carry the camera case. I realised, as I watched him wrap the strap around his hand and carry the bag over his shoulder, it was a gesture Marc would never have made. Men and women had been equals in our world. So equal, Marc wouldn't even offer to carry the shopping in from the car; I'd always had to ask.

In the shade of an overhanging willow tree, I quickly flicked back through the images I'd captured. 'Yes!' I declared, punching the air and beaming at Daniel.

'Something there?' he asked.

'Something stirring,' I answered, not missing the

flicker of his eyebrows. 'I feel a little badda-boom, badda-boom just here,' I said, patting my heart. 'And up here,' I pointed to the middle of my forehead, 'plans… plans for my first picture of the new era. Thank you, Daniel.' I threw an arm around his neck and hugged him. 'I think my mo is finally jo-ing.'

He grinned. 'Hey, happy to oblige.'

I bounced a little on the spot. 'I can't wait to get started.'

'We can forego lunch, if you like. Although the restaurant's only just at the next bridge.'

'No. Not at all. Lunch. Excellent. Lunch. Just what I need to set me up for an afternoon's painting.' I almost skipped along the river path. 'What sort of restaurant is it?'

'Small and traditional, with excellent foie gras.'

I stopped skipping. 'Ah. Small problem. I'm vegetarian and I'm beginning to realise France isn't the ideal destination for veggies, is it?'

'They do excellent fish dishes, too. And the best Vin de Pays in Limousin.'

'Marvellous!'

Over lunch we covered topics as diverse as Daniel's preference for cats over mine for dogs; if there was any likelihood society would swing in favour of women being the key breadwinners (bit of a sore point for me); and why whole nations were obsessed with football. 'If I were running the FA,' I said, tapping the salt cellar with my finger, 'I would insist all football shorts had a pocket with a hankie in. As a matter of hygiene.'

'Ah, but would they use it?'

'They'd bloody well have to, if I was in charge.'

'And so speaks Miss Marchant, Head of Art and

Football.'

I giggled. 'Once a teacher, always a teacher.'

'But you can become an artist. I'm sure, if you really want to.'

'I do.' I paused. 'I think.'

He dipped his head and looked at me, over invisible spectacles. 'Only think?'

I shook myself. 'It's self doubt, that's all.'

'Don't waste your time on that. Life's too short. I've told you, go for it and if it doesn't come off, you can say you tried.'

'So where does your confidence come from, Daniel?' I asked, although I had a sneaking suspicion it was down to his privileged upbringing. Who wouldn't be confident with lofty connections and no financial worries?

He tipped his head to one side. After a moment, he narrowed his eyes and said, 'Life's all about survival of the fittest. Show weakness and someone will spot it, they'll seize their opportunity and rub you out.'

'Wow. That's a pretty dark view of the world.'

'I learned it at an early age. Remember, at boarding school, we had no Mummy and Daddy to fight our battles for us. It was sink or swim, do or die.'

I realised his background wasn't so different from Christophe's. However, I'd spent my life in state education but I didn't recall many parents strolling into school like the Mafia to stick up for their progeny. 'Are you saying, bully or be bullied?'

He frowned. 'No. Absolutely not. No. That's cowardly. No.'

He pushed his empty plate away and signalled to the waiter for the bill.

'You see,' he went on, 'I had an older brother who went through it all before me. I learned from his mistakes.' He frowned as he glanced at his watch, before grinning up at me. 'Listen, if I get you home in the next half hour, you'll have three good hours of daylight to start that painting. What do you think?'

I smiled and nodded. 'Sure.'

Plucking raw nerves wasn't the kind of activity I liked to engage in.

Chapter 13

Having left the table set for dinner, I returned to my studio and began flicking through the pictures on my screen, rocking back and forth between the ones of the young fisherman and his father. I chose one of the images taken with the telephoto lens and started working out my composition on paper, before placing a new blank canvas on the easel. Within an hour, I had my principal structure and colours blocked in. There wasn't much to see but I was bouncing again. I would use misty colours to suggest the autumn light and sharp focus on the main characters. I was humming to myself and jumped when Christophe tapped on the open door. I looked up and grinned. 'Hi.'

'Good afternoon. You have been busy, I see. May I come in?'

'Of course.' I stepped back from my canvas.

He studied it for a moment. 'I see it is not the château.'

'No. Daniel took me down to the river, this morning. I saw a father and son, fishing. This is the start of that picture.'

'Very good,' he said. 'You are inspired, non?'

'I am. And it's very exciting.'

He nodded. 'So, were the pictures of the château not up to standard?'

'Aha! Yes. They were very good but I want to

study them and decide which scenes I want to revisit. The château is such a beautiful building, but it's really what goes on there that interests me.'

Christophe rolled his eyes. '*Mon Dieu*! I doubt that would make an attractive image.' He turned abruptly. 'I will leave you to your work.'

I shrugged and focussed again on my canvas. He didn't leave, instead he said, more quietly, 'Would you like something to drink – red, white?'

'Red. Thank you.'

He returned with a glass and the bowl of fruit from the kitchen. 'I don't want you forgetting to eat,' he teased, flashing his most practised and spine-tingling smile.

Nice one, I thought. But I'm an artist, now. I'm immune.

The following morning, keen to top up my bank of images, I took advantage of the crisp, bright morning to visit the weekly market. It really was an uplifting kaleidoscope of colour as it meandered through the small town. I thought back to the vast market I went to in Bristol – all noisy vendors and cheap clothes, the kind a girl might wear on a Hen Weekend in Magaluf.

There were neat rows of fruit and veg in a patchwork of texture and earthy colours. An elderly stall-holder nodded and mumbled '*Bonjour*' in a deep, gruff voice as I wandered towards him. His face was so lined from a life in the outdoors, he looked shockingly like one of his Savoy cabbages.

Moving on, I smelt the unmistakable and, frankly, repellent smell of raw meat. I scanned the chiller cabinet displaying butchered birds and animals: duck hearts, rabbits complete with their own offal, great shiny slabs of muscle and bone. Yuk! I dragged my eyes away settled on a stall festooned with lush scarves and shawls.

I raised my camera and clicked. A woman, layered up in grey wool, stepped out to promote her merchandise with an encouraging smile, so I was drawn in to touch the sumptuous fabrics. Tempted by a cerise, chenille shawl with tiny blue birds embroidered along the edge, I lifted it, felt its weight and absolutely knew it would drape perfectly.

It would look great with jeans and with my Best Winter Coat. But I'd left the Best Winter Coat in England. Would I really wear this out here? Reluctantly, I let it go and watched if fall back. I smiled, thanked the woman and moved away.

A cat was dozing beneath the fish stall, cunningly opening one eye, now and again – ever the opportunist. I bought a couple of red mullet and some huge, glossy grey prawns.

The next stall was Italian, with hunks of parmesan piled up like Cotswold stones, and racks of polenta, gnocchi and domed panettone. I bought some fresh pasta – it would be great with the prawns.

At the end of the market, when I turned and looked back, there was a sudden burst of winter sunshine warming the canopies. I clicked away – thrilled by the potential for another painting.

I had done my shopping so I could concentrate on snapping more pictures. I say 'done my shopping' but truth was, I'd not quite finished. Drawn – as I knew I would be – back to the cerise shawl. It's not as if I'd treated myself to much, recently. Okay, there was the rail ticket to France, new brushes, canvases and paint.

But, without my Best Winter Coat I might freeze to death. This shawl was an investment. An absolute bloody necessity. '*Oui*,' I said to the woman. '*Je voudrais ceci*,' I would like this.

'Bien sur,' she replied with a knowing wink.

Back at the house, I could see Christophe in his dove grey vet's scrubs walking across the courtyard towards the house. It was the first time I'd seen him in uniform. It didn't exactly have the impact of the military but it had a certain appeal. I plonked my shopping on the table and reached for the kettle, just as he came through the back door.

'Coffee?' I asked.

'Thanks, but I have one going cold at the surgery,' he said, with a polite smile, as he carried on through to his study.

Fair enough.

I packed the food away in the fridge and opened a tin of nutty flapjack I'd made the morning before. It was one of those delicious winter treats that always reminded me of home. As I leaned against the counter, chomping on a sweet, buttery mouthful of oats and toffee, Christophe reappeared. His eyes did a quick flick in my direction. He stopped, sidled over to see what I was eating and raised an eyebrow.

I held the open tin towards him. 'Nutty Flapjack. Packed with calories and hazardous to teeth but really scrummy.'

'Mmm,' he murmured in anticipation, as he dipped his hand into the tin and pulled a piece out. He studied it for a second and took a bite. It wasn't easy; the texture of my nutty flapjack has been likened to concrete. He frowned and then a piece snapped off into his mouth. As his jaws worked a little harder, the taste delivered its magic, and his face relaxed. 'Mmm,' he repeated.

'Sure you don't want a hot coffee to dunk it in?' I asked.

He shook his head, jaws still working on the flapjack. Finally, he said. 'You had the description about right, I think.'

'Do you want to take the tin with you – share it with your colleagues?'

He looked at the tin and he looked at me. 'Probably safer I don't, huh?' He went to move away then paused, turned back and smiled. 'Maybe I will. We have a long day ahead of us.'

As he walked out of the door with the tin under his arm, I'm pretty sure he said, 'Scrummy.'

Days later, to say I was pleased with my first, proper painting of the new season would be an understatement. It was singing to me. If my painting had a voice, it would be belting out *Stayin' Alive*. Okay, so I'd had to repaint the boy's face a couple of times to get it right, but in the preceding years, I'd been so bogged down with educational admin and wedding plans, I wouldn't have been surprised if all I could muster was a psychedelic spreadsheet in the style of Mondrian. I bounced around the attic like Tigger. 'Go girl!'

My mobile rang.

'Daniel,' I yelped into the phone. 'You've called me just at the right time.'

'Delighted to hear it. Why's that?'

'I've nearly finished my first painting and I'm really pleased with it.'

'There you go. I'm sure it'll be the first of many.'

'I do hope so.'

'How do you fancy coming with me to see a small gallery?'

'Yes, please. That's just what I could do with – more stimulation.'

'Truth is, the gallery owner's a bit of a bore – obsessive over his artistic choices yet always has his eye on business. With me, of course, he knows he's unlikely to make a sale but he labours under the illusion I have some influence in getting others to buy.'

'Oh dear, I hope he won't think I've got that kind of money.'

'Ha, no. I was thinking more along the lines of you getting to know him; preparing the ground for your future exhibition, while I check out the exhibits. I happen to know, he doesn't have a full calendar for next year.'

I raised my eyes to heaven in silent thanks. 'Brilliant! Count me in. You're an absolute star.'

'Oh, God, yes,' he said with mock emphasis, 'I'm a regular bloody saint.'

I started pacing a small circle. 'Daniel, are you sure it's not too soon?'

'It's never too soon to put your plans in motion.'

'No, of course. You're absolutely right.'

'Good. I'll set up an appointment with Raimond and let you know.'

I heard the slow rumble of a car engine, followed by the excited barks of the dogs as Christophe pulled onto the drive. I ran downstairs, arriving in the hall just as he entered. 'Guess what?'

'I don't know, tell me.'

So I did.

'Very good,' he replied. 'Daniel is proving to be quite a useful contact, non?'

'It's serendipity.'

The look he gave me only lacked a curled lip and a snort of scorn.

Miserable bugger! I thought, beaming more broadly as I headed towards the kitchen. 'Artichoke and mushroom flan – how does that grab you?' I called over my shoulder, not waiting to hear his reply.

I'd swapped several texts with Izzy during the day but felt a full-on dialogue was essential. So once dinner was over, I excused myself and shot up to my studio to call her. Unfortunately, it was one of those days when my mood was completely at odds with hers. I'm not saying she deliberately deflated the balloon of my excitement but she was definitely straining to match my enthusiasm.

'Babe, are you not having such a good day?' I asked, concern for her nudging my euphoria aside.

She sighed. 'I'm just very tired, and I have a headache. I'm really hoping I don't get sick because I have these two big clients who are so demanding, and one of them is promising me more of their brands to represent, just so long as I get this one right. My boss, Miriam, is watching me like a hawk. Sometimes I think she's banking on me bringing in more business, and yet she won't offer me any help. And that makes me think she wants me to fail. It's so stressful.'

Izzy didn't do stress like normal mortals. When she was on a deadline you'd be forgiven for thinking she'd inhaled a yard of coke when, in reality, the worst she'd done was drink bottles of the fizzy stuff. However, with her efficiency and attention to detail, I assumed she thrived on it.

Miriam was her boss. There seemed to be a grudging respect between them so it wasn't the ideal working relationship.

'Have you asked her for help?' I edged in, quietly.

'Non.'

'Could you?'

Another sigh. 'I shouldn't have to. Miriam should be right behind me on this. It's her business, after all.'

'Exactly. Work out what you need, then ask her for it. I know you can present the case really well, so she'd be shooting herself in the foot if she refused.'

Silence.

'You know I'm right, Izzy.'

'Maybe.'

'Come on, you're fantastic at what you do but even you can't do it all alone. And if you bring these new brands in, surely Miriam will have to promote you, won't she?'

'That could be the problem. I'm not sure Miriam wants to.'

'Oh. That's a whole other story.'

'Oui. I think I need a new career.'

'Such as?'

'I'm still thinking about that one. But right now, I have a couple of press releases to write. Long ones.'

'Okay, Izzy, I'll let you get on with it. Night, babe. Love you.'

'You too.'

Not for the first time, I wished Izzy lived down the road. Even though she had work to do, I could have been there to make her coffee while she worked; celebrate with a glass of wine when she finished. Maybe, if I decided to stay in France (my heart thrilled at the possibility), I should find myself a piedà-terre in Paris. I settled down to type her a supportive email.

I thought Daniel had rather pulled the stops out with his appearance on Tuesday, when he came to take me to the gallery. He looked more arty than usual, in a black polo-neck sweater and black jeans under his sludge green tweed jacket. Yes, smart and very nearly handsome, I thought, basing my opinion purely on aesthetics.

As we set off, he said, 'We're heading towards Angoulême, it's quite a drive, I hope you don't mind.'

'Not at all. I'm very grateful you're taking me.'

'This chap we're going to see, Raimond Fournier, I can't promise he'll book you…'

'No, of course,' I cut in. 'I have to get there on merit, I know. But you're doing me a huge favour just making the introduction.'

'My pleasure. You need contacts in this game.'

I picked at a crust of paint in my thumb cuticle. I was already hatching a plot to ask Colette if Daniel could see her collection. Fair dos – one good turn deserves another and all that. But I wouldn't mention it to him, yet. Just in case.

Raimond, at over six foot six tall, looked as butch as a Rottweiler on steroids but as camp as a black satin ridge-tent with scarlet guy ropes. He wore a black suit with a red shirt, and each pinkie of his expressive hands was adorned with a signet ring. His dark eyes scanned me swiftly. '*Enchanté*,' he said, with a twitch of his top lip before turning back to Daniel. 'The artist I am exhibiting has a wonderful way with colour. He's quite a find. His next exhibition is in Paris, Daniel. You know what that means; his profile will go up and so will his prices. Here,' he gestured to the archway into the gallery, 'come and experience his genius for yourself.'

I tried to catch Daniel's eye. Raimond's sales patter was as brazen as the scarlet and black, hand-stitched cowboy boots on his feet.

The artwork though, I had to admit, was impressive. In contrast to the gloomy work of Florin, these were vivid and bold, full of rhythm and sharp points of light. I loved them. I glanced at the price-list; lower than Florin's. If I'd been flush I might have been tempted to buy one of the smaller pieces. Just as with François' work, this artist attacked his canvases like a man possessed. I thought of my own work, idling on the easel; how would it match up? I felt a buzz of excitement travel through my spine. Now was my time. I was finally mixing with professionals in the art world. Wasn't this what I'd always wanted? I was here and now, and I intended to make the most of it. Those canvases up in my studio wouldn't know what had hit them.

After gazing at the paintings and making positive noises, Daniel finally turned the spotlight on me and my plans. 'So, Raimond, I thought you might consider Vicki for an exhibition, next summer? Be the first to introduce her work to the world.'

I swallowed. Just a few months away. How could they possibly take me seriously?

Raimond stroked a finger across his eyebrow and looked at me. 'Do you have anything to show me?'

'No. My early work is back in England. I'm starting fresh over here.'

He didn't look impressed, and who could blame him? 'Do you have a website?'

'No.'

'You need one. It's the best way to promote yourself.'

'Good idea.'

'Then you can send me a link and I'll take a look at your work.'

'Thank you.'

'I might take a couple of pieces for a mixed exhibition. Give them a try. If I think you have something to offer.'

'Great. I'd appreciate that.' I was smiling back at him but honestly felt he didn't like me. I was sure he had absolutely no interest in my work and everything he said was to keep Daniel sweet.

I took his business card and before leaving, made a last, wistful tour of the exhibition. When I came back to the entrance, the two men were nodding and shaking hands – Raimond beaming like a schoolgirl at her latest crush.

I was tempted to mention this to Daniel, as we drove away, but since I currently had no data on his own sexuality, thought it prudent to keep schtum. However, before we'd passed through the gates, he said, 'I really don't mean to trifle with old Raimond's affections, but,' he sighed, 'how shall I put it?'

I chipped in, 'He's better a friend than an enemy?'

'Ha! No. Although, you may be right. No, I actually think the guy has good judgement.'

I laughed. 'And that's why you don't mind him finding you so attractive.'

Daniel laughed even harder. 'Well, there is that, of course. But I was going to say, it doesn't worry me if he fancies me. I should be flattered. The important thing is to keep the professional relationship ticking along nicely.'

'I thought you made a lovely couple,' I teased. 'He only had eyes for you.'

'Behave yourself, Vicki, or that's the last gallery I'm taking you to,' he joked. As we drew up at a junction, his sidelong glance, teamed with a half smile, did surprising and unsettling things to my insides. Wow! I hadn't expected that. I smiled back, whilst silently realigning my chakras, which seemed to have been knocked sideways by this astonishing reaction to one simple look from Daniel.

* * *

Daniel loved boosting Vicki's confidence; it had quite a kick. When Jeanne had suggested they meet, he'd agreed purely on the basis of building his network. Contacts were everything, especially in his world. He certainly hadn't pictured himself becoming a mentor. True, he'd helped artists before; steered them in one direction or stopped them taking another. He liked using his knowledge. Why keep it all to himself? But he'd never really considered how he might benefit his protégée – until now. Vicki was like an open book. She was fresh, unadulterated by the current art scene, keen to develop and grow.

'Daniel,' he said to himself as he drove away, 'this girl is an absolute bloody gift, so don't screw it up!'

Chapter 14

Lying in bed that night – alone – I checked the clock. It was one-thirty and I didn't feel remotely close to sleep. Daniel had latched onto a part of my brain or possibly my heart, and I couldn't budge him. I wasn't used to my emotions being captured by stealth. I was used to a more Wham! Bam! approach to selecting a mate, which was possibly where I'd been going wrong. Christophe had charm and looks but being around him seemed to upset my equilibrium. Whereas Daniel was steady, supportive and made me feel at home – or had done until that look in the car had knocked my senses off balance. Since then, his lopsided smile had been playing on a loop inside my head.

I scrambled out of bed and pulled a thick sweater on, stuffed my feet into my slippers and crept downstairs to fix some hot milk and honey. Taking it back up to the attic, I turned the light on and studied my painting. I really was pleased with it. Was it okay to feel good about my own work, I wondered, or did it show arrogance and complete lack of objectivity?

I turned my back on it, bent over and viewed it upside down, through my legs. No. It had balance, it had structure. I really liked it. And what was the point of creating something I hated?

I'd allowed Daniel to view it when he'd brought me home. He'd nodded for a few moments, and finally declared, 'You've captured a moment in time. Well done!' And then he'd stood next to me and put a companionable arm around my shoulder and hugged me against him. 'It's fabulous, Vicki. I can't wait to see more from you.'

I also felt like I wanted to see more of him. Who'd have thought buckets of praise could be such an aphrodisiac? Despite the pheromones multiplying through my body, I had thanked him graciously and offered him a cup of tea.

Tea? Oh, how I cringed.

As we'd sat at the kitchen table, drinking tea and eating home-made ginger biscuits, Christophe had picked that very moment to come home. I'd thought he looked a tad preposterous, standing there all cool and arrogant in his smelly waxed jacket, and boots coated in layers of farmyard excrement. '*Bon soir*,' he'd said allowing his eyes to scan the scene before calling the dogs, and heading out for a walk.

'He can be so rude,' I muttered to his departing back.

'Forget it. The guy's probably just tired after a long day,' said Daniel. 'And that, I think, is a good cue for me to leave.'

I'd held my breath as he'd kissed me on both cheeks, and watched, almost dewy-eyed as he'd driven away.

Wow! I needed to get a grip.

I unscrewed the clamp on the easel, took my completed canvas down and placed it by the wall. 'Next!' I declared, sounding like the nit nurse on a busy day.

So… what to paint?

I fired up my laptop and flicked through the

images I'd taken in the market that cold morning. I'd never imagined Limousin could be so chilly in winter. Surely, that was the preserve of my mother's homeland – Aberdeen – not central France, over a thousand miles further south?

Before deciding which to paint, I found myself on Google and typing in Daniel Keane Art Critic. There were several listings under the Modern Cultural Review website. I clicked through and read a couple. His mug shot wasn't exactly flattering; he appeared older and his eyes looked a bit shifty. Odd how some people were amazingly photogenic but a bit ugly in the flesh, while others had great appeal with a pulse beating through them yet looked decidedly dodgy when frozen in two dimensions. Hmm... maybe I could suggest taking a more up-to-date shot. I closed the laptop, picked up my mug, and went back to bed.

The following afternoon, having elected to paint the fruit stall and its well-weathered owner, I was just blocking in the green for the pears when I heard Christophe jogging up the stairs. He was home early.

'Vicki,' he called up to my attic. 'Would you like to visit a farm with me?'

I moved over to the landing and looked down the stairs at him. He was leaning against the banister, waxed jacket over muddy jeans and boots. 'D'you mean, right now?'

'Yes. I'm on my way to a pig farm. Do you want to come too? I know you're always looking for subjects for your painting. We need to leave in the next five minutes.'

I looked at my filthy hands. 'Okay. I'm on my way.' I plunged my brushes into a bucket of water, and rinsed them through, grabbed my camera and belted downstairs.

'Why are you visiting this farm?' I asked.

'It sounds like I'll have to treat some of the sows for mastitis.'

'Ouch!'

'Yes. Not good for the sow, and even worse for the piglets – they'll be hungry and squealing. They could even die.'

My excitement dulled. 'So... you're actually taking me to witness something really distressing?'

He glanced across, his expression opening up. 'No. No, not at all. I'm taking you because some of the sows are still farrowing – giving birth – that's the part I thought you'd be interested in. I'm sure we'll be able to do something for the sick ones. Please, don't worry.'

Easier said than done. He was inviting me, a vegetarian with a conscience, to a pig farm, to see diddy little piglets coming into the world, while there was the spectre of life-threatening mastitis hanging over them.

As we drove through the darkened countryside I could feel my gloom increasing. I needed to brace up and be brave. Not for the first time, I realised how sheltered my life had been.

It's a pity nostrils can't be closed voluntarily. The pig shed had a whiff you couldn't and shouldn't bottle. At least it wasn't as noisy as I expected. The pigs were in pens, some containing sows and pups, others just sows. When Christophe asked if there were any sows actually in labour, the farmer – Monsieur Blanc – pointed over to pen number twelve. With a flick of his hand, he gestured me to go and see for myself. I looked at Christophe. He nodded. 'Monsieur Blanc and I are going to see the sick ones. You go ahead.'

In pen twelve, a farm hand had crouched down to watch the process from a safe distance. I'd heard pigs could be pretty aggressive when riled; from the little I knew about childbirth, I'm guessing a sow in labour wouldn't take kindly to being messed with. No gas and air for her, or the choice of a birthing pool. Yet she was lying there, with very little drama, as two piglets were already suckling. Down at the business end, a little head popped out, followed very quickly by two legs. After some wiggling around, it scrambled out – like a prisoner tunnelling out of Stalag Luft – then it flopped down on the floor to take a breather. The farm hand kept watch, and moments later, the little thing started trying to stand until, very soon, it was shoved out of the way by the arrival of another one. The farm hand, slowly moved across and lifted the first one, rubbed it with a cloth and positioned it alongside its siblings. Then the process continued.

It wasn't until another appeared that it dawned on me I hadn't taken a photo. I dropped to my knees, lifted out my camera, and began snapping away.

Some time later, Christophe came to find me. He crouched down next to me and looked through the bars of the pen. 'Pretty amazing, huh?'

'Yes.' It was lovely and bittersweet. It was an experience tainted by the certainty these little creatures were only here because they were destined for the table. I was squirming from the guilty memory of bacon and egg sandwiches I'd so relished in my earlier life. 'But I think I've seen enough, now,' I said, returning my camera to its case.

'More of your little friends, huh?'

'Something like that.'

We both stood up. 'Well, you'll be pleased to know that they're going to foster out some of the undernourished piglets, and we can treat the sows for mastitis.'

'So nobody died today?'

He smiled. 'No. Not today.'

'Good. Then that's something to celebrate.'

Monsieur Blanc joined us and asked me, in a very strong accent, if I'd enjoyed watching the birth.

'*Oui. Magnifique.*' I replied. '*Merci beaucoup.*'

Monsieur Blanc frowned and nodded. Christophe smiled, which I took as approval, and we said our goodbyes. As we headed towards the car he said, 'I'm afraid you've just told the farmer you'd quite like having ten babies at a time, and thanked him for the suggestion.'

'You're kidding?'

He chuckled. 'No. Why would I make it up?'

'I guess I need more practice with my French.'

So he called my bluff and insisted on no more English for the rest of the day, which was great but exhausting. We lasted until after dinner, when he took pity on me and lifted the ban on my native language. 'You've done very well,' he said, raising his wine glass to me.

'So have you. I must have really tested your patience.'

'Don't forget, I went to an English boarding school. When I arrived, my English language skills were pretty basic.'

'Of course.' I remembered how François had suggested Christophe had been lonely. 'I would have hated being away from home at that age. Was it awful?'

'To begin with, they teased me about my accent and using the wrong words. But I was quite used to being without my parents.'

'Really?'

'You've met Colette.' He shook his head but there was a smile softening the corners of his eyes. 'She often went away on little vacations without my father – who couldn't or wouldn't leave the stables. Her trips offered wonderful opportunities for her infidelities. But, of course, it also meant she couldn't be around for me.'

'That's why she sent you to school in England.'

'Sometimes she wasn't even there in the school holidays. By the time my beloved grandmère died, I was twelve and my mother felt I was old enough to come back to France to be looked after by my father and the housekeeper, so she was still free to take her trips whenever she wished. Which was often.'

'Did you hate her for going away?' I asked.

'I didn't like the situation but I didn't hate her. I was as much under her spell as everyone else. I adored her.'

I watched him as he rotated his glass, his eyes focusing somewhere in his past.

After a moment he continued, 'You've seen what she's like – so colourful and lively. I missed her. I used to go into her empty room, just to smell her fragrance.' He looked up. 'Can you believe I would even swap her pillow with mine, when she went away, so I could feel her a little bit closer? I would lie there and imagine her kissing me goodnight and telling me her fanciful stories.'

I found it painfully easy to picture a young, dark-eyed boy, curled up in bed, cuddling his mother's pillow.

Christophe lined up the salt and pepper pot beside his glass. 'Sometimes, I used to imagine she would send for me. When she telephoned and spoke to my father, I would hold my breath, waiting to hear him say, "Yes, I will send Christophe to join you." But, of course, that never happened. I wanted to visit the pyramids and ride on a camel with her – she made it sound so exciting – but…' He let out a little chuckle before looking back at me, just as my eyes began to fill. He tilted his head and he smiled. 'Vicki. Please don't be upset.'

I blinked, spilling a tear and wiped it away quickly. 'Sorry.'

His smile broadened. 'Don't worry. I got over it.'

I guessed he might think he had but truthfully, I thought it explained a lot.

Chapter 15

The following day, I returned to my painting of the market stall with renewed energy. Christophe and I seemed to have buried the hatchet over my drunken pass plus, I had more pictures to work on and this latest canvas was taking shape really well.

I was on fire.

What's more, Daniel was very keen to see my work in progress. I managed to buy a few days until the composition started pleased me, before I allowed him over the threshold. Part of me was super anxious at what he might think, but the larger part of me was enjoying his investment of time, his interest and his encouragement. He stood back to scan the image before him. He nodded. He smiled. 'You have a talent for capturing the moment; for fixing the mood of a place on canvas. There's a nod to Toulouse Lautrec and Renoir in this.'

'Toulouse-Lautrec is my hero,' I gasped as my ego inflated. I'd fallen in love with him when I was fifteen, on a school trip to Paris. He may have been a bit on the short side – not to mention, dead – but his paintings drew me right into his world.

Daniel placed a hand on my shoulder and squeezed it as he said, 'Thank you, so much, for letting me see your work. I realise it's not always easy to share a work in progress. And knowing how critical I can be, I imagine it might even be quite daunting.

Good on you for having the balls to show me.' He smiled straight into my eyes, then. It was a heady feeling – a boosted ego. 'You're going to have to put your work out there, one day, and it's not just the art world that can be critical. You'll need to grow a thick skin for all those people who won't like what you do. And you can bet there'll be some.'

He was right but, at that moment, all I could think about was the satisfaction of seeing my work hanging in a gallery, and people like Daniel – well Daniel, chiefly – saying positive things about it, which would make the sacrifices worthwhile. If I never had another exhibition, I at least had a fighting chance of hitting this year's target. My life with Marc Morrison was history. I smiled to myself. I had a lot to thank Marc for. If he'd done the decent thing, I'd still be answering plaintive cries of, 'Miss, how do you make brown?' and going home to wash Marc's socks. It was in this state of self-congratulation and gratitude that I said, 'Listen…' Daniel's eyebrows flexed, a bit like Boz's did when I talked to him, 'I know you said you didn't need to see Colette Dubois' collection of art, but you know, I think she'd be thrilled if you showed an interest. Why don't I ask her if we can go over, some time?'

'I certainly wouldn't refuse the opportunity. Thank you.'

'No problem.'

We went back downstairs to find my phone. Daniel crouched down to fuss the dogs, pulling biscuits from his pockets to make them sit. 'You old softie,' I said.

'Love dogs. We always had at least three at home. I find the odd biscuit is a great ice-breaker.'

'I thought you were more of a cat person?'

'Yes, well, on balance, I prefer cats – much more independent.'

I watched as the dogs wolfed down the biscuits. 'You'll be their new best friend, now,' I said and went into Christophe's study to make the call, because my mobile was out of battery. It was one of the nicest rooms in the house – possibly because he had to spend so much time in there. A set of bookshelves filled one wall; a contemporary desk stood in the centre of the room and behind it was an old fireplace, which had been bricked up. There were a couple of pencil drawings on another wall. While I waited for the call to connect, Daniel wandered over to view them more closely. 'Anyone you know?' I asked.

He shook his head.

Just when I was about to hang up, Colette answered. As ever, she was oozing charm and energy. Eventually, I broached the subject of taking Daniel to see her collection. She was absolutely delighted and suggested we go over the following day. I turned to Daniel, who was by the bookcase and browsing through a large, leather-bound volume. 'Are you free to go tomorrow afternoon?' I asked.

He smiled and nodded. So we arranged to be at the château for three o'clock.

'Thank you for organising that, Vicki,' he said, slipping the book back onto the end of the shelf.

'My pleasure.'

He sniffed the air. 'What can I smell? It reminds me of Sundays at my grandmother's house. She always baked while she was preparing the roast – too mean to put the oven on any other time.'

'Wow! You've got one helluva sense of smell. I

made nutty flapjack, this morning. It's my attempt at keeping Christophe sweet, he's been a bit grumpy lately.'

'Well, if he doesn't like your nutty flapjack, I'll happily take it off your hands,' he said, wiggling his eyebrows in a mischievous way.

'Of course you can have some.'

'Don't suppose you've got any hot chocolate, too? It's the best way to eat flapjack – if you don't mind me dunking?'

'I think I can rustle up some hot chocolate.'

We moved back into the kitchen and while I was watching the pan of milk, he said, 'I've just remembered, I've got a book in the car for you. Won't be a minute.'

I don't mind admitting, there may have been a modicum of self-interest in my arranging for Daniel to see Colette's art collection. Yes, I did feel under some slight obligation, after his interest and efforts on my behalf. However, against my better judgement, I was also beginning to feel a need to see him again and this seemed like an excellent way to guarantee it would happen. I certainly didn't imagine he'd want to come over for a weekly update on my work. He must be a busy man, with his book and his articles to write. I was busy, too. The sands were steadily slipping through my sabbatical-timer. I was already into my second month. A year had seemed so daunting when I set out, yet I was hurtling towards Halloween with only one completed canvas. Could I improve on one painting a month? Was it realistic? What number of paintings would be considered a reasonable output?

Daniel returned just as I was stirring in the chocolate. He handed me a book he'd written called

Art College Graduates. He looked a little apologetic. 'Please forgive the self promotion,' he said, 'but I thought you might find it interesting. I wrote it a few years ago; it was funded by The Arts Programme. I had the joy of trekking round a load of final year shows, selecting up-and-coming artists to feature on the programme. We produced this little catalogue as a memento for them and the colleges. Look,' he opened the book at a page where he'd stuck a small post-it note, 'This is one of the guys who's actually doing quite well. He's exhibited in Liverpool, twice, since he graduated. I like his stuff.'

The work was graphical rather than emotional and left me cold. It was the kind of work I imagined would sell well to corporates. 'Neatly executed,' I said.

He laughed. 'Oh dear. You don't like it, then?'

'I wouldn't want to spend hours meditating on it.'

He studied me with a lopsided smile and for a moment, I really wished I could read his mind. I sensed I might have enjoyed what it was saying. And, just in case he *could* read my mind, I announced, 'Hot chocolate and flapjack, coming up!'

I'd had a feeling Colette and Daniel would hit it off straight away; what with his impeccable English manners and her irresistible French charm. I was right. You could say her flame fully blazed, fanned as it was by the attention of Daniel Keane. Boy, he was knowledgeable. I confess, art history had never been my strong point. I was an artist. I knew about the painters I liked, because I'd studied them, so I was agog with interest as Daniel trotted out fact after anecdote relating to different painters. He was especially keen on three paintings by a Russian artist

I'd never heard of, and whose name now escapes me, who had been a student of the famous artist Briullov – I'd not heard of him, either – but Daniel was clearly thrilled by the find.

'So much of his work disappeared during the Russian Revolution. I've often anticipated discovering such gems in private collections.'

Colette, like me, was hanging on his every word and looked at him wide-eyed. 'I'm afraid I have no idea where they came from. My father travelled such a lot. I do hope this isn't a case for Interpol!' Her warm and husky laugh suggested she wasn't remotely worried. I'd almost go as far as to say there was a frisson of something decidedly saucy rippling between them but that might just have been paranoia, born out of my realisation that I now fancied the moleskin pants off Daniel. Yes. There was something unquestionably attractive about a man who knows his stuff and shares it without sounding like a pompous prat.

But there I was – again – checking out some man's mating potential. Would I never focus on the key purpose of my life?

Eventually, Colette turned to me. 'Vicki, how opportune for you – meeting Daniel. Sometimes, these things are meant to be.' She caught my hand in hers. 'Now, I don't know about you, but I'm ready for a Martini.'

'How lovely,' I replied, thinking there was a massive benefit to not driving. I should do it more often when I went back to Bristol. Bristol – the home of my birth; the setting for my life story, so far, but was it to be the backdrop for my future? I glanced at Daniel, who was still peering closely at the Tzatziki,

Jetski or whatever the artist's name was. Let's face it, so far, Daniel had been an enhancement to my plans. He was like a catalyst – the linseed oil making the pigment of my life flow more smoothly. Okay, so I'd told myself I would concentrate on my painting, and I'd promised not to let a man get in the way but…

We sat in Colette's salon, sipping Martinis from fabulously kitsch Art Deco glasses – with ruby red stems and gold rims, complete with two olives on red cocktail sticks. Daniel drank only one but I had three – just to be sociable. We were roaring with laughter at a story about Daniel's old art master, when Christophe walked in. His grim gaze swept the room like the laser beam of a gun sight, and almost as deadly. Spoilsport.

'Chéri,' Colette crooned, reaching her hand out to draw him closer. 'I wasn't expecting you, today. What a lovely surprise.'

He came forward and dropped a kiss on each of her cheeks.

I found my back straightening in defence of my being there. Although why I felt like I'd been caught rolling a joint in the choir pew was totally unjustified.

He nodded to me and then to Daniel.

'I have something to discuss with Alain. Now I see you have guests, I will leave you.'

'No. Stay,' Colette urged. 'We're having a lovely chat. Daniel can tell you all about the wonderful Russian art we have. You know that trio, in the old dining room? It seems they're quite extraordinarily special.'

Christophe pulled a taut, unfriendly smile. 'You can tell me later, Maman. Alain is just finishing a conversation with…' he glanced at his watch and frowned. 'No matter.' He looked at me. 'Vicki, I will be home around seven-thirty, if that is okay with you?'

'Fine. Absolutely.'

'Good. I will leave you.' Having effectively peed on the strawberries of our good humour, he walked out.

Daniel, clearly sensitive to Christophe's antipathy took the hint, like a true gent would, and instigated our own departure.

In the car, he made no reference to Christophe's grumpy interruption but I did. Three martinis had loosened my tongue. 'He's such a moody beggar. I don't know why he had to act like he'd got a wasp up his arse.'

'No?'

'No,' I said, although I had an inkling. I suspected Christophe's mistrust of journalists was so ingrained he couldn't help himself. Although, the argument didn't quite hold water when I thought about Jeanne. 'Do you?'

Daniel shrugged. 'He's French?'

'Daniel, you surprise me. That's such a blokeish statement to make.'

He laughed. 'You're right.'

'I do know he's not keen on journalists, which might be the problem.'

He took a deep breath, and I got the impression he was considering whether or not to be indiscreet. 'I suppose you're aware his family has quite a history?'

'Well…' did I want to be indiscreet? Even after three martinis, I hated to gossip. Despite Christophe being an arrogant, moody sod, I still remembered how upset he'd appeared when relating the infidelities of his grandfather and how it had hurt his grandmother. 'I know his mother has a bit of a reputation. Is there more in the same vein?' I ventured, wondering what Daniel might spill.

He threw his head back with a loud, 'Cuh!' and tapped the steering wheel with his thumbs. 'Vein, artery and alimentary canal, darling. You haven't heard the half of it.'

Did I want to? Could I bear to continue living under the same roof as the most recent in a long line of reprobates? Well, of course I did. 'Tell me more.'

***

Daniel hadn't planned on divulging the seedy history of Christophe's family to Vicki, just yet. But that conceited, self-satisfied bastard had really got up his nose. How dare he look down on them like he had some God-given superiority? Look at those glorious Russian paintings – undoubtedly acquired through some dodgy, black-market dealings during the war. How many more of the family collection had come to them via disreputable routes? Christophe Dubois had absolutely no moral high ground on which to parade his arrogance.

'Let's just say, infidelity runs through their genes like curls on a French poodle.'

'But why would that make him such a misery guts?'

'Bitterness, I should imagine. His girlfriend – not known to be genetically related – still managed to cuckold him with his own cousin. The biter – bit, one might say. I understand she only recently married the guy.'

He glanced across at Vicki, who was nodding

pensively. He wondered whether, perhaps, he'd overstepped the mark. He didn't want her to think him petty and small-minded.

Finally, she said, 'It can still hurt, though; if he really loved her. Having a legacy of deception in his own family still wouldn't ease the feeling of betrayal. And even now, now he knows the kind of woman she is, it won't necessarily make him feel he had a lucky escape. He'll probably be questioning his judgement. Wondering how he could have been so stupid to get taken in by her.' She paused for a moment. 'I think you're right about his grumpiness. He's feeling like a proper chump and hurting into the bargain. Poor guy.'

Poor guy? He wanted to say, save your pity. Instead, he said, 'Vicki. I never had you down as the armchair psychologist.'

'No? Well, stick around!' She winked at him then; a cheeky, matey gesture.

And she was clearly pleased with herself for setting up their meeting with Colette. He liked that about her. She was repaying his kindness. It showed a commendable sense of integrity, which is just how he'd imagined she'd be. These were all very good signs.

Chapter 16

Christophe returned to his mother's salon an hour after Vicki and Daniel had departed. He slumped onto the sofa opposite where she sat, and let out a heavy sigh.

'Chéri, have you been working too hard? You're so out of sorts, today.'

'Sorry.'

'Being sorry is no explanation.'

'No.' He leaned forward, moved a magazine along the coffee table and sat up straight again. 'So, Maman, how was your visit from our English friends? You seemed to be enjoying yourself.'

'It was fascinating.' She proceeded to tell him about the Russian paintings. 'It looks like we may be playing host to some illicitly acquired artwork.'

'Did you ever doubt it?'

'To be honest, I never gave it a thought. Wouldn't you love to know the story behind them, how they got here?'

'Not particularly. But I have a feeling Mr Keane will soon be able to tell us. You know he's a journalist, don't you?'

'Of course.'

'Then don't be taken in by him.'

'Oh, chéri, have no fear. He may be charming and knowledgeable but he has the manner of someone not to be trusted.'

Christophe's eyebrows dropped. 'Really? Why do you say that?'

'He speaks too evenly. You can't trust a man who measures every word that comes out of his mouth. Give me a man who speaks quickly, passionately – he hasn't time to fabricate lies.'

'Then I suggest you keep him at arm's length. Assuming no damage has already been done.'

'What do you mean?'

'Journalists never let up on a good story. Before you know it, we'll be the subject of some vile documentary exposing another chapter of my grandfather's shameful past.'

'Enough! My father may have led a colourful life,' Christophe suppressed a snort, 'but he was a hard-working man. You wouldn't have what you have now, without his work ethic. Show some respect for that, at least!' Colette's red hair might, these days, owe its brilliance to Wella technology but her temper could still flare in an instant.

Christophe felt a rare stabbing of something inside; the result of a maternal reprimand finding its mark. 'I apologise. You're right. He had some fine and admirable qualities. And I will always be grateful for what I have inherited.' All the same, Christophe hated the legacy of the man's disloyalties, and the prurient interest his peccadilloes generated for the masses. He'd hoped the notoriety attached to the name *de Castillon* was fading but Daniel Keane could stir it all up in an instant.

When he returned home, Vicki was wiping down the kitchen work surface, singing along to a Celine Dion track, in French. She called it developing her language skills. Her voice was soft, sweet and occasionally she dipped into a perfect harmony. Judging by the smell of things, fish was on the menu – again. He'd eaten more fish since Vicki had arrived than he had all year. She cooked it well, though. Beyond grilling, roasting and frying, she used Thai and South American recipes, bringing new and interesting flavours to his palate. 'It's smelling good. What do we have, tonight?' he asked.

Vicki barely glanced at him and ran the cloth under the tap. 'Tilapia with lime, coriander and garlic, and peppers stuffed with savoury rice.'

'Sounds and smells delicious,' he said cheerfully, hoping to lighten the atmosphere.

'Yes, it's one of my favourites,' she replied, wringing the cloth out with alarming force.

Whilst driving home, he'd speculated on whether his behaviour at the château might have bothered her – clearly it had. Why, he wondered for the hundredth time in his life, could he not be more diplomatic? Why had he not inherited his mother's skill for tact when faced with individuals like Keane?

As they sat to eat, Vicki leaned forward in her chair and said quietly, 'Do you think I was out of line, asking Colette to show Daniel her collection?'

She wasn't out of line, exactly, but he hadn't liked finding Daniel so cosily ensconced in his mother's salon. In fact, he wished she'd at least told him of her intention. Whilst Vicki wasn't answerable to him, he couldn't shake the feeling she'd taken advantage of her situation. After all, it was he who had made room for her in his house, and he who had introduced her to his mother. If he'd known she'd infiltrate his family home with bloody journalists, he'd have at least advised her against it. 'No.'

'But I got the distinct feeling you didn't like us being there.'

Christophe filtered his thoughts. 'I have no problem with you visiting my mother.'

'But you do have a problem with Daniel, right? Because he's a journalist.'

He drew a deep breath. 'Journalist or not – I don't trust him.'

Vicki recoiled. 'What?'

'You did ask.'

'How can you not trust him? What's he done to make you feel that way – other than being a journalist? It makes no sense.'

He drew a deep breath. 'Fine. Well, you clearly do trust him, and that's your prerogative. But for my part, and for my family's part, I choose not to. If you want my honest opinion, I think you should be cautious in your dealings with him.'

He watched Vicki frown as she considered her response. 'Look, I can't see that I have anything to fear from Daniel. He's done nothing but help and support me since I met him. However,' She slid her plate away and smoothed her hands over the painted pine table, 'out of respect for you and your family, I promise I won't invite him to the château again. Although, I can't speak for your mother – she seemed quite taken with him.'

'Don't worry about my mother. She feels as I do.'

'What? She doesn't trust Daniel either?'

Christophe shrugged in response. He really wasn't enjoying this debate over Daniel's virtue.

Vicki shook her head. 'Okay. You have your opinions, I can't argue with that. But right now, I'm finding his input useful and stimulating. So,' she pulled a taut smile and shrugged, 'I'm afraid I can't agree with you.'

She stood then, gathered up their plates and carried them to the dishwasher. There was an unnecessary clatter as she loaded the plates into the machine. He hadn't wanted to upset her but, equally, he did want her to know his feelings about Daniel. 'Of course, Daniel moves in your artistic world, I wouldn't expect you to ignore him. But…'

Vicki spun round. 'It's okay. I get the picture – pardon the pun. But I hope you won't be upset if, occasionally, I bring him to my studio to see my work. I don't want to have to carry my canvases out to the car to show him my progress.'

Christophe didn't want Daniel anywhere near the house but he knew, in the circumstances, such a request would be unreasonable. 'Fine.'

Vicki pulled open the oven door and said politely, 'I've made an apple tart for pudding, would you like some?'

He brightened his voice. 'Bien sur. That will be very nice.'

She carved a slice out and planted it onto a plate, before carrying it over to the table. 'Enjoy!' she said, with a forced smile. 'If you'll excuse me, I'm having an early night.'

He closed his eyes as she strode out of the kitchen and wondered why he was getting so uptight about it.

Chapter 17

I was barely out of the kitchen before tears were welling up. And that annoyed me even more. Why was I letting Christophe's obsession over journalists upset me? And what about Colette – she didn't trust Daniel either? Well, you could have fooled me!

I flopped onto my bed and hurled a few sobs of frustration into my pillow before thumping it hard. Then I sat up, blew my nose and threw the balled up tissue at the waste paper bin. Bang on target.

How could Colette have been so enthusiastic, so charming – not to mention charmed – with Daniel and then declare him untrustworthy? I couldn't believe it.

My breathing was starting to calm but my mind was still racing. For the first time, in a long time, I recognised that grim old feeling of homesickness. When had I last felt that? The first week at college, maybe? I was in a foreign country, accepting hospitality from a man who was laying down the law over my selection of friends, and I couldn't even be sure his mother wasn't two-faced, into the bargain. Did she even like me? Did it matter? I was only here for another ten months. It wasn't essential to bond with my landlord and his family. I looked at my watch. It would be just after seven at home, Mum and Dad would have finished their dinner. I snatched up my phone from the bedside table and dialled.

As soon as I heard Mum's voice, I knew I'd made a mistake. Calling in such a fragile state was asking for trouble. I didn't want her to worry about me now – as she surely would – any more than I'd wanted her worrying about me after my aborted wedding. So I was forced to put on a brave face and brazen it out. I majored on the good fortune of meeting Daniel and went into raptures over the possibility of a future exhibition.

'How marvellous,' she said. 'Let me put you on speaker-phone so you can tell your dad. Don, listen to this.'

I heard a click and the atmospherics of Mum and Dad hutching up together on the sofa to share the call.

'Hi, Dad.'

'Has my girl sold a painting?' he asked. I could hear the smile in his voice, and the prickle in the back of my nose threatened more tears.

'Nooo!' I exclaimed loudly, thinking if I made a lot of noise I could disguise the emotion in my voice, and went on to tell him about Daniel. 'It means I don't feel quite so isolated. To be honest, it's given me a bit of a boost.'

'I am pleased,' he said. 'And are you still happy where you're living – are you getting on okay?'

'Yesss! All's fine there, too,' I lied. 'What about you two? What am I missing in sunny Bristol?'

At last they took up the conversational baton so I was able to listen and smile and dab the odd stray tear from my cheek until, finally, Mum signed off with, 'We're so happy you've put all that misery behind you and are following your heart. You know we only want the best for you, love.'

Oh boy, how I kept myself together through the final farewells was a miracle. The minute my thumb hit the OFF button, my face crumpled again and homed in on the pillow.

Through my snuffles, I heard Christophe coming up the stairs. I gulped and held my breath. I may have imagined he was hovering on the landing, it was hard to tell. It only creaked in two places, outside his door and at the bottom of the second flight of stairs. There was a long gap before I heard the creak outside his room and the low thud as he closed his door.

In a shameful act of avoidance, I shut myself in the bathroom, ran the shower at full blast and spent a good five minutes leaning against the wall, watching the water gush and gurgle down the plughole. Finally, I undressed, stepped under the stinging jets and allowed the water to flow over me.

My weekend picked up with a totally-out-of-the-blue visit from Isabelle. We'd planned on getting together nearer to Christmas, so I was thrilled she'd found time, in her manic schedule, to leave the throb of Paris to slum it with the peasants in Limousin. She heralded her arrival with a text message on Friday morning, asking if I was around over the weekend and, if so, she'd be with me by 21:00hrs.

Did I have anywhere else to go? Gratitude poured into my return text.

I had a strong suspicion Christophe had secretly invited her down. Relations had been cool and cordial between us since the Daniel thing. Maybe it was his way of making amends. François had said he was thoughtful. If I wasn't so pissed off at his high and mighty attitude, my feelings might have thawed towards him. Truth was, I was more inclined to think he was hoping to get Isabelle onside; a sort of French solidarity against the English journalist.

Whatever the reason, I was stoked that she'd decided to come.

She arrived, dressed for the weekend – all boho-chic, in layered shirt, vest, draping cardigan, paisley skirt, scarf and fringed boots – and I cried; I was so pleased to see a friendly face. I hugged her until the boulder of her Tiger Eye pendant bruised my sternum. I wondered the weight of it didn't give her backache.

'Vicki!' she exclaimed, 'Don't cry – are you unhappy?'

'No,' I said, fanning away my tears and laughing. 'Come on, have a drink, I'm already two V&Ts ahead of you.'

'Then that's why you're crying.'

She handed over a bottle of brandy she'd brought with her.

'Brandy? It's not Christmas,' I said.

'No, but I feel like I've been battling a cold for the last week, so it might as well be. I always get sick over Christmas.'

'Here, let me put hot water and honey in your brandy.'

She shrugged and leaned against the fridge while I boiled some water. She did look pale.

As Christophe was still not back from Toulouse, we settled down in his salon, curled up together on the sofa.

I hadn't intended to taint the evening with talk about Christophe's feelings over Daniel but since Izzy already knew about Daniel, it wasn't long before she said, 'Now, tell me more about Daniel. Is he handsome?' She wouldn't be Isabelle if she didn't consider a member of the opposite sex an eligible partner for me. I imagined it might even have been her motivation in pairing me up with Christophe. Maybe that's why she'd come down – to safeguard her matchmaking plans.

'He has a very engaging smile,' I answered.

'Has he?' She raised her eyebrows. 'Are we being just a little bit inscrutable, Miss Marchant?'

Oh boy. Did I launch into a defensive proclamation then; stating my case for the friendship with Daniel, championing the benefits of his connections and eulogising his support for my work.

When, finally, I paused to draw breath, Isabelle nodded, raised her arms and yelled, 'Hallelujah! Praise be to Daniel!' which popped the hot air from my evangelical balloon, and we both curled up, snickering with laughter.

'Don't mock me,' I gasped.

Isabelle levelled me with a look only she (and possibly my mother) could give. 'Tell me, honestly, do you see romance on the cards?'

Isn't it strange how our minds can compute the whole range of our thoughts and feelings, just as we pause, inhale and open our mouths to answer? 'I'm not sure,' I said.

'Clearly you like him.'

'Yes.'

'He's tolerably good looking?'

'Yes.'

'Thinking of him keeps you awake at nights?'

'Once or twice.'

'Have you practised your marital signature?'

'Vicki Keane,' I offered, grinning at how adolescent we sounded. 'Noooo.'

'Have you slept with him?'

Another range of thoughts whipped across the screen of my imagination. 'Nooo! It's way too early.'

'Don't tell me Marc's still the last man you slept with?'

'Your point being?'

She shrugged. 'Don't you want to exorcise him? Wipe the slate clean?'

'Okay, I do quite fancy a nice healing dose of rumpy-pumpy but I came here to paint – not to screw up my ambition with a bit of reckless mattress gymnastics.'

'What about Christophe?'

I witnessed an instant replay of my drunken assault on him, and felt a simultaneous rush of blood to my face and sensitive regions.

Isabelle lunged forward. 'Vicki. You're blushing. Is it him? You've slept with Christophe? I knew it!'

'Nooo. That's ridiculous!'

'Mon Dieu! It had to be. Of course. Fantastic!'

'I said, no! Forget it, Isabelle. We don't see eye-to-eye, never mind pelvis to pelvis.' And out came the story of our differences over Daniel. 'Although I guess you already knew that. Isn't it why he asked you to come down here – to talk some sense into me?'

She gave me one of her haughty looks. 'Vicki, what is this paranoia? I haven't spoken to him for weeks.'

'No? I thought… your sudden decision to come down here…'

She rolled her eyes. 'I've arranged a meeting with a client in Limoges on Monday. It seemed like a good opportunity to visit you on company expenses.'

'Oh. That makes me feel really wanted.'

'Tch! Now you're feeling sorry for yourself. I didn't think I'd see you till Christmas. This is a bonus for me and I thought it would be for you. Was I wrong?'

'Of course not. I'm sorry.'

We hugged until Isabelle ploughed on with her inquisition. 'So, what else has been going on between you and Monsieur Dubois? Because I definitely detect something's going on. And don't tell me you didn't react at the mention of his name.'

'That's because he's difficult.'

'But you still think he cares enough about you to invite me down to help iron out your differences.'

I could feel myself sobering up. 'I don't like him passing judgement on Daniel. And he says his mother feels the same way. It's uncomfortable.' I focussed on her eyes. 'So, he definitely hasn't asked you to press home his point?'

'Not at all. Don't worry about it. Remember, "Seize the day!" Ignore what they think.'

'I intend to.'

'Good. That's my Vicki.' She picked up the brandy. 'So, are you going to invite this Daniel over so I can meet him?'

Relentless. The woman was relentless. 'No, this is a girlie weekend.'

She pouted. 'Indulge me. Take me to see him.'

'I can't. He's away.'

'Pity.' After a slurp of brandy, she continued. 'Okay, let's suppose, in a year's time, you're still in touch with Daniel, could he be the man for you? What's he like?'

I ran down a list of his qualities, which made me sound like I was weighing up a candidate for a job, so I finished off with, 'Daniel's nothing like Marc. He seems like the kind of guy who would put me first. And that is a very good sign.'

'I'll drink to that,' she said and winked.

Yes, I thought, it is a very good sign.

My resolve to eschew all intimate dealings with men was wobbling precariously, I realised. All the same, I allowed myself to mull over how and when I might progress things with Daniel Keane. Maybe Easter?

Chapter 18

Daniel wondered how Vicki would take the good news. Raimond had pencilled in space for three of Vicki's pictures at an exhibition he was planning for the following July – dependant upon viewing of her work before February. Daniel was confident she would jump at the chance, and it gave him a boost to know he had engineered it. Another diamond in his crown. The exhibition was to be called '*De Nouvelles Perspectives*' – New Perspectives.

He toyed with the idea of setting up a nice, intimate moment to share the news with her, but maybe that was going over the top. Vicki might be an attractive, savvy young woman but she had a sensitive side and he wasn't about to go crashing in like Zorro with his heroic news and have her backing off in terror. No. He'd save it for Con's birthday party. He'd take her aside and tell her he had some good news. He wouldn't make a huge thing of it – just suggest she might like to take him up on the offer. Yes. That was the way. He picked up the phone to invite her.

'Really?' Vicki squealed, a week later, over the reggae track thumping through the wall of Con's house.

'Yes, really. Although, like I said, he needs to see some of your work, first.'

'But I don't have a website.'

'You have a camera, an email account. Send something to him.'

'Okay. Okay. Okay.' Vicki stepped back, stepped forward and back again, her feet scrunching on the gravel. 'Oh, wow! What an opportunity.'

Daniel smiled, pleased with her reaction.

She looked up and beamed back at him. 'Oh Daniel, you're such a good guy. Thank you. Thank you from the bottom of my heart.'

She threw her arms out and hugged him to her. He could feel the strength of her gratitude in that hug. How satisfying, he thought, and allowed the smile to spread across his face. 'You're very welcome.'

* * *

Yay! Daniel was my hero. Had any man (other than my dad) ever made such an effort on my behalf; ever championed my corner quite like he had? Without a doubt, Daniel was on my side. I felt a shift in my attention from the news he'd just delivered to the feeling of his arms around my waist. How cosy it felt. How secure. Yes. Daniel offered me the kind of security I'd never experienced with Marc. I relaxed the squeeze I was subjecting him to and rested my head against him. He was a few inches taller than me, so my head fitted snugly on his shoulder.

Daniel wouldn't stand me up. Daniel made a habit of calling when he said he would and turning up on time. Daniel kept his word. More than that, he anticipated my needs and went out of his way to meet them.

I could feel myself relaxing even more into the shape of him, and the weight of his head shifted to lean against mine.

The music volume increased as someone came out from the party. Just my luck. There I was, in the first truly romantic moment of my life since... well, Christophe didn't count. That was an aberration on my part, since the early days with Marc. I opened my eyes to see Jeanne, her unblinking stare boring into us before settling on me. Her mouth lifted into a glittering but irregular smile – like the dermal filler in her lips had just melted. Then she moved past us, bathing us in the wake of her pungent fragrance.

I stepped back and whispered, 'I wonder why she's suddenly looking so pleased with life.'

'Who knows?' He smiled. 'Fancy some champagne? I snuck a bottle into the boot of my car to stop all this lot guzzling it.'

Champagne. What a gent. 'Ooh, yes please.'

Daniel offered me two champagne flutes to hold, before working the cork off with a loud pop. 'Here,' he guided the flutes towards the stream of foam. 'I've started writing an article. About you.'

'Me?'

'Your work. You and your work.'

My work. Humble little art teacher, Vicki Marchant.

'Careful,' he said, righting the flute that was about to dispense fizz over the gravel.

'But, who'd want to read it?'

'Lots of people, I hope. He took one of the glasses from me and held it up in a toast. 'To your future.'

I raised my glass and took a sip. It was chilled to a crisp, straight out of the coolbox. 'Thank you, Daniel.'

His eyes twinkled back at me. 'It's a pleasure.'

I took another sip. 'What kind of thing would you

write about me, though? Struggling artist makes stab at the big time?' Disbelief and insecurity were winning out over pride and excitement.

'Come on, I'll show you,' he said, tucking the bottle under one arm and slipping the other around my waist to guide me back into the house, and up to his room.

Okay, even though it was almost *Come up and see my etchings*, I was perfectly happy to comply.

His room was furnished with old furniture. None of it matched. Still holding his arm around me, we moved towards a bureau on which sat a laptop and small printer. After putting his glass down, he one-handedly brought the laptop back to life, clicked through to a document and set the printer running. As it whirred and chuntered, I looked from it to Daniel, and felt a delicious and warming glow spreading through me.

'What?' he said, that lopsided smile tweaking my neural pathways.

'I don't know,' I whispered, feeling un-characteristically shy.

'Here.' He leaned across to lift the paper from the printer. I didn't move out of his way. If anything, I pressed a little closer as my body switched into hussy mode.

The title of the piece was, Vicki Marchant – An Emerging Talent.

* * *

Daniel could feel the pounding of Vicki's heart through her rib-cage, and smiled to himself. As she hesitated, looking first at the page and then back at him, he said, 'You don't have to read it now, if you don't want to.'

She placed her glass down on the bureau and took the paper from him. He couldn't be sure how much of the first page she'd read, because moments later he saw a tear trickle over her cheek. She placed the paper back on the desk and wiped the tear away. She sniffed. It was a much stronger reaction than he'd expected; delight – yes, conceit – possibly but tears? 'Hey, it's just an article,' he said quietly.

She nodded and looked up at him, a watery smile softening her face. He felt her cool fingers touch his cheek. And as her lips came up to meet his, pressing gently against his mouth, he felt a new ripple of satisfaction. It wasn't a deep or wild kiss but a soft, sweet kiss – of what – gratitude, promise? He lifted his head and looked back down at her. Yes, if he wasn't mistaken, of promise! He leaned in and kissed her again.

* * *

Historically speaking, it's not like me to take the slowly-slowly approach with men; probably because it's been my custom to be half-trolleyed before making a move. Looking back, guys don't usually make plays for me unless they're well-trolleyed. Neither Daniel nor I were even close to being trolleyed, barely even roller-skated. But there we were, in the comparative tranquillity of his room, the floor pulsating to Beyoncé belting out *Single Ladies* and I thought, Vicki, you may not be single for much longer.

Although, it really wasn't in my plan to get involved, at least, not this year.

The thought pulled me back, ever so slightly.

Daniel backed off too, one hand moving up to push a strand of hair behind my ear, which I found rather sweet. Maybe I could lighten up a little on my resolution to abstain from male company; a bit like the time I went on my alcohol-free month and allowed myself one bottle of wine at the weekend. I'd certainly felt better for it. Maybe I could ration myself to one man-filled day a week…

'I've never had that kind of reaction to my work, before,' Daniel said, quietly. 'If I had, I might have been inspired to write a few more biographical pieces.'

'Best not write one about Raimond, then.'

He laughed and I noticed that crooked tooth which gave his smile character. 'Why not take this home with you to read. It's not quite finished yet but maybe it will make you believe in yourself a little bit more.'

I took it from him, rolled it up and held it against my chest. 'If it's as good as it sounds, I'll frame it.'

'Wait till it comes out in print. It'll be more impressive with Modern Cultural Review in the header.'

Little old me in Modern Cultural Review. I leaned up to kiss him again, just as the music downstairs stopped abruptly and we heard Connor yelling, 'Fireworks! Everybody outside! Outside, NOW, for fireworks!'

'Oo-er,' I said, noticing Daniel's eyes roll. 'He should be in the army.'

'Oh, no, too much discipline for Connor. Come on.' He picked up both our champagne flutes. 'These bloody fireworks have cost me an arm and a leg. I want to get my money's worth.'

They were impressive. Not quite Olympic but they sure beat the family pack of Standard fireworks Dad used to buy when I was a kid. I had hoped to nestle into Daniel while we watched, but the minute Connor saw him, he was marshalled over to help with the display. So I hugged my jacket around me, sipped my champagne, and smiled every time I caught Jeanne's eye.

I had no doubt she was well stoked to think her machinations to partner me off with Daniel appeared to be bearing fruit. I also had no doubt it was engineered to keep my hands off Christophe. I tried to picture them together. It wasn't a pretty sight. She was too prickly for him, too detached. He needed someone funnier and friendlier but someone he could respect. He'd already told me he didn't like journalists so Jeanne seemed totally the wrong match.

Still, what did I know?

After the last rocket faded in the sky, she sauntered over and began speaking to me in French, the gist of it being, 'How are your paintings coming along?'

'I'm making some progress.'

'You seem like the kind of person who has her life all planned out.'

'Do I?'

'I admire you for that; for taking charge of your destiny.'

'You do?' Excuse my disbelief but it didn't feel like she admired me at all.

A beatific smile emerged on her face. It was scary in its mesmeric quality. 'And Daniel could be a very good ally.'

'Yes. I realise that. Thank you for introducing us.' I

added, because I felt she was fishing for it.

'My pleasure.' As Daniel approached, she inclined her head towards me and whispered, in English, 'I recommend you maintain that confident front – I think you'll need it.'

I didn't like her conspiratorial nose wrinkling, one bit.

She smiled at Daniel, slid a hand down his arm and said something along the lines of, 'I'm glad you two are getting along so well.'

'Vicki could be a star of the future,' he said.

'Marvellous. Well, if you'll excuse me, I'm going to see Christophe. No reason why he should miss out on all the fun.' She waved a packet of sparklers and winked at me.

I watched as she hurried to her car, and as she checked her reflection in the rear-view mirror. What did she mean about maintaining a confident front? I could hear the embers of any self confidence I possessed hissing into dust. I looked to Daniel for re-ignition. 'Great fireworks,' I said, slapping on my broadest smile. 'But the party's not over, is it?'

'Not unless you want it to be,' he said.

I felt I had three choices: would it be upstairs with Daniel for an introductory romp to the rhythm of nineties' disco hits, or take him back to Chez Christophe for a cheeky coupling that might just put Monsieur Dubois' nose even further out of joint, or should I go for a thrash around the dance floor with the fizz of champagne in my veins?

Despite my throbbing hormones, I plumped for the last option. There was plenty of time for a spot of mattress dancing, later.

By midnight I was in charge of the music and by

two o'clock, I was the last one standing, doing the Macarena all on my own. Daniel had disappeared – up to bed, I guessed, and Connor lay on the sofa, his shirt open to his corpulent belly, snoring intermittently. Two others had crashed on the floor. I staggered to a standstill, looked around me and felt a wave of self-pity wash over me. It was a wave laced with alcohol. Had I learned nothing in this life of mine?

I turned off the music and, rather than listen to the post-party silence and inhale the stench of alcohol and smoke, I grabbed my coat and went outside. In the distance was the drone of traffic from the A20 motorway, heading north to Paris and south to Toulouse. Toulouse – where Christophe spent so much of his time.

I imagined he was an excellent vet. I'd seen how gentle he was with his dogs and how professional he had been at the farm. Veterinary work was clearly a vocation for him and he must be quite accomplished to lecture at the college.

I'd left him a beef casserole for dinner, feeling unnecessarily guilty for abandoning him on a Saturday night. How had that happened, and why had I worried when he had Jeanne swooping in on him for dessert?

No, it was still not a pretty picture.

Leaning against the wall, the soles of my feet felt like they'd been bashed with a baseball bat and my eyelids were heavy. I wondered if it would be acceptable for me to slip upstairs and catch a nap with Daniel. I weighed up the pros and cons: comfortable bed and handsome mentor versus my reputation.

Daniel was tucked up and lying in the middle of

his bed. In the interests of modesty, I only took off my shoes and jeans. It wasn't a full-sized double so when I slipped in beside him, there was no avoiding close contact. His body was firm and comfortingly warm. As I lay down, he turned away in his sleep and pulled the duvet with him. After gently coaxing a few inches of it back for myself, I lay listening to the shrill whine in my ears until I fell asleep.

Chapter 19

Christophe peered out of his study window when he heard the car pull up. Daniel Keane was quickly round to hold open the passenger door before Vicki had chance to swing her legs out. He offered her a hand, guiding her towards him before leaning in for a kiss. Christophe's lip curled, even though he knew it was exactly the kind of thing he'd do himself.

It was gone mid-day. No guessing what they'd been up to, last night. Who could blame the guy? Vicki was very tempting. Although that assumed Vicki wanted to get involved with Daniel, and from what he knew about her, she was much more determined to concentrate on her painting.

He turned back but couldn't focus on his laptop screen. The car engine revved and Daniel drove away. Good. At least she had the decency not to bring him indoors.

He listened to her murmured greetings to the dogs; that silly baby-talk she adopted for them – 'Herculey-wooley' and 'little Bozzy-wozzy'. Mon Dieu!

Would she prepare lunch, today? He heard the stairs creak as she headed up to her room. How long before she moved in with Keane? He shook his head. Maybe that would be for the best.

He clicked through from one document to another, trying to get his mind back into his report.

Just as his fingers settled again on the keyboard, he heard a creak on the landing above as Vicki headed back downstairs. Moments later, there was a tap on his door.

'Come!' he barked.

Her head appeared, blonde waves ragged around her pretty but pale face. He'd seen her like that once before and pushed the memory back. She smiled and said, 'Hi. How are you?'

'Very well, and you?'

'I'm good, thanks.'

'Good.'

She may have been looking pale but she was sickeningly cheerful. 'Would you like some pumpkin soup?'

He glanced at his watch, knowing full-well it was almost quarter to one. 'No rush.'

'It's okay. I'm ready for it, so I'll heat it up and you can come and get it when you want it.' Her smile flickered. 'The soup. Obviously.'

'Thank you.' He focussed again on his computer screen. He would miss her cooking when she went, that was all. But as the door closed, he stared at the back of it for several moments before shaking himself and scowling at his laptop.

* * *

I've never actually tried to cut an atmosphere with a knife. All I'd ever had was my bravado, which I'd just deployed in Christophe's study; bravado and a seriously misplaced sense of humour. Of course, I knew he wasn't going to be remotely pleased to see me roll up with Daniel. I'd been praying I might come home to an empty house but God must have been busy on something more important.

I'd made the soup the day before so all I had to do was reheat it. A simple enough task – except I was working with a hangover, a guilt complex and confusion... confusion over Daniel. I'd woken an hour earlier to an empty bed. Nothing much wrong with that, but when I went downstairs and found him chatting over coffee with Connor, all he'd done was pour me a cup and continue his conversation. And after coffee, he offered to drive me home; no 'shall we go back to bed' or even 'that was a wonderful evening, let's do it again'. Just coffee.

On the way home, he'd warmed up a bit; wanting to know if I still had the copy of his article and would I let him know what I thought about it. It was only when I stuck my neck out and offered to cook him dinner, while Christophe was away in Toulouse, that he livened up. I tried to put it down to his gauche, public school background but hell, he was over thirty, he'd surely cracked the dating game by now.

As I stirred the soup, my memory randomly fired off Jeanne's words from last night, 'I recommend you maintain that confident front.' A front, indeed. Is that how I came across – a confident pain in the arse? And even if it was, she didn't have to be so patronising about it.

I pulled out the bread board and attacked the loaf with a knife. Saw. Saw. Saw. Bang! into the bread basket. Saw. Saw. Saw. Bang! Saw. Saw...

'Ayayay!' Christophe said in alarm as he walked into the kitchen.

'Hungry?' I asked, slowing down on the sawing front.

He grunted in reply then asked, 'What did the

bread do to upset you?'

'It's not the bread. Somebody said something that bugged me.'

'Not me, I hope?'

'No. And before you ask, not Daniel, either.' I looked for a reaction but he'd already turned away and was rifling through the dishwasher for clean cutlery. He started laying the table. Finally, I filled the silence. 'Christophe, do I seem confident to you – like overly confident, like I've got it all figured out?'

He carried on, lining the spoons and knives up on the table. Eventually, he looked at me. 'I think you have confidence but that's not necessarily the same as being confident.'

'What d'you mean?'

'I've no doubt you could get up in front of a class and command their attention and demonstrate a skill. That shows confidence. You can walk into a room full of strangers and charm them with your personality. But do I think you are confident in who you are? Non.'

And to think I was looking for reassurance that I wasn't a pain in the arse.

I filled the bowls with soup and Christophe carried them to the table.

As I sat down, he said, 'Vicki, you know, very few people are truly confident in who they are.'

'Exactly.'

He stirred his soup for a moment before looking up at me. 'The question is, do you have the confidence and the application to fulfil your dreams?' The way he looked at me, reminded me of my headmistress, Mrs Pope, when she'd asked me if I was going to knuckle down to my GCSEs. He could have been channelling her when he said: 'Only you can control that, Vicki.'

That proved it – I was no further advanced than I had been at fifteen. Just older. Older and more battle-scarred. 'I know. And I will.'

'So, who has upset you?' he asked.

'Just someone at the party last night.' I wasn't going to mention Jeanne's name.

He shrugged. 'Sometimes it's good when people challenge our perceptions, non? It makes us more resolved to…what do you say? Plough our own field.'

'Furrow. Plough your own furrow.'

'*Voilà.*'

For a few moments, the only sound was that of slurping soup but my mind was feverishly active.

'Trouble is, it's made me wonder whether I'm deluding myself, like those girls you see on talent shows – the bloaters who sing like a cow in labour but still think they're the next Lady Gaga.'

He smiled.

'I'm serious.'

'I know.' He stretched out his hand and put it over my wrist. 'But Vicki, you'll never be happy until you've tried, will you? This could be an important year for you. You're here to paint and to get your life back on track. Cooking for me is incidental.'

I wasn't about to brood on his dismissal of my culinary efforts as 'incidental' although it registered momentarily in my brain. Uppermost was the fact his hand remained on my arm and the frisson I was feeling from his touch was more electric than anything I'd felt from Daniel. But lust was transitory, wasn't it? And anything developing between me and Christophe would just complicate things.

He was right. This could be an important year for me. It was my year. 'Well said. I'm just wobbling in my convictions. Thank you for putting me back on track.' With a nod of my head, I withdrew my arm and reached across to grab some bread.

'You've had major changes in your life. You're bound to have the occasional moment of uncertainty.'

I was having more than one.

I smiled and wiped the bread around the bottom of my soup bowl. 'Well one thing's certain – there's a canvas upstairs waiting to be completed, and I have all afternoon to work on it.'

'There you go. *Vouloir, c'est pouvoir.*' Where there's a will, there's a way.

'Indeed,' I said as a massive yawn broke over me.

'I expect you're tired.'

I was. Although judging by the look on his face, not in quite the way he imagined.

'Yes, I was dancing till the early hours,' Not that an explanation was necessary. It was my life, after all.

Chapter 20

A few nights later, when Christophe was away at the veterinary school, Daniel came over. My feeling of disloyalty over entertaining him in Christophe's house almost drove me to cancel. But I reasoned that it wasn't as if I was inviting the Gestapo into the headquarters of the French Resistance. It was just a meal. I set the table in the dining room with a vase full of green leaves and wild honeysuckle on a linen tablecloth. I backed away from going all flash with the meal, though – keeping it simple with smoked salmon blinis to start, followed by paella.

Daniel arrived bang on time, bless him, presenting me with a bottle of Pinot Grigio, which I thought a brave move considering we were in one of the proudest wine-making countries in the world. He'd chilled it in advance so we cracked it open immediately and sipped it over the blinis.

'I liked your article,' I said. 'If that's not too immodest of me to admit. Thank you for writing it.'

'Hey – it's what I do.'

'Well, thank you for wanting to write it. It means a lot to me.'

He smiled his lopsided smile, catching my hormones off guard. 'I think you're worth it, don't you?'

'Hah!' I scoffed, but felt a thrill all the same. To hide my embarrassment, I pushed a whole blini in my mouth and nearly gagged so I swallowed it and felt like a snake on a binge.

Daniel's hand reached across and covered mine. 'From the little I've seen, you should believe in yourself more. You might find it opens up the floodgates of your creativity.'

I squirmed at his over-the-top enthusiasm. I'm not used to such praise. As if sensing it, he squeezed my hand. 'Truly. Confidence works wonders.'

I nodded. Confidence. That bloody word again; the one that had me debating the value of my dreams with Christophe. The difference tonight was that Daniel knew what he was talking about.

I used my other hand to raise my wine glass and took a sip of wine or two. My affirmations kaleidoscoped through my brain. 'I do believe in myself, just like I believed in my students.'

'Exactly.' He removed his hand and reached for his own glass. After a sip, he grinned at me, 'I must say, this wine's brilliant with the salmon, isn't it?'

'It is.' I savoured another mouthful.

Life was good – as was the paella. The rice wasn't too squishy and had slightly caught on the pan, giving that delicious, treacly taste to the bottom crust.

As we cleared away the dishes, Daniel said, 'I have an important question to ask.'

I stood still, wondering what on earth was coming next.

He tipped his head to one side and said, 'Would you agree that the best thing about being in France, is being able to eat crêpes, any day, in almost any town?'

'You're talking a lot of crêpe there, Daniel.'

He laughed. 'I just love them. Crêpes with syrup, crêpes with cream, bananas, chocolate, booze… any way they come. I'm not crazy for all that French haute cuisine but crêpes...' he kissed his fingers. '*Magnifique.*'

I'd made apple tarts for dessert but they'd keep. 'Are you dropping hints, Mr Keane?'

'Good lord, no. It's just that once the main course is over, my thoughts naturally turn to pud. Especially after all those years at school; sponge and custard, fruit and jelly, cake and cream. Never got a bloody crêpe, though. Even on Shrove Tuesday, if we wanted pancakes we had to twist Matron's arm to make them in the boarding house. Matron taught us all a big lesson – that favours could be reciprocated.'

'Favours – from Matron? Sounds dubious.'

'No. Favours from us. We'd do little jobs for her.'

'What, like running errands?'

'You could say that. We'd bring duty-free fags back from foreign holidays for her. She had a regular supply of marijuana too, thanks to Greenaway. His brother grew it in a barn in Portugal.'

'What, might I ask, did she do for you?' I asked, wide eyed with anticipation.

'Turned a blind eye to booze in the wardrobe, fags under the pillows, that kind of thing. She always had a stock of Fernet Branca for the morning after. And, of course, spoiled us with pancakes, occasionally.'

'How did she get away with it?'

'Shagging the Bursar. Oh, and Hancock, Head of Seniors for a while, till his wife found out and blew the whistle. Matron was evicted and replaced by Attila the Nun; she had the moral code of a saint and the temper of Miss Trunchbull.'

I was seeing a new and much funnier side to Daniel.

'So, no more pancakes.'

'No, but I only had two terms left, so I didn't suffer for long.'

'Would you like pancakes, now?' I smiled.

'Well…' he moved closer to me and ran a hand down my arm. 'I did write a very flattering piece on you.'

I grinned. 'Just don't call me Matron!'

He grinned and leaned closer still. 'Wouldn't dream of it. You're far too sexy for that.' Then he closed the gap and kissed me, his hand travelling up my spine and pulling me in. He was a good kisser; firm and soft at the same time. As he pulled away, he slid a strand of hair behind my ear, stroked my face and said quietly, 'My pretty girl, Vicki.'

'You're only saying that for extra pancakes.'

He smiled. 'My pretty and very talented Vicki. Who will, one day, be a celebrated artist.'

'Are you after Crêpes Suzette, now?'

He held both my arms then and stood back, his eyes suddenly still and focussed on mine. 'I mean it, Vicki. You truly have talent. Trust me on this. I know.'

I could feel the prickle of tears behind my eyes and dropped my head. He pulled me to him then and hugged me. 'Vicki, you're special.'

After reining in my emotions, I said, 'Daniel, you've definitely earned your pancakes but there's something I want to give you, even more.'

I looked up into his face, slid my hands away from his body and stepped back to peel off my sweater. His eyes drifted over me as he watched my t-shirt follow the sweater and the bra drop to the floor. I'd only had one glass of wine. I was fully in the moment. For the first time in a long time, where a man was concerned, I was in control of my actions.

'I'll take pancakes for breakfast,' he said and, like Rhett Butler, lifted me into his arms and carried me upstairs.

I never got around to making pancakes. Daniel thought it best not to stay the night. As we lay in our post-coital knot, he said, 'In a little town like this, nobody misses a thing. I wouldn't want you getting a reputation.'

'Spoilsport.'

'We want people talking about you for the right reasons – your work.'

I traced the line of his arm with my finger. 'Think of all the great artists with a reputation for loose morals – Gauguin, Lautrec and don't get me started on Sickert. Actually, scrub Sickert, he was a creep. But I think I'd quite like history to remember the artist, Vicki Marchant, as a bit of goer.'

'Odd,' he said, and drew my hand to his lips for a kiss, 'how there are very few truly great female artists.'

'Well, don't bet on me being one of them. I might be good but I'm not that good.'

He smiled, kissed my hand again and said, 'Never undersell yourself, Vicki.' He turned to me and kissed me full on the mouth. I could feel my body brewing up again but he pulled back and said, 'I really should be off, but no need for you to move, lovely girl. I'll let myself out.'

So I lay there, watching him dress; fascinated by the brisk, matter-of-fact way he pulled on each item of clothing. Nothing like Marc, who'd made getting dressed a performance – rolling his hips into his jeans and whipping the zipper up accompanied by a double click of his tongue; sliding into a sweatshirt, shrugging it to a neat fit on his shoulders and smoothing down the front, before checking the result in the mirror. I hadn't watched a man dress for over a year. Too long.

In a lazy stupor, I must have nodded off really quickly because I didn't even hear Daniel's car start.

The following morning, I was up before it got light, straight into the shower and singing my head off. I just loved the acoustics in that bathroom. Downstairs, I found Hercules and Boz whipping their tails back and forth. I lobbed them each a chunk of stale bread from the basket. Coffee-maker on, I cleaned up the detritus from last night's meal and put the vase from the dining room onto the kitchen table. I drank my coffee and crunched through some muesli and blueberries, as daylight slowly spread through the windows.

Once it was light enough to head off up the hill, I wrapped myself in a jacket, scarf and gloves, calling the lovely dogs after me. The only way to approach that hill on a frosty morning was with enthusiasm. Up we went, listening to the swish-swish-swish of my sleeves against my jacket. From the top we looked back at the little town, where lights were still twinkling in windows. Life was good. Life had never been better. 'This is great,' I said aloud.

Finally, I'd hit the groove. Ahead of me was a whole day of painting, and I knew exactly what I wanted to achieve. 'Geronimo!' I hollered, before running haphazardly down the hill, Hercules and Boz bounding along in front.

I was working on the detail of the market stallholder when I heard Christophe climbing the stairs to my floor. I turned to wait for his appearance in the doorway. Was it the pale fabric of his white shirt reflected in his face, or did he look more drawn than he had the last time I saw him? He hovered in the doorway.

I beamed at him, my spirits buoyed up by the progress I had made. 'Hi.'

He smiled. 'Wow! It's going well, huh?' He stepped forward, scrutinizing the canvas. I waited for his reaction, watching as his eyes travelled over and around the image. He raised his eyebrows. 'It's looking good. I think you are pleased with it.'

'Still a lot to do, though.' Despite his saying all the right things, I felt his mind was elsewhere. 'How were things in Toulouse?'

'Fine.'

'You sound tired.'

'Do I?' he shrugged. 'I have been riding.'

There was a frown on his face. 'Would that be Léopard or Belle?'

He glanced at me, one corner of his mouth lifting, before he turned to sit on the edge of table. 'Which do you think?'

'Judging by your mood, I'd say Léopard.' He nodded slowly, his eyes locked on mine. This close, I could practically feel his emotional turmoil. 'O…kay.' I stepped forward and offered him my brush and palette. 'Wanna paint a picture? It's very therapeutic.'

Christophe glanced down at the palette and let out a muffled snort of humour. He looked back at me. I realised my clothes were a mess and my hair was scrunched up in a shambolic sprout on top of my head, but hey – I was busy working there. 'You think I need therapy?' he asked.

I grinned back at him. 'Not if your ride on Léopard did the trick.'

He still looked troubled. 'It helped.'

'I'm glad. Oh shit!' I said as one of the brushes slid off the palette and hit the floor – taking a detour via his leg. A smear of cream paint added a unique touch to his trousers. 'Jeez! Sorry!' I shoved the palette on the table so I could sort out the mess.

He stepped away. 'Hey. Don't worry,' he said, moving towards the door.

'It's only acrylic, I can wash it out straight away.'

'I said, don't worry. You carry on with your painting.'

'But you must let me clean them, it was my fault, after all.'

'Non!' he barked, sounding thoroughly cheesed off, not that I blamed him. Then he raised his hand apologetically. 'Really, I will sort it out. I shouldn't have disturbed you.' He turned away but stopped in the doorway. 'I also came up to see if you wanted anything.'

'Oh. Thank you but no, I'm okay.'

I listened to him descend the stairs and called out, 'Get those trousers in water, straight away!' But he didn't reply.

I wondered if Christophe knew about Daniel's visit? Had someone said something? Was I transmitting guilty conscience? Actually, scratch that. Was I broadcasting 'woman with re-awakened libido gagging for more'? Oh lord, that would be it. My aura had a phosphorescent glow from rampant hormonal activity. My pores were oozing post-sex pheromones with all the potency of Samsara.

I leapt over to the mirror to investigate. Crap! I looked a bloody mess. Oh well. That would negate any sexual tension that might have been brewing. And I'm sure it had been. I wasn't imagining it. Christophe had a kind of vibe about him, which set my hormones on red alert – red for danger – and I didn't need danger in my life, thank you very much. I needed my life to remain on an even keel. Daniel was a steadying influence in my world and that, I decided, was invaluable.

Although…

I had to admit, my coupling with Daniel, whilst it had been lovely – a welcome release of sexual tension and shared intimacy with a man I liked – it hadn't been momentous.

I pulled a face at my reflection.

'I am an artist,' I began reciting my affirmations.

Daniel encouraged and supported me in my work. He understood me.

'There is an audience for my work and the Universe is bringing us together.' The affirmations were working.

I would clean up, cook dinner and then phone Izzy. I was dying to tell her about the latest developments. I might need to brace myself for her whoop of approval.

Bracing was unnecessary. A husky 'At last' was her only comment.

'Yes,' I said, although I doubt she heard it over her dry cough. 'You've had that cold for two weeks, Izzy. You should see a doctor.'

'I saw one today.'

'Why haven't you been before?'

'Too busy.'

'That's why you're still sick.'

'I know. This job is killing me.'

'Are you still thinking of changing?'

There was a long pause. 'If I can find the energy, I might.'

I could hear her slurping a drink. 'I hope that's a hot toddy you're drinking. You sound like you need one.'

'Herbal tea. Echinacea and liquorice.'

'Dear Doris! You must be ill. Why don't I come up for a couple of days? I could cook you some healthy soups and make sure you take it easy.'

'No, don't. I have a severe case of influenza. If you catch this too, I'll feel even worse. No. I'm going to spend the weekend in bed. Don't worry.'

'Not working, I hope.'

I heard another slurp. 'No. I'll be resting.'

'Promise me you will not work?'

Izzy didn't do resting. 'Cross my heart. I'm too sick to work. Miriam's delighted – not.'

'Stuff Miriam. You be kind to yourself. I won't call you in case I wake you but please, promise you'll call me – every day?'

'I promise.'

As soon as I came off the phone, I googled influenza with bronchial complications. I wanted to know just what the poor girl was going through and whether I should be more concerned than I already was.

Yep. It was *very* concerning.

Chapter 21

Back in the studio, I was on a roll with my painting. Daniel kept a polite distance from the house when Christophe was about, which wasn't often, and my love muscles were getting a welcome workout.

Of course, I'd always known how important encouragement was for bringing out the best in my own students. Yet I'd forgotten it on a personal level. Looking back, Marc's support had been rare and shallow. He never volunteered it. 'What do you think of this?' I'd say, after producing a series of sketches as teaching aids. 'Oh, great, babe,' he'd say, 'you're wasted on those kids.' Or after hours spent icing a Christmas cake with meticulous precision, he'd managed a 'Cool' as he'd peered into the tin.

Daniel, on the other hand, was positively happy to praise my efforts; delighted to see progress in my work and never needed prompting. Suddenly, my life felt like an all-in luxury cruise instead of a self-catering school trip. Even cooking for Christophe only happened two or three times a week. He was either out (sometimes all night) or down at Toulouse. I had to wonder if he still had a thing going with Sylvie – although where on earth they would conduct it, I had no idea, since the château was just bulging with relatives.

I didn't like to imagine Christophe was carrying on with Sylvie – it tainted him. It was bad enough Jeanne appeared to hold his affections, a woman I would never have associated with him. No. I wanted to believe I was sharing a house with a decent guy. Hell – I wanted to believe my brief aberration with him at Francois and Marie's could have held some promise beyond a tipsy tumble on his heavy blue bedspread. Because that would have tainted me.

Not that any of it mattered. The crucial point was – my painting was coming on in leaps and bounds. I had support from Daniel and life was, in many ways, sweeter than it had been in ages. He'd even set up a meeting for me with some friends near Bergerac, who held painting, photography and writing courses.

'Their regular art tutor's emigrating to South Africa, and they want to run two, one-week residential courses in the spring,' he told me over the phone. 'You never know, it might lead to more.'

'Would I be paid?'

'Of course.'

Any fees would be very handy. 'Fantastic. Should I send them an email?'

'Yes. His name's Bruno. I'll text his email to you. He's coming up this way in a week or so. You could meet him.'

Life was getting sweeter by the day.

The next time Christophe was away at the veterinary school, I cooked Daniel a special dinner. We had scallops on puy lentils, grilled sole with samphire and sauté potatoes, followed by Crêpes Suzette. I knew my way to a man's heart.

When it came to the washing up, he insisted on helping. 'I can't sit around watching you toil, darling. My mother would have a fit. She's always had a bit of a thing against cavemen.'

'Don't tell me you're a mummy's boy?'

'In so far as my father spent most of his time at work, I suppose I must be. Though, to be honest, my older brother Jamie's umbilical cord is much tighter.'

'What's he like?'

'Dull.'

'That's a terrible thing to say about your brother.'

'Alright, he's not dull. He's tall, dark and handsome, achingly funny and a lawyer. I had to leave England to maintain an uninterrupted love life. Too much competition at home.'

'I don't believe it. You're lovely.'

'And you're sweet.' He kissed me. 'Plus, you haven't been Jamied, yet.'

'Ha-ha! Now, if you go and sit in the salon, I'll bring the coffee through.'

He gave me a parting peck on the nose. 'Don't be long.'

I buzzed around the kitchen, arranging dinky little coffee cups and saucers on a tray, along with a plate of petit-fours I'd knocked up with some marzipan and Armagnac syrup. I congratulated myself on it all looking pretty stylish, and headed off to the salon.

Daniel wasn't there. But there was a light under Christophe's study door so I put the tray down and went in. He was standing by the book shelves, leafing through a small, leather-bound volume and looked up, grinning, when I entered. 'Nice collection,' he said.

'Really? There are more books in the salon, if you want something to read,' I said holding the door open, eager for him to move and wondering why on earth he wanted something to read tonight.

He slipped the book back onto the shelf and continued browsing.

I propped the door open with my body. 'Look, I'm a bit uncomfortable with you being in here. It's very much Christophe's territory.'

'Don't worry, it's not like he's here to see me.'

'I know but…' I was there to see him, and it went against my sense of decency. 'Daniel, please. For me.'

'Oh, darling,' he said, coming over to me and stroking my arm. 'The thing is, I have this wonderful opportunity to do a documentary on great art collectors. Colette's father acquired those famous Russian paintings and, judging by some of the books here, he was very keen on that particular school of Russian art.'

'Then, why don't you ask Colette? Better still, ask Christophe. He knows you're helping me. I'm sure he wouldn't mind.'

'You know as well as I do, he'd probably mind like hell.'

'Then, all the more reason why you shouldn't be in here, at all.' I could feel the soft, mellow mood of the evening stiffen like over-whipped cream.

'Look,' he took hold of my hand, 'I just wanted to get the details straight before I completed my proposal for the documentary. That way, when I show it to the Dubois family, it will be factually correct and they'll have confidence in me. Ergo, they'll give their approval.'

'Then why didn't you ask me to find out?'

'I didn't want to trouble you. In any case, if Dubois didn't approve, it could have caused a problem between you and him. You could lose your studio, and that wouldn't be fair. You're doing so well up there.'

I wriggled my hand free of his. 'I'm sorry Daniel. But I'd much rather you broached the subject directly with Christophe or Colette. It makes me uncomfortable. This is his private office.'

He shrugged. 'Sorry, sweetheart. I guess it comes as second nature to a journalist. We do like to take the most expedient route to the evidence.' He smiled his lopsided smile but the magic didn't quite sparkle as much as before.

In an attempt to lift the mood, I wagged my finger at him and said, 'Well, young man, I want it on record that I'm registering my disapproval of your methods.'

'Duly noted,' he said as he mimed scribbling on a notepad. 'Miss Marchant.'

'Come on, let's have coffee,' I said, taking him by the hand out of the study and letting the door close behind us.

The following morning, I called Isabelle. She had, as promised, rung me every day – not for very long since she was so exhausted from her regimen of painkillers, no alcohol and lots of rest. Each time we spoke, I offered to go and look after her but she swatted me away with the contagion argument. However, this time she said, 'You can stop worrying, my mother arrived today.'

'What if she catches it? She's nearly sixty and much more vulnerable than I am.'

'She's been vaccinated. In any case, she was a nurse, she's immune to most things.'

'Okay. And, to be honest, you already sound brighter – even with your mum in residence.' Muriel Masson was one of those bright, efficient mothers who could smother you with love one minute and bawl you out the next for leaving a magazine on the floor. I had no doubt Izzy's resourcefulness came from her mother's side.

'So, my little pumpkin,' Izzy said, imitating my father's Bristolian accent and using his pet name for me. 'How are things with you?'

'Okay.'

'Not good, then. What's happening?'

'It's complicated.'

'It's a man, then. Daniel or Christophe?'

'Both, kind of.'

'Mon Dieu! You're sleeping with both of them now?'

'Only Daniel.'

'So, what's wrong?'

I sighed. It was never easy for me to open up to people, especially when it meant fessing up to a possible error in judgement.

Isabelle cut in. 'Are you okay?'

The story tumbled out. Finally, I said, 'Daniel has been wonderful to me, but I can't get over how uneasy I feel about him sneaking around in Christophe's study.'

'Surely, if he was really sneaking about, he'd do it when you weren't there. Not right under your nose.'

She had a point. The study door was on a self-closer; it wasn't as if he'd shut himself in there. 'If only Christophe liked Daniel, I wouldn't feel so bad.'

'It's just macho rivalry.'

'But Christophe's only my landlord,' I said, imagining my nose growing a couple of inches as I pictured our earlier liaison.

'Maybe he'd like to be more.'

'Has he said so?'

'No. But you know what men are like.'

'Well, he'll just have to get over it,' I said, although I wasn't entirely convinced she was right. 'What about you, any more thoughts on your future?'

'I don't think it's wise to plan anything while I feel like this. Next week, I have a big event…'

I cut across her. 'You can't go to that. You're sick. You know you can't.'

'I've been planning it for months, I have to at least show my face.'

'You can't. You're contagious. It would be irresponsible.'

Izzy sighed. 'Not according to the doctor. He says the flu is passed. I'm just weak.'

'Then you should stay home. In bed. What's so important, anyway?'

'I'm running an exhibition stand for my main client.'

'Brief someone else.'

'They could screw it up or worse, steal my client.'

'No. How could they?'

'You'd better believe it.'

'Then brief me. I'll do it.' What was I saying?! I'd never done PR in my life but it couldn't be worse than the average parents' evening, could it?

Izzy chuckled and then immediately coughed. 'You're funny.'

'Why not?'

'No, chérie. Thank you but I'll cope. Honestly. I'm much better. You said so yourself.'

Which was typical of Isabelle Masson. Bloody-minded, stubborn and always in charge. If I didn't love her so much, I could cheerfully give her a good lecture on being kind to herself, but it would be a complete waste of energy.

Chapter 22

As Christophe returned on Friday evening, he saw light shining into the night sky from Vicki's studio, the rest of the house was in darkness. When he entered the hall, Hercules and Boz leapt around him like excited puppies. Although exhausted from three days of field visits with students, he dropped to his haunches and fussed them vigorously, breathing in their warm, doggy smell and, above that, picking up notes of something savoury cooking in the kitchen – predominantly sage and garlic. But the only light in there came from the oven. Vicki must be upstairs, painting.

He gave the dogs a final rub, hung his coat on the stand and carried his briefcase into the study. He felt a drop in temperature, and touched the radiator. It was warm enough but then he noticed the window was open a crack, its latch undone. Frowning, he pulled it closed and rammed the latch down, tight. He surveyed the room. Everything looked as it should. He opened each drawer of his desk in turn. Nothing appeared to have been moved. After another scan of the room, he wandered over to the kitchen to find a beer. He pulled the cap from the bottle and peered into the oven, where a casserole simmered in its clear glass dish, and he grinned to himself. Good. It looked like there was meat on the menu tonight.

With a scuffle of paws the dogs trotted back into

the hall to greet Vicki as she came downstairs. Christophe straightened up and took a swig from the bottle as she walked in. 'Good evening,' he said.

'Welcome home.' She beamed at him. Her hair, with a shock of blue paint above the temple, was scrunched on top of her head in a clip, and she'd swapped her painting clothes for clean jeans and a chunky red sweater. 'Did you have a good trip?' she asked.

He nodded. 'Busy.'

'Aha – better to wear out than go rusty, as my grandmother always says.' She moved past him to reach the fridge, leaving a blend of linseed oil and sweet sandalwood in her wake.

He took another swig of beer, swallowed it and clenched his teeth. Philippe had mentioned he'd seen a lot of Daniel Keane over here, recently. He didn't like to attribute Vicki's cheerfulness to that odious journalist.

He stepped back and leaned on the counter. 'Vicki, I noticed the window in the study wasn't fastened properly. It's quite old, so you need to ram the handle down hard to make sure it's secure.'

Vicki looked up from the fridge, a deep frown forming on her face. He guessed she didn't like being told what to do. 'Oh. Okay.'

'It's not that I have much of any great value in the house, but I wouldn't want to clear up the mess if somebody did break in.'

'No. Of course. Absolutely.' She closed the fridge door and took a cabbage out of the vegetable rack and ran water into the sink. He watched as she wrenched the cabbage apart, tearing hard, white stems from soft, dark green leaves, before plunging them into the water.

'How's the painting going?'

'Fine.' She held the leaves under the water, like she was trying to drown them. 'It's going well.'

He passed her a saucepan, hoping the gesture might help lift her suddenly altered mood. He hadn't meant to criticize her about the window, he just wanted to point it out. Somehow, since Keane had come onto the scene, his own relationship with Vicki had become brittle.

'How long till dinner?' he ventured.

'Twenty minutes.'

'Right. I'll just go and change.'

* * *

Shit! What was that about the window in the study? I hadn't opened it. Could Hercules have dislodged the latch? I'd not had him pegged as a particularly dexterous animal. Maybe it had been undone for some time and a sudden gust of wind had displaced it.

Sadly, a grim and more worrying thought shadowed my brain: Daniel.

Crap! Crap! Crap! Was he capable of leaving it open so he could sneak back in and have another nosy around the study? Around the house, even?

There'd been a cold lurch in my stomach the moment Christophe mentioned the window, and the more I thought about the possibilities, the more it lurched. It felt like crossing the English Channel on a hovercraft in a force six.

I went and stood in the kitchen doorway, listening for Christophe. When I heard the hiss of water in his bathroom, I scampered across to his study and flicked on the light. I looked around. Everything seemed the same, didn't it? Had Daniel snuck in here and rifled through private papers while I was sleeping? He could have driven round the corner, walked back, let himself in and spent hours in there, and I wouldn't have known. As for the dogs, just a couple of biscuits tossed their way and they'd roll over and grin.

Bloody-hell, Daniel, I thought. You've taken this a bit far. More than that, if my suspicions were right, there was absolutely no future for us. No matter how good he'd been to me.

I stood, breathing heavily at the possibilities.

Just how far would a journalist go for a good story?

A massive penny dropped down the well of my being, and landed with a sickening splat. Would he go as far as to sweet-talk an aspiring artist?

I slammed off the study light and belted back upstairs. I rifled through my bag and fumbled for my phone. Daniel, Daniel! Where's your bloody number? Eventually, I punched the dial button and waited. Message only. 'Shit!' I spat before leaving as controlled a message as my pounding heart and heaving lungs could manage. 'Daniel. Vicki here. Please will you call me?'

I flopped onto the bed. Would he call? Of course he would. He always returned my calls. And probably had no idea that my suspicions were roused.

Maybe I was over-reacting.

Being dumped at the altar had sure put a massive dent in my self-esteem.

I managed to get through dinner by cross-questioning Christophe on his latest excursion to Toulouse. Never before had an English art teacher been more fascinated by the machinations of the

French veterinary training process. Every question I asked deflected any possibility of him quizzing me on the state of his study window. Every answer distracted me from the horrors of Daniel's potential culpability. He complimented me on the chicken casserole, while I chomped my way through a tasteless heap of cabbage with hummus and walnuts. My mind had been too preoccupied to serve up a half-decent meal for myself.

He left the table in a more buoyant mood, I think, than I'd found him in. So job done. Only Daniel Keane to sort out now. I checked my phone for service – five bars – but no missed calls. I toyed with the idea of asking Christophe if I could borrow his car. But even if I drove to Connor's there was no guarantee I'd find Daniel at home. I'd just have to wait.

I fixed myself a coffee and resisted the urge to lob a slug of brandy in it. I wanted a clear mind if Daniel rang me back. I headed up to my studio to tidy the mess I'd left before dinner. Moments later, I heard the second flight of stairs creak as Christophe came for a visit. I turned to see him in the doorway, his face blank and taut. 'Vicki,' he said in the dullest tone ever. Either someone had died or I was about to.

'Yes?'

'Forgive me for asking but have you taken a photograph album from my study?'

A photograph album? I swallowed. 'Was it leather bound?'

'So you have it, then?' his face seemed to relax. 'Were you looking for more inspiration for your paintings?'

'You know me,' I said, shrugging, as my mind

raced to assimilate this new development.

He sighed. 'I'd prefer you to ask before taking my things. That was my grandfather's album. It means a lot to me.'

'Of course. I'm really sorry. It was stupid of me. I just got carried away.' I could hear a peculiar note in my voice, as fear and guilt clutched my vocal chords.

He glanced around the room. 'I hope you haven't got paint on it.'

'No. Not at all.'

He continued scanning the room. 'So, where is it, please?'

'The thing is…' I could see his mouth flatten as I began. 'It was precisely because I didn't want to get paint on it that I asked someone to scan a few of the pictures for me. Then I could work from those, and not the originals.'

'By "someone" I assume you mean Daniel Keane.'

Oh kerrist! Could he make his name sound more evil? 'Well, yes, but…'

'*Merde*!' I'd never heard him swear before. 'Of all the people, Vicki! You know what I think about him. Where's he taken it?'

'To his home, I imagine…' My voice paled with uncertainty.

'We're going there, right now, to get it back. Viens!' he turned towards the stairs and waited for me to move.

'I'm not sure he's there.'

'Phone him!'

'I tried earlier, I left a message but he hasn't called back.'

His eyes narrowed. 'You do remember where he lives, don't you?'

'Roughly.'
'Good.'

* * *

Christophe could not believe Vicki's naïveté. He'd learned that Daniel had never been top-drawer in the cabinet of journalism, family connections had smoothed the way for his career to continue. Rumour had it he was just biding his time until a bigger, juicier story came up to catapult him into the big-time. How convenient that he had access to the family art collection and now, through the photo album, the private life of Antoine de Castillon. A name that would mean little to a British audience but Keane had plenty of contacts in France.

Vicki sat in the passenger seat, politely offering directions, dithering slightly at junctions until finally, she said, 'I do know it's outside a town with a very ugly war memorial,' after which, Christophe did a U-turn and headed straight for the location.

Lights were on at Connor's house and Daniel's car sat outside. Christophe parked behind it and switched off the engine.

'Will you let me go in on my own,' Vicki said, with a slight wobble in her voice. 'It might be better.'

'Of course not,'

'Why?'

'I'm sorry, Vicki, but my family's privacy is more important to me than your pride. He may have fooled you but not me.'

'He's an art critic not a tabloid journalist. I've seen some of his cuttings.' As the words tumbled out of her mouth, he noticed her eyes were glistening more than usual.

He didn't need the complication of her muddled emotions. All the same, he drew a breath and softened his voice. 'Please, Vicki, don't challenge me on this. Let's just get the album back.'

She shook her head and, to his surprise, hissed, 'Shit! Why am I so stupid? Stupid, stupid, stupid!'

'Let's not do this, now, Vicki. Come on. I need you to get that album back. If he thinks he's doing a favour for you, it should be easy. '

She shook her head. 'He isn't.'

'What?'

'Doing me a favour. I didn't give him the album. He took it without me knowing. Seems you're right about his methods.'

Christophe slammed one hand on the steering wheel, shoved his door open with the other and headed up to the house. Moments later, as he hammered on the door, he felt Vicki's hand on his arm. 'Easy,' she said. 'Let's just ask for it, nicely.'

'He's stolen my property. I don't have to be nice.'

* * *

Why had I been born with a knack for screwing up? Was it karmic justice for a transgression in an earlier life? That's what Isabelle might say. Shafted by Marc, taken in by Daniel and now on the receiving end of Christophe's anger – though with some justification. Unfortunately, I didn't have time to worry about it right then, as the door swung open and Connor swayed in the hallway. He frowned at Christophe before spotting me. 'Hello, gorgeous girl. Are you here for young Daniel?'

I pulled a smile and stepped in before he had chance to close the door. 'Please. Is he in his room?'

'Sure, go on up.'

I headed towards the stairs with Christophe close behind. I tapped on Daniel's door but opened it without waiting. He was seated at the bureau, his laptop open. His look of surprise was switched, in an instant, to a phoney smile.

'Hello,' he said, pulling down the lid of his laptop. Either he was working on a story about Christophe's grandfather or surfing porn sites. If only it had been the latter.

I'd been considering what I might say all the way up the stairs but needn't have bothered. Christophe steamed straight in with, 'I want my grandfather's photo album and anything else you've taken.'

Daniel pulled a wide-eyed face and shrugged. 'What are you talking about?'

Above Christophe's response I slammed the door for dramatic effect – an old teaching trick – and pushed past him. 'Give it up Daniel, I know you've taken it. You were looking at it the other night and now it's gone.' I stared down into his face. His eyes didn't flicker. I'd seen that look often enough on year nines, who equally had no scruples.

He gave a little snort of laughter. 'You do remind me of Matron.'

'The album,' Christophe and I said in unison.

'Why would I want your family album?' he asked, glancing at Christophe. 'I'm an art critic not a genealogist.'

'Who knows why you do anything?' Christophe said. 'You're a journalist who'll stop at nothing to get a story.'

'Really? I'm not sure you're in a position to take the high ground on this, Dubois. Your family isn't exactly the model of morality, is it?'

'You have my property, and I want it back,' he said through gritted teeth.

It was starting to feel like an episode of *The Sopranos*. I decided if they could keep on with the conflictual dialogue, I'd have chance to scan the room for stolen goods.

'Sorry. Can't help you,' he said, but flinched when I lunged under the bureau to grab a package. It was only a fresh box of paper. 'Happy now?' he asked.

Christophe moved to the other side of him, rifling through some documents beside the laptop. '*Crotte!*' He held up a sheaf of paper. 'Not interested in genealogy? So what's this?'

Daniel pulled a cock-eyed smile and shrugged. 'Too late, Dubois. The cat's out of the bag, I'm afraid.'

'What cat?' I said.

'You'll have to wait and see. I'd hate to spoil the surprise.'

Christophe began studying the papers in more detail. 'Dorothea de Castillon was my grandmother. She was a wonderful woman. Why would you want to dig around in her life?'

'A wonderful woman, indeed,' Daniel nodded. 'A woman wronged. A woman shamed by your grandfather's smutty little affairs.'

'That's old news.'

'Yes it is.' There was a smirk on Daniel's face I would have gladly swatted with a damp rag, if only I'd had one. And I don't consider myself a violent woman.

Christophe carried on reading. An eerie weight of silence descended. Finally, a deep frown forged between his brows. He looked at Daniel who grinned, 'Surprise!'

Christophe shook his head and backed away. 'I don't believe it.'

'Too bad, Dubois. I'm afraid it's true. The following pages will give you all the facts you need.' He chuckled. 'I was only looking for a story about stolen Russian paintings, and instead I came across something much more juicy.'

'What is it?' I squeaked.

'Old Grandpa de Castillon wasn't the only one playing away from home. It seems Grandma couldn't keep her knickers on, either.'

Christophe seized Daniel by his shirt collar, swung him round and pinned him against the wall, his forearm rammed against Daniel's throat.

'No!' I yelled, 'Don't kill him!' which, in hindsight, may have been a bit over the top.

'Where's the album?' he barked in Daniel's face, which was not looking quite so smug under the force of Christophe's anger. He didn't attempt a reply so I began searching the room, discovering the album beneath his bed.

'Here!' I called, dragging it out.

Christophe glanced over. 'Check they're all in there. Check every page.'

I went through the contents; a mixture of monochrome and colour pictures. Some were official press shots but mostly they were domestic, family scenes. 'They're all here. No gaps.'

'What else have you taken?' he asked Daniel, who shook his head. 'If I discover anything missing, it won't be me coming back, I'll send in the police. Capitaine Mathis is a very good client of mine. And he's not too fond of journalists, either.' This made Daniel's lip curl. 'And I'll borrow your laptop, too. Vicki…?'

I nodded and disconnected the laptop from the plug socket. Then I gathered the papers up and piled everything onto the album.

'You're wasting your time,' Daniel said through a restricted larynx. 'All my research is backed up.'

'Good,' said Christophe. 'More evidence.' And he pushed himself off Daniel, who gave him an ineffectual shove. 'Vicki, take those down to the car, please.'

I hesitated. I didn't fancy leaving him there in case a punch-up ensued. Christophe must have read my tennis-match eyes moving from one testosterone fuelled male to the other.

'Okay,' he said and turned to Daniel. 'You're going to wait here until we've gone. And you're not going to report your laptop stolen because it will be returned to you.'

'You know, I could make this all go away. Couple of mill should do it.'

Christophe's hand tightened on my arm but I don't think he knew just how tight. 'Would you like to put that in writing, too?'

'We could discuss it.'

'Yes. With a lawyer.' Then he guided me out of the room. I could feel the heat coming off him and hear the breath chafing his lungs.

When we reached the bottom of the stairs, the television was on but there was no sign of Connor. We let ourselves out and hurried to the car. Behind us, I heard a window open and Daniel's voice crowing, 'Have a nice life, Vicki. I'm sure you'll make a great art teacher.'

I stumbled forward as his words hit home. Christophe grabbed my arm to steady me and to prevent the spoils from our raid hitting the deck. We drove away quickly, heading in the opposite direction from the one we'd come in.

'Where are we going?' I asked.

'To the château. The security's better there.'

'You think he'll come after us?'

Christophe let out a huff of contempt. 'No. Not him. But I don't know what kind of people he mixes with.'

I thought of Connor, Jeanne and Raimond but couldn't imagine any of them coming after us wielding a Smith & Wesson.

Chapter 23

The further away from the scene we drove, the more my body began to react. Adrenalin had been flushing through it as if my glands had sprung a leak. Muscles that had been on red-alert now began to relax and judder. Invisible goldfish were swimming a marathon inside my head and Daniel's papers were sticking to the palms of my hands.

'What about the dogs?' I asked, the pressure in my chest forced it out like a squeak.

'I'll go back for them, later.'

'On your own?'

He glanced over at me. 'I'll take Alain.'

The gates of the château glistened in the headlights as we approached. I could feel my rib-cage deflate as I finally let out my pent up breath. Once we were through and they'd closed behind us, Christophe pulled the car over and switched off the engine. He placed both hands on the top of the steering wheel and sank his head onto them.

After a moment, I said, 'I'm so very sorry for all of this. I never, ever wanted to cause you any trouble.' My voice was getting fainter with each word. 'You've been really good to me, and all I've done is screw things up. Sorry.'

I knew, with absolute, crushing certainty, my dream was well and truly over. Worse, I'd visited my lousy, Marchant misfortune on Christophe's family, too.

He didn't speak for ages and I wasn't about to fill the silence with more apologies and pathetic excuses. I'd let him down, very badly, and I was letting Izzy down too. They'd both gone out of their way to help me in my quest for fulfilment, and trouble had been my contribution.

I stared out at the dark silhouette of trees and fast-forwarded through the process of packing, sitting on a train hurling me further and further from everything I'd hoped for. Back to Mum and Dad, to scour the Educational Supplement for another job. Jeez! I hoped to the Almighty I wouldn't have to do supply teaching. There wasn't enough money in the education authority's coffers to compensate for the indignities suffered by a supply teacher. Although, I probably deserved to do a month or two in the Strangeways of comprehensive education, as penance for my latest misdemeanour.

Just as I was conjuring up a scenario of fourteen year old girls backing me against a wall with the force of their 'attitood', Christophe straightened up. 'Do you know what Keane found out about my grandmother?'

'No. I've no idea.' My own anxieties had rather eclipsed the skeletons in his family closet. 'Is it really bad?'

He stared out of the window. 'My grandfather was very close to a man in his company, called Jacques Valois. You can see photos of them in the album. Apparently, he and my grandmother had an affair, back in the sixties.'

I waited. That didn't seem such a ghastly crime in the light of her husband's conduct.

He continued. 'She had a daughter by him in 1965. The daughter, Albina, was severely handicapped and sent to a private hospital in Surrey. Years later, as you know, my grandmother moved back to England. I always thought it was to avoid the glare of scandal from my grandfather's latest liaison but now I see it was to spend time with her daughter.'

'That's not such a terrible thing, Christophe.'

He tossed his head back and laughed, before turning to look at me. 'No. If only that's all it were. But you see, it's much worse than that.'

'How much worse?'

'It seems that back in the sixties, my grandfather's company was producing LSD. Jacques was his chief chemist, you see, and Jacques had masterminded its production. It wasn't illegal when they started but after it became illegal, they continued to supply it on the black-market, sharing the profits of this lucrative little side-line. But when Jacques' brother died from an overdose he was filled with remorse and told my grandfather he wasn't prepared to continue with production. They fell out and my grandfather paid him hush money and continued alone, for a while.'

'Surely other chemists in the lab must have known what was going on?'

'Not necessarily. Pharmaceutical companies back then could be very cagey with their "research".'

'You say he carried on for a while, when did he stop?'

'According to Daniel's report, Albina was born soon after Jacques left the company. Jacques believed her disability was God's way of punishing him. He went on a massive LSD trip. He never came back from it.'

'Oh, how awful.'

'Ironically, Jacques had left all his estate – and it was quite sizeable, thanks to his creative lab work – to set up a charitable organisation to help victims of drug abuse. It became the Jacques Valois Federation, of which my grandfather, and then my mother became president.'

'Your grandfather? I thought they'd fallen out?'

Christophe almost smiled. 'It was Jacques' way of making sure my grandfather paid, too. It seems his will insisted on it. There was a private letter accompanying the will, which detailed my grandfather's obligations. I don't believe Daniel has that letter, but I think we can guess what it said.'

'Is Albina still alive?'

He shook his head. 'I don't know. But I intend to find out.'

'But, what's in it for Daniel?'

'Money.' He let out a sigh. I had a feeling there would be a lot of sighing still to come. He restarted the car. 'Come on. Let's get you settled and then I need to talk to my mother.'

Colette was thrilled by our arrival but her face slackened off when she saw Christophe's pale, grim features. 'Chéri, what on earth is the matter?'

'We'll speak later. Are any of the guest rooms made up?'

'*Le Rubis*. What's happening?'

'Later!' he snapped. I got the feeling he suspected she knew the full story.

I was installed in a cosy little room on the side of the château. It had a stone fireplace and a dark, canopied bed in ruby red satin and marble topped bedside cabinets. The en-suite had a huge claw-footed bath and an array of expensive toiletries. Everything a girl might need, apart from English TV and a mini-bar.

Christophe stood in the doorway. 'Would you like a hot drink? Something stronger?'

'Brandy, maybe?' I asked, secretly hoping for the full bottle.

He nodded. 'See you tomorrow.'

I assumed from that, it would be someone else serving the brandy. I didn't really qualify for VIP treatment. I slumped onto the bed when he left and indulged in a smorgasbord of self-recrimination and emotional flagellation. I saved the tears until after the brandy, which was brought to me by his aunt, Anne. A woman of few words at any time, she handed the bulbous glass to me and merely said, 'I hope you sleep well.'

I smiled and waited till the door closed, before swallowing half the brandy. Then I ran a hot bath, lay down in it and gave way to a tsunami of misery. The Ruby room (*le Rubis*) was so far from Colette's apartment, nobody would hear me and I couldn't hear them. Instead, I could only imagine the scenes playing out in her salon; the accusations, the blame-laying- undoubtedly some of it aimed at me.

And then I remembered, on Sunday I was supposed to be meeting the guy who ran the arts courses in Bergerac. He was going to come and see my work. So long as Daniel didn't sabotage that, I was still in with a chance of continuing with my painting. I would phone Bruno tomorrow to confirm our meeting. Whatever Daniel had done to me, there was no reason why I couldn't get that tutoring job on my own merit. After all, even Daniel had said I'd make a good art teacher. Plus, if my stay in Limousin was about to end, perhaps I could persuade Bruno to give me accommodation in exchange for hard graft. I'd do almost anything rather than shuffle back home in disgrace.

Later, around eleven, I climbed up onto the bed, still wearing the complimentary towelling robe, which had seen much better days, and pulled the sheets over me. I didn't anticipate sweet dreams. I didn't hold out much hope for sleep either. There were three books on the cabinet – all in French. No uplifting Marian Keyes; just a Sartre, a Camus and a Stephen King. I'd read the English version so I pulled it towards me and opened it. Soon, words swam out of focus and I started blubbing all over again.

I groaned. This was all too familiar. Where was my bumper pack of chocolate chip cookies, now? I lay back and stared at the canopy above, feeling tears trickle down over my temples and into my ears. 'What a bloody mess,' I muttered into the silence. A silence soon broken by the distinctive rhythm of paws trundling down the corridor outside. 'The dogs,' I bleated, my chin puckering anew. I could hear them sniffing at the base of my door and nobody seemed to be calling them back. I sniffed as well, threw off the bedclothes and jumped down to let them in. Boz yapped with delight and Hercules head butted my thigh. I crumpled to the floor, hugged him to me and ignored Boz's infantile tugging on the end of the robe's belt. 'Lovely boys,' I sobbed into Hercules' furry neck. 'You are the sweetest dogs in the world. I'm going to miss you so much.'

There was a cough. I looked up. Christophe was standing in the doorway, he appeared slightly less grim but still pale. The dogs, knowing their rightful place, deserted me and sidled back to him. 'You okay?' he asked.

I shrugged. Puffy red eyes and nostrils weren't my idea of a good look. I felt a draught over my chest and realised the robe was gaping. I snatched it shut although, with my boobs on show, he probably wouldn't have noticed my eyes. 'I'll be fine. I just feel so dreadful about this whole business. You were right, Daniel is a creep.'

He nodded slowly and with no sense of victory.

I stood up. Despite my transgressions, the humiliation of crouching at his feet was more than even I could take. 'How are you?'

He ran a hand through his hair and leaned on the door-frame – more from exhaustion, I imagined, than any desire to appear cool which, of course, he did anyway. 'Still assimilating the news. Preparing myself for the fallout.'

'And Colette?'

'She knew all about it.'

'Where is the girl now – Albina?'

'She died in her early twenties.'

After digesting the implications, I said, 'I guess it's really hard to associate such a deception with your grandmother.'

He shrugged. 'Soon after the birth, my grandfather told her the baby had died because of her deformities.'

I took this in. 'That's despicable.'

'Exactly. But he made sure the Foundation paid for Albina's care, in Surrey. She was passed off as the child of a drug addict, which meant she qualified for funding.'

'So, it was a massive cover-up for a tragedy that his company had been responsible for?'

'Oui.'

'Christophe, I can't apologise enough. If I'd had the slightest idea Daniel was…'

Christophe held his hand up to stop me. 'He was a man on a mission. He'd have got the story, sooner or later.'

'You were right about him, though. I was wrong.' I could feel myself start to implode from humiliation.

He shrugged. 'Don't beat yourself up over it, Vicki. We all make mistakes.'

Yes, like he'd made one by taking me into his home.

'See you in the morning,' he said before stepping out with the dogs and closing the door. I sat back on the bed and listened to them retreat down the corridor and stop for a moment before heading back in my direction.

Oh, no. I thought. This is it, the ultimatum: 'Pack your bags and leave tomorrow!' I held my breath. He tapped on the door. 'Yes.' I croaked.

The door opened. 'Would you like the dogs to stay in here, tonight?'

I nodded like my head was on springs.

He signalled them in before saying, 'Goodnight' and left us.

Hercules sat at my feet and grinned up at me. I lifted Boz with one hand, nuzzled my nose into the woolly fur on the back of his neck and scrambled onto the bed. I drew the covers over me and sat him by my feet, at which point, Hercules immediately leapt up, circled and plopped down next to me. 'You darling, darling dogs,' I whispered, snuggling up to

Hercules' back. Maybe, just maybe, Christophe didn't hate me, after all.

I couldn't believe my luck. As I lay in the dark, wallowing in my trough of shame and self-pity but slightly comforted by the rhythm of Hercules' snores, Izzy texted me. She wanted to know if there was any chance I'd meant what I'd said about helping her out on that PR job in Paris.

Any chance?

If time travel were possible, I'd hit the transporter button and dematerialise from Limousin, immediately – dogs or no dogs. I re-read the text. It's not like Izzy to do such a marked about-turn, she must have been sicker than she made out.

I hit the call button and sat up.

'Allo.'

'Izzy, babe, how are you?'

'Better than before. You got my text then?'

'Yes. Tell me exactly what you need me to do.'

'Bring your best clothes. Be charming. Schmooze the clientele. Easy stuff. You could do it with your eyes closed.'

My heart sank. 'I've never schmoozed in French, before.'

'They're coming from all over Europe. What the French don't understand, the Brits, the Dutch and the Germans will.'

'When do you need me to be there?'

'Tomorrow – until Tuesday. Is that possible?'

Well, that would shaft my meeting with Bruno into oblivion.

'Absolutely. I'll be there.'

I asked a whole bunch of questions to clarify the situation. The product was a new beauty range. I would need a convincing makeover to pull this one off. She was emailing me all the gen, the press releases and a cheat sheet of things to say. Her company would pay for my rail fare and accommodation.

'Can't I stay with you?'

'You need to be on site.'

'Who else will be there?'

'Me, of course.'

'But you're ill!'

'I won't be there all day – just when I need to be. Don't worry, I won't be snogging anyone. Nobody will die,' she added with emphasis. 'So is that a yes?'

'Erm...' There was just one problem – Christophe. How would he take it? I'd put a match to the blue touch paper, launched the turd rocket at the fan, and was doing a runner before the fallout landed.

'Vicki, what's stopping you?'

'Nothing, really. To be honest, it's exactly what I need, right now.'

'Good. You're not worried about cooking Christophe his dinner, are you?'

'Well, there is that.'

'Listen, I'll call him in the morning and talk him round. I've got him out of some scrapes in the past, I'm sure he'll give you a break.'

'No! No, I should be the one to ask him.'

'Suit yourself. I'll ring you in the morning.'

She hung up so I didn't have chance to pour out my sordid and sorry tale. Although, on reflection, it might be better told face to face. Preferably when we were old, grey and senile.

Chapter 24

You can do a lot of thinking on a train hurtling through France in the driving rain. I certainly did. I replayed every flattering, encouraging, dishonest word Daniel had ever spoken to me. I took every one of those words, negated it and alighted at Paris Austerlitz Station, convinced I'd been kidding myself I could become a proper artist. I wasn't even sure I was fit to teach. My suitcase felt lead-lined as I dragged it behind me.

In the station concourse, I spotted a man holding a large white and red sign with my name printed on it – printed – not scrawled in marker pen. I smiled and headed towards him.

'Mademoiselle Marchant,' he said, using that same soft 'ch' Christophe used. I felt a pang – a poignancy for lost opportunities. Christophe had actually looked relieved when I'd asked if he'd mind me going to Paris for a few days. 'Stay longer, if you like,' he'd said. 'Probably best if you do. That way, Daniel can't cause you any trouble.'

So he'd taken me back to the house to pack my best clothes, which amounted to half my wardrobe and barely filled my case. Then he'd dropped me at Limoges station and driven off without as much as a wave.

The taxi moved slowly through the streets of Paris until we reached the hotel, where huge, branded flags fluttered outside and massive posters of beautiful women beamed sunnily through the grey drizzle.

Once inside the hotel, I whipped off my jacket – it was several seasons old and very much in the school teacher mode – just in time, as Isabelle rushed over to me. Her face was so hollow-cheeked beneath her immaculate make-up, you'd be forgiven for thinking it was still Halloween. Thank heavens I managed not to gasp but my face may have dropped momentarily before lifting into the brightest smile I could manage. She was wearing a buttercup yellow dress that hung loosely on her normally curvy frame. I threw my arms around her and began to hug her tightly, but slackened off for fear I might snap her in two. 'Izzy, there's nothing of you,' I said stepping back and holding her hands.

'Great, isn't it?' she smiled. 'All those years I've stayed off carbs and one dose of flu does the trick.'

Now was not the time to say I preferred the fuller version. 'Honey, you always look gorgeous.'

She smiled a grateful but knowing smile. 'I'm greeting the client at twelve,' she said. 'Here's your room key, it's fourth floor, the lift's over there. Freshen up then meet me on stand number six. Okay?'

'Okay.'

She squeezed my hand and said, 'So glad you're here.' Then she whipped round and speed-walked back into the main hall.

The room was splendid. Izzy had left a comprehensive array of cosmetics on the dressing table and a name badge for me. I opened my case. The Dyed Wedding Dress lay clean on top. Beneath it my shoes shimmered crimson. Third time lucky, I thought as I lifted them out of the case.

I dressed, swept my hair up into a silver butterfly clasp and applied some of the expensive lipstick. I thought I looked the part. Yes. I was going to schmooze the silk socks off those corporate honchos. I really hoped I wouldn't let Izzy down. My recent record on reliability wasn't exactly stellar.

If I'd thought teaching was tough on the feet, I hadn't experienced handing out leaflets at a trade show whilst wearing cripplingly high, crimson stilettos. But I really had nothing to moan about because, by lunchtime, Izzy looked done in. She'd sailed through her thirty minutes with the client and appeared to chatter comfortably with other celebs of the cosmetic cosmos, but I could see perspiration glistening on her face. 'Here,' I said, pressing my room key into her hand, 'go and lie down.'

I watched in wonder as she took it from me without argument. 'Thanks, pumpkin. You're a star.'

I'd ear-wigged a lot during the last hour and picked up enough from my cheat-sheet and Izzy's patter to make a passable impact during the following three hours. I was particularly proud of my performance with Margo – a buyer from a large chain of Dutch department stores. Descriptors like glowing, silky, dewy and radiant dripped into my spiel like beauty serum.

'Well, of course,' Margo said – clearly jaded from a decade or two listening to sales patter, 'most products make these claims, but I want to know why our clientele would choose Mineral Cosmetics over their usual brand?'

'It's the new, ingenious science they've applied to the development of their products, enriching the formula so that it truly has a rejuvenating quality. Eighty percent of the ingredients are derived from organically grown resources.'

Margo nodded and fondled one of the sample tubes in the complimentary goody basket. 'And...?'

'There's been concentrated research on our improved use of flavanoids, which as we all know,' I rushed on, since I had absolutely no idea what they were and prayed she wouldn't ask, 'are essential for improved skin texture.'

She picked up the freebie lip balm and made eye contact.

I smiled but her look said she wanted more. 'As you'll see, that particular product is rich in Omega 3, for nourishing the lips.'

'Hmmmm.' She replaced the lip balm and glanced around the stand. I was losing her.

Amongst the beautifully shot botanical photos, were images of *Tre Cantate* – Europe's leading classical singing trio of gorgeous women. Minerals Cosmetics had signed them for their launch campaign. I decided to busk it. '*Tre Cantate* have been using the products since the first trials. Just their association with the range will guarantee superb coverage and instant absorption by the cosmetic buying public.'

Margo glanced back at me, a glimmer in her eye. 'How agreeable would *Tre Cantate* be to a personal appearance in our flagship store?'

'I'm very glad you asked,' I said and then leaned forward, dropping my voice to a more intimate level. I didn't want anybody overhearing the bullshit I was about to spread. 'They have pencilled in a couple of dates for such appearances. But it's yet to be decided where those events will take place. If you'd like your store to be considered, give me your card and I'll make sure Isabelle Masson gets it.'

'Who's she?' Margo asked, rather rudely.

'Isabelle Masson is running all PR for this product launch. She will be very influential in the decision.'

'Is she here?'

I wasn't about to drag Izzy from her bed so I spread some more of the smelly stuff. 'You've just missed her. She's in tele-conferences for the rest of today, negotiating with some top Hollywood actors about representing a forthcoming range of male grooming products.'

That got her eyebrows moving. 'I see.' She handed her basket of freebies to me so she could fish in her bag for a business card. As she passed it over, she said, 'Perhaps Isabelle could call me tomorrow?'

'I'm sure she'll call you just as soon as she is free.'

'Thank you…' she peered at my badge as she retrieved the basket, '… Vicki. Enjoy the rest of your day.'

'You too, Margo.' I beamed after her, and stuffed the business card into my bra.

When the first day's event came to a close, I couldn't get up to my room fast enough but I practically had to perform a military tattoo on the door, to rouse Izzy. To say she looked rough would be charitable. She'd slept in her dress which was so crumpled that, over her newly skeletal frame, she looked like a street urchin, and she had a consumptive cough to go with it.

'What can I get you?' I asked as she stepped back to sit on the edge of the bed. 'A hot drink? Do you have any medicine?'

'I have some water. I'll be fine. I've just woken up.'

The last time I saw Izzy looking this bad was after her twenty-first birthday, which had involved a tray of Margaritas and a Havana cigar the size of a marrow.

'Get into that bed, now, while I order you a hot drink. What would you like?'

She scrambled back up the bed and lay against the pillows. 'Just mint tea, please.'

'In bed would be best, Izzy. But take the dress off first.'

At the pathetic look she gave me, I leapt over and hugged her, then helped her out of the dress; not letting her see my reaction to the sight of her angular shoulder blades, and the bra cups dimpling over her reduced cleavage.

She wasn't supposed to be staying at the hotel, but no way was I bundling her into a taxi to go home. Especially since I knew her mother had gone back to Bordeaux. If necessary, I would sleep on the little couch. 'Are you sure you don't need a doctor?' I asked as she settled into bed.

'No. I have some antibiotics for my chest infection but there's nothing else he can do.'

'You're sure it's just flu?' I asked tentatively, convinced she should be tucked up in bed under medical supervision – and I was no Florence Nightingale.

'Positive. I just had it badly.'

I rang down for some mint tea and a coffee for myself. Then, with massive relief, kicked off my shoes and felt my toes spreading, like little sponges, back into their natural form.

'Thanks for helping me out,' she said.

'Absolute pleasure.' I bent forward to loosen the kinks in my spine.

'I know, it's hard on the feet and back, isn't it?' she reached out and stroked my back. 'You should have a bath.'

After an indulgent groan, I unfolded. 'Nope, a shower's fine. But first, let's look at the room service menu.'

'You choose,' she said, closing her eyes.

I selected tomato soup, two Caesar salads – we both needed our greens – mushroom risotto for me and chicken casserole for Izzy, and two fruit salads. She was surely going to eat something from that selection. Oh, and half a bottle of Sancerre for me.

I left her dozing while I had my shower, then pulled on my jimmies. Izzy stirred and said, 'Feeling refreshed?'

'Very.' I sat on the bed next to her and put my feet up. 'Do you do these events all the time?' I asked, despairing for my friend's sanity.

'Ugh, no.' She hauled herself up into a sitting position. 'The real work is in the preparation, the copywriting, the press chats. The shows are a necessary evil. You have to be seen at them – especially with a new product.'

'Well, hats off to you. I thought facing year nines on a windy day was bad enough, but at least I didn't have to be relentlessly cheerful. Poor you.'

'Hmmm, poor me.'

I handed her Margo Nieman's business card. 'I have a confession to make...' and trotted out my *Tre Cantate* story, along with the Hollywood idol subplot.

Izzy grinned back at me. 'Who told you about the personal appearances?'

'What? You mean, they're for real. I didn't just make it up?'

'It's our special telepathy at work.' My jaw dropped as she continued. 'They're actually doing six dates, coinciding with their European tour but it's not public knowledge – yet.'

'Wow! Mineral Cosmetics must be throwing a load of dosh at this new range.'

'Oh yes. It's why I absolutely have to be here.' She sank the dregs of her water bottle and leaned her head on my shoulder. I leaned my head on her head. We stared at each other in the mirror opposite. She gave me one of her, I'm-glad-you're-my-friend smiles, which I returned. There was a pause. Inevitably, the story about Daniel would have to come out, so I don't know why I was sitting there waiting for it. I wasn't keen on having to fess up to yet another miscalculation of human nature. I felt like a fly bashing itself against a window but never learning anything.

Sure enough, she said, 'How're things with Daniel?'

I was tempted to say 'fine', and change the subject. I'd even considered my story – we were cooling it; he had a book to write; I was concentrating on my painting, blah, blah, cough, cough. But I knew it would come out in the end so I said, 'Oh, you know. Exactly how you'd expect them to be. He's a lying shit and I'm getting over him. By the way, have you taken your antibiotics, this evening?'

She blinked and sat up. 'Yes. Now, tell me what happened with Daniel.'

I had thought very carefully about this. Christophe's family secret might stay a secret, if he could pay Daniel enough money to bury the story. It wasn't my place to air their dirty linen on the Champs

Elysées. Hence, my version of events concentrated on the reason for Daniel's espionage being Colette's art collection. 'So you see,' I concluded, 'I'm not quite the Next Great Thing in the art world, after all.'

Izzy, pragmatic as ever said, 'But you never expected to be, did you?'

'Not really.'

'The guy sounds like a creep.'

'That's what Christophe said.'

'Good. There's hope for him, after all.'

'What do you mean?' I said, hackles rising.

'I mean, Christophe and I don't usually see eye to eye.'

'Oh.'

'On the up-side, you can carry on painting without the complication of a relationship. You got something out of it, didn't you – he introduced you to that guy with the gallery?'

'I think that was just a set-up.'

'Maybe, maybe not. Depends how long Daniel was planning on… you know…'

'Using me. You can say it.'

After a brief coughing fit, she asked, 'Did he take you anywhere nice?'

'Couple of restaurants, the museum.' I thought about the lovely river walk we'd done and my first painting of the boy fishing. 'Yes, I got something out of it.'

'And don't forget the sex; sex to exorcise the spectre of Marc. It's good for the soul and very good for the complexion – you do look better for it, you know.'

I peered at my reflection. My hair was out of the clip and messy around my flushed face. The expensive lipstick had stained my lips. 'Yes, quite gorgeous. Any man would, don't you think?'

There was a knock at the door. 'And here's one now,' Izzy said, winking at my reflection.

I got up and opened the door. A young waiter entered, wheeling a food trolley. He set out some cutlery on the table and opened the wine. At his polite bow, we thanked him and watched him go.

'Too young,' I said after the door closed.

'You're too choosy.'

'I do hope so – at least, I hope I'm getting better. Right,' I moved over to the trolley. 'Tomato soup?'

Under pressure from me, she consumed most of the soup, all of the salad and half of the casserole. I, on the other hand, ate everything else. Some people lose their appetites when stressed, I usually find one belonging to an athlete.

As I tidied up the plates, Izzy said, 'I need to call a taxi.'

'No you don't. You're staying here.'

'No. I'll be coughing all night. You won't get any sleep.'

'I'll be absolutely fine. I'm so tired I could sleep through a hurricane.'

'No,' she said, swinging her legs out of bed, displaying a spine not unlike that of a stegosaurus. 'I'll go.'

'Isabelle Masson. Get back into bed. Now!' She cast me a baleful look over her bony shoulder. 'Do as you're told. I'll sleep on the couch.'

'But my clothes!'

'I can lend you some clean knickers, and,' I said, peering into the wardrobe for the ironing board, 'I'll iron your dress.'

She didn't need a second telling. 'Vicki, you're a star. We're doing ten till four, tomorrow.'

'Oh, good. I'm really looking forward to it,' I said, exercising my charming smile before opening up the ironing board. What I really wanted to say was, Oh crap.

Chapter 25

On Monday evening, Christophe walked around the kitchen in his house by the surgery, looking for any food Vicki might have made before the bombshell had dropped. There was flapjack in a tin and fruit salad starting to ferment in the fridge. He threw it out. There was cheese, bread and some pâté too. It was sitting next to another helping of the chicken casserole Vicki had made him. He put the radio on to fill the silence.

He'd moved back to the surgery after handing all the material over to his lawyers. There was no point in trying to cover up what had gone before. Once his shock at the news had faded, he'd acknowledged there were times when you just had to face the music. And that stood for Daniel, too. He didn't see why he should get off scot-free after snooping around and stealing private documents. So he'd called in Captain Mathis.

Colette had known all about Albina. She'd even visited her on the few occasions she went to England. It irked him that he'd been kept in the dark for so long. 'Why?' he'd asked her.

'Chéri, neither mother nor I knew about her until the scandal broke over my father's Italian affair. During a row, he threw some spiteful comments at her about her own affair with Jacques and it all came out. She packed her bags and returned to England to care for Albina. I was happily married by then and you were barely six.'

He remembered how, while other grandmothers were off playing golf or going on cruises, his had been performing acts of altruism at the 'special hospital', where she volunteered. It was one of the things he'd most admired about her. He shook his head.

'Christophe, darling, there was nothing to gain by telling you, it kept things simpler.'

'And where is Albina now?'

'It was very sad. She died from pneumonia, four years later.'

He was trying to remember anything significant from that time, which might be evidence of his grandmother's grief, but nothing stood out. He would still have been at prep school then. His grandmother had kept her secret well.

Hercules and Boz became alert, jumping from their beds and barking at the door. Christophe peered into the hall as a silhouette formed behind the frosted glass. The doorbell chimed. More barking. '*Taisez-vous*!' he snapped at the dogs and signalled them back to their beds. He drew a deep breath before opening the door.

Jeanne stood frowning on the doorstep and clutching a bottle of expensive brandy. 'Christophe, I am so very sorry to have brought Daniel Keane into your circle. I had absolutely no idea he was such a despicable man. Please,' she said, thrusting the bottle towards him, 'will you accept this as a very small gesture of apology?'

Christophe managed a smile. 'Come in, Jeanne. We've been friends long enough for me to know you wouldn't have set me up on purpose.' As she stepped over the threshold, he welcomed her into a warm embrace, and inhaled the heady, musky fragrance of her perfume.

'Oh, Christophe, I don't know which is stronger – my embarrassment or my anger.'

'I think you should concentrate on the anger, it will probably be more useful,' he said, as they stepped apart.

'I've just heard, Keane's not staying at Connor Kennedy's any more. Nobody knows where he is.'

'I'm not surprised. Even though I informed the police, I doubt they'll consider it a serious enough offence to involve the border police. After all, I got my photographs back and, as far as I can see, nothing else has gone missing.'

'Good. I've told all my contacts in the International Federation of Journalists about it, and I spoke to a friend who's a member of the NUJ in England. Unfortunately, Keane has some good contacts of his own, so he'll be well protected.'

'In fairness, you did say he might not be a very principled character and, when I met him, I got the same feeling.'

'I know. I wish I'd followed my gut instinct. But with you having an artist coming to stay, I thought…'

'Of course. And I really appreciated the introduction, at the time.'

'According to my contact in England, there's some British gagging order on a story Keane was pursuing. He was planning to dish the dirt on an English businessman – drove the poor guy to suicide. The family's taken legal action to prevent publication of any material he'd unearthed but rumours are still churning.'

'What an odious little snake.'

She shrugged and pulled an apologetic smile. 'I'm so sorry, Christophe.'

He put a hand to her elbow. 'Come on. Let's go and discuss this in the salon. That brandy looks too good not to be opened.'

He was pleased to see Jeanne's face soften, at last.

* * *

Once the show was over, and we returned to Izzy's apartment, it was clear she had passed the worst of her illness. I knew this because she was starting to boss me around. 'So, when are you going to make a decision about your future, Vicki? Are you going to stay here and carry on painting or give up and go home?'

I didn't like the words give up, and she knew it. 'Of course I'll stay,' I replied, although I wasn't convinced I would be welcome. I'd had two brief phone conversations with Christophe over the weekend. He'd told me that the Daniel situation was in hand, and that I didn't need to worry about it. Fat chance. He wanted me to enjoy my stay in Paris. In fact, he assured me I didn't need to rush back on his account. Whilst that was very magnanimous of him, I couldn't help seeing it as a form of rejection. Particularly when he said Jeanne was helping him to repair the damage. 'Like you, she feels responsible for the situation – having brought Daniel into our lives.'

Of course. Bloody Jeanne. I wondered whether she planned on being as helpful to me.

'Oh good,' I said. 'How is she helping?'

'She has first-class journalistic connections. Which is probably why Daniel contacted her to start with.'

'So they're not life-long friends, then?'

Christophe had let out a harsh laugh. 'No. Jeanne is my friend. It was she who warned me Daniel might not strictly be on the up and up. But she had no idea what his true motivations were.'

Pity she hadn't warned me. Once again, I wondered if her sole reason for fobbing me off onto Daniel was to annexe Christophe for herself.

'If it's okay with you, I'd like to come back on Friday,' I said. That gave me three more days in Paris to recharge my creative batteries.

'Of course. Let me know when your train gets in, and I'll pick you up.'

I'd heard that one before. 'Thank you,' I said, all the while wondering if it might actually be Jeanne waiting for me the Bénédictins railway station.

I had, up my sleeve, the vague possibility that I could decamp to Bergerac and work for Bruno. I'd phoned him when I was on the train to Paris. It would be menial, cleaning work in exchange for a bit of studio space and the chance to run his painting workshops. There were only six residential courses over Easter and Summer but the fees for those would cover my accommodation and food. I say vague possibility, because he had yet to sign up enough delegates for the courses and, more importantly, he needed to discuss it with his business partner – aka his wife.

Now that Izzy appeared to be on the mend, I thought it was safe to ask about her future plans. 'You said you were thinking of making a career change. What did you have in mind?'

She looked over at the bookcase beside her for a moment.

Writing? I thought. Publishing, perhaps?

Finally, she said, 'Charity work. Helping get medical aid to Africa, something like that.'

'Oh,' was all I could say. Izzy – sharp-suited, silky-haired, uber-efficient, corporate dynamo – was thinking of swapping it all for loose linen, mud huts and amoebic dysentery.

'I expend all this energy, but what for? Money. Money for me, money for The Suits. I could be working just as hard but for a more worthy cause. Charities need PR just as much as any other business.'

'Then I think you should do it.'

She nodded, thoughtfully.

'But not,' I added, 'till you're in tip-top condition.'

'No, well, I need to see this Minerals project through. The contract is up for renewal in March.'

'So have you started looking?'

She leaned over and pulled her tablet from the top of the bookcase. 'I started my research today.' She tapped the screen a couple of times and brought up a charity job website. 'Some of these are based in London, too.'

'Really?' So no risk of dengue fever, then.

'The PR function is usually run from a central office in a developed country. But I'd still get to travel, and see projects first-hand.'

'I think that's really exciting. Scary – but exciting. Good for you!'

She smiled back at me. 'You know, you're partly responsible for my decision.'

'I am?'

'You took a chance on a different future. And it made me think, maybe I should pursue something that had been in the back of my mind, too.'

Oh wow. 'So I really do have to see this year in France through to the end, don't I?'

'Yes. Christophe and I spent a whole bloody weekend cleaning that room up for you.'

'You did?'

'Yes. Truckloads of stuff. Up and down those stairs. Up, down. Up, down.' She bounced in her seat, her arms outstretched holding the tablet like a tray.

'I didn't know.'

'Eh bien. You do now.'

My love for Izzy bubbled up and spilled out of my tear ducts. I leaned over and hugged her hard. 'You're absolutely right. I should go back. You're such a good friend.'

She squeezed me tightly. 'But don't do it for me, pumpkin, do it for yourself.'

'Okay.'

'I don't want your poxy paintings, anyway,' she added with a smile.

After six days in Paris, my waistline was expanding after matching Izzy, carb for carb, calorie for calorie, as she started to put her weight back on. I'd spent a day on the sofa watching old French movies that I almost understood; several hours in galleries gazing wistfully at the works of the Impressionists, and countless hours wondering if I had the strength of character to get back in the artist's saddle.

I returned to Limoges with some trepidation. Even though I'd spoken to Christophe on the phone, and he'd said he didn't blame me for all the trouble I knew I'd caused, I was still anxious about seeing him, face to face.

He'd promised to meet me at the station and this

time, he actually did.

Although Daniel was back in the UK, I did wonder if Christophe was still concerned for my safety – or maybe our safety – because he definitely looked relieved to see me. Not ecstatic, of course, it wasn't exactly the return of the prodigal lodger but his smile was genuinely friendly. He even hugged me in a brotherly kind of way and he'd insisted I put the Daniel problem behind me, which was far more than I deserved. As was the dinner he insisted on taking me out for, that evening.

'You don't have to,' I said as he drove us into the heart of the countryside. 'I've bought you a big piece of steak from a really smart butcher in Paris.'

'Thank you. It will keep. You've had a long journey and I think, after all the cooking you've done for me, you've earned a meal out, don't you?' He smiled across at me.

'Well, no, not really. But it's very kind of you to suggest it.'

'It's a Friday night and it's my favourite restaurant. Indulge me.'

La Chaumière was a small, thatched cottage nestling amongst trees beside a straight, country road. We were guided to a table tucked in beside the fireplace, where a large chunk of wood smouldered in the grate. I looked around – there was space for about eighteen diners. Despite the impressive wine list, I opted to drink water. Based on recent experience, I no longer trusted myself in mixed company with even the whiff of a wine cork.

I studied the menu like I was cramming for *Who Wants to be a Millionaire*. There were three fish dishes: crab, bream or salmon, which should I have? Crab, bream or salmon; how long could I avoid Christophe's eyes and the inevitable conversation about Daniel? Maybe I should start it, get it over with.

I looked up. He was watching me.

'Have you decided?' he asked.

'Crab.' I never ate crab. 'Please.'

'Good. And I will have the lamb.'

The waitress came back with the drinks and took our order.

I could feel the huge weight of The Daniel Topic pressing against me, like a sweaty commuter on the Tube – really distasteful but unavoidable. Finally, I said, 'I'm not finding it easy to move on from the Daniel thing. To be honest, I'm mortified.'

'Don't be. You aren't the first and you won't be the last to be taken in by a journalist.'

'But the fallout has been…'

He put a hand up to stop me saying any more. 'Nothing. There is no fallout. All that's happened is I've learned more about my family, that's all.'

'But the scandal!'

'None. It's old news.'

'But the whole drug thing…'

He shrugged. 'Something good came out of it – the Foundation – it's still doing good work today.'

It seemed I wasn't allowed to feel guilty. But I've never been very good at doing forbidden things.

'Vicki. You're still frowning,' he smiled. 'Are you sure you don't want a glass of wine?'

I forced a smile. 'Absolutely certain. But I promise I won't mention it again.'

Tonight, I added mentally. I didn't believe it was off the agenda for good.

The crab was a challenge. I'd once had it in a

sandwich. I'd never actually wanted to tackle one, claws and all. 'This will be fun,' I said, surveying the crustacean and an interesting selection of hardware. 'Where do I start?'

Christophe leaned across and discarded the underside of the body onto my side plate. 'All this in here is edible, and inside the claws.'

'Right. Thank you.'

I must have burned more calories mining the damn thing for meat than I consumed. But it was fun. Probably the most fun I've had eating a meal since my days playing with Alphabetti Spaghetti.

At the end of the meal Christophe said, 'So you brought me some steak back from Paris, huh?'

'Yes, I went to this fabulous butcher in the fourteenth arrondissement. He came highly recommended.' He smiled at me. He was clearly impressed. Maybe I'd got something right, at last. His smile broadened into a grin. 'What?' I asked.

'You do know, all the best beef is bred in Limousin?'

I didn't. Beef wasn't exactly my specialist subject. 'So, I've brought you a steak, all the way from Paris, that I could have got down the road?'

He was still smiling. 'But I'm touched that you thought of me. And I look forward to eating it.'

Bollox. I bet I'd paid way over the odds, too.

Chapter 26

So, I was back in my studio with a reprieve from Christophe but my enthusiasm for painting lasted about three days. After getting off to a cracking start with my next picture, I was languishing in the doldrums of self-doubt and creative inertia. No matter which way I looked at the canvas, I couldn't bring myself to apply any more paint.

I re-read my affirmations and said them aloud but the voice in my head was Daniel's: 'I'm sure you'll make a great art teacher.'

I looked at my canvas. It was a second study of the boy with the fish – only this time, from a distance – a tableau of father and son, lost in their dreams as they patiently watched the water. The scenery – for which I had previously applauded myself for its moody and autumnal appearance – now looked like random, amateur daubs and my attempts to strike the right attitude in the young boy's body had failed miserably. I would sit, for minutes on end, staring glumly at my work, unable to raise any interest in it. At the end of each day, I had to soak my palette in fabric softener to release huge blobs of unused acrylic.

For two days, I busied myself in the kitchen. I baked my favourite chocolate layer cake and made lemon curd. I washed and ironed anything I could lay my hands on. I spring-cleaned the fridge and tidied all the cupboards. Now and again, I would return to my studio in the vain hope my enthusiasm would resurface. But each step up the second staircase felt harder to make.

I invited Louise over for supper on an evening when Christophe was in Toulouse, and spent most of the day preparing food, cleaning the silver and setting the table in the dining room. But it was too formal so I set it again in the kitchen.

She was impressed with my home-made pumpkin soup. 'You must give me your recipe, it's delicious,' she said. She was so sweet, I had the feeling she would have been impressed even if I'd just opened a can of supermarket special.

I didn't want to talk about me or my painting, so now that my French was so much better, I quizzed her on her childhood, her family and her hobbies. When she said she liked line dancing, I said, 'Really. Can you teach me?'

Minutes later, we had moved the coffee table from the centre of the salon and there was music blaring from the speakers, and we were stomping, wheeling, kicking and slapping for all we were worth. Just as we were hacking back on our heels, I noticed the dogs circling and barking in the hall.

Wiping my forehead with my sleeve, I walked over to answer the door. It was Jeanne – in a dress. It was in slate grey wool with a scooping cowl neck, which she'd teamed with a pair of fabulous black bondage boots. Okay, they were lace-up with modest heels but they had the whole shiny leather and silver eyelets thing going on.

'I don't see Christophe's car,' she said – a touch proprietorially. 'Is he out?'

'He's in Toulouse. Would you like to come in?' I

quite fancied the challenge of getting her doh-si-dohing with us.

She stepped over the threshold with some authority, closed the door and ignored the dogs. 'He asked me to come round. Perhaps I got the date wrong.'

'He's back tomorrow.'

She nodded a smile at Louise, who had turned the music down and joined us in the hall. 'You're having a girls' night in,' she stated. 'How nice.'

I offered her a glass of wine. After some hesitation, and watch-gazing, she declined. I got the impression she had more important places to be. 'Tomorrow night, you say? I must call him and check our plans. It's been a very busy week, made even more hectic by this wretched Daniel Keane.'

'Yes. I can imagine.' Beneath her business-like surface, I could almost see Jeanne twitching. For once, I actually didn't feel to blame over Daniel. I couldn't be, since she appeared to be shouldering that responsibility herself.

She glanced at her watch for maybe the sixth time since she'd arrived. 'Well, I'll leave you. Enjoy the rest of your night.' With one hand on the door handle, she stopped and looked back at me. 'Oh, I meant to ask, how is your artwork progressing?'

'Really well, thanks. I'm loving it,' I lied.

She nodded and flared a quick smile. 'Good. That's good.'

Moments later, she was in her car and roaring off up the road.

'She can't seem to keep away from him,' Louise remarked as we turned look at each other.

'Really?'

'I think she was here every day, last week.'

'Didn't Christophe go to Toulouse?'

Louise looked thoughtful. 'Ah yes, he did, but she was here as soon as he came back.'

'Are they lovers?' I couldn't help myself.

She shrugged. 'It looks that way, don't you think?'

With a surprising lurch in my stomach, I had to agree, it did.

Despite Christophe's apparent interest in the progress of my work, I had banned him from my studio until the picture was finished, fixing a taut smile on my face and saying, 'You won't appreciate the final piece if you see it through all its stages of development.' When what I'd really meant was, through all my futile attempts to turn this piece of rubbish into a work of art.

On Friday evening, as I stood in the kitchen, gazing out into the courtyard and questioning my talent, Christophe's voice jolted me from my thoughts. I turned and tugged a mouth-only smile in his direction, before I focused again on stirring my tea.

He continued, 'I'm going over to the château to pick something up, why don't you come with me?'

I raised my eyebrows. I was sure he'd never needed an escort before. Maybe he wanted to parade me in front of Sylvie. I'd heard The Elopers were now home and settled into Gerard's apartment. Still, if it helped Christophe to feel more comfortable about facing his ex, I didn't mind playing along. Although reasoned that if it were the case, he should be taking Jeanne with him. Still, what else was I going to do, spend another evening fretting about my painting? 'Sure. I'll just go and get changed.'

I tugged off my sweatshirt and looked at my make-up bag. Should I make an effort? I swept a little blusher over my cheeks, applied smoky-grey liner and soft pink lip-gloss. Removing my hair from its clasp, I attempted to brush it into an alluring shape about my face – but there was a big kink above my right ear and another just below my left. I groaned, rolled it back up and fixed it with a clasp. I tested a sultry, oh-so-cool look but dropped it hastily. 'That's it, Vicki, looking dozy is seriously on trend.'

At the château, Christophe parked alongside an old, red Citroën, which I hadn't seen last time we'd visited. I assumed it must be Sylvie's. Surprising, really, I'd imagined she'd drive something much more sophisticated. Christophe walked round to my side of the car and opened my door. He had a curious look on his face. I glanced up at him as I stepped out. What did he have to be so cheerful about?

He closed the door after me. 'Tell me, how do you like surprises?'

I turned around, half expecting my family to leap out from behind the trees. It would be so lovely to see them. The very possibility suddenly made me feel homesick. 'What…' I began, swallowing a lump of emotion, '… what are you talking about?'

Christophe stepped towards me and gestured to the red Citroën. 'I think you need a car – so you can go out and take pictures whenever you want. It's not much, but it's reliable.'

I looked from him to the old car. In the twilight, its paintwork was glistening from the recent rainfall. Oh. He'd actually taken the trouble to find me a car. I'd had to sell my own to make ends meet. Now I could tootle about the French countryside to my heart's content. I looked back at his smiling face and threw my arms around his neck and hugged him. 'It's lovely, lovely, lovely. Thank you so much.'

'It's just an old car, Vicki. I'm sorry it's nothing smarter.'

'I don't care. It's great. But there's a problem; I don't have any car insurance.'

'It's okay, I've sorted that out.'

'Really? How much do I owe you?'

He tilted his head and gave me a look. 'Nothing.'

'No, wait. You can't get insurance for free, it doesn't work like that. Please let me cover the cost.'

'You can paint me a picture.'

I thought for a moment and grinned. 'Wow, French insurance must be seriously expensive.'

He smiled down at me. Killer smile, actually. The kind of smile gets a girl into all sorts of trouble. Suddenly, my tummy was tipping sideways and back again and my heart picked up a beat or two. Alarm bells screamed in my head and I stepped away quickly. There was the sound of footfall on gravel and Christophe's back stiffened as a woman's smooth, clear voice said, 'Bonsoir.'

It could only be Sylvie. He was looking at her over the top of my head. I don't know why I felt guilty; it was hardly the same as when I was found kissing Jason Cartwright at the fairground – by his girlfriend.

The woman I saw approaching was wearing a thick, cream, woollen sweater, with fern coloured breeches tucked into black riding boots. She was almost as tall as Christophe, with long, dark hair smoothed into a plait, which hung forward over her shoulder. She walked with the grace of a model and the tone of an athlete. Less than an hour earlier, I had fantasised about flooring her with a pathetic don't-mess-with-me look. I now realised it would take the might of Boadicea and her tribe to floor this woman.

After a brief exchange, Christophe introduced us. She came forward and stretched out her hand. I took it, noticing how warm and dry it felt against my own, chilly one. I had built up a grossly unpleasant image of Sylvie and now, here she was in the flesh, smiling kindly down on me. *Merde!*

'I'm so pleased to meet you, at last.'

'And it's a pleasure to meet you.' After everything I've heard, I added silently.

'Unfortunately, I can't stop to talk, now. We're going out. We'll catch up some other time.' She smiled briefly at Christophe. It was one of those, we've-got-a-past smiles. '*A tout à l'heure.*'

There followed a moment's silence in due respect for the departure of this splendid creature. Finally, he looked at me and said, 'Do you want to get in and see if you like it?'

Of course. The car. I shook my head, as if waking from a trance. 'Wait a minute. Where did it come from?'

'We've had it for years – but it's an excellent little car.'

'This is so kind of you.'

He shrugged, his eyes smiling down at me, 'It makes sense. I don't know why I didn't think of it before.'

I sat in the driver's seat. My feet were so far from the pedals I might as well have been sitting in the boot. I adjusted my position and looked at the gear knob, which was on a short stem jutting out from the dashboard. 'Weird,' I said, tracing my hand over the switches and dials.

He sat in the passenger seat and demonstrated the position of the gears. 'Now, we take it for a spin.'

It took me a couple of minutes to get used to it but I loved the throaty noise of its engine and the quirky way I had to change gear. When we parked back in the driveway I beamed at him. 'Thank you so much. It was really thoughtful of you. I'll take very great care of it.'

He laughed. 'You'll be the first person who has. We all learned to drive in this car, even my mother, it has quite a history.'

I could well imagine.

'Come,' he said, pulling on the door handle. 'We should say hello to Colette before we leave. She will never forgive me if we don't.'

We found Colette in the salon, reading a travel magazine. As soon as I'd said '*Salut*' to her, I launched into a grovelling apology for all the trouble I'd caused. Before I was fully into my stride, she leaned over and took hold of my hand. 'Chérie, you could not have known.'

'But I've caused a lot of upset for you.'

She shook her head. 'We have grown thick skins in this family. And we have come to know the people we trust and the people we don't. Now, why don't you and I go out for lunch, next week?'

'Erm…'

'We'll go to Limoges, and I can show you some of my favourite shops.'

That sounded expensive. 'Thank you. That would be lovely.'

'Chérie – I can hardly wait,' she said as we parted.

'And perhaps you will let me see your current masterpiece. My son tells me you are really quite talented.'

Had he? Oh dear. The clouds were gathering once more. That wretched picture was waiting at home for me. It was sitting there on the easel, like a big, fat bully with its arms folded and a curl on its lip, goading me to try and tackle it again.

The gloom continued to roll over me as I followed Christophe home in my little car, talking to it as I went. 'How did I ever believe I was an artist? I must want my head testing. I gave up a perfectly good job. Daniel was right. I'd make a much better teacher.'

As I pulled onto the drive next to Christophe's car, and switched off the engine, I suddenly became aware of him standing outside, head bowed, watching in fascination as I chattered away to the dashboard. He opened the door and leaned on the top of it, looking down at me. 'You know, they say it's the first sign of madness – talking to yourself.' There was just the ghost of a smile on his face.

'Then, I must be absolutely barking – I've been doing it for years.' I stepped out of the car. There was only the driver's door separating us and so very little room between the car and the house wall. I spluttered on. 'I've called him Tom, it's short for Tomato – you know, red car – red tomato. Is that okay?'

'You can call it whatever you like.' He was closing the door and advancing on me as I backed off into the space behind the car. I'd already discussed with Tom that my attraction to Christophe was just a symptom of my emotional confusion. If I acted on it, I might as well hit the self-destruct button. He was just one of those men who attracted women. We were like wasps to a picnic. I hurried round to the front door, where Hercules and Boz were waiting, excitedly. Christophe greeted his dogs while I escaped into the kitchen.

It was getting late and we hadn't eaten yet. I began gathering the ingredients for a spicy prawn pasta, acutely conscious of Christophe's presence in the hallway. I prayed he would go into his study and leave me in peace to make supper. God wasn't listening.

'Talk to me, Vicki.' He came and stood right in my bubble – heating the space between us.

I busied myself at the chopping board, aware my hands were doing things with peppers and onions but I couldn't be sure if they were doing the right things. 'What about?'

'Earlier, when we left my mother's, you let out a huge sigh, like you were dreading coming back here.'

'Did I?'

'Yes.'

I'd never chopped pepper so finely – or so fast. 'Agh!' I had overshot the pepper and sliced into my finger.

Quick as a flash, Christophe took the knife from me and steered me to the tap. Pulling off several squares of kitchen roll, he dried my hand and pressed a piece firmly to the cut. 'I don't think it will need stitches. We'll put a tight plaster on it, here.' He delved into a drawer to find some plasters, and carefully smoothed one around my finger. Finally he looked up. I flicked my focus to the finger.

'Thanks,' I said, not wanting to look at him. 'I can't believe I just did that.'

'Let's forget about cooking, for now. This whole situation with… Keane,' he said the name with a blend of reluctance and venom, 'has clearly upset you, and I can understand that, but you have to believe me when I say neither my mother nor I hold you responsible. So, put it behind you.'

'I may not be totally responsible but you are still having to deal with the outcome – the lawyers, the other journalists. If I hadn't come to France and got involved with Daniel, you wouldn't be in this mess.'

'You think so?' he asked. 'You don't think Jeanne might have introduced Daniel to me anyway? Remember, it was my mother's collection he was interested in. He got lucky – he met you first.'

I took a deep, shaky breath and continued to stare at my plastered finger, pressing against the wound with my thumb. Daniel had got lucky in more ways than one, but Christophe had a point. 'I suppose so.'

'*Exactement*,' he said, as if to close the subject. 'Now, I don't think you should be allowed near sharp instruments tonight, do you?'

'Are you saying, you want to chop the vegetables?'

'Why not? Time for a cooking lesson, huh?'

'I guess.'

After dinner, as we cleared away the dishes, I shared my fears with him about my painting. 'Daniel was so supportive, I honestly believed I could do it, but now... I don't know, maybe I was deluding myself.'

'Hey! You believed you could do it before you ever met that man. Erase it. Go back to how you felt when you first arrived. You were bursting with enthusiasm.' I was surprised at how effusive he was in his opinion. 'If you give up now, then he'll have done even more damage, won't he?' he said, fixing both hands on my shoulders.

The heat from his hands was travelling at great velocity down through my spine and pooling in my pelvis. His eyes were intensely fixed on mine. My head was saying 'move' but my body misinterpreted the command and I stepped closer to him. 'Thanks,' I whispered, looking from his darkening eyes to the curve of his top lip and down to the feint vertical crease in the centre of his chin. And he seemed to be contemplating this electric moment between us just as intently as I was. As his hand drifted up and touched my neck, I was a goner.

A kiss every bit as delicious as the one we'd shared before, sent a vibrant hum through all my senses. This time, we'd come to this point together and it had nothing to do with me consuming every wine in Limousin. I could feel the stroke of his thumb beneath my ear, and the pressure of his other hand in the small of my back. He drew me so close I could feel the thumping of his heart against my chest.

His hands were moving over my back, hugging me even more tightly to him as his mouth moved so skilfully – searching and tasting mine. I was in heaven, a whole different place from where Daniel had taken me. This took pulse-quickening to a whole new level.

No wonder he had claimed so many hearts in Limousin.

Had he?

I was breaking the spell. Why did I do that? This was my moment, I should enjoy it.

My moment or my turn?

Damn!

Sylvie's cool figure drifted in from the corner of my mind, followed swiftly by Jeanne's.

Stop it!

Stop what? Kissing him or analysing this?

It was no good. I pulled back. My breathing was every bit as laboured as his. I shook my head. 'Christophe, I don't think I'm ready for this.'

He frowned. 'You're not ready or you won't let yourself? Just like you won't let yourself paint.'

That stung. I pushed myself back from him. 'It's entirely different.'

'I don't think so. You are so full of talent. You are passionate about your work. I've seen it. Then you have a small break in your confidence and look at you! You are giving up too easily. You ran away from Bristol to find your answers, and now, perhaps you are running away again.'

'Maybe I'm just a realist. Maybe I know my limitations and have the balls to face up to them and move on.'

'Yes. And you moved on from Marc, didn't you? You came here to create a new future for yourself. Stay with it, Vicki.'

We had a moment's standoff. I could hear his breath over my own. I knew he was right and yet the whole Daniel scenario had seriously winded me. 'Maybe I need a break. Maybe I should go home for a week. Come back refreshed.'

'You've just had a week in Paris.'

Right again.

He stepped further back and whistled to the dogs, who stirred quickly from their beds and obediently trotted into the kitchen. 'Think very seriously about why you came to France before you give up on your dream.'

He pulled two leads from a hook on the wall and headed out into the courtyard, slamming the door behind him.

I stared at the door long after he'd gone. I did think about it. And about him.

That kiss had been good, hadn't it? Hadn't it been knee-tremblingly, heart-swellingly, mind-blowingly fantastic? So what was all this about not being ready?

I opened my eyes and let out a yell of frustration.

I ran up to my room and showered. When I got out, I rubbed myself punishingly with a towel. I snatched up my toothbrush, squirted on a glob of paste and scrubbed my teeth vigorously. Finally, I lay back on the bed and replayed the evening in my mind, fast-forwarding to the lovely parts and rewinding over the final few minutes.

What had he said that really hurt – I was talented? No, what hurt was that he said I was running away. I slapped myself on the forehead. I'd never considered myself a quitter. But he was right. My relationship with Marc had failed. I'd run from my life in Bristol, thinking a fresh start was the answer but here I was, with all this opportunity in front of me and I was preparing to run away from my painting too, and I was sure as hell trying to run away from Christophe – just not fast enough. Maybe the answer was right here in Limousin.

I was becoming breathless at the thought. Possibilities tumbled through my mind like clothes in a dryer. I recalled our kiss. If I hadn't pulled back, what might we be doing now? If he was just looking for another notch on his bedpost, why tackle an emotional nut-job like me?

Maybe he really cared. I'd been so thrown by the Daniel thing, I wasn't sure I was qualified to judge. I studied the evidence and let out a moan as I realised that even after all I'd done, Christophe was still prepared to give me a home and showed every sign of being attracted to me. I shivered. What a wasted opportunity.

I lay listening for him to come home, trying all the time to think of a way to redeem the situation – whether to sit on the stairs and wait for him to come back and shame-facedly admit he was right, or whether to wait until tomorrow. Tomorrow, I could make amends with a truly spectacular dinner and a little careful seduction.

I sat up and started smoothing body lotion into my skin, and wondered if it was logically possible to seduce the same person, twice. I heard movement downstairs. He was back. Hastily, I slapped the cream onto my thighs and smeared it the length of my legs. Jumping up, I grabbed my dressing gown and struggled into it.

Damn! Why hadn't I pulled the sleeves the right way round this morning? I quickly checked my reflection. Yep – still flushed – but at least my hair was clean and drying into a nice, softly curling frame around my face. Taking a deep breath, I opened the bedroom door – trembling but resolute. I took the stairs slowly, I didn't want to fall base over apex into his arms. As I reached the bottom step, there was a chilling sound from outside. Christophe had gunned the engine of his car and was now reversing – fast – into the road.

'No!' I cried, and ran to the front door. Hell! Why did it have to be so stiff? I yanked it open just in time to see the car's tail-lights speeding away down the road, with Christophe on board, quite probably heading off to consol himself with Jeanne.

All was not lost. I sprinted back up the stairs and rifled through my bag for my phone. Pulling it out I flicked it open. No life. I hurled the clothes off the chair to get at the charger beneath. Plugging the lead into my phone, I waited impatiently for it to register. Finally, and with heart thumping, I selected Christophe's mobile number and pressed the key.

I waited.

It connected.

Bzz. Bzz.

I dropped my head. Downstairs, I could clearly hear his phone vibrating on the hall table.

Chapter 27

I woke with a nagging feeling in the back of my mind that all was not well in my world. I forced my eyelids open, which felt sticky and swollen from crying. It was then I remembered and pulled the covers back over my head. I'd fallen asleep around dawn, having played through a number of possible scenarios in my head – not least of which featured me packing up and heading for home.

I summoned up the energy to face the world and, in particular, Christophe. I guessed he'd gone to see Jeanne, although he could equally have gone to the château. A vision of Sylvie floated into my head. Was he hoping to confide in her? No. That couldn't possibly happen, could it? But something tugged at my insides, all the same. I groaned and dragged myself out of bed, washed and dressed in my best jeans with my most flattering, soft lilac sweater and headed downstairs.

The first thing to catch my eye, was the hall table – now missing the mobile phone that had been mocking me last night. So, he was back. My heartbeat quickened as I began walking about the house looking for him.

I made myself some peppermint tea. It was now eleven-thirty, and the low-slanting winter sun shone hazily through the damp air from last night's rain. I decided to take my tea outside to drink it in the courtyard, thinking it would be so much nicer to meet Christophe there, than at the scene of last night's misunderstanding. To my surprise, the door from the kitchen was locked, with the key still in place. Christophe didn't usually lock it after walking the dogs. I turned around and noticed, for the first time, a small note on the table, beneath the pepper-pot.

Sorry for last night. My mistake. I will see you next week.
I believe you are a painter – don't give up.
Christophe.

Next week? Yes. I could wait. He was putting distance and time between us. After all, I had told him I wasn't ready – hadn't I?

I let out a sigh. He was being thoughtful, just like François said.

Up in my studio, I turned the easel round, so I didn't have to look at the picture. I fired up my laptop and navigated straight to the photos of Christophe. The last time I'd pored over pictures like this was when I was fourteen and drooling over pictures of Ronan Keating. I reached for my sketch-pad and began drafting the outline of his profile, studying the strong straight line of his nose and the slate-grey shading on his jaw. Half an hour later I held it at arms' length. It was a good portrait. Pencil drawing had always come easily to me. I glanced over at the back of my canvas – shame about my skill with paint. Disconsolately, my eyes drifted across to the mirror on the end wall.

I gasped.

Reflected back at me, was the painting – only in this reversed view, it looked quite different. Suddenly, I saw in it a beauty I hadn't appreciated before. I stared aghast – seeing immediately that the picture only needed more angles in the principal characters. It was astonishing. Looking at the image back-to-front, was like seeing it for the first time. And I knew exactly what needed to be done. Before I lost the vision, I flipped over the page of my sketchpad and hastily made some notes.

Long after sunset, I ran down to the sitting room and put on a Tchaikovsky CD – loud. With my stomach hollow from hunger, I danced about the kitchen, while a jacket potato sat heating in the microwave.

'Wait till I show him what I've done. He won't believe it.' I announced to the empty room. 'Even I don't believe it!'

A couple of nights later, my phone rang. I was onto it like shot from a catapult.

'Salut,' I chimed into the receiver.

'Salut, Chérie!' It was Isabelle. 'How is it going? Have you started another painting yet?'

'Almost finished one.'

'*C'est magnifique!* And how is Christophe?'

'Fine.'

'Has he forgiven you for the Daniel situation?'

That set me thinking. I supposed he had. There wasn't much evidence of grudge-bearing the other evening.

'Vicki?' Isabelle's voice rose inquisitively. 'Have you fallen out?

'No. Why would you say that?'

'Because Xavier says he's moved back into the château. He saw him yesterday.'

I was relieved to know he wasn't with Jeanne.

'Oh, he often spends time over there,' I lied. 'He has a really smart apartment.'

'I know. Xavier says his ex is living there, too. Don't you think that's weird?'

'Extremely.' My heart began to plummet at the possibilities and it reminded me of something else. 'Izzy, what does the phrase, *croceuse dedi amant*, mean?'

'*Croqueuse de diamants*? It's not very nice, it means gold-digger – like a woman who's after money. Has somebody called you that?' she sounded concerned.

'No. It was a phrase I heard someone use to describe Sylvie.'

'Ahh. Could be. I've never met her. So, you haven't fallen out with Christophe. And you're happy with your painting?'

'Yes. But how are you, Izzy? Are you feeling better?'

'Much better. I'm finally catching up on my sleep.'

'Great,' I said, suppressing a yawn. I hadn't slept properly for days.

On Sunday morning, I reviewed my painting in the mirror. After adding just a few highlights to the fishing basket, I stood back and grinned with satisfaction. An artist can always find something more to do to a picture but I resisted. The move from where I was on Tuesday, to where I was now, had been huge. Feeling as if a load had been lifted from my shoulders, I made myself a sandwich then packed it, some water and my camera into my new friend, Tom the Citroën, and headed off into the countryside for some fresh air.

* * *

Over at the château, Colette was admonishing Christophe for deserting Vicki. He scratched dried mud from his riding breeches. 'She needs space and time to work on her painting. That's the only reason I came here.'

'Well, I think it's very inhospitable of you. We must invite her over to lunch.' She held out a bangled arm. 'Chéri, pass me the telephone.'

'Maman, please don't interfere.'

'What's interfering about inviting someone to lunch? If she doesn't want to come, she's entitled to say so.'

'And I'm sure she will.' He stood and passed the phone to his mother.

Colette tapped the receiver as she waited for the call to connect. With a heavy sigh, Christophe strode out of the room. 'I'm going riding,' he barked over his shoulder.

'Christophe,' she crooned after him, but he took the stairs two at a time and headed out.

As he was tightening the girth strap on Léopold, he heard his mother's voice behind him. 'Chéri, do you have Vicki's mobile number? Nobody answered at the house.'

Why couldn't she just drop it? He busied himself about the horse. 'Maman – if she didn't answer, I think it means she doesn't want to be disturbed.'

Colette came over and patted the horse's cheek. 'Perhaps. Or maybe she's lonely and has gone out looking for company. If I were her, I would hate to be on my own.'

'Well, that's you. Vicki is an artist. Artists spend hours in their own company. It's how they work.' All the same, he wondered why she hadn't answered the phone.

His mother sighed. 'What a pity. Seeing her would have cheered me up, considerably. Especially as you're so snappy this weekend.'

Christophe plugged his foot into the stirrup and swung himself onto the horse, steering it back and away from his mother. 'I apologise. It's all this business with Sylvie and Gerard. I promise I'll be more cheerful when I get back.'

Colette raised her eyebrows and shrugged.

He urged the horse forward and out of the yard.

* * *

Even though I thought I'd followed the only roads in the area I knew, I ended up on an unfamiliar, winding hill with a long curving bend. Eventually, it opened out to reveal a magnificent view across open fields with Christophe's family château nestling comfortably within trees beyond. From that angle, as the sun blazed through a gap between the clouds, it looked spectacular. I pulled over onto the grass verge and took out my camera. I was probably half a mile away but the telephoto lens gave me a wonderful, clear shot of the old building. I supported the camera on Tom's roof as I selected my shots.

Over to the right, a horse and rider was galloping away from the château. My heart skipped as I trained the lens on them, discovering it was, indeed, Christophe. I hastily made some adjustments to the camera settings, and snapped as many pictures as I could, before he disappeared into an area of woodland. Once he was out of sight, I switched the camera to view mode and back-tracked through the images. Only one of the five I had taken was really good – excellent, in fact. His head had almost come down to meet Léopard's, and there was a wonderful sense of shared purpose about the two of them. There was no getting away from it, he looked sensational, with those riding breeches stretched taut across the muscles of his thigh and all the primal strength he was displaying.

I pushed a strand of hair behind my ear and looked over to judge where he might emerge from the trees. Further to the left, and coming from the other direction was another rider. Great! Two for the price of one. I manoeuvred the camera again, steadied it and focused.

There was no mistaking the tall, elegant figure of Sylvie. I lifted my head from the camera and watched the scene unfolding before my eyes. As Christophe galloped out from the trees and saw Sylvie, both riders slowed their horses to a canter – as if choreographed by some unseen director.

I lowered my head to watch it in close-up. They reined in their horses until they came alongside. I couldn't see Sylvie's face but there was clearly a look of intensity on Christophe's. My finger instinctively pressed the shutter. He dismounted and held both horses as Sylvie jumped down.

My mouth went dry.

I watched as they talked for a moment, my heart hammering so hard, my body was rocking and I struggled to steady the camera. Sylvie's hand lifted and rested on his shoulder. They were about the same height and, although I couldn't feel it, I could imagine oceans of passion swelling between them. Then Sylvie's hand slid around his neck and Christophe drew her to him.

Click. Click. Click.

I couldn't see the detail through the film of tears, but I knew the lens would.

Moments later, they had remounted and were cantering off across the field – together – away from the château. Beyond them lay another crop of trees, which very soon swallowed them up.

I hung my head. At least I knew where I stood now. For that, I was very grateful.

I had to hand it to him, when it came to seducing women, he had style. There was I, feeling sorry for him because his cousin had run off with Sylvie. Now, I stood watching while he galloped off with his cousin's bride. He'd got it all.

And to think, on Friday night, I had come so close to taking the next step. I blew the air from my lungs. Thank heavens for the sixth sense that had told me to pull back. I'd had a narrow escape. I let out a long, grating groan, and stared at the thicket of trees. Who knew what was going on in there?

A sudden, chilly wind whipped at my hair. I sniffed and picked up my camera, switched it off and replaced the lens cap. Automatically, I put it carefully in the case, pushing aside my notepad as I did so.

Another cramp in my heart reminded me of our cosy chats over dinner and the night he gave me the car. The car! I'd thought he was thinking of me. All the time, he'd been looking for a way to move out of the house. Now he'd provided me with transport, his conscience was clear.

And what was Jeanne's reference to Sylvie being a gold-digger? She gets to marry Gerard and screw Christophe on the side? I guessed Gerard had the bigger bank balance. Jeanne obviously had the whole situation weighed up and was simmering with jealousy.

Dear Doris – who was I to judge?

Sitting back in the car, I stared unseeingly out of the window.

All's fair in love and war.

But I wasn't in love, was I?

'Don't cry!' I screeched, sniffing as I raked both hands through my hair. 'He was never yours, Vicki. Don't!' I was in danger of hyper-ventilating, as I assimilated this latest development. 'Some men are just like that. Who can blame him? He's spent a lifetime being successful with women – and Sylvie got the measure of him. Good for her.

'Don't get miserable, get mad! I am mad. I must be. Ha-ha! There's a funny side to this, somewhere.' I'd probably discover it in a year or so.

No matter how much I tried to convince myself that Christophe was a player, I couldn't get away from the fact that he'd been really kind to me. But then, so had Daniel. Hang on, didn't everyone think Daniel was a creep? Had I thought that? I rewound to the first night I'd met him. He'd seemed a little... was it – wary? A little chilly, to begin with? Had I warmed to him instantly? Well, for that matter, I hadn't warmed to Christophe, either. Although my physical attraction to him had been there instantly. I sighed.

So, just how close had I come to letting myself be completely taken in by him too?

I let out another groan and leaned back on the headrest.

Why did I have such bad judgement? I must remember to write a checklist of all the good things to look out for in future, and all the warning signs.

Never again would I let my heart rule my head.

I started the car and revved it unnecessarily hard. I lurched out onto the road and drove, with tunnel vision, deliberately turning away from the château. Several miles later, when I found myself driving down a rapidly narrowing lane, I realised I had no idea where I was going. A quick glance at the petrol gauge told me, 'not far'. I pulled up, closed my eyes and counted to ten.

There was a funny side, after all – this was turning into a farce. I'd be laughing soon.

It made sense to leave the car and conserve petrol, while I headed off on foot to find someone and ask for directions to a filling station. Had I passed any houses recently?

After walking for twenty minutes and not seeing a single house, roof or chimneypot to give me encouragement, I stopped and considered my only realistic option – to phone Christophe and ask for help. I flipped open my phone and wondered whether I might be interrupting an intimate moment…

Maybe not such a bad idea after all, then. I selected his number, took a deep breath and pressed the connect button.

Nothing. No signal. No little bars on my screen. As the French would say, *Rien*.

I snapped it closed and cast an accusatory look at the heavens for their lack of support. Although, I couldn't be absolutely sure the heavens had finished with me yet. What had been a glorious blue was fast being replaced by something further along the spectrum. By the time I had walked back to within two hundred metres of the car, rain began falling in big, fat drops onto my head; by the time I'd halved the distance, thick painful pellets, yes – pellets, of water were smacking against my body and urging me to beat my own land-speed record. By the time I stood struggling with the antique Citroën lock, I could feel water seeping into my underwear.

Slamming the car door, I checked my phone again. One bar. One glorious little bar. Surely I was due a break?

Once again, I selected his number and waited.

Quelle surprise. Voicemail.

There was nothing left to do, but to turn the car round and hope I had enough petrol to get me to the château – or at least to someone who could help me. I started the engine and consoled myself that it was often the case that cars had more in their tanks than the petrol gauge suggested. The empty mark was like a cautionary tale; designed to teach slack drivers like me, a lesson. Well, thank you Citroën, I'd learned my lesson and I wouldn't be doing this again.

Apparently, that just wasn't enough.

Tom coughed and struggled to clear his tubes but, just at the point in the road where I'd given the heavens my dirty look, he shuddered, croaked and trundled to a stop.

I dropped my head onto the wheel and bellowed in defeat.

After a few minutes' silent meditation, interjected with the odd swear word, I switched the ignition off, took my sandwich out and began nibbling at it. If only I were a poet, I could probably write a very moving stanza or two from this experience. Clutching at creative straws, I swapped the lens on my camera and snapped a few shots through the streaming wet windows. You never know, I thought.

Eventually, the rain relented enough for me to set off again on foot. On and on I walked. Could there really be this much uninhabited countryside? I spotted a well-trodden footpath to my right. That bode well for fellow walkers who might just be able to send me in the right direction or, better still, give me a lift. I walked quickly down the path until it came to a stile. Over it I went, intermittently studying my phone for a signal. Two bars. Maybe there were enough microwaves or whatever was required to connect me to the satellites so I could turn on the mapping program. I made all the right connections and hit the location button. Yes, there I was, a little pulsing blue button in the middle of a field. It knew where I was, I just needed to work it out for myself now. I zoomed out and disappeared into a mesh of gridlines. 'Come on!' I yelled at the thing. 'Give me a break!'

As if in response to my cry, I heard the unmistakable, 'gerdunk, gerdunk, gerdunk' of a horse's footfall on damp turf. Could this be Christophe?

I looked up and a handsome, large, brown beast was thundering my way; head bobbing, mane bouncing, teeth shining. Actually, I couldn't see his teeth but I knew they were in there somewhere. 'Nice pony,' I muttered, backing up towards the stile. It seemed wise not to run. 'Lovely boy,' I said in a soothing but wobbly voice. In reverse, my foot hit a soggy patch of mud and went sideways. I teetered, over-corrected and toppled to the ground. Four strong legs were heading my way, and they didn't belong to a pair of knights in shining armour. I watched, mesmerised. The horse slowed to a trot and then a walk, before coming to a standstill in front of me. I stared at his knees, uncertain whether eye contact was advisable. His breath snorted through his nostrils. I felt like a prisoner, waiting to learn my fate. I saw a foot move closer. Then his head dropped towards mine, his hot breath shifting my hair. My body was paralysed but I could still feel my backside chilling from the soggy soil beneath it. And then… then his large, warm head slid gently down and up the side of mine. I could feel the restrained weight of it; the firm, flat cheek grazing mine with its fine, bristly hairs.

'Bonjour,' I croaked.

Despite such intimacy, I still couldn't bring myself to look at him. He indicated his objection with a nudge.

I weighed up the situation: I was beneath him and he was above me. Aside from nuzzling my ear, he wasn't taking advantage; I posed no threat to him in this position and he didn't appear to be threatening me; finally, I reminded myself, horses were not carnivores.

I turned my head slowly. Jeez! Those nostrils were huge. His breath wasn't too fragrant either. He flexed his upper lip, which I hoped wasn't a come-on. When I finally made eye contact, he blinked, bowed politely and stepped back.

I remained still, watching for any intent to charge and trample. After a moment, I spoke quietly, 'If it's okay with you, I'm going to get up v-e-r-y slowly.'

He bowed again.

Putting my hand into the mud, I gradually levered myself out, fully expecting a squishy popping sound as my bum left the pocket of sludge it had been sucked into. I kept a watchful eye on my equine buddy until I was upright. He gave me a look of grudging approval, nodded again and made a quarter turn away, which I took to be my dismissal. It was either that or the pre-cursor to a new move on me.

'Thank you, kindly,' I said, inclining my head deferentially, like we were performing a scene from Pride and Prejudice.

Then, with apparent indifference, he wandered several feet away and chomped some grass. I took the opportunity to side-step my way to the stile and whipped my legs over it as fast as a gymnast. Safely on the other side, I slumped against it and drew fresh air into my lungs. 'Darcy' and I exchanged another look and, like Elizabeth Bennett, I began to re-evaluate my opinion of him and acknowledged that this had been a significant moment in my life. I smiled and said, 'A pleasure meeting you, sir.' I'd like to say he raised his head in acknowledgement but he carried on grazing, which shows just how fickle these creatures can be.

I tugged at my damp trouser-seat which was clinging to my newly-chilled buttocks. 'Yuk!' I stepped away from the stile and headed back to the road.

Just as I was contemplating a night under the stars, my phone rang. It was Christophe.

'Hello!' I said with some enthusiasm.

'I see that you called me?' his voice was as mellow as you might expect after a grapple with his lover.

I glanced at the time – that was well over an hour ago. 'Yes, look, I really didn't want to bother you, but the thing is – I've run out of petrol.'

'Where are you?'

It was a relief he was neither angry nor amused.

'Umm...' oh dear, this was going to sound as wet as I was. 'I'm not exactly sure. But I think it's quite near the château.'

'If you were on your way here, there's only two roads you could be on. Don't worry, I'll come and find you.'

'Wait!' I realised he would drive down the road back to his house – and I was nowhere near there. 'I really don't know where I am. I was driving around, looking for nice pictures to take and I saw the château in the distance. But that was ages ago.'

'Can you describe where you are?'

I turned slowly through 360°. 'Trees, hedges, fields, one large, brown horse. Sound familiar?' I managed a weak, laugh. I heard him let out a sigh of exasperation. Of course, this was absolutely the last thing he needed. 'Listen, Christophe, I've been walking for a little while, I'm bound to find a house soon and then they can tell me where I am. Why don't I call you later?'

'Don't do that. You might walk for a long time. Do you remember how you got there?'

I swallowed. I had no idea but I described where I was when I looked down on the château and the direction I'd headed off in.

Finally, he asked, 'Did you pass an old house – a ruin?'

'Yes! Yes! It was on my right. All beams and old stone.'

'Good. The road forks after that, which way did you go?'

My heart sank. I had no idea. What an idiot. I tried to think but shook my head.

'Vicki?'

'Sorry, I can't remember.'

'If you wait in the car, I'll come and find you. We can keep in touch by phone, okay?'

I pulled a face. 'The car's miles away, I've been walking for ages.'

'How far?'

'Five kilometres – maybe more.'

'Then stay where you are.' He sounded tired. 'I'll ask Alain to help me. He can take a different route.'

Oh dear. That was another person's Sunday afternoon ruined. 'Thank you. I'm so sorry.'

'Don't worry.'

My misfortune continued, as the rain returned. I sheltered under a tree until, eventually, Alain's four-by-four came into view. My relief at being discovered was only slightly marred by my irrational disappointment that it wasn't Christophe. How mad was I? Alain immediately handed me a large, heavy jacket to wear and rang Christophe. Then, he drove me back to the little red car and emptied a can of petrol into the tank.

As I mumbled my thanks and apologies he said kindly, 'It's something we all do at least once in our lives.' His weathered face lifted as he smiled, reminding me he was still a handsome man. 'Colette has told me to bring you back to the château. She's worried in case you have a chill.'

'Oh I couldn't. Really, I'll be fine.' It was the last place I wanted to go now. I'd just caught sight of my soggy reflection in the car window. I looked like a weary scold, fresh off the ducking stool.

'She feels responsible. Come on, she wants to see you.'

I drove behind Alain, half expecting to see

Christophe at every junction but he had returned to the château ahead of us. Who could blame him?

Chapter 28

When we arrived at the château and before getting out of the car, I swivelled the rear-view mirror to remind myself how ghastly I looked. As I scrunched across the gravel with Alain, I spotted Christophe, leaning casually in the back doorway of the château, still wearing his riding gear. Even now, he made my stomach tumble – which was more than he had a right to. I held my head up and walked with as much dignity as I could gather. This really hadn't been in my plan, at all.

He stepped out to greet me. 'You had a bad afternoon, huh?'

That was putting it mildly. 'All part of life's rich tapestry.' I said. 'Sorry for the disruption. I'll just say hello to Colette and then I'll go.' I barely made eye contact as I swept past him into the house, my wet shoes making ghastly squishy noises as I walked, and my stiffening trouser-seat chafing my bottom.

Colette had already run a deep, hot bath for me and wouldn't hear of me going home. 'I can't believe my son gave you a car with no petrol in. This is the least we can do.'

'It was my fault. I should have checked.'

'Nonsense. You were unfamiliar with the car.' Colette draped a Japanese silk kimono over the chair in the bathroom, her gold bangles rattling on her wrist as she did so. Today she looked striking in a jade green trouser suit, with a plunging neckline. 'Take as long as you like. Now, would you like some herbal tea or maybe a little brandy?'

'Tea, please.'

'Darling, I will bring you both.'

The bath was glorious. I almost nodded off twice and only got out when the temperature dropped below body heat. The kimono was a couple of sizes too large for me, but since Colette had taken my damp clothes somewhere to dry, I didn't have any choice but to wear it.

There was no sign of Christophe when I emerged from the bathroom and padded into the salon. Colette was reading a book, with Amy Winehouse playing quietly in the background. She looked up as soon as I entered. 'Vicki! Chérie! You look lovely and you have some colour back in your cheeks. Do you feel better?'

'Much better, thanks.'

She put her book down, kicked off a pair of mules and tucked her feet underneath her. 'Come and talk to me. How is your painting coming along?'

I sat next to her and related the story of the latest picture's progress. I covered my early frustrations and how Christophe had encouraged me to continue, but I skipped over our little disagreement and hurdled the part with the romantic clinch. But like a counter-melody, the scene of the two horse-riders kept playing in my head.

Colette was fascinated to learn how the mirror had come to the rescue. 'Then you must always use a mirror from now on. Although, perhaps you won't lose your inspiration again.' She leaned forward and covered my hand with her own. 'I know how deeply involved you artists can become. I once had an affair with François, you know.'

I did know. Half of France knew. I'm surprised the sexual shenanigans of the Dubois clan didn't have a reality TV show all of its own.

Colette continued, 'He used to become so worked up if a piece wasn't going well. Of course, he handles it with…' she raised her hand as if drinking from a bottle. 'Such a dangerous combination – talent and addiction. Marie is talented too – but so much more controlled. And rather cool,' she added, as an afterthought.

'I like her,' I responded, honestly.

Colette picked up my hand in both of hers. 'Chérie, I love Marie. She's a wonderful woman,' she smiled warmly and whispered, 'but you know, some men need more warmth in their lovers – more passion, do you understand me?'

As I opened my mouth to answer, Christophe appeared in the doorway, wearing a black sweater over black chinos, accentuating his Mediterranean colouring. The impact was as troubling for me as had been the sight of him in the tuxedo, on my first night. The difference being, I now knew the kind of man I was dealing with. I straightened my back and continued, 'Yes, I understand you.'

Colette gave my hand a little squeeze and turned to her son. 'Vicki tells me she has finished another painting.'

'That is good news.' He crossed the room and sat on the other sofa. 'And you are pleased with it?'

I nodded, forcing myself to look at him but focusing on the line of his jaw. 'I am.' I tugged at the front of my kimono. Another thought occurred to me as I battled with my feelings. I lifted my head a little higher to make my point. 'Although, I'm sure I can do better.' I punctuated my statement with a direct look into his eyes.

Of course, he couldn't possibly read my meaning. Annoyingly, he smiled back at me. 'Isn't that the way every artist feels?'

I shrugged. 'Perhaps.'

Colette was watching our interchange like a spectator at Wimbledon. 'Please excuse me for a moment.' She released my hand and slipped the mules back on her feet. 'I promised Anne I would do something.' She left the room, closing the door behind her.

Both Christophe and I knew a set-up when we saw one. Trouble is, he didn't look half as awkward or pissed off as he should have done. That was my role. 'So,' he said, with a smile lighting up his face, 'you completed your picture – I think you must be feeling good, yes?'

'Good' was a very inappropriate word for how I was feeling, right then; confused and disappointed but above all, angry. I stared at the closed door, repeatedly smoothing the silky belt of the kimono between my finger and thumb. I wanted to confront him, find out what was going on with Sylvie, even though I was pretty sure he probably just couldn't resist her any more than he could resist flirting with every other woman who crossed his path. He was a serial philanderer. I forced a smile and stuck my chin out saying, brightly, 'Yes. I've proved to myself I can do it. And now that I'm really fired up – I feel I could do anything.' I fixed him with my eyes. Yes, I thought, Vicki's on her way back.

'Anything?' he asked, quietly – one edge of a double-entendre nudging its way forward.

I closed my eyes in exasperation. 'Don't go there, Christophe!' I fixed my eyes back on him. 'Stop looking on me as just one more girl in a long line of romantic conquests.'

His mouth dropped with surprise and then he clenched his jaw before saying, 'It didn't seem to bother you the other night. I thought you were quite enthusiastic, until you decided you weren't ready to get involved.'

I stood up. 'Maybe I was taken in by you.' A dramatic exit was on my mind, but where would I go? As I hesitated, he had moved to within inches of me.

'Taken in? I'm not trying to fool you. I am attracted to you.' He lowered his voice. 'But it would seem that you don't have any good feelings for me. Clearly, you were right – you are not ready.'

He had a nerve. 'And you think you are?' I said through gritted teeth.

'What?' he asked. 'Why wouldn't I be?'

It was on the tip of my tongue to say, I've seen you. I have the photographs to prove it. But in light of his opinion on journalists and photographers, I knew how unwelcome that would be. No, I had the upper hand. I didn't need to tell him. 'Nothing. Forget it.' I said.

'You're talking about Jeanne, aren't you?'

Oh, and there was her too. 'Isn't she important in your life?'

He looked at me for a moment and then his voice became very soft, 'She's a friend, an old friend. I admit she may have wanted to be something more but, I assure you, Jeanne is only a friend.'

At least I'd been right on that score. But I doubt my face registered much relief, since he was barking up the wrong tree.

'Hey…' he put a hand up as if to touch me but stopped before he made contact. 'Let's not be enemies.'

His hand was hovering within inches of mine. My treacherous body tingled in anticipation but I stepped back and folded my arms. 'Of course we're not enemies,' I said, equally quietly.

'Then, don't run away.'

I took another step back and bumped against the sofa. 'You're crowding me.'

'Sorry.' He stepped back too, and ran a hand through his hair. 'Okay.' He looked around the room and pointed distractedly towards the coffee table. 'Why don't you relax with a magazine and wait for Colette. I have a feeling she will be back as soon as I'm gone.'

At the door he turned back. 'I must apologise for not telling you where to find petrol. There is one garage on the Limoges side of the town but nothing else for about twenty kilometres.'

'Thanks.'

He nodded and left.

As the door shut, I slid down onto the sofa and reached out for a magazine. I flipped through its pages unseeingly. I realised staying with Christophe was going to be impossible. He was clearly unable to take the hint for more than twenty-four hours at a time, and I would never be able to concentrate on my work, living in such an atmosphere. I would have to find somewhere else to live. I would chase up Bruno and hope Daniel hadn't rubbished my chances of working for him. I was damned if I was going to let this drive me back to Bristol. Marc had already bombed one big plan in my life, Daniel had nearly succeeded with this one, no way was I going to let Christophe torpedo it now.

As he had predicted, Colette reappeared with a small tray of canapés. 'I thought you might be feeling hungry.' She set the tray down on the coffee table and offered me a plate. It was hours since my sandwich but I wasn't hungry. Out of politeness, I took a couple of crackers garnished with fish pâté and dill. Colette perched on the sofa opposite. 'Where did my son go? I wanted to ask him something.'

'He didn't say.'

She was fiddling with her bracelets. 'I hope you don't find him too difficult to live with. He's always been very good-natured – sometimes a little preoccupied, perhaps but who isn't?'

Colette was fishing. I wondered if she'd make as good a composition as the scene I'd just painted. 'He's absolutely fine.' I said, before pushing a cracker into my mouth and moving it round with a dry tongue.

Colette started drumming her fingers on the cushion beside her. 'Excuse me for being so direct, Vicki, but I feel that something…' she gestured with her hands as she sought for the right words. I wasn't sure where she was going with this. 'I feel there is a tension between you and my son. If he is a little ill-tempered at the moment, it is because he is dealing with some complicated family issues.'

She could say that again. I swallowed the cracker, which lodged below my windpipe. 'Yes, I know.' I swallowed again. 'The…erm… Albina thing… and the Gerard and Sylvie thing… and the Foundation… thing' for every instance of thing, insert scandal. 'Don't worry, it doesn't affect me,' I lied. 'I've just been a bit grumpy with my painting and I probably took it out on him. We had a few words on Friday but everything's fine.'

'Good. I'm pleased. Now,' she clasped her hands together, jangling her bracelets emphatically, 'will you stay for dinner? We have a lovely wild salmon from one of the local lakes.'

I shook my head. 'It's very kind of you, but I must go back. I need to seal the painting and prepare another canvas for my next one.'

Colette's head tilted. 'Are you sure? We would be delighted to have you stay. And I don't think your clothes are quite dry yet.'

'Honestly. I wouldn't be very good company.'

'But we still have a lunch date for Thursday?'

I slapped a smile on my face. 'Definitely. And if you come to the house, I'll show you my painting.' Assuming I was still there.

'Wonderful. I shall look forward to it.'

I borrowed a pair of Colette's navy jogging bottoms, which I doubt had ever been jogging, and a cream sweater. Both were too large, so I turned them up at the ankles and cuffs. As I prepared to leave, there was no sign of Christophe. Despite everything that had happened, I still felt it would be impolite to leave without saying goodbye.

The door to his apartment was on the ground floor. I waited, biting the inside of my lip until he appeared. His smile was slight. 'Do you want to come in?'

'No. Thank you. I just wanted to say thanks for

organising the search party. And... um... I'm going back now.' Everything about me felt awkward, from my still-damp shoes to my oversized clothing.

He gripped the edge of the door and leaned his head against it. 'Don't get lost, huh?'

I smiled. 'Nooo!' I wavered in the hallway. 'Will you... I mean... When...' I looked at my feet momentarily, before fixing my eyes back on his. 'Will you be coming back to the house?'

His eyes narrowed a little. 'Why don't I give you a bit of space for a while? So you have chance to get involved with your painting.'

'But that's your home.'

He shrugged. 'So is this.'

And much more handy for Sylvie, I thought. 'Well, that means I'll be staying under false pretences. So, if I'm not cooking for you, I must pay you rent.'

'Absolutely not. You are a friend.' Then his smile broadened. 'You don't eat your friends, I don't take money from mine.'

I really wanted to stop liking him but he made it impossible. 'Thank you.'

'*De rien.*'

I stepped back. 'See you, whenever?'

He nodded but said nothing. I turned and walked away, an unwelcome stinging sensation prickling at the back of my eyes, and an undignified squelch in my shoes.

Chapter 29

I was up to my wrists in paint as I attempted to kick-start my creativity with finger-painting. The muse had abandoned me – again. Occasionally, I would scroll through my growing archive of photographs for inspiration, but always ended up loitering over the wonderful picture of Christophe riding Léopard. Then I would torture myself by clicking forward to the shot of him with Sylvie. Each time, I could feel my pulse increase before I reached it and each time I felt sick as I looked at it, knowing how close I'd come to falling for him – big time. I returned to the one of him riding. I really wanted to paint this. I didn't know if I could capture the sense of power and speed but I was more turned on by this image – creatively of course – than anything else.

What the heck. I needed to get it out of my system. I was an artist, after all, and this was how artists worked – through their emotions. Removing the practice canvas and securing a new one, I settled in front of it to draw it out.

On Thursday, Colette arrived for lunch in a haze of expensive fragrance – and late. I had vacillated between leaving the incomplete picture of Christophe on the easel or concealing it. Coward that I was, I stuck it behind the empty canvases. Artist or no artist, I didn't want to subject myself to more speculation from Colette. She clapped her hands at my first painting of the fishermen. 'C'est magnifique! I love it. Will you sell it to me?'

I was taken aback. 'I haven't even thought about selling any paintings yet.'

'When you do decide to sell it, please, think of me first.'

The restaurant she took me to in Limoges was in an old part of the city, with dark panelled wood and stained-glass windows. I chose onion soup, followed by soft scallops with lavender cream, while Colette chose garlic prawns and stuffed breast of pheasant. Once the waitress had departed with our order, Colette placed her elbow on the table, rested her chin on her hand and said discreetly, 'I must tell you – Alain has finally accepted the marriage between Gerard and Sylvie.'

I smiled. 'How lovely.' My thoughts were replaying our lunch at the château, when I'd detected an atmosphere between Alain and Christophe. Alain had been the first to discover Sylvie with Gerard. Had he also discovered she was screwing Christophe behind Gerard's back? Why not continue a family tradition, now she had married into it?

Colette nodded. 'It has been difficult. Of course, you know Alain strongly believed Sylvie was only after the Dubois fortune?'

I didn't but it certainly matched Jeanne's opinion.

She stroked a large tear-drop of gold, hanging from her earlobe. 'Christophe has had to work very hard to change Alain's point of view.'

Wow! I thought. That was pretty magnanimous of him, not to mention, convenient, bearing in mind he was rogering her in the woods.

Colette continued. 'So now it looks as if I shall have my party after all. We're celebrating their wedding, next weekend. I can't wait! And you, chérie, must be there.'

I forced a smile. Deep joy. My first wedding party since my own. Another opportunity to pretend all was well in my world.

I cleared my throat. 'Do you think Christophe has got over Sylvie?'

Colette had just raised her wine glass but put it down again. 'Of course. She was not right for him. Too cool – very much like Marie and François. Oh, I'm sure they would have managed, but Gerard is a far better match for her. Christophe is too sensitive.'

I was surprised Colette believed she knew her son so well, especially since she had been absent for most of his childhood.

Colette continued, 'He takes after my mother. She was a wonderful lady.'

I frowned, as Colette continued, 'I'm afraid I take after my father,' she laughed heartily, shaking back her rich, auburn hair, and winking at me over her wine glass.

'Christophe told me about his grandmother. He was very fond of her.'

'And not so fond of my father. He disapproved of all his infidelities. Mind you, so did half of France, at one time. The other half were jealous.' Colette laughed again.

Her glee was infectious, I laughed too.

'My dear, my father and I chose to have fun. Unfortunately, as we have discovered, he was also something of a rogue. On the other hand,

Christophe's own father was a very good man but also very serious. I think I found that attractive at first, he was so different from me I was sure we would have a wonderful, passionate marriage but,' she stopped for a moment and considered, 'we were much too different. *Eh bien.*' She shrugged before raising her wine glass. 'To life's pleasures!'

After lunch, we wandered around the older part of Limoges, stopping at a créperie close to the St Aurelien chapel, for dessert. As I tucked into my crépe with crème de marron and Chantilly cream, she confided, 'I shall never be thin again but I don't care. It's so important to live life, eat life, for tomorrow – who knows?'

I leaned forward. 'But Colette, you have a great figure.'

'That's because I keep active.' She winked as she closed her mouth on another spoonful.

Returning full but refreshed from my trip into Limoges, I contemplated my work with renewed enthusiasm even though I was painting it in the shadow of my own disappointment. Colette had reminded me that it was important to make the most of the here and now. And right now, I was producing my fourth painting – that alone was a joy.

I worked right through the weekend investing all my energy into the new painting. Sometimes I missed Christophe. I saw him briefly, when he visited the surgery and passed through the house to collect something but most of the time I was so absorbed that the hours flew by. All the same, on Sunday evening, while I was cleaning my brushes, I found myself pining for a cosy chat over a bottle of wine.

Instead, I rang Isabelle, who was very pleased to hear I was still painting. 'Fantastic! And what about men – have you set up a force field to deflect them?'

'Of course. I'm through with men.'

'What a pity. I was so looking forward to your next wedding. The last one was such fun. You do weddings so well.'

'Thanks. I'm going to a wedding party next weekend.'

'With Christophe?'

'He'll be there. It's to celebrate his cousin's marriage to the ex – Sylvie.' And a complete hypocrisy, I was tempted to add but didn't want my gossip getting back to the family, and I certainly didn't want to be responsible for triggering another family drama. I would leave that to Christophe and Sylvie.

'Oooh!' Isabelle was intrigued. 'That will be interesting. Make sure you take lots of pictures.'

I hadn't even thought about it. The party was low on my list of priorities. Every time the subject came up, I pushed it back down again. Isabelle asked me what I was going to wear.

'No idea.'

'Wonderful! You can go shopping. Don't forget: shoes, handbag, ear-rings, manicure. You must do everything properly.'

'On my budget? I'll just go for the essentials.'

'Whatever you buy – make it a real *clou du spectacle*!'

'What's that?'

'A showstopper.'

Chapter 30

Friday was, possibly, leaving it late to buy an outfit but shopping under pressure seemed to suit me. Isabelle's advice had driven me to write a list of everything I needed, from leg-waxing strips to nail varnish. Limoges was alight with Christmas decorations and heaving with shoppers.

I had a few euros in my pocket. Mum and Dad had finally sold Marc's electronic keyboard. I'd held on to it out of some misguided sense of loyalty – possibly even hope that he might return – but Dad had persuaded me he wouldn't be back and, even if he tried, I was fully within my rights to sell it. So I toured the fashion shops in search of something special.

I knew, the minute I fastened the zip on a truly scrumptious dress, and saw every seam fit beautifully, that I'd found the perfect thing. It was full-length. Exactly the length Marc had hated on me but which I'd secretly wanted to wear for my wedding. The soft, crimson chiffon over satin was sprinkled with tiny sequins across the bodice. It was an absolute knockout. I'd show Christophe and Sylvie I was not beaten.

More practically, it would match my wedding shoes.

* * *

Christophe drove over to the house, on Friday, to

collect his tuxedo. As he turned into the drive, he realised Vicki wasn't home. Wandering around the house, he noticed small Vicki touches – an arrangement of ivy leaves and wild heather in the hall; fruit salad in the fridge; a discarded magazine on the armchair. He walked upstairs to his room, pulled his suit from the wardrobe and carried it back onto the landing. He listened. Vicki was definitely not home. He loitered. He draped his suit over the banister and walked to the bottom of the second flight of stairs. Had she been painting?

He carried on up to the studio to look at the second painting of the fisherman – he'd not seen it completed. As he stepped into the room, he stopped dead in his tracks. On the easel, was an unfinished, but unmistakable painting of him on Léopard. He stood, frowning, studying it, taking in the accuracy of her depiction. Her style avoided fine detail, but she had still captured movement and energy.

When had she taken the picture? Goodness knows he'd ridden Léopard more in the last couple of weeks than he had for months.

Finally, he found the impetus to move from the doorway and towards the easel, peering closely at the thousands of brushstrokes that went into creating the image. He backed away and leaned against the table, jolting the laptop out of screensaver mode. There, on the screen, was the photograph she'd been using for inspiration. He pressed the arrow key to look through more pictures of him riding away from the château. He clicked on again and stopped at a picture of him with Sylvie, and then another. Within the frame, there was not much to see of the horses, just a powerful close-up of the two of them.

She must have taken the picture the day she ran out of petrol.

He closed his eyes, shook his head and let out a big sigh. 'Ah, non!' Then, he clicked on to the original picture and, with a last look at the painting, headed downstairs to pick up his tuxedo.

* * *

The night before the wedding party, I had the worst night's sleep. I could feel a whole can of emotionally charged worms stirring up – not least because it was the first wedding celebration since my own. It brought back memories of what I'd thought would be my last-night-as-a-single-girl. I shed a tear for the heart-to-heart I'd had, first with Mum and then with Dad; both of them being so positive about a future that would never happen.

'Stop being wet!' I told myself as I turned over. 'You've moved on. Live in the moment.' I plumped the pillow vigorously.

How exactly, I wondered, was Christophe going to behave around Sylvie – and would I be able to resist watching them all night, looking for flaws in their performance? I turned onto my back, bashed the pillow with my head a couple of times for comfort and closed my eyes.

Late on Saturday afternoon, as I applied the first coat of nail varnish, Colette phoned. 'Vicki, darling, I'm sending a car to pick you up this evening.'

'You don't have to do that. I'm quite happy to drive.' In any case, it would give me an incentive to stay sober and in control.

'Not at all. You must relax and enjoy the evening. I absolutely insist. It will be there for seven-thirty.'

'Thank you.'

Just before seven-thirty, I checked my reflection in the wardrobe mirror. My hair was loose over my shoulders. The dress hung beautifully, the hem drifting as I moved. I smiled. I might not cut such a striking figure as Sylvie – but I could definitely give her a run for her money.

What was I thinking? And why on earth did I feel like I was preparing to go into battle against Sylvie?

A flush crept up my cheeks. Oh, nuts! I still wanted him. How could that be possible? I was truly hell-bent on self-destruction and deserved all the pain coming my way. Was insanity an artist's natural state? Think: Gauguin, Van Gogh, Dali.

Outside I heard the low rumble of an engine and the scuffle of excited dog paws on the hall floor. I took a deep breath and blew it out slowly. 'Just enjoy the party,' I muttered as I left my bedroom.

As I was halfway down the stairs, Christophe walked through the front door and looked up. What was he doing here and how dare he look so gorgeous in his tuxedo? I paused for a split second and then overcompensated by quickening my pace and almost fell off the bottom step. He held out a hand to steady me.

'Sorry. It's the shoes.' I gasped, mentally clouting myself.

He bent and kissed me on both cheeks. He smelled delicious. 'You look beautiful,' he said.

'Really?' I asked, breathily, wondering who'd stolen the oxygen.

He studied me for a little longer. 'Very beautiful.'

The oxygen thief had also turned the boiler up. I shook my head and croaked, 'Thank you.'

He stepped away and lifted my jacket from where it hung by the door. As I shrugged my arms into the sleeves, I felt a random shudder as he held the collar a fraction too long.

His deep voice was close to my ear. 'I hope you like the car – it took me an hour to get it started.'

'You're driving me?'

'Of course. Didn't Colette say?'

'No. She just said she was sending a car.'

'Well, it is a very special car.'

Outside was a gleaming vintage Rolls Royce. I loved it. It was big and boxy, in black and burgundy, with a fabulously long bonnet and huge, shiny headlamps. 'Oh, wow!' I said. 'What is it?'

'It's a 1930 Phantom.'

'You didn't fancy lending me this one, then?'

He smiled and opened the passenger door. As I sat inside, I noticed the smell of old leather and felt the resonance of history in its fabric. The door made a satisfying 'clunk' as it closed. I studied the dials and switches on the dashboard; walnut and chrome gleaming from years of care.

I sank back into the seat and felt the throb of the engine as it started up. 'Has this always been in the family?' I asked.

'Not from new. My grandmère, Dorothea, brought it over from England when she married my grandpère. It was a wedding present from her father.'

'She didn't take it back with her, then?'

'She left in haste. I don't think it was important to her.'

We pulled up in front of the château, where ranks of candle-stands lit the entrance. As I moved to open my door, a footman came forward and opened it for me. '*Bon soir, mam'selle,*' he said as I stepped out.

Straight away, Christophe came round and was offering his arm to escort me into the house. I took it, still drawn to him by some perverse, cosmic force despite my brain computing the irony that we were about to celebrate the marriage of his lover to the cousin who had pinched her from him. I felt like a character walking into a Jilly Cooper novel.

The grand entrance hall was festooned with cream and apricot roses. We could hear the strains of a band playing in the ballroom. Alain and Anne were politely greeting guests in the hall, while Colette sashayed in and out of the ballroom to check who was arriving. She wore a midnight blue gown, slashed to the thigh and glittering with beads. I hope I look that sensational at her age, I thought as she wrapped me in a fragrant embrace.

'Now, you beautiful darlings,' Colette began, as she stood between us, 'I want a picture,' and summoned the photographer. After posing like a professional, she stepped back and steered us together. 'Have some champagne, lots of it, and enjoy yourselves!'

As she headed off to capture another couple, the bride and groom appeared at the top of the staircase. Sylvie was wearing a plain ivory dress, with gold detail around the neckline. She looked beautiful – classically beautiful.

I suddenly felt vivid and cheap, like a Christmas bauble.

Christophe's arm settled easily around my waist. This time, instead of my tummy flipping with desire, it sank with disappointment. If only it were for real, I thought, when I knew he was just putting on a show to maintain a pretence. Well, he'd got a nerve. I wasn't prepared to be an accomplice in his crumby deception.

I lifted his hand from my hip. 'Excuse me.' I said, moving away from him to greet the bride and groom. Gerard was a similar build to Christophe, but less toned. His short hair was fair and styled neatly with a side parting. When he smiled, his cool blue eyes glinted with a roguish charm – so in that respect, he was clearly family.

Sylvie held out her hand to me, 'I am pleased to meet you again, Vicki,' she said. 'This is my husband, Gerard.'

Gerard's hand was hotter and sweatier than Sylvie's. 'Congratulations. I hope you had a lovely honeymoon,' I said, smiling up at him.

Gerard beamed back at me, revealing perfect white teeth but the twitch of his lip and a glance at Sylvie suggested he was far less confident than his wife. 'Thank you very much,' he said.

As I asked Gerard about Madrid, Christophe stepped forward to embrace Sylvie – completely throwing me into confusion and mucking up my attempt at polite conversation. Gerard seemed not to notice and held out his hand to Christophe and hugged him.

A distasteful lump formed in my throat at Christophe's treachery. I backed away and headed for the ballroom. Nobody was dancing, apart from Colette, who was swaying rhythmically inside the huge double doors. 'Chérie, isn't it a bore, Alain says we can't start dancing until after dinner. Who ever heard anything so ridiculous!' She put her arm through mine. 'Vicki, you look adorable tonight.' I smiled and sipped my champagne. 'I think my son will have to fight off a few opponents, don't you?'

My sip became a gulp. Eventually, I said, 'I doubt it.'

Colette leaned in to me and whispered. 'You must let him fight a little. Men like that.'

I swallowed. Every indication suggested Christophe did, indeed, want me – just not in the right way. It might be his family's practice to pursue several relationships at once, like some people hold down different jobs, but it wasn't mine. I managed a smile for Colette just as the great bulk of François appeared with Marie on his arm. Colette threw out her arms in greeting, and we were all indulging in cheek-kisses as dinner was announced.

Chapter 31

Lucky me – I was seated between Christophe and Louise, with François and Marie opposite. There were two narrow tables running the length of the dining room, with the bride and groom seated at the centre of theirs. And, for once, there was no Jeanne.

The food was presented in spectacular fashion, and I had been specially catered for with a seafood risotto.

François was, of course, most interested to hear how my painting was progressing, raving generously about the ones he'd seen. 'And what are you working on at the moment,' he asked.

'Well,' I began, instantly aware of Christophe turning towards me to hear what I had to say. 'It's in your field of work, François – a horse and rider.'

François let out an overloud 'Aha!' followed by. 'I definitely want to see that. I might have some competition, eh?'

'I don't think so,' I smiled, conscious that Christophe was poised to ask a question. I lifted my glass. 'Could you pour me a little more wine please, François?'

'So, where did you find your inspiration for the horse and rider?' Christophe asked.

'When I went out for a drive, one day.'

'Really? Where did you find them?'

'Oh, I can't remember exactly. You know how

terrible my sense of direction is.'

'Perhaps it was Henri Maigny – was he fat?'

I shook my head.

'Then I think you must have had a long drive. Maybe you went to St Léonard, huh?'

I stopped rolling the hem of my napkin and gritted my teeth. Sooner or later, he would see it. I took a deep breath and turned part-way towards him. 'Actually, it was…' I couldn't bring myself to say the word, so pointed my finger at his chest instead.

He turned and smiled in what I took to be a rather self-satisfied way, damn him. 'You painted a picture of me?'

'Yes.'

He leaned over and his breath brushed my cheek, as he whispered, 'I know.'

I nearly cricked my neck as my head spun towards him. He was close, very close, his gaze moving from my eyes, to my mouth and back again. Damn him, he was still flirting with me. I frowned. 'What do you mean, you know?'

'I came over yesterday to collect my dinner jacket. I was hoping to see you, instead I saw your work.'

My mouth had popped open, so I snapped it shut. 'That's despicable,' I hissed back.

'What is?'

'You sneaking around, looking at my work, without telling me.'

'I'm telling you now.'

I could feel the heat of his leg, and his hand was only a hair's breadth from mine. 'Yes but…'

He cut in. 'You can't accuse me of sneaking around my own house. If you'd been there, I would still have come to your studio.'

I knew he was right but it didn't stop me from feeling exposed. 'You could have said something earlier instead of pretending you didn't know anything about it. Still, I suppose you've become quite accomplished at keeping things quiet.'

Further along the table, Alain stood up and began tapping his glass with a spoon. There was a rumble around the room as everyone turned and settled themselves into position for the speeches. I took the opportunity to move away from Christophe and adjust my chair. He too changed position, turning his chair so he was behind me but practically leaning over my shoulder to see the speakers.

Much of what was said went straight over my head. You could blame my dodgy grasp of the language but more likely, it was the way my skin tingled with the nearness of Christophe. I wanted to move further away, but Louise's chair was blocking me.

I picked up snippets in the speech about the couple's deep love for one another and even the announcement of a child to be born in the spring. Wow! They'd moved fast. Of course, one assumed it was Gérard's baby. A shudder ran through me. I really didn't need that kind of complication in my life.

As soon as the speeches were over, and it was polite to do so, I stood up to leave the table. Christophe caught my hand and rose to meet me. He was still smiling, God rot him! I looked down at our hands and briefly at him. I was not smiling. 'If you'll excuse me, I'd like to go to the Ladies.'

He let go of my hand and I escaped to one of the bathrooms. By the time I emerged, the band was playing again. As I expected, The Happy Couple were swaying in the middle of the floor and gradually others joined them. I sidled over to Marie and surreptitiously scanned the room for Christophe, but he was nowhere to be seen. As the music changed to something more lively, I said, 'Come on, Marie. Shall we dance?'

She laughed. 'Not me. I don't dance.'

'No?' I hated to be at a party and not dancing, so I ventured out on my own, joining Colette, who was as lithe as a serpent on Speed.

Two songs later, I caught sight of Christophe, leaning against the wall watching me. I had no idea how long he'd been there. The next time I looked, Louise was leading him into the throng. I began dancing in retreat, but Louise was determined to join us.

Okay, it was a big room, I didn't have to dance with him or even look at him. All the same, my skin was prickling from his presence and the expert way he was manoeuvring Louise to the music. Colette, beside me, was vamping it up like Tina Turner, and flashing bedroom eyes at a tall, goat of a man, who was wearing a bright green bow-tie, and looked easily two decades younger.

When the number ended, I shot off to the bar for a reviving vodka-tonic. As I raised the glass to my lips, I watched as Christophe walked into the room and headed straight for me. Just what I didn't need. I took a gulp and placed the glass back down on the bar, but kept hold of it for support. He put a hand on my arm and leaned towards me. 'Vicki, what I'm going to say now, may not change the way you feel about me but I still have to tell you.'

I raised my eyebrows in an if-you-must kind of

way.

He went on, 'I know you saw me with Sylvie because I've seen the photographs. And I know how it might have appeared.'

I concentrated on my glass, rather than him.

'My uncle is a very honourable man. He believed Sylvie had wronged me and had no right to marry his son. He totally misread her motives and has been threatening to disinherit Gerard. But he was wrong. Sylvie is absolutely the right person for Gerard. I knew that, months ago.'

I swallowed.

He continued. 'I've been acting as go-between for them all. On Sunday, I finally made a breakthrough with Alain. When you saw me with Sylvie, she was giving me the good news.' He loosened his hand on my arm as he said, 'You accused me of snooping round my own house. How do you think I felt about you spying on me?' Then he walked away, leaving me shuffling from one foot to the other.

I took my drink and slumped into the nearest chair, my eyes darting from side to side as I chewed over this latest news. Did he really think I'd been spying on him? I wasn't sure which was worse – his arrogance or how my actions reflected on me. Replaying his words in my mind I let out a little groan. He had been doing the decent thing – thoughtful as ever – and I'd seen the absolute worst in him. I'd very nearly accused him of it to his face, too. I leaned forward and held my head in my hands. It was a natural mistake to make, wasn't it? I nearly imploded with shame as I imagined how he'd have taken my suggestion the baby might be his.

Sometimes in life you just have to suck up the

shame and admit to being wrong.

I may not have been deliberately spying on him but I'd definitely drawn the wrong conclusion.

Yes. The wrong conclusion.

A glimmer of light filtered through the gloom of my mortification. What had he said? 'What I'm going to say now, may not change the way you feel about me.' How did I feel about him?

A kaleidoscope of images flashed across my mind and my heart pitter-pattered in my chest.

Well, I knew the answer to that. The question was, did I have the stomach for the large slice of humble pie I was about to eat?

François strode up to the bar and ordered a bottle of red wine, before spotting me. 'Aha! my beautiful young friend. What are you doing sitting here, drinking on your own?'

I smiled up at him. 'Just having a moment of reflection.'

'You should be dancing.'

I stood up. 'You know François, you're absolutely right. And that's exactly where I'm going.'

I took a deep breath followed by a bracing gulp of V&T and walked as calmly as I could back to the ballroom. I tucked myself against a marble pillar and scanned the room for Christophe, finally spotting him dancing with his aunt, amongst the rest of his family.

I watched him, just like he'd watched me. After a moment he looked up and held my gaze briefly. The tune must have been the longest on record but throughout it, I'm pretty sure my intentions were telegraphed across the room to him. Even though his dance movements compelled him to turn away from me, he looked back every time he had the opportunity. Each time, I was still watching him.

The moment the music ended, he kissed his aunt's hand and turned to face me. He stood and waited, his head tilted in expectation. It was my big moment. I set off, knees wobbling with each step... each step nearer to those heavenly molten chocolate eyes and a man who'd turned my world topsy turvy – but in a good way. As I reached him, he scanned my face, picking up my apologetic smile, which may also have been a little starry-eyed. It was a good job he caught hold of me, or my legs might have given out.

As he pulled me close, and the band started another foot-tapping number, he pressed his mouth close to my ear and said, 'You wanted to dance jive, huh?' I leaned into him and he dropped a hot kiss against my temple. In the next moment, he had caught hold of my hand and was moving me round to the music, launching me away from him and drawing me back in.

I couldn't stop giggling, it was the best kind of dancing and he was superb at it, guiding me like a pro. Round we went, close and then apart. I didn't want to stop.

When eventually we did, Christophe threw me back over his arm, like he was Patrick Swayze and I was Jennifer Grey. Swear to God, I might have died happy in that moment. Then he pulled me back up against his chest and looked down into my eyes. 'Did you like that?' he asked.

'I loved it!' I shrieked, slipping my arms around his neck and feeling hot, hot heat radiating between us.

'Come on, I want to take you somewhere quiet.' He said, looking meaningfully down at my mouth, before steering me away from the dance floor.

Every organ, every vein, every fibre in my body was supercharged. Okay, so the exertion of the dance was partly responsible but the promise of being alone with Christophe had me at fever pitch.

He guided me through the milling party guests to his apartment. He struggled to unlock the door with one hand, because I was selfishly clutching and kissing the fingers of his other hand. Finally, the key turned in the lock and he drew me inside and pushed the door closed.

The only light came from a small lamp in the corner of the room. Running his free hand down my arm he caught my other hand and looked down into my face. Very quietly, he said, 'You told me you were not ready, if that's still the case?'

Was I ready? Hugh Jackman and Rafa Nadal in a hot tub couldn't have dragged me away. What's more, I knew right then, that ambition or no ambition, I wanted Christophe – for keeps. He was a good man.

I leaned up towards him and felt the catch of his breath, before I pressed my lips against his.

I'd never felt more ready in my life.

The End

♥ ♥ ♥

Thank you for taking time to read *Chloe's Rescue Mission*. If you enjoyed it, please consider telling your friends or posting a short review. Word of mouth is an author's best friend and much appreciated.

Thank you, again.
Rosie Dean.

Millie's Game Plan

Does your life lack fun and love? Does your mother fix you up with her priest's middle-aged nephew?

Millie's does – so she takes a grip on her own future and draws up a plan to find Mr Right.

When the first guy to float her boat, Josh Warwick, doesn't match her wish-list, she moves on to wine merchant, Lex Marshall, who ticks all the boxes - he's sexy, rich and unable to keep his hands off her. But when Millie faces danger and betrayal, she wonders if her dream man might not be Mr Right after all.
So, who will be...?

> *"Loved it, loved it, loved it."* Best Chick Lit

> *"Author Rosie Dean's debut book is a hit!"*
> *Stephanie Lasley – Kindle Book Review*

Chloe's Rescue Mission

Can Scottish leisure tycoon, Duncan Thorsen, help Chloe save her family's crumbling theatre?

Can she resist his notorious charms?

And just how much exposure will satisfy the paparazzi's lust for headlines?

Chloe is about to find out...

> *'Rosie Dean is fast becoming one of my most favourite romantic fiction writers'*
> *Heidi at CosmoChicklitan*
>
> *5/5 'kept me smiling throughout'*
> *Shona at `Booky Ramblings*

Vicki's Work of Heart

What if you found yourself stranded at the altar, knee-deep in your absent fiancé's gambling debts?

Vicki Marchant, humble art teacher and jilted bride carries on with the reception because she likes a good party. Then she seizes her freedom and leaves teaching to paint – in France.

It's her time and there's nobody to get in the way of her ambition. Definitely, no men…

She learns two things: some men are hard to resist and her judgement of them is still on the dodgy side.

'A beautiful and emotional story' – CosmoChicklitan

'The book is a sheer joy to read' – Best Chic Lit

Gigi's Island Dream

Gabriella Gill-Martin – Gigi to her friends – ditches her privileged life in London's fast lane, to live on an island, in her dream house, where she will build beautiful sculptures and grow vegetables. But she soon learns life in the fast lane is not all she has to give up.

When dreams become nightmares – what's a girl to do?

Winner of 2017 ACRA
Heart of Excellence Readers' Choice Award
Romance Writers of America

"Lively, easy reading with unexpected twists and comedy. Perfect scene setting with the references to Isle of Wight locations and events, you can almost imagine you're there."
Amazon reviewer

Toni's Blind Date

Second Chance Romance

Toni Spielman and Will Thomas have no plans to date -- anyone -- but when fate throws them together on a TV dating show, they have to smile, pretend, and rethink their plans.

Having loved and lost before, maybe they're just what each other needs.

'Great story, a most enjoyable read. Couldn't put it down.'
Amazon Customer

'When I got to the end of the book it felt as though I was leaving behind some really good friends.'
Amazon Customer

Acknowledgements

Firstly, thanks to the Romantic Novelists' Association who encouraged me on my journey into print.

Secondly, to Kirsty Greenwood and the Novelicious team: in 2012, the beginning of this novel was runner-up in the public vote in their *Undiscovered* competition. My prize included a critique from Kirsty, which helped shape the finished result.

To my editor, Hannah M Davis, for her insights; and to my beta readers, Noëlle Chambers and Carolyn Gray, for their essential observations.

To my own sister under the sun – Anne de Guernon – and staying with the French theme, Janie and Mike Wilson, who host wonderful writing courses and retreats at Chez Castillon.

As always, to fellow writers – too many to name here but in particular, Anita Burgh, Wendy Cartmell, Giselle Green, Jenny Harper, Nina Harrington and fabulous new author, Rebecca Leith.

Once again, massive thanks to Joe Brown for his illustration and cover designs.

Love to my own hero – Chris – for his unfailing support.

www.rosie-dean.com

Printed in Great Britain
by Amazon